NUT

FOR

FRAUD

To Jim

Love Thomas

DAN

THOMAS

NURTURED FOR FRAUD

ISBN: 0 9666741-9-7

Library of Congress Catalog Card Number: 98-87175

PRINTED IN THE UNITED STATES OF AMERICA

COVER ILLUSTRATION BY STEVE HECKMAN; LIBERAL, KA

> This is a work of fiction--none of the characters are real,
> and none of the events ever happened.

This book is dedicated to my friends who were both nice enough to give me encouragement and to tell me what they didn't like.

PART ONE:

VINCE

DAN THOMAS

1

Colorado – 1949

The dragsters roared down the runway. Smoke drifted toward Linda. She let the sound die down and then began walking past the boy's car. She ran her hands down the outside of her tight pedal-pushers confirming everything was firm, smooth and round, and hoping to draw the boy's attention.

"Hi, Billy," Linda said over her shoulder with a lascivious smile. Her hips were swaying and her ponytail was dancing.

Billy sat behind the wheel of his souped-up 36 Buick. "Hey, Linda," he said. He punched the boy standing next to his window.

The boy left with obvious reluctance.

Linda spun on a heel, threw her ample chest out, her head and shoulders back, and walked to him. "This was a beat up old wreck when you got it," she said. "Now look at it." Her fingers drifted delicately back and forth across the deep-red, glossy finish of his car.

"Sure is a pretty sweater," Billy said.

"Glad you like it." She looked into his dark eyes, then at the empty passenger's seat.

"See you around," Billy said, searching for the key.

"Wait. Brett's being a jerk. I might have to catch a ride home with you."

Billy looked around nervously. It was a several-hour drive to Ft. Collins on the other side of the Rocky Mountains, and the road was slow, narrow and winding.

"Afraid the mohair in my sweater'll come off on your new seat covers?" Linda said. "Don't be. Feel it." She placed her arm on the driver's window and bent over revealing cleavage.

"Aren't you going steady?" Billy said.

"Not anymore. Told you, he's being a jerk." Brett's class ring was in her pocket where she'd put it as she approached Billy's car.

Linda looked up and in the distance saw the girl Billy had been talking to earlier. She was leaving in a car with a *Rawhide Indians* banner in the window. Linda had heard Billy was driving over to Rawhide on weekends. Now she knew why.

"Who's that girl I saw you talking to?" Linda said. Billy gave her a blank stare. "The short, brown-eyed one with the buckteeth?"

"Buckteeth?" Billy laughed. "Her name's Ann Holtz, and she was Rawhide's homecoming queen. I bet they don't think she has buckteeth--and she's not that short. Everybody can't have blue eyes and be as tall as you."

"What would people from Rawhide know? They're all a bunch of hick farmers. Town doesn't have more than ten thousand people."

"So what's going on with Brett?"

"You beat hell out of him. Says you're an egg-head and a football player, and you got no business fooling with cars."

Billy smiled a big, satisfied grin. He and Brett had both participated in the drag races at the Rawhide, Colorado airport. They'd all driven over from Ft. Collins on the other side of the Rocky Mountains.

"Hear you're going to play football in college at Wyoming," Linda said. "Get a scholarship?"

"Sure did," Billy said, smiling broadly at her midsection. "Got a full ride."

"So how about a ride home?" Linda said, in a low voice.

Billy looked around. "Didn't you ride over with Brett?"

Linda sighed, and gave Billy a disgusted look.

"Jump in," he said, pursing his mouth.

Billy had the car started before she opened the passenger door, and they departed the second her door closed. Billy turned quickly, bypassing the spectators who were scattered along the runway. He drove through town and into the countryside.

"You've been coming over here on the weekends?" Linda said with a scowl, looking out her window. "How can you stand this shit anyway?"

"What do you mean?"

"I mean look at this place. Nebraska's prettier."

They were driving across a desert on the western slope of the Rocky Mountains in an area called Devil's Kitchen. Heat waves rose off the mostly bare soil that had absorbed the sun's mid-day energy and was now radiating it back. In sharp contrast, the country around Ft. Collins on the far side of the mountain was green and pretty.

"It's public land, so you can go anywhere on it. And it's neat country," Billy said as they crossed a bridge over a large dry stream. "This is Hell's Creek. I've never seen water in it, but I've heard that it really goes sometimes."

"And it's hot." Linda could feel sweat trickling around her breasts and down her spine. She looked at Billy and thought about making love in the desert, and how his sweat-lubricated body would feel. She looked at the mountain, which loomed high ahead and pictured a meadow of flowers nestled in green grass, and thought it would be better to wait. Besides, she thought, the boy might need to be convinced that it was the right thing to do.

"I'm not hot," Billy said, tugging at his white T-shirt and looking at her sweater.

Before the races, Linda had gone into Rawhide and shopped at the store with the plastic palomino horse on top. When she tried on a sweater, she left her blouse in the dressing room. As she studied her pretty picture in the mirror, the owner went into the back. Linda slipped quickly out the door, leaving her old blouse behind.

"I like this country," Billy said. "The history of the world's laid open here. See that bluff over there?" He pointed to a towering cliff of gray shale. "That was the bottom of the sea when dinosaurs roamed."

Linda gave him a blank look, and wondered what he was talking about. She tugged on her sweater. "I have to take it off."

Billy looked with hungry eyes.

"Keep your eyes on the road," she said, pulling the sweater off. "Eyes on the road. Be a gentleman." She patted him on the thigh. Billy looked back down the road, eyes wide.

"I'm in a bad mood, Brett and all. Let's stop in Shell. I'll get a bottle of peppermint schnapps."

"How'll you do that?"

"Fake ID," Linda said, smiling.

Shell, Colorado was a little cowtown snuggled against the mountains. Shell Creek flowed through the center of the town. It was a beautiful trout stream lined with towering cottonwood trees. Ranchers took water from the creek and irrigated hay fields around the little town. As a consequence, Shell was ten degrees cooler than the desert they'd just come across.

"I'll go down the alley so nobody sees you going in," Billy said, taking a detour from the main road. He stopped fifty yards away behind some unkempt bushes.

Linda looked at him. "It costs three bucks," she said pulling her sweater on.

Billy sighed. "Only have two, and I need one for gas."

Linda put her hand out. Billy stared for a second then struggled to reach into the pocket of his jeans. He pulled out a green square not much bigger than his thumbnail, unfolded it, and handed her a crinkled dollar bill.

She was back in no time, brown bag in hand. "I love this stuff," she said, taking a swig.

From Shell, the road followed a rugged canyon carved out by Shell Creek. It was a tiny, twisty road with occasional fallen rocks.

"Can I have some?" Billy said, as Linda took another swig.

"Watch the road." There was barely room to pass and the turns were so tight they had little warning of oncoming cars.

"What if I slow down?" He lifted his foot from the accelerator.

"Just drive."

Billy furrowed his brow and looked at her.

"If you stop, you can have some."

"My parents have a cabin in the forest on this side of the mountain."

"The one with the warm spring nearby?"

"That's the one." Billy's eyes were shining.

"Got a key?"

"Know where it's hid."

Linda smiled and slid lower in her seat. The air was getting cooler as they climbed the big mountain. Just past Shell Creek Falls, Billy turned onto the main Forest Service road. It crossed Shell Creek that was lined with towering spruce, fir, and aspen.

After a few miles, Billy turned onto a much smaller road. "I maintain this road," Billy said. "I come up here every year with a pick and shovel. Takes me about a week to get it all smoothed out. Don't get paid. Dad says it's my share for using the cabin."

Linda sipped on the schnapps and gave him a smile. "You can have some now," she said.

When they got to the old bridge, Billy got out and looked it over. Satisfied, he came back and drove across slowly.

"We're going to have to replace this old bridge pretty soon," Billy said.

Linda smiled at him indulgently, and combed her hair with her fingers.

"The cabin isn't much farther," Billy said.

The cabin had no running water and no electricity. It was constructed of logs cut from the surrounding forest, and it had a chimney made from rocks that had been gathered from the nearby stream. It blended perfectly with the mountain scenery. An outhouse stood twenty-five yards away.

Billy quickly had the cabin door open. It smelled funny. Not musty--more like stale wood. Billy got a couple shot glasses and plunked them onto a roughhewn table that occupied most of the kitchen's space. "Aren't you hot?" he said, looking at her sweater.

"Get your mind out of the gutter." Linda slurred her words. She looked around. "So where's the warm spring?"

"I'll show you." Billy opened the cabin door. The room was flooded with light from the sun, which had moved low on the horizon.

The path alternately went through grass and wildflower-covered meadows and a forest full of big boulders. Many of the evergreen trees were old, twisted, and gnarled. The spring was at the bottom of a cliff. The water was perfectly clear. Steam rose in thin wisps.

Linda tested the water. "Feels good."

"My parents sit in here and drink cocktails. See the rocks make seats. My dad thinks the Indians set it up that way. Couldn't hardly be natural."

"Your mom have a swim suit I could borrow?"

"Dad says there's an Indian curse that gets people who go in with clothes."

When Billy gave Linda a stern look, she stepped from ankle-deep water onto dry land and smiled at him. "Turn around," she said, slugging down the contents of the shot glass she was holding. "Don't look 'til I tell you it's okay."

Linda tossed her clothes in some bushes. "Oh, this is wonderful," she said, sliding into the warm water.

Billy turned, wide eyed. "Now turn your head," he said, taking a swig.

"You can't get in. You don't like me."

"What?"

"You like that girl from Rawhide." Linda looked at Billy and rose in the water until her breasts floated near the surface.

Billy took another swig, wiped his mouth, and looked back with narrow eyes. "I don't get drunk with people I don't like."

"I want to hear you say it," she said, twisting slightly back and forth. She smiled coyly as she noted the bulge in his crotch.

"I've always liked you."

"That's better," she said. She stood up in waist-deep water, a forearm across her breasts, and turned around.

"That was quick," she said, hearing him splash.

He was standing behind her taking another swig of schnapps. Linda sat back down. Billy slipped in close.

"Not too close," Linda said.

"Want some schnapps?" Billy said.

"You go ahead."

Linda lay back and glanced over at Billy as she closed her eyes. His jaws were clenching, and he was breathing nervously.

"Want to see the Indian skull?" Billy said.

Linda opened her eyes.

"Just below the water over there," Billy said, pointing to the cliff face on the opposite side of the pond.

"I can't swim." It was a lie. Linda had grown up skinny-dipping in the big stock pond behind her folks' ranch house.

"There's a ledge to walk on."

Linda hesitated.

"I won't look. Come on."

Linda rose quickly. Billy took a big lusty look before he turned, took a clumsy step, and fell into the water.

They walked in the shallows to the cliff face, then along the shelf that was initially knee-deep. As it got deeper, it also became narrower.

"Wait," Linda said. "If I fall, I'll drown."

"Hold onto me."

She placed a hand on his shoulder. As they walked, she allowed her body to occasionally rub his.

When the water was chest high, he stopped at a place where the cliff face took a right turn. "It's right here," Billy said. "Hold onto the side."

She looked at him with a worried look.

"Don't worry, see the hand-holds?" He pointed out places where she could hold onto the cliff. "I'll take a look."

Linda nodded nervously.

Billy's form was visible under the water. It looked like he was looking into a small cave. In a moment he surfaced.

"I saw it," he said.

"Really?" she said, amused, thinking the Indian skull was a clever ploy. "Can I see it?"

"Sure." They looked at each other. It meant she had to pass him on the narrow ledge. "I'll step around you," he said.

"I'd feel better stepping around you."

"Okay," he said, pressing his back against the cliff. She looked with a little smile, faced the cliff, and put a foot between his. Their thighs were touching. She let her breasts brush his chest lightly as she feigned difficulties. It felt good, and she could tell he liked it. When she felt something pushing on her thigh, she grabbed a loose rock and dropped it in the pond.

"Oh," Linda said. "I almost fell in."

Linda pressed her body against his. He was fully erect, and big, the way she liked them. She took one more step with her right foot. Now she was straddling him.

His slightly glazed eyes told her his mind was in no condition to detect her guile. He wasn't as cool around women as he let on, and the schnapps was having its affect.

When she started to step again, he put his hands on her waist and said, "Linda, wait."

"What is it?"

Their lips were inches apart and moving slowly together until they were kissing. She was surprised at how good Billy felt. His body was solid, including his buttocks, which she took the opportunity to caress as he fondled hers.

She guided him as well as she could with her thighs. When he barely made penetration, she broke away from the kiss. "No." she said, reaching down with both hands. "I've loved you since the fifth grade. You know that. But I can't sleep with you."

"Why not?" Billy's voice was quavering.

"You don't love me." The head of his penis was inside of her. She caressed its shaft with one hand--with the other she fondled his testicles. "Do you?"

Billy's mouth was hanging open, and his breath was coming in spurts.

"Well?" she asked.

Linda nibbled on an ear, still caressing him with her hands.

"Can't we just do it?" Billy said.

"Not unless you love me." She was kissing his closed eyes. "You don't, do you?"

"I love you," Billy said.

"Oh, I love you, too."

Billy gave a sigh of relief and pulled her close.

"But we can't do it here, Darling. The first time has to be just right. Let's go back to the cabin." She'd done it in the water before. She thought the water had gotten inside of her, and washed out the semen. Linda stepped away and lithely made her way along the ledge. Billy stood and watched. She made her moves as sexy as she could. She pulled her sweater, pants and shoes onto her wet body and grabbed her panties and bra. "You coming?" she said, starting down the trail, and smiling sweetly.

Billy shook his head and started moving.

Linda looked at the brilliant orange and yellow sunset and thought about how she'd wanted this boy for years. Her dad said she could never have him because his family ran in the same bunch with the banker. He was talking about the banker who'd smiled sweetly when he loaned her family money on their ranch lands, then snubbed them, and sneered as Linda's father begged for a little more time to pay. Linda was eight when the banker took her tire swing that hung from a cottonwood tree on the banks of a Rocky Mountain brook and made them move onto the treeless prairie where the wind blew.

Just before they got to the cabin, Billy stopped and threw a rock in the direction of a robin that was singing. The rock didn't hit close enough to make the bird fly, but it quit singing.

"Dumb bird doesn't know when to shut up," Billy said. "If an owl's around it might discover where the robin has chosen to perch for the night. When it's dark, the owl will catch the robin and eat it."

The two continued down the trail. Just a few steps farther, on the other side of a big tree, Linda stopped and stared straight into the big, yellow eyes of a gray owl sitting on a low branch. Its long talons were clearly visible. It made Linda feel good when she thought about how the talons would find the little robin.

Linda grabbed both Billy's hands, and guided him past the owl. She was happy when the owl didn't fly. The cabin was just a little farther.

"I'll be right in," Billy said, stopping at his car. Linda wondered what he was up to. She watched from a window. He pulled something from the glove box and brought it inside.

"There you are," Linda said as Billy walked in. She wrapped her arms around him, pressed her body close, kissed him, and then pulled him into the bedroom. He was carrying a little toiletry bag. He set it on the dresser, returned her hug, and started tugging on her clothes.

"Give a girl a chance," Linda said, maneuvering him out the bedroom door. She had the door closed before he could protest. The bedroom was dark, situated in the cabin on the opposite side of the setting sun. She cracked the door open. Billy was still standing right outside.

"Honey, it's dark in here."

"Be right back," Billy said. Soon he was back with a lit candle.

"Thanks, Honey." She smiled sweetly and closed the door. "I'll just be a minute."

She opened the little bag. It contained a razor, shaving cream and, as she suspected, prophylactics. She rummaged around at his mother's dresser, found a four-inch long hatpin, stacked the prophylactics, and quickly punched several holes in the stack. When she put them back a couple of the little packets dropped into the drawer where she'd found the hatpin. She wanted to grab them and put them back, but Billy was tapping on the door. She pushed the drawer closed, threw off her clothes, and jumped on the bed.

"I'm ready," she said, in a sweet voice.

He came in with a starved look, started for her, stopped, grabbed the bag, and stepped outside.

"Just a minute," he said.

When he came back in, she was sitting up in bed, her back straight. She extended a hand. "I'm waiting."

She had dreamt about this moment for some time. She'd imagined him gently fondling and kissing the breasts that she'd so carefully showcased with her pose and the candle's light. Instead, he put his arm around her waist and roughly pulled her down.

"Not so fast," she said.

"I'm a man," Billy said, moving on top of her.

She squeezed him with her thighs, and held him back.

"But you're not being nice," Linda said.

"What do you mean?"

"Touching gently, saying you love me." She felt his body relax.

"You're right," he said, kissing her face, then her breasts. She still didn't relax the grip she had with her legs.

"I love you, Linda," he said.

When she relaxed, he fumbled around again. When he finally found the right place, he was too big to enter quickly. Nevertheless, he pushed hard, hurting her.

She squeezed with her thighs again, and held him back as she kissed and caressed him. When she finally felt more receptive, she relaxed, and as he slipped deeply inside of her, she squealed with delight.

She was in heaven; building toward what she knew would be a terrific climax when he stopped and his body became tense. She sighed deeply when his body went limp.

He started to roll off, but she held on tight, hoping he'd be ready for more after a short rest.

"Oh, Darling," she said, "that was wonderful. Stay here. I never want you to leave." As she kissed him and rubbed his back, she felt him slipping away. "Hey, don't pass out." He didn't move.

When she felt him going flaccid inside her, she tried to wake him up, but he wasn't stirring. Waves of disgust pulsed through her. She punched him, but he still didn't react. Her frustration was intense.

An automobile light flickered on the bedroom wall. She heard a car approach, and found herself wishing it was Brett. She figured Brett knew where the cabin was, because he had spent time in these mountains tending his grandfather's sheep.

She got her clothes on and ran outside. It was Brett, and his face showed rage, so she changed hers to match.

"You son of a bitch," Linda said. "You left me. I had to catch a ride. Thought I'd be stuck here all night. He's passed out."

"What do you mean?"

"You left me, that's what I mean. You lost the race and went off pouting. I had to catch a ride with some jerk who can't hold his liquor." She paused. Brett was looking contrite. She ran around the car, jumped in and snuggled up to him.

"But you're here now, Honey Pumpkin." Linda squeezed his neck. "And I need you. Have a rubber? You'll need one. I'm in the middle of my cycle." She kissed him passionately.

"Wait, look over there," Brett said, pointing to the valley where bolts of lightning were twisting and flashing and illuminating big billowing clouds. "There's rain in those clouds," Brett said, "and they're coming this way. That old bridge I just came across can't take much high water. It was raining so hard in the Devil's Kitchen I could hardly see to drive. Hell's Creek was so full of water it looked like the bridge across it was ready to wash out."

Linda smiled indulgently, and rubbed his thigh.

100

2 – Vince Longto

The ovum was huge in comparison to the tiny sperm cell that was swimming toward her. She was like a mother space ship hovering in the darkness, although she wasn't in the cold of space, but in a warm liquid sea with a chemical composition similar to the ocean that had existed when life was new. The sperm cell had no brain, and no way to feel, hear, or see. But he could smell, and he could move his body in a purposeful way that let him follow her scent.

He swam until his head was against her enormous body where her intense smell motivated him to work harder to try to gain entry. He had no sense of time, no anguish over her failure to let him in, and when he was finally admitted, he felt no joy.

Others like him were also trying. They would swim against her massive body until their lives were exhausted. She knew instinctively to grant entry to only one.

With the union, there was a complete organism. It lacked a brain, muscles, bones, skin, eyes, and ears, but it was human. It was a zygote and it was drifting slowly and absorbing nutrients and oxygen from its surroundings the same as any primitive bacterium or one-celled animal. Its assignment, and ultimate goal in life was simple, to survive and reproduce.

The zygote communicated with chemicals. It told its host, its mother, of its existence, and asked her to save the nutrient rich lining in her womb. Mother responded by releasing her own chemicals that caused her body to begin to change in ways that would assure the zygote's survival.

Mother was everywhere, the zygote's entire universe. It was surrounded by protein molecules each bearing her unique

signature, all similar in nature to the protein molecules the tiny
sperm cell had smelled in order to find the ovum.

ᘳ ᘳ ᘳ

It was three weeks before Billy called, and it was about time,
because Linda couldn't give Brett excuses forever.

She thought from his voice that he wanted to make love
again.

Linda walked down the lane and met Billy about a mile from
her house. The sun was low when they went for a drive. Billy
didn't want to drive into town. He said he'd always wanted to
get a good look at the prairie.

It all looked pretty much the same to Linda, one rolling hill
after another. Linda figured he didn't want to be seen with her.
He must have sensed her concern, she thought, because he told
her it wouldn't be good if Brett saw them together. She directed
him to a small pond. When they arrived, the sun was setting.
Magpies were squabbling in nearby cottonwood trees.

This time it was just like her dreams. He kissed her gently,
and slowly removed her clothes. He even gave out a reverent
gasp as her breasts were revealed. He pulled them together with
his hands, and gently kissed and suckled them until Linda could
stand it no longer, and she pulled him down.

When he came before she did, he apologized and said if she
could wait just a little while, he would make sure she had her
turn. She had three wonderful climaxes before he finished
again. She'd been worried she was doing the wrong thing.
Finally she felt good about it.

They were naked in the cavernous back seat of his car.
Linda had situated herself so the moon was illuminating her
best features. At his request, they were waiting a little while
before making love again.

"Billy, Honey," Linda said. "Think you're going to be a
daddy."

"You're pregnant?"

"Accidents happen, but look on the bright side. You're going
to be a father." Linda thought she might have trouble getting
him to think of himself as a family man, so she was ready with
her arguments. She talked about the nice house they'd live in,

how he'd be her man, and how happy they'd be. The more she talked, the more distant he became.

"What makes you think it's mine?" Billy said.

"Whose could it be?"

"Brett's? How about Benny Bullock?"

"Benny Bullock's a lying sack of shit. He asked me out three times before my dad yelled at him. He hasn't called since. And Brett and I didn't do it last month. Told you he was being a jerk. And when we do it he uses new rubbers, not old moth-eaten ones."

"What do you mean?"

"How long have these been in here?" Linda opened the glove box, then the little bag. "They get holes in them when they sit too long." She pulled out a packet, tore it open and stretched the rubber, revealing five little holes. She knew this ploy had risks. He was smarter than the boys she was used to. He might wonder how she knew so much, and worse, he might examine the outside of a packet and see the little holes going through everything. She didn't want him seeing the advertisement either that said: *Guaranteed Fresh for Forty Years.*

"Get new ones," Linda said, tossing them all out a window.

"I can't be a father now. I'm going to play football in college and I have to get through college. My dad says once us kids get married, we're on our own. How could I go to college without his support?"

"You'd walk away from your child?"

When their arguing grew intense, Billy said, "Because my mom and dad think you're a low-class hick."

Linda knew it was what he thought. She also knew she could use the words to her advantage. She jumped from the vehicle, and began walking slowly, crying into her hands.

"God, I'm sorry, Linda," Billy said.

Billy walked her back to the car, pulled her close and kissed her gently. "I don't have to do what my parents want. Let me think about it. I guess I don't need those things now," he said, looking out the window at the little packets strewn around. "Would you like to make love again?"

"Do you still love me?" She was fondling him.

"I do."

☒☐ ☐☒ ☒☐

It was a week before he called again. His voice was strained. He said they needed to talk.

"So, I'll see you in about thirty minutes?" She wanted him where she could apply pressure. "Know where the little pond is?" Linda said. "Where we went parking? Why don't I meet you there?" She thought about the condom packets at the pond and decided to get there first to dispose of them. She also thought about the two packets that had fallen into the bottom drawer at the mountain cabin and wondered if she should drive up there and get them.

Billy hesitated, then agreed to meet her at the pond. She didn't want him coming to her house during the day because it was so ugly. There was no lawn, just a dirt yard with chicken droppings.

Linda thought about the pretty mountain yard she'd had as a child, and she felt happiness. Suddenly, she was a child again, swinging under her tree. Everything was beautiful. Birds sang-- flowers were everywhere. The nearby stream babbled quietly. She sensed trouble and looked at dust on the road. A car with an evil looking grill came up the drive. The car drove on the grass and crushed a flower. It was the banker and he jumped out, and ran past Linda like she didn't exist, then pounded impatiently on the door. He showed no respect as he told her father with a strangely contorted face that they would have to leave.

The look on the banker's face had become burned into Linda's mind. Now, as she got in her car and headed down the road, she tried out the look on Billy's face, and she felt disgust when it appeared to fit. She wanted desperately to have again the beauty that she'd had as a child. She didn't know why, but this boy seemed like her best chance to recapture what she'd lost.

Dust billowed behind Linda's vehicle as she drove across the parched prairie. Heat warped the view close to the horizon. When she arrived, the packets were gone. There were some unusual looking tire tracks that appeared to be a day or two old. She figured they were Billy's.

He wouldn't mention the holes, Linda thought. How could he? He'd only have suspicions. Wasn't he too drunk to put it all together from that night in the mountains? She saw dust on the horizon. She had to think of something. When Billy's car stopped, Linda ran around the back. The tracks were the same.

She jumped in and wrapped her arms around his neck. "Oh, I've missed you," Linda said.

He was stiff.

"I have a friend in Rawhide," Linda said. "She told me about a girl named Holtz. Been poking holes in rubbers for the fun of it. Some sick mind, I'd say."

Billy gave her a blank stare, then looked away. When he turned back, his eyelids were low. It was the banker's look, and Linda felt rage building. She couldn't bear to hear what she thought he was about to say.

"Going to tell me you love me again so you can get into my pants?" Linda said. "Think I'm somebody to use and throw away?"

His face grew softer.

"Why haven't you called?"

He started to talk. It was the banker's look again.

"My daddy says he'll kill you if you don't marry me."

He gave her a blank stare.

"Oh, Darling," she threw her arms around his neck, "I'm sorry. Make love to me."

He was still stiff. He looked at her and started to talk.

She could see what was coming. She couldn't bear it. "If you won't make love to me, I'll find somebody who will." Linda jumped out, went to her car, and left in a swirl of dust.

🜨 🜨 🜨

The zygote had become an embryo. It had a head, a primitive brain, and a skeleton with muscles. Its form was not uniquely human. It still had the remnants of gill slits, and only an expert could tell it from a sheep or a dog. It had no ears, internal or external, although it could sometimes feel vibrations on its body. It had dark spots where its eyes would form, but it could not see.

It detected smells and tasted the fluid that surrounded it. Sometimes it smelled Mother.

It moved gracefully, and seemed to swim, and even jump when its stubby little feet hit the end of its watery world. It had no apparent reason to move, although it most likely did something to increase the probability that it would survive and reproduce.

Sometimes Mother's heart raced, and she became anxious. It caused the embryo also to become agitated. The hormones of fear filled its veins and its heart raced, too. Billions of neurons in its developing brain fired until the experience was incorporated into the neural network that would eventually become a human mind.

ゴゴ ゴゴ ゴゴ

Linda sat in her doctor's waiting room, fidgeting. The older ladies were looking at her like they knew why she was there. The door opened, and the doctor came in. He was a middle-aged, balding man. He smiled broadly.

"Miss Peterson," the doctor said to Linda, "you're next." He held the door and smiled nervously as she entered the examining room.

"Do you have a cold?" the doctor said in a way that was friendlier than necessary.

The last time she had come in with a cold, the nurse had her strip to the waist, and gave her a paper cloth to cover her chest. When the doctor came in he removed it, and without saying a word, dropped it on the floor.

"I need an abortion," she now said, a little too coldly, feeling naked before him.

Everyone knew he'd given the mayor's daughter an abortion, but the doctor denied doing such a thing.

"Young lady," he said in a self-righteous tone, "I didn't get you pregnant. You did it yourself. Now you have to bear the consequences."

Linda sneered at him. He was obviously punishing her for his own thoughts, for wishing he'd been the one. She could tell he wanted her by the way he looked at her and touched her.

She felt aggression and wanted to inflict pain. She jumped to her feet and opened the door. "You pervert," she screamed.

"Get your hands off of me." She rushed through the waiting room. When she could see that none waiting were blaming the doctor, she wished she'd ripped her blouse before opening the door.

As the days past, Linda became desperate. She used a clothes hanger, but, when she began to bleed, she got scared and quit. She punched herself in the stomach, thinking the thing inside her would die, but it didn't work.

When the fetus began to kick, she saw reality. If she had the baby, it would have to go for adoption. She'd have to go away, and when she came back, there would be suspicions. Her reputation would suffer. Having the baby out of wedlock was out of the question. On the other hand, she *was* carrying Billy's baby. Maybe he'd be back? Should she call him? Bump into him?

Linda's world changed forever when she heard about the necessary wedding. She drove to Rawhide, sat outside the church, and watched as Billy came out with his bride. She was the pretty, brown-eyed girl Linda had seen Billy talking to at the races.

Linda gasped when she saw the girl's swollen abdomen. It seemed to be the same size as her own. Linda couldn't help finding it mildly amusing that Billy had probably gotten this girl pregnant too, with the rubbers she'd punctured.

Linda winced as Billy looked at his new bride with love and tenderness. He didn't even notice Linda, who was parked right across the street. Billy kissed his bride tenderly before driving away. Cans rattled behind. Everyone cheered.

Linda's fate was sealed. She'd have to marry Brett Longto. Brett was a good man, good-looking, hard-working and honest, but she would never love him. He balked at first and demanded to know how the child could be his, and what really happened that night at the cabin. Linda had little trouble getting Brett's mind on the right track, and they were married within three weeks of Billy's wedding.

Brett worked for his father as a sign maker. He didn't make much. The newlyweds bought a run-down little house along with a couple acres of land near a tree-lined mountain brook called the Cache la Poudre River just outside Ft. Collins, Colorado.

Linda quickly decided that she hated her situation. She knew it was Billy's fault. She hated the idea that the thing inside was going to cause her pain, which again was Billy's fault. Linda dwelled on her hatred for Billy. Linda's father was right, Billy was "banker-folk," never to be trusted. In her imagination, she reveled in the pain she would inflict on Billy when she had the chance.

ᗊ ᗊ ᗊ

The embryo had become a fetus, and had taken on a human male form. The fetus had ears that could not hear and eyes that could not see. Only his sense of smell was well developed, and he was very familiar with the smell of his mother. He could perceive that his body was placed into motion by forces other than his own, although he still had no sense of "self. "

Once he smelled something foreign. It was a nasty metallic smell. He knew it must be a threat to his survival because his mother's heart was racing, and her blood was full of the familiar chemicals of fear. His own fear became intense when he felt the thing next to him. It was long, thin and hard. His heart raced, and he kicked at the thing and pushed it away until it withdrew.

Several days later, the fetus became alert when he felt a tickling sensation in his ears. Within days, he could clearly hear his mother's voice. At first the sound was nothing but a cacophony of stimuli, having no order, making no sense.

Gradually the little fetus learned the sounds of language and the rhythm of his mother's speech. He liked hearing it. He moved his arms and legs with the rhythm of her voice.

The fetus was beginning to perceive the individual that was his mother. He "knew" instinctively that the voice he heard, and the smell that was not his own was "Mother." He knew, just like any non-thinking animal "knew," that Mother existed for the sole purpose of looking after his survival until he could look after himself.

Once in a while he heard other voices, and he could tell they were different from his mother's voice. The fetus discovered that if he kicked hard enough, he would hear Mother's voice, and he liked that.

Sometimes his mother's voice was loud. He knew these times were dangerous because he felt her heart race and sensed her chemicals of fear. His developing brain continued to incorporate these sensations of danger into his developing mind, which was gradually becoming hard-wired in a way that would better allow him to deal aggressively with a hostile world.

🙚 🙚 🙚

Linda was in labor for an hour when the baby came. There was pain, but it was nothing like she had dreaded. The doctor said he wasn't surprised. She had nice, big hips--plenty of room.

Linda looked at the tiny bundle of pink flesh, and waves of love poured from within. How could this be what had kicked her with the force of a little mule?

"I'm going to call you Vince," she said, with a little smile, "Vince Longto." Linda flinched as she said Brett's last name.

"Are you planning on nursing him?" the nurse said.

"Hadn't thought about it."

"Nursed all my babies. Such a happy time. You can talk to him and see the first glimmer in his eyes that he loves you as much as you love him. Want to try?"

"Okay," Linda said, tentatively.

The nurse picked up the baby and kissed him on his forehead.

"I love the way babies smell," the nurse said.

Vince was making cranky little noises.

"I think he's hungry," the nurse said. "We've been giving him sugar-water in a bottle, and he took right to it." She looked over at Linda. "This baby's special. I've seen thousands. I follow them to see what happens. I'm right most the time. Believe me, I've only seen a couple like this one."

Linda frowned at the old nurse, and held Vince to her nipple. The baby reacted when he felt it on his mouth, tried to suckle, then turned his head and began to cry.

"Sometimes it takes them a little while to get the hang of it. I'll leave him with you," the nurse said, then left.

"Come on baby," Linda said, trying not to look at his crying, contorted little face.

It was a half-hour of hell as she fought with him. As he cried and screamed, Linda became upset and her fleeting thoughts of love vanished.

ᗰ ᗰ ᗰ

The little fetus had a warm and comfortable home until one-day he awakened to a new sound. It was liquid--his liquid and it was running from his mother's body.

The walls of his home were closing in on him, and he felt pressure all over until he was squeezed so hard he couldn't move. He hated it, and he struggled hard against the sensation, but the squeezing continued, and when he wasn't being squeezed, he was still miserable because his home had become so tight and small he could barely move. His arms and legs ached with the pain of overexertion.

The squeezing got worse. His head was squeezed so tight it became a different shape. His ears rang with the pressure, and his skin stung where it was folded. Through all the pain and anguish came something pleasant. His mother's smell had grown intense.

Then, in his eyes, there was another new sensation. It was light, and every time he was squeezed, it got brighter until finally it was so bright it blinded. When the squeezing ended, he barely noticed, because the feeling of cold overwhelmed him. He hated it. He took a deep breath, and felt another new sensation--air rushing through his respiratory system.

In that instant the fetus became a baby. He was distressed and he did the only thing he could do: He let out a blood-curdling wail. The sound of his voice was yet another sensation. All these new stimuli bombarded and overloaded his infantile brain.

When a blanket went around him, he learned his first lesson in communication as a human. When he needed something, if he cried, he might get it. Crying, as a means to communicate, was instinctive. This would be almost his only way to communicate for a long time. It would take him months to learn how to coordinate the dozens of muscles that controlled speech, and to understand what words meant, and years to master it.

The baby could still talk to its mother with chemicals. One chemical was a perfume, and it covered his fuzzy head so that when she kissed him, her olfactory senses would be filled with a wonderful smell, making her feel good about her baby and helping her to bond tightly with him.

Vince stopped crying when he was finally warm. Someone was holding him, and he liked that, but he could smell and hear that it wasn't his mother, and he didn't like that. He was being jostled and touched. His skin had never felt so many things.

Suddenly he perceived another new feeling, taste. Something was in his mouth and he was sucking and tasting something sweet. He liked it, but he sensed that Mother was not near, and that made him uncomfortable because he knew instinctively that Mother had been programmed by their joint creator to have a concern for his survival that was second to none.

He wanted his mother. He couldn't find her with his eyes because he could only perceive light, and he wasn't very good at that. On the other hand, even if he could see where his mother was, he couldn't use that information to transport himself into her arms because he could not move his body in a purposeful way.

He cried for Mother until finally he heard her voice, and smelled her, and he was glad, because he was exhausted, and over-stimulated, and had to sleep. But every time he started to sleep, his mother jostled him, and poked something into his mouth. He didn't suck because his tummy was full of the sweet stuff. He didn't like what was happening so again he did the only thing he knew--he cried.

ᗡᗡ ᗡᗡ ᗡᗡ

Little Vince was asleep when the nurse came back.

"How's he doing?" the nurse said.

"He won't nurse," Linda said. "You said he was drinking from a bottle?"

"Yes."

"That's it then," Linda said, with a gesture indicating the nurse should take him.

"Try one more time," the nurse said, turning to avoid Linda's piercing glare.

When the baby woke again, he seemed to give Linda a blank stare.

Linda looked at him carefully. Her eyes narrowed and her mouth pursed when she saw that the baby had Billy's face. In that instant, Linda's anger toward Billy found a new target. The baby opened his mouth as if to talk. His eyelids were low. It was the banker's look, Linda thought, and the same look Billy had given her when he came to tell her she was no good for him. Linda couldn't stand it. She threw the baby to the bottom of the bed. The baby was relieved to be away from her, Linda thought.

"Nurse," Linda screamed.

"What is it?" the nurse said, taking the baby.

"He won't have me." Linda was wailing. Tears streamed down her face.

Linda looked up as the baby was carried away, and felt satisfaction that he was being ostracized, because hurting the baby was as close as she could get to hurting Billy.

இ இ இ

Baby Vince felt his body hit the bottom of the bed, and for an instant he stopped crying and contemplated the tension in his mother's voice, and as he did, tension in his own body rose until he felt discomfort. Again, he did the only thing he could, he cried.

Then he could tell he was in someone's arms who was not his mother, and he didn't like it. He cried until his energy reserves were depleted, then he slept. When he awoke, he was warm again. He was hungry, and when he cried, he was given warm milk, but he had no sense of Mother, and it made him feel uncomfortable, and he cried again until he was exhausted.

It was several days before he perceived his mother again. He could smell her, and when he heard her, he moved his arms and legs to the rhythm of her voice. He could feel his mother move him around. He heard other voices, but he didn't cry, because he felt good in his mother's arms.

இ இ இ

When Linda brought the baby home, she put him in his crib in a dark room, and that's where he stayed. He cried constantly, she thought. She worked in the garden so she didn't have to hear, or she went shopping. A part of her claimed to hate this baby but another part drew her to him, and when he was quiet and sleeping she would sometimes stand by his side and look with longing at his pretty little self and wish she could pick him up and love him the way a Mother was supposed to.

One day when she came home from shopping, Brett's mother was outside holding the baby. His mother didn't seem to like the baby, either. She had commented on how he didn't look like Brett. Still, she expressed shock that Linda had left him alone.

Linda got a baby carriage with a bonnet. When she took the baby after that, she grudgingly moved him without talking and stuck him into the carriage under the bonnet where she didn't have to see him.

$$\text{▨ ▨ ▨}$$

Vince immediately felt the lack of stimulation in his new home. He'd had enough excitement for the day, so he enjoyed the quiet and slept.

When Vince awoke the next day, he was still in the same dark and quiet room. Now he needed stimulation, and when he got none, he cried softly.

Baby Vince was motivated by two powerful desires, and few others. He wanted to be free of pain, including the pain of hunger, and he wanted to learn. Between these two desires, his will to learn was even stronger than his desire to avoid the mild pain of hunger. His instinct told him that he was in a hostile world where a lack of skills and knowledge would probably cause him to get eaten. He knew instinctively that without more stimulation he would grow up to be stupid, that stupid individuals were poor survivors, and did poorly in the mating game, and as a result his genetic code may vanish from the earth.

Vince wanted light for his eyes so he could learn to see, sound for his ears so he could learn to speak and understand speech, and motion to develop his notion of space and his ability to move his body within it. The longer Vince went without these things, the harder he cried.

Sometimes Vince was rewarded for crying with a little motion, some light, some sound. But it wasn't enough.

꧁ ꧂ ꧁

"Brett Honey," Linda said one evening, "your baby needs a nanny."

Brett shot her a piercing glance. Linda's own mother had pointed out that it looked like the baby would have brown eyes, and if it did, Brett could hardly be the Father.

Linda ignored Brett's look. "Someone who understands him." Linda's voice got low, "who can put up with him."

"If you can do it on ten bucks a week, go ahead," Brett said. Then he turned his back, and left the room.

Linda thought she knew where she could find a nanny. The Longto's had recently acquired new neighbors who lived in a house in the middle of an ox-bow loop on the Cache la Poudre River. They were poor Chinese peasants. Someone from San Francisco had recently purchased the house they were staying in. Gossip had it they were house-sitting. They only knew a couple words of English. They had chickens and someone said they ate dogs.

One of the Chinese women was stooped and walked with a cane. Linda thought it would be good if the Chinese watched the baby. It made her feel good inside when she thought about putting Billy's baby into a bad home.

3--Jin Yaping

Jin Yaping was born near Canton, China, in 1920 where her father had been a wealthy merchant. The Jin family lived on an estate near the Pearl River. Yaping's father owned a harbor with several piers for boats, and several large warehouses. A short, broad canal led from the river to the harbor.

Yaping's father had often told her the story about how she had become his only "male" heir. When she was born, her father was despondent. He had no boys, and he was sure he could have no more children. He contacted the headmaster of a school in the area. The headmaster was solemn and stroked his long, thin, white beard when her father asked if he could educate his oldest daughter to be a businessman.

"It's too late," the headmaster replied. "She has missed taking the path where she gains intelligence about such things."

Master Jin's face became long, and he prepared to depart.

"Wait," the headmaster said, "I understand you have a new child."

"It's another girl," Master Jin said.

"Ah, but it is a baby, and that is when they learn," the headmaster said. "That is when they gain their intelligence."

"But you said girls have no interest in business?"

"I said your oldest daughter has no interest. That doesn't mean your baby girl can't acquire an interest."

"But you said girls have no intelligence."

"I said your oldest daughter does not have intelligence when it comes to business. She is very smart when it comes to things that hold her interest, such as getting what she wants from her father, no doubt."

Master Jin perked up and he began listening intently.

"The solution is simple," the headmaster continued, his eyes flashing. "You must give the new baby an interest in your business. Nature tells her to be interested in those things her role model does. Since she's a girl, she will naturally be interested in those things her mother does. If you want her to learn about your business, you have to be her role model. Once she is interested in business, she will learn as well as any boy. If she's with you from infancy, she will have an intuitive feel for your business. She may even learn it better than you."

As a result of this, Yaping was with her father from the time she was an infant. When she was old enough, she worked hard to please him. She began conducting small portions of his business before reaching her teens, and from then on, her responsibilities grew. When she wasn't in school, she was working with her father. Upon graduation from college she joined him in his business in charge of foreign sales. She corresponded in Japanese, Korean, Mandarin, French and English. She had the power to sign for her father.

She was an expert negotiator. She knew how and when to squeeze her opponent, and she could do it smoothly without causing hard feelings. Her father learned to trust her with difficult negotiations. He was justifiably proud of his little girl, his only "boy."

For the most part, Yaping enjoyed her life. She was pretty and charming and attracted to men, but they astutely avoided her. She didn't like that part, because she wanted to have a family.

When the Communists came to power, her father decided their family would stay in China. Other entrepreneurs were leaving, but it was his home, he had said. He had ample properties outside of the country that the Communists couldn't take. He'd seen government fads come and go, and this one would go soon enough. It turned out worse than he expected.

As a large entrepreneur, Master Jin was "an enemy of the state," and he was sent away for "re-education." As old as he was, he was not considered educable. His re-education facility was little more than a prison he would never leave.

Yaping was assigned to a nearby farming village for re-education. It took her a long time to become accustomed to the physical work, and when she did, she worked hard for her new family. Twice a week she walked five miles to a nearby town for re-education classes. It was not easy for an educated person to be instructed by peasants.

A month after Yaping arrived, a baby was born in the home where she was staying, and Yaping helped with the delivery. It was the most beautiful, ugly little thing Yaping had ever seen, and it brought back the feelings Yaping had about her own infancy. It had been, she had thought, a wonderfully joyous time when the world's treasures were unfolded to her. It was the same thing Yaping wanted to give to her own infant as a very humble way to pay for the gift that had been given to her. Every day, Yaping's desire to have her own baby grew.

Yaping noticed one positive change at the farming community. She was finally getting looks from men, and it made her feel very good, although none of them would be acceptable as the Father of her babies.

Yaping was working in a field of rice when she felt a stare. She looked up and saw a man. He was far away in a wide field belonging to the next village. Yaping could see instantly that he was different. He was tall and he looked intelligent. Without hesitation, they walked toward each other, both studying the other as the distance closed.

"Walk on past," he said when she was close enough to hear. Then as they passed, he said: "Come to the buffalo pen in your village after dark."

Although their meetings were short and sporadic, Yaping quickly became bonded to the man. His name was Jianping, and he was a nuclear physicist. His re-education program was supposed to be a fast one. China needed his expertise so they could build nuclear bombs. When he discovered that Yaping was a large capitalist, he was depressed. The Communists would not allow their union, he said, because his work was crucial to China's national security. Yaping told him that she had access to money in banks in Europe and America, and if they could get out of China, their lives would be fine.

It was August when they made their move. They met by the side of the Pearl River. Each of them had a goat's stomach for flotation.

Yaping and Jianping had planned to get out of the river before reaching the sea, wait through the day, then, under the cover of darkness, gradually get to Macao, a Portuguese trading settlement on the Chinese mainland.

Hong Kong was closer, but they figured the route would be more carefully watched. When they finally came to the spot where Jianping wanted to get out, they saw soldiers on the shore and continued floating. Soon they could see nothing, and wondered where they were.

In the darkness, Yaping heard a whooshing sound. She strained to hear. It was in the air, moving fast. Then she heard the sound she knew to be the subtle call of a pelican.

"Pelicans," Yaping said.

"We are in the sea," Jianping said. "The water is saline, and it is cooler than the river."

"Is that why I'm so cold." Yaping was shivering.

As soon as it became light, they could see dark forms in the water around them and wondered if they were sharks. Jianping saw a small island. They tried swimming to it, but the current and the breeze carried them past. They continued into the great ocean, into what appeared to be certain death.

They came upon a sunken reef. It took effort to stand on it. The water came to their waist, but the tide was going out and in a little while, it was down to their knees. The sun was high. Gradually their shivering bodies became warmer. Every so often, a high wave knocked them down. The rocks were sharp and full of urchins. When Yaping fell on one, spines stuck in her side. She tried to pull them out, but they broke off. She saw dark spots just below the skin. One of them bled a little. There wasn't much pain.

She could deal with this, too, she thought, but she was having a hard time dealing with her inevitable death. When the tide came back, the water would be too high for them to continue standing on the small reef.

They huddled together, resigned to their fate. When they thought all was lost, a voice broke the silence.

"You two are the sorriest looking sight I've ever seen," the voice said in English. It was a well-dressed Chinese man in a little boat. Yaping and Jianping didn't care who it was. They just wanted to be warm again.

"Want to be saved?" the Chinese man said. Fine, you sign on with me in my factory."

He explained that they would manufacture shoes. They signed.

The Chinese gentleman took them to a houseboat in Aberdeen, on the other side of the island from Hong Kong. Yaping heard him leave orders with the man and woman who lived on the boat to nurse them back to health.

In a couple days, a nervous man approached the couple. "How do you do, Madam," he said in English.

It was the first time anyone had been nervous around them. The man was obviously a leader. Yaping figured they'd been identified and she wondered if she would be sold back to the Communists.

The man said: "My father is the man who pulled you from the sea. He's a trader, and he's very concerned about you. The Chinese have placed a reward upon your husband's head of two thousand dollars."

Yaping could see that it was not his intent to turn them over to the Communists, whom she could see he hated. On the other hand, they needed compensation for their costs and the risk they would take. Helping Yaping and Jianping could cost the shoemakers their lives. There was also the cost of the passage, and Yaping and her man would need money until she could get access to her foreign accounts. She knew a trader in San Francisco whom she was certain she could count on to help.

In short order, Yaping negotiated the deal. The shoemaker agreed to pay her cost of passage and advance funds for incidentals. She wasn't surprised. Good will with a large trader like Jin Yaping could pay off handsomely for him in years to come. Yaping signed a note for a thousand dollars, payable in sixty days. She had but one special request. She asked the shoemaker to procure for her a special baby book. It was a book that had been written more than five hundred years ago in northern China. It was this book the headmaster had used to advise her father in the way Yaping was raised. Yaping planned to have babies in America, and she wanted to raise them in the same way.

Within the week, Yaping and her man were on a trading vessel. At first Yaping was happier than she had ever been, then she became sick, and as the days passed, it got worse. Jianping attributed it to seasickness, but she knew it was something worse.

In the hospital in Chinatown in San Francisco, she was found to have an infection in her abdominal cavity. In surgery, diseased and necrotic tissue was removed. Both ovaries had to be removed. Muscle and connective tissue in her side and back were damaged. It would be difficult for her to hold good posture again. She was lucky to be alive.

"I found this protruding into your abdominal cavity," the doctor said, holding up a thin black rod.

"What is it?" Yaping said.

"Could it be an urchin's quill? Have you been near the ocean?"

Yaping realized that's what it was. The doctor explained that bacteria clinging to her skin had probably been pushed into her abdominal cavity by the quill.

Yaping finished her recuperation with the Chinese trader. He felt their lives were in danger, and said they must hide for at least five years. He helped them plan.

With the aid of an atlas, they found a possible location at a pretty spot in Colorado. Yaping hired an agent who found and purchased a suitable piece of land where they could grow their own food and keep to themselves.

They were delivered to the house late at night. There were three of them. Yaping had acquired a young woman named Yong Haua to act as a servant.

Yaping liked the house. It sat in the middle of a big loop in the stream. In the second story of the house there was a small room with a window, which looked over the road. The only way to the house was down that road. Yaping made the room into a sitting room where the road could be watched.

With time to think, Yaping became depressed. Much of her beauty was gone, but her main concern was her inability to have a baby. Jianping suggested they adopt. It would be easy to find one in China. It could even be a relative. But Yaping knew they would have to wait. Looking might give away their hiding place.

Yaping often took discreet walks along the Cache la Poudre. It was on one of these walks that Yaping saw a woman with a baby carriage. The baby was crying, but the woman didn't seem to care. The canopy on the baby carriage was situated so the woman couldn't see the baby.

Finally, and with an irritated look, the woman picked up a bottle and jammed it into the baby's face. Then with a mean look on her face, the woman returned to her position behind the carriage.

After that, Yaping went for walks often in hopes she would catch another glimpse of the baby that was so in need of love.

4—Ersatz Mother

A week later, Yaping was in the sitting room reading. She felt an emptiness that kept her from enjoying the pleasant afternoon. She was startled when she saw the woman with the baby coming down the road. Yaping watched until it was obvious the woman was coming to her house. She immediately went downstairs and met the woman in front of the house.

Her name was Linda Longto. Yaping's full attention was on the little bundle. "Your baby will have brown eyes," Yaping said in her accented English, bending over the infant.

"Brown eyes you say? That's cuz he's plumb full of shit," Linda said.

Yaping thought the woman actually had a desire to inflict pain upon her baby. She figured the woman might leave him with her if she thought her baby would be in bad hands. Yaping switched to Pidgin English. "I take your baby, please. Not charge too much."

"How much? He's a bad boy, you know."

Yaping hid her disgust. "There are meals," Yaping said, slowly. "What's the baby eat?"

"Have him on a bottle."

"Milk's expensive. It will cost about twenty-five cents per day. Then there's the cost of soap to wash the dishes, about five cents a day. That's thirty cents." Yaping went on listing numbers and watching Linda as she did. If Linda's face indicated she'd pay more, Yaping thought up another expense, and if it was too high, Yaping thought of a reason why that expense was not necessary.

In just a few moments, without Linda saying a word, Yaping knew the going rate for taking care of a baby, how much Linda would pay in cash, and how much she'd promise to pay on credit. Yaping and Linda struck a deal. It was more than Linda wanted to pay, but Yaping wanted it that way. She readily extended credit.

The next day, as Yaping waited, she walked back and forth and fidgeted. Linda was supposed to bring the baby at eight, and it was nine.

"She's coming," Haua reported.   Yaping rushed into the kitchen and waited. When Haua called to her, she came out casually, thanked Linda and had Haua take the baby. As soon as Linda was gone, Yaping took the baby.

He felt so good in Yaping's arms. She kissed him. He smelled good, just like a Chinese baby.

"Hello, Baby," she said in Cantonese, her mother's language, "My name's Yaping. You're such a precious baby." She squeezed him. "You have such a pretty nose." She touched his nose, "and you have a forehead, pretty eyes, and a mouth." She touched each part as she said it. Yaping got the feeling that Haua thought she was being foolish with the baby.

"A baby cannot learn a word he does not hear," Yaping said to Haua. Looking back at the baby, Yaping could see that Vince didn't seem to be responding well to her voice. She saw in the baby's eyes that no one was home. Concerned, Yaping consulted her book.

"This book," Yaping told Haua in a deep and reverent voice, "contains the wisdom of the ages." Yaping was satisfied with the way Haua became alert. "It says two important things about babies. It says babies are born good." Yaping paused. The old book appeared to be giving her words more authority. "The book says that *all* babies are born with the ability to grow up smart, and what happens to the baby in its first five years determines how smart it will be."

Haua watched closely as Yaping tested the baby's ability to track with his eyes, and his reaction to sounds. "This baby has not been exposed to the world," Yaping said. "We'll soon cure that." Yaping smiled confidently at the baby. But it was a show for Haua, because inside, Yaping wasn't so sure. Only one baby in a hundred was dumber than this baby, and it was also the wisdom of the ages that dumb babies grow up to be dumb adults, and maybe her efforts would go nowhere. The baby's mother was obviously stupid. Maybe this baby was doomed to stupidity, just like all other babies with stupid parents. Maybe her book was wrong. Then Yaping thought about how she was so much smarter than her sisters, at least where business and a man's world were concerned, and how the only difference was the way she was raised. Yaping took a deep breath, closed her eyes, and resolved to roll up her sleeves and do her best. It was her baby now, and she didn't intend for it to grow up to be stupid.

"You want to see the light?" Yaping said loudly in Cantonese as she walked outside. "Light," she said. She was relieved to see the baby's pupils contract. "Let's go back where it's *dark. Dark*," Yaping said again back inside, where she waited for his pupils to again adjust to the dark. Three trips outside and baby Vince was fast asleep. "Five minutes ago, his mind was a total blank," Yaping said, kissing him on his sweet-smelling head. "While he sleeps, he will learn what light is. Baby's learn at lightning speed."

Twice a day Yaping repeated this exercise. When, on the third day, the baby didn't fall asleep, Yaping held up a black and white checkerboard. "Look at this," she said. It was right in front of him but he obviously couldn't find it.

"Keep looking," Yaping said. His eyes wandered. He seemed to know something was there. Finally, his eyes fixed onto the boundary between white and black, and he stared at the contrast with big eyes as Yaping talked to him in a loud voice. Soon he was asleep.

"The first thing a baby must do is learn to see," Yaping said to Haua as she put the baby down to rest. "First he must learn black and white, then colors. We must start with the basics. Watch the baby carefully. When he loses interest, that's when we move on. A baby will not waste its precious time on something it already knows." Yaping was pleased to see that Haua was beginning to understand. Soon Haua was talking to the baby in Mandarin just like Vince understood every word.

In less than a month, Vince could follow Yaping across the room with his eyes and recognize his name.

"The next thing we have to teach him," Yaping said to Haua, "Is how to use his hands." Yaping ignored Haua's incredulous look, and went to work.

"Look baby, beads," Yaping said, holding up a string of big red beads. "The earlier a baby learns, the smarter he will be when he grows up," Yaping said as she eagerly watched the little baby.

🜚 🜚 🜚

Baby Vince knew to search when he heard the word "look." He quickly found the pretty beads, and his eyes locked on.

He opened and closed his mouth, trying desperately to bite them. *Red. Shiny and round*, he thought. *What to do? Not close enough to bite. But wait. The hand. The one with the thumb that is good to suck. It can grab, but where is it?*

🜚 🜚 🜚

"You want to taste them, don't you?" Yaping said to the baby with a smile. Vince was moving his mouth, and at his side, his hand was opening and closing. His face showed intense concentration. "You have to pull them to your mouth. Use your hand." Yaping squeezed his hand twice saying the word "hand" both times. "You can see how hard he's trying, can't you?" Yaping said to Haua, who had been watching closely.

🜚 🜚 🜚

Baby Vince wanted to grab the shiny red beads so he could feel the red, and taste the round. His hand opened and closed, but it was nowhere near the beads. It lay to the side of his head.

What's that? What's moving? Is that it? The hand?

Vince looked at the object at his side, and watched with awe as it moved in perfect step with the signals he was sending. He had to be looking at his hand.

"You *see* it, don't you?" Yaping said. "Now make it move the way you want it to move. You have to practice."

Vince understood he was being encouraged. At first his hand didn't do what Vince wanted it to do. He could make it move, but never where he wanted, when he wanted.

His first movements were spastic. He could pull his hand to his mouth but nothing more. It was a place to start. He touched his mouth then flung his hand into space. It hit the side of the crib. It hit his face. It hit another hand.

Another hand?

There are two hands!

Touch it.

He threw his hands toward each other, but they flew past. *OOPS.* Big baby eyes. *What happened?*

His arms flailed, but he continued to move them and practice. Every so often one hand crashed into the other, and when that happened, he repeated as best he could his last motion. They crashed into each other more and more frequently.

Every day he got better.

Finally the time came when he thought he could do it. He held his left hand in front. He reached with his right, and grabbed his left hand. It wasn't easy, but he did it.

He did it again. *Yes. It works. The hand works.* His hard practice was rewarded. He could finally make a purposeful movement, and if felt wonderful.

He looked around, waiting, watching, and listening. *Now, where are those beads?*

🛏 🛏 🛏

Yaping was happy when Vince finally grabbed the beads. In another week, he was grabbing them reliably. Yaping again consulted her book. She was delighted to find that he was no longer behind. She was equally happy with her progress with Jianping and Haua. Both were talking to the baby, and showing him things, just like he understood everything.

At the end of every month, Yaping gave Linda a bill. She wrote on the bill, "Take your time paying. There is no rush."

For the first two months, Linda had brought the baby to Yaping, then picked him up in the evening. Linda brought the baby at erratic times.

One day Linda didn't show up at all. Yaping marched up to Linda's house and presented a bill. "If you don't bring the baby, I'll need payment right away," Yaping said.

"I just didn't get him to you yesterday. You can take him now," Linda said.

"Take Haua to the baby. From now on, Haua will come to your house in the morning. It is best if she lets herself in. Then she can take the baby without disturbing anyone." Yaping figured that Linda slept past nine in the morning. Yaping stepped aside, holding the screen door open. Haua began walking with a pleasant but resolute look on her face, just as they'd rehearsed.

From then on, for six days of every week, Haua got the baby in the morning and brought him back in the evening. Vince soon became Yaping's reason for existence. Yaping showed the tiny baby pictures, read to him, and took him for long walks. She talked to him as she would to any adult. She listened intently to any sound the baby made.

"The first word he says will be my name," Yaping said confidently to Jianping and Haua. Yaping was right again, because when Vince was four months old, he was saying her name. It wasn't clearly articulated--it was nothing more than a blob of sound, but Yaping knew it was the best the baby could do.

Yaping had made up a nursery rhyme: "Little baby flies, and from the stars he swings. When he is tired he falls into the arms of Yaping." She said the rhyme to baby Vince twice a day.

When she thought he was ready, she stopped saying her name at the end. Then she waited. Instantly Vince froze and stared into space. He moved his mouth, trying to form a sound. He wiggled his arms and legs. Yaping saw he was trying. She waited. He'd say something soon, she thought.

His mouth was moving--he was trying so hard. Finally, Vince said, "Ing," then gave everyone a winning smile. He was awarded with a big round of applause.

"Next time," Yaping said, "his mind will have more power, and he'll be faster."

Baby Vince had gone quickly from being a dull baby to a baby who was alert. He looked for sounds and focused quickly on things moving nearby.

Soon Vince was crawling everywhere. Yaping moved only those things out of his reach that she thought might cause him to choke. She loved to watch him explore.

One day, Baby Vince crawled to Yaping and watched as she used her abacus. "Look, baby. One." Yaping pushed a bead out, and when Vince focused on it, she pushed out another, and said: "*Two*. Always feed a baby's interests," Yaping said to Haua. "When a baby is exposed to information, he will develop ways of using it. That's what intelligence is, ways of using information. You only get it when you are young."

After that, Vince regularly crawled to the abacus, shook it and said: "Numbers." Then he looked at Yaping, who kept his interest by adding another bead at each session. Yaping loved these sessions with the baby. Nevertheless, she was careful not to give him too much.   "Always quit showing it to them when they're still interested," Yaping told Haua. "Twice a day is plenty, even if he asks for more."

When Vince was still a toddler, he understood more than a thousand words, not just in Cantonese, but also in Mandarin, Haua's language, and he could speak hundreds of words in either language.

Haua couldn't understand how a baby could understand and speak so many words.

"A baby can't learn a word he doesn't hear," Yaping said. "The younger a baby is when he learns, the more intelligent he will be. The more words a baby hears, the more he will be able to learn when he's grown."

When Vince was two years old, her book said that only one baby in ten thousand had a larger vocabulary. The book said it was time for the baby to learn to read. Soon Yaping was deep into a reading program.

"Look baby," Yaping said, holding up a word in Chinese writing, and at the same time saying the word. Then, as quickly as she could, she'd show him several words. "When he quits looking," she told Haua, "That means he's learned it. That's when we show him new words."

Baby Vince always napped where Yaping worked. Often he slept in front of the hi-fi, as Yaping played classical music. "He doesn't belong in a quiet room," Yaping said, "babies learn in their sleep."

The contrast was striking between life with Yaping, who was all love and life with Linda who was all hate. For Vince at a young age, the difference caused him little concern. Linda's personality was like a wall that he couldn't walk through or a bird that he couldn't touch--something that just was. That all changed when Vince was two and Linda discovered that she was pregnant. Her joy was obvious, and she walked around the house singing and talking about the new one. She had Brett add a bedroom to their house.

When the bedroom was finished, Linda installed nice birchwood furniture. It was a beautiful room, decorated with bright wallpaper. Vince's room in comparison was little more than a broom closet, with barely enough room for the little cot he slept on. "This baby will be precious," Linda told Brett. She went on to explain that it was important that the baby's room be far from Vince's. Frowning at Vince, she said: "We don't want him hearing any stupid sounds." Vince watched and absorbed every detail. Linda's negative attitude and her derisive laughter had long since taught him not to speak Chinese around her.

As time passed, and Linda's attitude remained the same, Vince began to sense injustice and feel pain.

Yaping always found ways to entertain him. She took Vince with her when she worked her Chinese vegetable garden, which was just beyond the towering cottonwoods and spruce trees that encircled the house.

She put Vince in the grass surrounded by pieces of bread. Little gray squirrels came out of the trees and ate the bread. They let Vince get close. He reached out with a chubby little hand, but they always stayed just a little out of range.

Yaping always stayed within sight, because if Vince could not see her, he became upset. Yaping could see Vince was afraid of being left alone, and she wondered if she had done the right thing to tell him that one-day she would leave. Vince wanted to know why Linda loved his brother, but not him, and Yaping didn't know what to say or do.

Yaping knew there were risks in letting him explore. She had heard of a rabid rodent biting a child. But there were greater risks, Yaping thought, in not letting him learn about his world, and the chance of encountering a rabid rodent *and* being bitten was almost zero. Nevertheless, she always looked for unusual behavior in the squirrels that came around.

After the squirrels ate, brightly colored birds came. They didn't have the same trust in the baby as the squirrels, and kept their distance. After the songbirds, there were ants and other insects. The baby was entertained for as long as Yaping worked in her garden.

When Vince found a mass of frogs' eggs, Yaping put them in a little pool near the house so he could watch them. While he watched the tadpoles grow, he watched the water bugs, the whirligigs, toe biters, and dragonfly nymphs that sometimes ate one of his tadpoles, and wrigglers that became mosquitoes before his very eyes.

As Vince lay in the grass watching, he would hear neat sounds like woodpeckers and the wind whistling through the wings of the mourning doves as they flew.

Vince learned about plants, like the fact that spruce trees were sharp and sticky, almost like cactus. In May, the fruit trees would blossom: apple, crabapple and cherry, and bees would swarm over them. When Yaping saw his interest in the bees, she got a hive, and had Jianping put a window in the back of it. Jianping fashioned a "foyer" with a curtain to keep out the light. Vince could stick his head through the curtain and watch the bees inside. Yaping smiled when she saw him watching his bees. The boy watched for hours.

Whenever Vince showed an interest in a subject, Yaping sent off for books in Chinese from San Francisco. Sometimes she got books from Taiwan or Hong Kong. When they arrived, they spent hours reading and looking at the pictures.

When Vince was four years old, he was reading independently. From that point on, Yaping made sure he always had a new book to read.

Socially, Vince's environment was also rich. It was difficult for Vince to deal with Linda and Brett, but gradually he developed effective strategies. He also had to develop strategies that enabled him to switch back and forth between two quite different cultures.

One Sunday four-year-old Vince was with Linda, Brett, and two year-old Mike. At a pet store, Vince pointed to the puppies and said, "Look, Momma, yummy--" Vince stopped. He knew he'd said the wrong thing. He smiled at Mike, then took his chubby little hand.

"What'd he say?" Brett said.

Linda pursed her mouth, grabbed Mike and shielded him from Vince with her body. "He was going to say, 'Yummy dogs,'" Linda said with a look of disdain. "The little idiot wants to eat a puppy." Linda picked up Mike and kissed him affectionately as if he had just endured pain.

"I told you not to let him go to the Chinese," Brett said. "We'll end up with a little monster."

Vince watched his mother with sad eyes. She rarely hugged and kissed him.

Linda gave Brett a deadpan look. "End up with?" Linda said, sarcastically. She gave Vince a hateful look, then walked away.

Vince noticed that Linda never told anyone about Yaping, and skirted the issue when it came up. He understood that she thought she was doing the wrong thing in sending him to the Chinese, and he knew that in some ways she liked it and in other ways she didn't.

Vince wondered why eating puppy could be bad. Haua often kept a puppy in a wicker cage in the kitchen. If possible, the puppy was saved for a special occasion. Haua would get everything ready. Then, at the last minute, with little Vince "helping," she slaughtered the puppy for the meal. It was just like when he was at Grandma's and they slaughtered chickens and rabbits.

He knew the Chinese were not bad. Everyone was nicer at his Chinese home. No one was rude and there was no vicious shouting and never any hitting. He was certain the Chinese were better people. He didn't understand why his mother was of a different opinion.

First thing Monday morning, Vince talked to Yaping. "Why don't Americans eat puppy?" Vince said.

Yaping looked away quickly. With a look of resolve, she looked back and said, "Because Americans think it's wrong to eat puppy."

"Why?"

"Different people have different rules when it comes to eating. Lots of times, the rules don't make any sense. Americans eat pig. In Israel or anywhere in Arabia, that would be a very bad thing. Are there things you won't eat? Wait, let me change that," Yaping said, laughing. "Are there things your mother won't eat?"

"Earthworms."

"They are as nutritious as anything can be. In some places in the world they're a delicacy. If it isn't poisonous, or even if it is poisonous and there's a way to remove the poison, somebody, somewhere eats it."

"So, what do I do?"

"When you're with us, you eat by our rules. When you're with your other family, eat by their rules."

"But what if my family finds out I eat puppy?"

Yaping looked away, thinking. She took a deep breath, furrowed her brow, and then turned back, "You don't tell them." She gave him a big hug and left him to ponder what she had said.

Vince realized he already did that. He'd never tell Yaping his mother had hit him, even if she asked. It was okay to hit his little brother if Yaping didn't know about it. It was okay for lots of things so long as only the right people knew about it. Sometimes, the only right person was Vince.

By the time Vince was five, he'd developed skills for dealing with the people in his world. When he was with Linda, he was guarded and quiet. Honesty was rarely rewarded, and answers honestly given were often used against him. He learned that deception was best. He knew that if he lied to his mother while using the demeanor he used while telling the truth to Yaping, he could get an advantage. He usually told the truth to Yaping, but he discovered that sometimes a lie to her also gained him the advantage, but he had to be very clever to get away with lying to Yaping.

His personal rules concerning food were unique. He didn't resort to habit like other people when he decided if he should eat something. His rule was simple: If it wasn't poisonous, it was edible.

Vince also saw that the Chinese had different physical characteristics than he. From as early as he could remember, he was aware that he was not Chinese. As he thought about that, and the fact that Yaping would one day leave, his need for his mother's love grew. He realized that the only difference between Mike and him in his mother's eyes was that he had Yaping. He decided that if he no longer had Yaping, that his mother would love him just like she loved his brother.

Vince dreamed about the day that Yaping was gone and his mother would love him, too. Sometimes he felt anger toward Yaping, and the older he got, the more aggressive he became toward her.

When Vince turned seven, Yaping's book said his personality was set. She wished she had done something to insulate Vince from his mother's abuse, and especially from her sneers, snubs and rudeness. She tortured herself thinking she did the wrong thing when she pressured Linda into giving Vince to her, and wondered if Linda would have treated him differently if she had never intervened.

Yaping could see that she had been successful in making Vince smart. She could also see that Vince didn't have the most important ingredient for a smart person: He didn't have honor and integrity, and without these, Yaping knew he could not have nobility. She knew a great man without nobility was a threat to everyone around him. Yaping thought Vince had been damaged by his mother, that the damage had literally changed the structure of his brain.

Vince was eight years old when the time finally came for Yaping to leave. Leaving turned out to be more heart wrenching than the taking away of her father by the peasant communists.

"You're on your own, now," Yaping said to Vince just before leaving. "You're smart enough to control your own destiny, and make your life a good one. Good luck." With that, she was gone.

5 – Where the Rubber Meets the Road

The morning after Yaping had departed; Vince awoke with a start. He could feel that something was wrong. He lay on his cot and listened to his heartbeat. For eight years, his day had begun with the sound of Haua coming through the back door and saying in broken English: "Haua come for boy."

The sound had energized Vince. It meant to him another day of discovery and fulfillment. He would jump out of bed and holler to Haua in English as he pulled his clothes on. Then he'd chatter to Haua in English until they were down the road. Haua usually didn't understand what he was saying, so he would answer his own questions. He wanted everyone to think that he only spoke English when he was with the Chinese. He'd long since forgotten why.

When he knew Haua wasn't coming, he felt a little depressed; Vince pulled his clothes on and went to the kitchen. Dirty dishes on the table showed that everyone had already eaten breakfast.

"Hey, Mom," Vince said, wondering if he sounded too cheerful. "You forgot about me."

"Want breakfast?" his mother said, coming into the kitchen; "Fix it yourself." Linda was gruff and rude, as usual. This time it hit Vince almost like a physical blow. He had half expected that his mother would change the instant Yaping left. He tried hard to push the pain away. His mother wouldn't change overnight, he thought.

"Where's Mike," Vince said, "and everyone else?" He meant Brett. He didn't know why, but he felt uncomfortable calling him "Dad."

Linda said that Brett had taken Mike to pre-school, and that she had to have Vince in school soon so Vince had to hurry and get ready.

Vince was apprehensive as his mother led him to the school. The principal was a short, chubby man with a heavy beard.

"Your boy's eight," the principal said. "Should we put him in the second grade?"

"He's slow," Linda said.

Vince wanted to say that Yaping thought he was smart, but he didn't feel comfortable talking about Yaping in front of his mother. He sat quietly as the pain of their banter settled hard.

"I suppose we should test him," the principal said.

"We did that," Linda said. "That's why we didn't start him earlier."

Vince felt more pain as Linda lied, and wished there were some way to show his mother how smart he really was.

Linda watched with a smug smile as the principal wrote, "learning disabled" on Vince's folder.

"Then you did the right thing holding him back," the principal said. "We'll start him in the first grade."

The weeks passed, and Linda didn't change. Vince was never fond of his little brother, and now, every time his mother smiled at Mike, hugged him, and did something special for him, Vince felt a powerful surge of aggression. If it wasn't for Mike, he thought, he'd get his fair share of the hugs, and the special little favors. He couldn't help wishing that Mike were dead.

Before Yaping left, her love had kept his hate from growing. Now, he yearned to communicate with her. She had promised to write, but so far, he had received nothing. He had hated Chinese calligraphy, but Yaping made him learn it, saying it was how they would keep in touch when she was gone. In anticipation now, Vince wrote long letters to her. Thinking and writing in Chinese, and talking to Yaping made him feel good, the way he felt when he was with her and everything was beautiful. He was always worried the Chinese writing would be discovered, and he took great pains to hide the letters.

Every day, Vince ran home from school so he could check the mail himself and every day that there was no letter from Yaping, he felt a little smaller.

One Sunday morning, several months after Yaping had left, Vince awoke before anyone else. He was angry as he sat up. He was still in a tiny room, still on a cot. He went into Mike's bedroom, and as he marveled at his brother's surroundings, his anger grew. The room had pretty shelves full of toys, and his bed had fancy covers. Vince felt hatred. Mike was at fault, Vince thought, for keeping Linda's love for himself.

Vince couldn't help himself. He crept up, reached under the covers and pinched down hard. When Mike jumped up screaming, Vince slipped under the bed.

Linda was there instantly.

"Somebody pinched me," Mike said.

"Brett," Linda screamed. "Find Vince!"

Vince figured he'd make his getaway when Linda ran out looking for him.

"He's not in his room," Brett said.

"Go to your Daddy," Linda said to Mike.

Linda never referred to Brett as Vince's father with the same ease, and as Vince thought about that, his hatred for his brother grew. Vince heard Mike jump out of bed and walk across the room. The door closed, then it was quiet. Vince knew he was trapped. He only regretted that he hadn't inflicted more pain.

"Hey, Mom," Vince said, sliding out from under the bed, "what's going on?"

He looked her square in the face. When Linda looked at him, her face changed, showing revulsion. Her right hand shot out fast and knocked Vince into the corner. She beat him, then she yelled. "I should've let you die when I had the chance." She coughed a dry smoker's cough.

Vince was calm, more mature than his almost nine years should have allowed. He positioned himself so his face and head would take the next blows. Vince had developed many ways to handle his mother's rage. He was inwardly pleased to have this opportunity to learn more about his mother, and the way she thought about him and his brother. He knew the beating would end sooner if he showed pain and let her win, but pain didn't motivate him the way it did most small children. His tolerance was high. He looked up, his inner determination hidden behind big brown eyes.

"You stupid little monster, I hate you," she said. "See this?" She pointed to a picture of his little brother, and, as she looked, the hate on her face momentarily subsided. "This here's a good person, not bad like you. Smart, not stupid. He's gonna grow up to be handsome and athletic, not an ugly little wimp." Linda scowled at Vince. The last sound was frozen on her contorted mouth. A crooked little blood vessel bulged on her forehead.

Vince was sad to see her like this. He liked having a pretty mother. He could see it was his little brother's fault, and if his little brother were gone, or if his mother could be shown how stupid and bumbling he was, his parents would love him.

"You better never hurt him," Linda said, "never raise a finger against him because compared to him, you're dirt--nothing."

Linda raised her hand to strike, looked at her son with trepidation, and then withdrew. Vince's tactic was working. Visible bruises could cause problems for her. The anger on her face turned to frustration. Finally, she broke down.

As Linda cried, Vince came to her and touched her gently. He knew love was there. He'd seen it in her eyes, in the way she moved, but some hidden force kept it from coming out. When he thought it was safe, he moved in closer and hugged her and said it was okay. His mother's smell made Vince feel good, and touching her was exhilarating.

"Mother," his voice was soft and sincere. Linda seemed to relax and enjoy his touch. "I'm not going to hurt Mike." Instantly he felt Linda's body stiffen. It seemed to Vince like it was the mention of his brother's name that caused his mother's reaction.

"You dirty little liar," his mother said, and swung at him.

Vince was ready and jumped away.

"You'll burn in hell for lying. You think I'm stupid? I know what you've been doing."

The words had no apparent affect on Vince. He looked at his mother, and repeated the litany that he would never hurt his little brother. Vince knew she could not know otherwise. He knew it from watching her as she lied, and from the lessons taught him by Yaping. He knew he was the only person on earth who could see the thoughts in his head. Others could suspect otherwise, but his intent could only be known if he admitted to it, or showed it on his face.

After that, Vince was angry with his mother. He was angry with Brett for being stupid and indifferent. But most of all, he hated his brother for being the cause of it all.

For months after this incident, Vince couldn't stand to be around any of them. Their manners were terrible, he thought. They didn't give Vince the respect he deserved, and they stank. He was mad at Yaping, too, and one day, when his anger grew intense, he got out the letters he'd written to her and burned them.

Vince kept away from Linda, Brett and Mike, and played a hiding game. When it was warm, he liked to sit in the attic, where he sat cross-legged and allowed his brain to go fuzzy by letting his thoughts jump anywhere, everywhere, even many places at once. Yaping called it "monkey-brain." She was referring to a scared monkey who ran here and there and looked everywhere, never focusing on any one thing. Yaping had taught him ways to guard against monkey brain. She said one day he would be important, and the better he focused his brain, the more important he would become.

Vince found no relief from his anxiety when he went to school. He was bored there. He already knew most of what was being taught, and he was never appreciated for who he was. Sometimes teachers whispered silently about him. He knew they were talking about his learning problem.

When he was in the second grade, his teacher explained to the class that bones in the body weren't altogether necessary, that people could get along well without them, and the only difference is that their bodies would not be rigid, but limp like the body of an octopus.

Vince's hand shot up. He knew better, and this was a chance to show that he had no learning problem. He was wearing a short-sleeved shirt. When he was called on, he flexed his biceps and said: "See this biceps muscle?" The whole class was looking. "See this tendon?" He put a finger under it. "It goes from the muscle to the radius bone in my forearm. If there were no bone, how would it move my arm?"

The teacher glowered at Vince. For the rest of that year, she found every way possible to make him look dumb. In the middle of the year, Vince turned in a drawing that was better than the drawings of his classmates. He was very proud of it. He'd spent several nights working on it. Again, he wanted to show her what he could do. Later that day, the teacher reviewed the children's drawings with the class. When she got to Vince's, she looked quickly, threw it down, and said sarcastically: "This doesn't look like something Vince did." Vince came away from that grade with a negative feeling for school and an appreciation for the fact that success required much more than a string of good deeds.

Vince was ten when Brett brought home a World Book Encyclopedia. Linda said it would help Mike with school. Mike looked at it once. When Vince looked he was mesmerized. Within six months, Vince had read every interesting article at least once, and committed thousands of facts to memory. But his mother wasn't impressed when he spouted off facts, and said he was being a smart aleck. Vince knew that. Yaping had taught him differently, that for his mother to see how smart he was, he had to show her. He thought about the way his mother had been delighted with Mike recently when he showed her something he'd made. It was from school, made from paper. Glue bent it out of shape. It was haphazardly colored with crayon marks. Vince had no idea what it was. He knew he could do better.

He had things in his bedroom he could show her, he thought. He was proud of a little electric motor he'd made. He'd used old nails that he'd wrapped neatly with some wire he'd found. He was especially proud of the battery. It was homemade, too. He'd used an old ceramic cup his mother had thrown away. The encyclopedia had given him the idea and know-how for everything.

"See my motor?" Vince said when he thought the moment was right. Linda was sitting at the kitchen table. "I made it myself. Watch Mom." Vince took a deep breath and touched a wire to a piece of lead sticking out of the ceramic cup. He was elated as the rotor began to turn. He looked at Linda with a big happy smile.

Linda flicked the ash from her cigarette into a dirty dish, glanced apathetically at the thing, then balefully at Vince's battery. "You digging around in the trash again?" she said. "What's in this thing?" Linda grabbed the battery tearing wires lose. It was full of sand soaked with acid from an old car battery. When she smelled it, her head jerked back quickly and she made a face. "Goddamn it. I threw this thing away once, and that should be enough." She pitched the battery into the trash.

Vince felt bad. He grabbed his damaged motor and turned to run back to his room. Mike was standing in the doorway, and the look on his face indicated he'd seen the whole thing. Vince wanted to destroy the look. Before he reached Mike, Linda grabbed him. Her sharp fingernails hurt his shoulder.

"Get to your room," she said, and gave him a solid push past Mike.

Vince sat in his room. He felt like he was totally out of control--that others could hurt him any time, and he could do nothing about it. He needed a solution and focused on the problem. His mother needed to see that Mike was stupid. When he tried to tell his mother as much, she got mad at Vince. But wait, he thought, there were times when his actions got Mike in trouble. It was when he had no apparent motive to hurt Mike. Like the time Brett threw him a ball that he couldn't catch. When it hit Mike, he thought he was in trouble. But he wasn't. He wondered how to disguise motive. He had several ideas, and he couldn't wait to try them. He jumped from his bed, sneaked into Mike's room, hid his dirt shoes then went, head low, into the kitchen.

"I'm really sorry, Mom," he said. "I know I shouldn't have dug that cup out of the trash. Could Mike and I go to the pond?" It was on the neighbor's land, a watering hole for the horses.

"Yeah, Mom," Mike said coming into the kitchen.

Linda hesitated, looked at Mike's eager face, then said: "Get your old shoes on."

Vince followed Mike to his room where Mike searched frantically. "I won't tell Mom if you wear these," Vince said, pointing to Mike's good shoes. Mike pulled them on and the two hurried to the pond. When they returned, Vince was able to get Mike's old shoes back into the open without being noticed.

When Mike was caught, Vince made excuses for him, and told Linda Mike had searched but couldn't find his shoes. It worked great. Linda was mad and disgusted at Mike and Vince wasn't in trouble.

Another way to conceal motive was to have someone else carry the message. It was best if it was someone his mother trusted, like his grandma, Linda's mother. Problem was, Mike was too bland a child to do many bad things. And when Vince did plant the news, the message often didn't get back to Linda. Vince sat down again and thought. It's how Vince discovered the power of slight twists of the truth. Suddenly, everything Mike did was bad.

When a bully pushed Mike into the pond, Vince told everyone that the Bully was innocent, that Mike had dropped in to get the bully in trouble.

When Mike said he'd gotten one answer for a school test from a friend, Vince spread the word that Mike had copied the friend's entire paper.

Sometimes the best schemes took months to develop. One such scheme involved the school bus.

Vince stood with Mike and watched one day as the bus approached fast. The brakes of the old school bus squealed and gravel crunched. The door flew open even before it came to a stop. At first, the dust was too thick for the two boys to see. Then Buck's mean face became visible and Vince felt joy, because Buck only drove when there was a problem, and his eyes seemed to dwell on Mike.

"Come on, Mike," Vince said. He took Mike's hand and squeezed hard to keep him from sitting in the wrong seat. "Sit here, Mike, this is your usual seat." Vince said it loudly enough for Buck to hear. "I'll sit in my usual seat."

The "usual seat" announcement was part of Vince's plan. Vince thought he knew what was about to happen.

This particular opportunity for Vince to defame his little brother had arisen three months earlier. Mike was chewing gum and had asked Vince to open the window so he could throw it out. Vince talked Mike into putting it under the seat in front. Since then, Mike had missed riding the bus three times, and Vince took each opportunity to plant a whole package of gum under that seat and the one in front.

Vince had recently planted a seed with the bus's tattle tail; a twelve year-old thin-lipped little girl named Myrtle. Vince had told her that Mike was putting his gum under the seat. Vince could see that Myrtle had bought his act that telling her was a slip of the tongue.

Now, Vince knew that the emotions he displayed would decide the outcome. He'd spent hours practicing because it was crucial that it appear that Vince was his brother's loving protector.

As Vince went to a seat, he heard Buck walking down the aisle. When Vince looked up, Buck was bearing down on Mike with an even meaner look.

"This your seat?" Buck said. Mike seemed too scared to talk.

"You know it's his usual seat," Vince said, stepping forward making it clear in his expression that he wasn't going to let anyone push his little brother around.

"What's this?" Buck said, as he unpinned the frame of the seat in front and rolled it forward. Gum blobs were everywhere.

"I only did one," Mike said, "This one."

"That's right," Vince said with less enthusiasm. Vince blinked his eyes, and cast his gaze away from Buck. "Just that one." Vince put his hands on his hips and looked resolutely at Mike, then glanced up at Buck with a guilty look.

"You are grounded from this bus for a month, Buster," Buck said to Mike.

"You throw him off, you gotta throw me off, too," Vince said, careful not to let the joy he felt show on his face.

"Git," Buck said, pointing to the door. Both of you--git."

"You'll be hearing from our mother," Vince said as the two left the bus.

"He can't get away with it, Mike," Vince said. Vince kept his mind focused on the injustice. He knew that if he contemplated the victory, his whole plan would either become apparent, or suspicions would be raised.

His plan worked perfectly. Not only had Mike admitted to doing it, everyone knew he'd lied about not doing most of it. A liar and a property destroyer. Their mother would know and be furious because for the next month, she'd have to drag herself out of bed in order to drive them to school.

After a year or so of Vince's new tactic, he began noticing changes. People began acting differently toward Mike, and talked differently about Mike. Without saying a thing, people were sending the message to Linda that Mike was a bumbling dummy. The messages were very subtle, but incredibly powerful. Like the time Linda told her mother how good Mike was. Grandma agreed, but not vigorously, and it provided Vince with a new tool--faint praise. Everyone was doing it--the bus driver, even the dogs seemed to be treating Mike differently.

As time went on, Vince's skill grew. He felt guilty at the things he did, but he couldn't stop. Each success gave him a greater feeling of control, and he could see that gradually his efforts were eroding Linda's image of Mike. He still spent long moments thinking of ways to kill Mike. It was a habit he couldn't shake.

One day, Linda looked at Vince, walked up to him and hugged him. "You know, I shouldn't have--" Her voice trailed off.

Vince knew she was going to say she shouldn't have sent him to the Chinese. He thought he could relieve her feelings of guilt by telling her how wonderful the Chinese were. But he didn't. He liked the idea that something she had done to him made her feel guilty.

"What I'm saying," Linda said, with a determined look, "I should have brought you up myself because you've learned some bad habits. It isn't going to be easy, but I mean to break every one of them. It's all for your own good. First thing I want you to do is clean up that filthy room of yours. Now get."

Vince went happily to his room and cleaned and cleaned. When Linda inspected, she found little right, and told him he was lazy.

For the next several months, Linda stuck to her plan to rectify past misdoings. It quickly became a reign of terror. Vince rarely did anything right. The more she yelled at him, and made him do well and be good, the better she seemed to feel. At first, Vince liked it. Then the realization sank in that she was doing it to pacify her own guilt, not out of any love for him. Vince began finding ways to escape.

Brett had started his own sign company and operated the business from the old tool shed behind the house. Vince hid behind the shop and stared through the window watching Brett work for hours. Vince thought Brett didn't see him, because Linda never found him there.

One day, Vince watched as Brett struggled to do something that a third hand would have made easier. Brett cussed, then kicked the thing, then tried again, but nothing worked. Without looking up, he commanded Vince to come and help.

After that, Vince helped out by cleaning, answering the phone, and handing tools to Brett when he needed them. Soon Vince was doing a little bit of everything and Brett was acting civil. Vince spent all of his spare time in the shop. He loved every second because he was learning neat new things.

Building a large sign required knowledge of many different skills. Signs made from wood required knowledge of carpentry. Signs made from metal required knowledge of sheet metal and welding. Knowledge of commercial art was needed to paint it. The sign had to be wired up and the neon tubes filled with chemicals. Best of all, Vince thought, no two signs were alike, and no two installations were the same. But what amazed Vince was how good Brett was at it all. Brett didn't know about books, but he sure knew about signs.

Brett never said it, but Vince could see that he was very impressed with Vince's quick grasp of everything. Vince liked it when he did things that made him look smart. He'd since forgotten why.

Gradually, Vince became friends with Brett, although he didn't feel about him the way he thought a Son was supposed to feel about a Father. It was one reason Vince often felt empty inside, and soon he was again writing letters to Yaping. It made him feel the way he felt when he was very small. When a letter was finished, he burned it.

ᴆᴈ ᴈᴆ ᴆᴈ

It was a pretty, fall afternoon. Brett had run to the bank. Vince, an energetic thirteen year-old boy, was in the shop working on a sign. He felt anxiety as he worked. His mother still favored his little brother even though it was obvious even to her that Vince was smart, and Mike was dumb. If only Mike was dead, Vince thought.

The quiet was broken by a powerful baritone voice. "The owner around?" the visitor said. He was a big Greek man with an air of confidence. Vince knew who he was. He owned restaurants and had a kid in school.

"He'll be right back."

"You make signs?" the man said.

Vince was holding a long glass tube in a gas fire. When it glowed red, he bent it into the shape he needed to form the words of the sign.

"This is a sign for a Laundromat," Vince said, studying the man's response. "This glass tube will glow blue." A salesman should talk about the thing the customer's interested in, Vince thought. He may be able to find out the most important thing, what the customer wants.

"How much will this sign cost?" the man said.

Vince's eyes were sparkling. Vince had been reading books about sales, and he'd been watching Brett for years. This was his chance. First establish value, Vince thought, then determine if there's competition. Finally discuss price.

"Brett, the owner, handles that end," Vince said. He knew it was best not to have too much authority in a negotiation. "But I can tell you the buyer was in yesterday, and he was overjoyed with the sign. And he was sure it would make him money."

"I'm starting a pizza parlor," the Greek said.

Vince glanced up and saw Brett outside, looking through the window. Brett nodded to the table near the fridge. Vince knew what to do.

Vince walked over to the old fridge they kept in the shop, and opened it. "Like a soft drink? We also have coffee."

The Greek was looking at the beer. Without hesitation, Vince popped the top off a bottle of beer and placed it on the table. He positioned the chairs just right, then took one and motioned to another for his guest.

When the Greek sat in the seat offered, Vince began showing him information about the sign he was interested in. "A sign's the all-important part of any business," Vince said. "It's the symbol people use when they think about your business. If they like the symbol, they'll like your business. You know what your sign will look like?"

The Greek shrugged.

"Here are the drawings of the sign I'm working on. I think you'll find them interesting. Once the logo's chosen, we decide how to express it."

"Who designed this logo?" the Greek said.

He doesn't have a logo, Vince thought, then resisted the urge to tell the man that the design was his own.

Brett came in, walked up to the table, and extended his hand.

"Hi, Brett," Vince said. "This man needs a sign for a new restaurant. This is Brett Longto, the owner."

"Don't stand up," Brett said, "I'll just sit here and listen. Looks like the kid's doing fine." Brett took the seat that trapped the Greek at the table. It's the way Vince had planned it.

"The first thing we have to find for you is a logo," Vince said, "because the logo is the most important part of a business."

"I thought the sign was?" The question told Vince the man was listening.

"Once the logo's decided upon," Vince said, "the sign becomes the most important. A logo doesn't have to say anything. It allows a person to remember your restaurant and the last good meal he had there."

"Tell us about your product," Brett said.

The Greek told them about pizza, and how it was getting popular in America.

"Our whole family participates in the logo design," Brett said, pointing to a recent family portrait, his finger tapping right below the pretty face of his wife. "It would be best if we all sampled your product together. That way we'll know better how to design it."

The Greek looked closely at the photo. "Will your bushy tailed hired-hand be there?" the Greek said, indicating he meant Vince.

"Of course," Brett said. "He's family." Brett looked at the photo. Vince wasn't in it. He started to speak, but didn't.

"Excellent," the Greek said. "I'll have you all to my restaurant Saturday night for pizza dinner. You'll love it."

The Greek left happy, and Brett was, too. Even if they didn't make the sale, the whole family was going to get an evening out.

Vince spent the evening at the drafting table. He was good at designing logos. Many had hints of an oriental motif. Chinese writing had thousands of shapes that Vince often drew upon. If he could come up with a logo the Greek liked, it would eliminate the competition.

"Who's the logo for?" Linda asked Vince as he worked. Vince told her eagerly about the Greek, and his new restaurant.

"You mean the fat cat, Anthropoulis?" Linda said with a sneer. "He's nothing but a big shot, spelled with an 'i.'"

"And that's why he's going to pay more than the sign's worth," Vince said.

"Good," Linda said. She smiled, and walked away.

Vince liked the smile he got. He became determined to make the sale at twice the sign's value. The next day, he struck up a conversation with the Son of the Greek, and discovered that Paul Blake, a pompous middle-aged man who always wore a coat and tie, was their competition. Vince also discovered that the Greek had a teenage Daughter named Andrea who was home from college.

That evening, Vince prepared an order for six red roses. He also prepared a card that said, "Andrea, These flowers are a *sign* of my affection. PB." Vince put the order with a cash payment into the mail slot of a flower shop early the next morning.

Before dinner that Saturday night, Vince prepared two prices for the new sign. One of the prices was twice as much as the other. Vince convinced Brett to first ask for the higher price. They could always fall back, Vince explained if they sensed that Blake's offer was more attractive. When Brett was reluctant, Vince enlisted Linda's support. She liked the idea, and told Brett to do it. It was the first time Vince's mother had supported him.

When the Greek accepted the offer with the higher price, Vince was ecstatic, and so was Linda.

This new allegiance with his mother temporarily alleviated much of Vince's anguish, but her friendliness was short-lived. Although Linda's outward displays of affection for Mike had waned, Vince still wanted to see him dead, and still dreamed about ways to kill him.

There were many possibilities, especially when the two went hunting in the nearby hills. There were rabbits with tularemia, a deadly disease. There were mushrooms that Yaping had warned him about. There was the possibility of a hunting accident.

One time, Vince "accidentally" shot and hit Mike with a BB gun. The pellet lodged in Mike's hand under the skin. Mike said he thought Vince had done it on purpose. Mike told Vince that his intent to do harm was in his eyes. From that point on, Vince worked hard at controlling his face. Vince wasn't mad at a rabbit when he shot it--he just wanted to eat. In fact, when Vince killed a rabbit or a quail, he was happy and he greeted the dead or wounded animal with a happy face. Vince devised a simple trick. When he thought about something bad, like another scheme to kill or injure his little brother, or a way to smear his reputation, he pictured his victim as a prey animal, nothing more. That would keep his face from giving his thoughts away. And there was an added benefit. If his own mind were fooled, he could tell lies as if they were the truth.

Vince had continued the practice learned long ago to let everyone know that he loved his little brother deeply and that he would do anything for him. As time passed, he discovered over and over that the ruse did an excellent job of hiding motive, and disguising his true feelings and intentions. He knew it would keep him out of trouble and allow him to do what he knew he had to do.

6 – The Seductress

Linda Longto had two brothers and four sisters. Linda's mother had been a controlling tyrant with her and the older kids. Leslie was the youngest and from the time Leslie was a toddler, she could figure out a way to do anything she wanted.

Linda was uptight, controlling, and neurotic, while Leslie was carefree and spoiled.

When their mother died, their father asked around among her siblings if they'd take Leslie. Linda didn't like the idea. She was jealous of Leslie and intolerant of her spoiled nature.

Leslie was fifteen and nubile, not as pretty as Linda, but she had traits that made her interesting to men. Her mouth was full, sexy, and curled up at the corners, creating a perpetual pouty smile.

"She could help around the house, and she could watch the kids," Brett said. "Grandpa would give you more support money than you'd need to take care of her."

Linda gave Brett a disgusted look. "If seventeen will get you twenty," Linda said, "what'll fifteen do?"

"She's a child," Brett said indignantly.

Linda gave him a look that said otherwise. Linda thought back to when she was fifteen, and how she'd succeeded in seducing several older men. She figured her little sister wouldn't be any different. Linda thought about how boring Brett had become, and how she yearned to be with other men, and she thought she knew how to use the young girl to her advantage. Brett was surprised when Linda suddenly changed her mind about Leslie. Within a week Leslie was all moved in.

"We only have one bathroom in this house," Linda said to Leslie, "so don't be shy. We run around the house undressed."

The first hot day, Linda told Leslie she needed cooler clothes, and found her skimpy shorts and tops. Linda was delighted when Brett unwittingly played his role, and gawked every time Leslie walked by.

"I wish Brett would find a mistress," Linda said to Leslie. "Too bad you're not older. I'm tired of sex."

From then on, Leslie taunted Brett. She wore shorts and sometimes just panties. She experimented with different ways of walking. She giggled as Brett struggled not to look.

The chairs in the living room were formed in a circle. Leslie sat across from Brett, feet up, legs spread, and occasionally gave him a smile that said he could have her if he wanted.

When Linda thought the time was right, she told Brett that she was taking the kids to Denver for the weekend, but that Leslie had to stay home because she was grounded.

☒☒ ☒☒ ☒☒

Brett couldn't understand why Linda was so jovial as she left. The kids were noisy as they tumbled out of the house. Brett waved from the front door. When they were gone and all was quiet, he continued standing in the doorway. In the corner of his eye he could see Leslie's round face. He looked and confirmed that she'd been watching him.

Leslie gave him a sexy smile. She looked spectacular in short-shorts and a tight cotton shirt tied at the waist. Brett had already forgotten that he'd heard Linda picking these clothes out for her.

Linda had cut him off from sex the day Leslie had moved in, and his need was intense. But he knew he couldn't get involved.

"Looks like it's just us," Leslie said, with an inviting tone in her voice.

"Guess you're the cook," Brett said, his voice a little shaky.

Leslie smiled and walked slowly to the fridge. "Want a hot dog? I'm making one for myself."

"Okay," Brett said.

"How about a bun?" Her voice was low.

"Sure," Brett said, his voice quavering a little.

"Beer?"

"Okay." Brett's eyes were a little wide.

As Leslie poured, her hip brushed against Brett. She poured for awhile, stopped and talked, then poured again. After awhile she walked slowly back to the kitchen.

"I like mine without the bun," Leslie said, nibbling on a hot dog, her lips greasy.

Brett's eyes were wider.

"Another beer?"

Brett tried to speak to decline the offer, but couldn't get the words out. Leslie leaned a hip against him again as she poured, pausing occasionally to talk. "There's something in your beer," Leslie said. When she leaned over to have a closer look, her breast rubbed the side of his face.

Brett was frozen in fright. Her smell filled his nasal cavities and seemed to be the final ingredient in switching off his brain. He reached up and placed his hand on her hip, and pulled her close. Every time he moved, he shook. His breathing was labored.

Leslie looked down at him with a knowing look and smiled. She set the beer aside and held his left hand on her hip. She placed his free hand on the opposite hip, and slowly undid her shirt.

When she offered her bare breasts just inches from his face, she giggled and said, "Why Brett, your eyes look like they're gonna pop out of your head."

Brett struggled for a minute trying to decide what to do. When he looked away, Leslie grabbed his head and turned it back.

"Don't look away," she said. "You've been dreaming about this moment from the time they were half as big. A girl always knows."

It was more than Brett could handle.

Linda hadn't given up sex--she just found it elsewhere. She picked up men in bars, day and night. She enjoyed the variety.

When Linda drank too much, she talked. She told a lover, maybe two, about Leslie and Brett.

Before long, half the county was talking about the Longtos. Brett's business suffered. His income couldn't sustain their expenses and Linda's bar bills. They fought until Brett packed up his tools and moved over the mountain to Rawhide. The town needed a sign maker. He hoped Leslie would follow when she got out of school. Six months later, Linda showed up in Rawhide with Vince and Mike, and things went back to the way they'd been. Vince was fourteen.

Shortly after Vince arrived in Rawhide, a few simple words from a pretty girl initiated a change in his basic attitude toward his younger brother. The girl had blue eyes and bouncy hair.

"Are you Mike Longto's big brother? He's on the football team in junior high."

It was the first time Vince thought of his little brother as a possible asset. Pretty girls rarely talked to Vince. He wasn't athletic like Mike. Yaping didn't know about teaching athleticism. Brett had spent hours and hours with Mike. Using Mike to increase his own esteem didn't change his desire to see him dead, but it did help him realize that the desire was irrational.

When Vince learned to drive, he found a new way to try to soothe the turmoil in his mind. He went into the desert hills around Rawhide and walked and thought. It was in the desert, at a place he called his Shrine, where he finally learned to control his aggressive feelings toward his little brother.

It didn't matter that Vince was smart, he didn't do well in school. He was bored at the courses and the teachers were all well beneath his intellectual level. One day the principal of the high school called him in. "I just don't understand it," the principal said, "your test scores are off the chart, but you struggle with freshman courses."

Vince thought he knew why he hadn't done well. His boredom gave him an attitude, which caused the teachers to focus on him.

When Vince was sixteen, he dropped out of school. He felt no loss doing this. He'd never thought of getting a college degree. His mother had none, nor Brett. It was something "banker-folk" did. Out of school, Vince learned much faster, because he was no longer confined to studying material he already knew, or learning new things at a fraction of the speed necessary to keep his interest.

Vince worked construction. He heard a lot of Spanish, became interested, got books from the library, and within a year he was speaking it fluently.

"Hey," a Hispanic worker said, "How'd you learn Spanish so fast?"

"I've always learned things fast," Vince said.

"Speak any other languages?"

"Just Spanish and English," Vince said.

"How come you know Spanish grammar?"

"Learned it."

"But your Spanish grammar's better than your English grammar."

"What do you know?" Vince said, pointedly.

"I studied English in Mexico, and you don't speak the way I studied."

It was the first time Vince had thought about the fact that he spoke three foreign languages more correctly than English. Vince wasn't surprised at how easily he'd learned Spanish, but he was surprised at the fuss everyone made. Vince vaguely thought it would be impressive if he suddenly "learned" Chinese. He knew he could still speak it, because he still wrote long letters to Yaping, and he spent hours speaking Chinese to her at his Shrine in the desert.

It wasn't long after that Vince stopped by a Chinese restaurant in Grand Junction, Colorado. Vince was given a menu written solely in Chinese. It said "Master Menu," at the top. Vince had no trouble reading the menu, and he quickly gave his order in English. The cook immediately said in Cantonese from the kitchen that they were out of the item that Vince had just ordered. The waiter answered the cook in Mandarin, and the two talked like that for a while.

Vince understood every word that was said. When the two were done talking, Vince gave another order in English, one that utilized the information he'd just gained from the conversation between the cook and the waiter.

The waiter wrote down Vince's order and took his menu. Half-way to the kitchen the waiter stopped, looked at the menu, then turned slowly and began talking in Cantonese to Vince.

Vince laughed. He didn't want to reveal his knowledge of Chinese, so he repeated what the waiter had just said, creating, as best he could, an American accent. The waiter's eyes got big, and he hollered for his wife to join him. Vince repeated everything they said to him. Within an hour they were conversing in simple phrases.

Vince spent eight months in Grand Junction, and at least six hours of each day was spent in that restaurant. The Chinese told everyone they saw how Vince had learned two Chinese languages in just a few months. They were amazed at how fast he'd learned, and also by the way he learned a phrase perfectly upon hearing it once.

For several years after that, Vince roamed Colorado and other states in the Rocky Mountain area. He used his idle time to good advantage reading, studying, and learning. He liked doing that so much he cut back on his drinking so his hangovers offered less interference. The more Vince read, the greater became his desire to learn.

When Vince was twenty-one, he bought a welding truck. The owner of the truck was so desperate to sell, he didn't require a down payment. These were Vince's carefree years, and he should have enjoyed every minute. But he was not happy. The anguish in his mind kept his guts twisted tightly. Vince didn't sleep well at night, and when he had idle time his heart pounded inside his chest.

Vince had no idea how to fix his anguish, nor did he have a good idea why he had to endure it.

One day, when he handed a work ticket to the foreman, he noticed a hundred-dollar mistake. Before Vince could pull the ticket back, the man had it. Vince felt a rush when he thought about getting an extra hundred dollars.

"This math looks wrong," the man said.

Vince wasn't about to lose the high he was feeling. "Let me fix that," Vince said in a practiced voice that even Yaping would think was sincere. "Should have been twelve hours welding, not ten, which adds a hundred dollars to it." Vince made changes and handed back the ticket.

The man was scowling at him.

"Seriously," Vince said. "I did it in my head. I didn't add the column." Vince looked at the man, put out his hand and said, "Here, I'll delete it. Don't want no trouble. You guys've been too good to me."

The rush Vince felt when the man apologized and drew the ticket back made him feel good for the rest of the day.

The incident made Vince think about a change, but he had no specific long-term goals or desires other than the desire to escape the indescribable anguish in his mind that grew stronger every day.

7 – Tom Patton

Manderson, Colorado had a population of one hundred and twenty-three. The little town was beneath the white caps of the Rocky Mountains, twenty miles north from Rawhide. Vince stopped in Manderson often at the Hiway Bar and Grill as he went to and from welding jobs at oil wells in the surrounding countryside. He was twenty-three years old, and beginning to look like a man. He'd had fleeting love interests, but he wasn't ready for anything permanent. He still had no idea where he wanted to go in life.

There was an old Chinese lady at the Hiway Bar who washed dishes for the attached restaurant. Vince had gotten her the job. She didn't speak a word of English, and that's the way Vince wanted it. Vince had to translate whenever there was a problem, and in that way, everyone knew about Vince's ability to speak Chinese, and how he'd learned it in just a few months. It always irritated Vince that everyone thought he'd learned just one Chinese language, when he'd learned three, because Chinese writing was another language again.

On every visit, Vince slipped into the kitchen and talked to her. She'd get to laughing so hard, Keith, the owner, would come in to see what was going on.

One warm, early fall afternoon, Vince was in the Hiway Bar playing pool. He was on his third beer. The place was full of farm and ranch hands who smelled like the back end of a farm animal. The ranch hands were outnumbered by oil field workers who smelled of crude oil and other foul smells that had come from the bowels of the earth through long, narrow pipes. Oil hands were just a little rougher and grubbier looking than the ranch hands. It was 1974, and things were hopping in the oil patch. The price of oil had been rising rapidly with the trouble in the Middle East.

Vince was chalking up his pool cue when the front door of the little bar opened, and a slick-looking fellow with straight, white teeth walked in. Vince couldn't help staring for an instant into the man's eyes. There was something about them, Vince thought.

Vince had known the fellow from high school. His name had been Tom Patton, and he was a sophomore when Vince was a freshman.

Patton had been one of the "in" crowd who hung out with the other preppy boys and dated the girls who wouldn't give Vince Longto a second look.

Vince had heard that Patton had quit law school in order to go into the oil business. Somebody said he'd studied geology at the University of Wyoming. On his first try, he'd discovered oil in the hills not far away. Talk was he had more oil than he knew what to do with, but so far he hadn't sold a drop.

Patton was dressed in jeans and wearing work boots just like everyone else in the bar, plus his clothes were splattered with black oil. His face and hands were dirty, just like some of the other men, but Vince could see from the looks of others that they recognized Patton to be different from themselves.

Vince shifted uneasily when Patton seemed to pick him from the crowd to look at. Vince didn't like him. He was definitely in the "banker-folk" category.

Patton greeted the bartender, then continued through the crowded room. As he passed the pool table, a big, overweight, longhaired farm hand in coveralls jabbed the butt end of a pool cue toward Patton's midsection.

Patton deftly caught the cue handle in his left hand before it reached his gut, and diverted the thrust into the air at his side. At the same time, his right hand doubled into a fist and he swiftly came to a fighting position. He crouched slightly as his head and eyes locked onto the big man.

"Did I get you?" the big man said laughing, then scowling.

The farm hand did the same thing to every stranger who walked into the bar. Everyone had laughed when his victim recoiled in fright. This time, it was different.

For an instant, Vince thought the farm hand was going to get decked, but Patton seemed to think as quickly as he reacted. Patton tugged on the cue pulling the larger man toward him. He put his left forearm on the man's chest, then "playfully" slapped him hard on the neck and ear with his right hand.

"You almost got me," Patton said, grinning.

The man was still recoiling, and wondering what to do when Patton turned and disappeared into the bathroom.

The next time Vince saw Patton, he was sitting at the bar, his face and hands clean and his hair nicely combed. Patton was talking to the bartender, a blond, country girl with big breasts. Patton had her blushing, smiling, and laughing like Vince had never seen. She had stayed aloof from most that frequented the little bar.

Vince was in the middle of a pool game with the big farm hand when Patton walked to the pool table and put his quarter into the little slot reserved for challengers. Vince couldn't help noticing that he was quite a bit taller than Patton. Vince also knew he'd be no match in a fight.

"Ten bucks a stick," the farm hand bellowed.

Patton returned to the bar, smiled at the buxom bartender, then belatedly nodded his consent to the big man's challenge. When the farm hand sank the eight ball, Vince threw down his ten bucks, and put his quarter into the challenger's slot.

Soon Patton was collecting the ten dollars Vince had lost. Vince put in his quarter and racked up the balls. It wasn't long before Patton was close to taking another ten dollars from Vince.

"Hear you're a welder," Patton said, sizing up the eight ball shot.

Vince nodded.

"Got a job?"

"Just finished one."

Patton missed the eight ball shot. Vince was incredulous. He figured Patton was trying to sucker him into a bigger bet.

"You want to come out in the morning and do some welding?" Patton asked. Patton had the ten bucks in his hand, ready to throw it on the pool table. Vince had an easy shot at the eight ball.

"Fifty bucks an hour," Vince said, sinking the eight ball. He brushed the end of his beard away, chalked up his cue tip, and looked defiantly at Patton.

"I'll see you in the morning," Patton said.

Patton dropped the ten dollars on the table, gave the blond bartender a nice smile, and headed out the door.

Vince went to the window. Patton was driving an old two-wheel drive Chevy truck painted an ugly green color. There was a shovel in the back. Vince figured Patton needed the shovel to dig himself out when he got stuck. Everyone else around Manderson drove four-wheel drive vehicles.

Vince couldn't help wondering what was going on. He was a little worried that he might not get paid, so that night he called around and discovered that Patton was current with his suppliers.

♱ ♱ ♱

Patton looked like he'd already done a half-day's work when Vince arrived at eight the next morning. There were four, four-hundred-barrel tanks on location, a treater, and a four hundred-barrel tank near the wellhead. Everything looked like it had been hooked up in a temporary fashion. Vince could see there was a lot of work to be done.

Patton put Vince to work making a pipe-wrack. Vince could see Patton needed a pipe-wrack, but there were many other things the location needed first. Vince watched as Patton worked on an oil tank near the wellhead. After a while, Vince wandered over. It was a big tank, more than two stories high.

"Smoke break," Vince said, grinning at Patton and putting a wad of chewing tobacco under his lip. Vince's beard, from the corners of his mouth down, was discolored from tobacco juice. He didn't have to stand there long before Patton started telling him what was going on.

"This well flows and makes a thousand barrels of water a day, along with fifty-three barrels of oil," Patton said. "I designed this vessel to knock most of the water out of the oil before the oil goes to the treater, but the oil line broke on me."

"This is the strangest looking gun-barrel I ever saw," Vince said. Vince could tell that Patton had never heard the term "gun-barrel." "A gun-barrel," Vince said, "is standard oil field equipment. Usually they're made a little different."

Vince looked at Patton, who was eager to know more. Vince still hadn't decided about this fellow.

"See this big opening for this water-off siphon?" Vince had entered the tank and was pointing to a big six-inch pipe at the bottom of the tank. "It'll cause the water to swirl in this vessel, and big drops of oil will get sucked into it."

Patton nodded enthusiastically like he'd been having that problem. The water went from the gun-barrel to a pit system. Oil on the surface of the pits would be a problem.

"So, you need to 'L' off here with a sweep," Vince said, "and put a length of perforated pipe across the bottom of this tank. You should also have some baffles above it to keep currents from forming."

Vince walked over and examined a break in a three-inch PVC line. "This the broken oil-off line?" he said. When Patton nodded, Vince said, "My guess is you shut the well in, then continued to pump oil until this plastic line was empty."

"Right," Patton said with a surprised look.

"PVC has good tensile strength, but it's poor in compression. When this pipe was empty, the fluid around it compressed it until it broke. You either have to make this line out of steel, or put it outside the tank."

Vince looked at Patton. In spite of a good physique, he looked out of place wearing gloves and holding a pipe wrench.

"Why don't you hire somebody to do this?" Vince said.

"Ran out of money drilling the well. I got four tanks full of oil, but I haven't had any luck getting the water out so it will sell."

"Where you going to put your new oil production when you get this gun-barrel fixed?" Vince said, laughing. Now he couldn't help liking Patton, nor could he quit wondering if there was a way he could cheat him out of his oil well.

Patton shrugged, and explained that all of his tanks were full of wet oil that nobody would buy.

"I always wanted to learn about the oil business," Vince said. "Why don't you put me to work? If you're making fifty-three barrels a day flowing, you should make four times as much on pump. If your oil sells for eleven dollars, that's two thousand three hundred and thirty-two dollars a day."

Vince noticed Patton's suspicious look. Vince figured he'd catch him a little later checking his math with a calculator.

"Pumps cost fifty-thousand dollars apiece," Patton said dryly, "then there's taxes and royalties."

"All right, flowing you'll gross five hundred and eighty-three dollars a day. That'll cover my wages. Seems like all you have to do is sell some oil."

Patton explained his problem. The oil was very heavy, almost as heavy as water, which made it hard to get the water out of the oil. The pipeline wouldn't take oil that had more than a small trace of water; otherwise, their main, cross-country transportation pipeline might freeze up in the winter.

Vince said he had a friend who worked at the Torchlight oil field just a few miles away, that it produced heavy oil, too. Before Patton could protest, Vince jumped into his vehicle and headed down the road, saying he'd be back.

Before they went home that evening, Patton rummaged around in his pickup and came out with a book about the dehydration of oil, published by The Society of Petroleum Engineers. The book looked beautiful to Vince. By the end of the week, Vince had a tank of oil sold, and Patton told Vince to find a roustabout to help them out.

Next day, Vince showed up with a Hispanic fellow. Vince made a show of the fact that he hadn't discovered earlier that the man couldn't speak English. Actually, Vince had picked the man that way because it would give him more control at Patton's new oil field. When Patton didn't seem impressed with Vince's Spanish, Vince talked to Keith, the owner of the Hiway Bar, in a subtle way and got Keith to tell Patton that Vince had learned Chinese in less than a year. People usually got nervous around Vince when all this came out. Vince found Patton's reaction unsettling. Patton seemed to think it was neat and he became friendlier.

The next day, as the three were working, Vince looked at a row of pipe collars on a cable. "Reminds me of beads on an abacus," Vince said.

Patton stared at Vince, big-eyed.

Vince laughed. "Had a Chinese nanny. She had an abacus. She said when I was a baby I'd crawl up to it and say 'numbers.' She'd slide a couple beads out and say, 'two beads, baby.' She said she had to limit me to two sessions a day with the abacus. Said I was enthralled with it."

"Did she speak English?"

Vince froze, and knew immediately he'd said too much. "How do you suppose she talked to me?" Vince said.

"You probably heard them speak Chinese when you were a baby," Patton said, "and that's why you learned it so fast."

Vince concealed a sudden flash of anger, and said: "Could be, but I doubt it. Don't remember nothing like that, that's for sure."

"Did you say your nanny had a maid?"

Vince scrunched up his face. His anger caused him to speak without thinking and he said, "My nanny was more like my real mother."

Again Vince recoiled at his own words. He felt pain, and turned away in case his face showed it. He'd inadvertently told Patton one of his deepest secrets.

ꀜ ꀜ ꀜ

A week later, Patton broached the subject again. "I read an article recently about intelligence. The article said intelligence is mostly acquired in infancy. I'll bet that's why you learned Spanish so quickly, because you were introduced to other languages as a baby. Same thing with math."

Vince shot Patton a piercing look, and stomped off. Patton seemed to think that any child in Vince's position could have learned three languages with ease. It made Vince feel better if people thought he was born smart, that nobody else could have what he had even with the right stimulation as a baby.

A little later, Vince came back and apologized. "Sorry I got mad," Vince said, "but I learned Chinese just like I learned Spanish. Next time you're in Grand Junction, stop in at the Chinese restaurant. They'll tell you all about it."

Patton gave Vince a queer look that told Vince he wasn't buying the lie. Before he could speak, Vince said, "This production stuff's Chinese, though. I need more books. Look here."

Vince showed Patton a book list. The list was on the inside cover of the book from the Society of Petroleum Engineers that Patton had given him. Vince had five hundred dollars worth of books marked off, all books on oil field production practices.

"I'll buy one at a time," Patton said.

Vince read a book a week. It both irritated and pleased him when Patton was skeptical and asked Vince questions when he finished a book. Vince always knew the answers, and tried hard not to gloat when Patton seemed amazed. Vince had no trouble getting Patton to keep buying new books. When Vince had trouble with calculus, he hired a math teacher to tutor him. By the end of six months, he knew more about production practices than any engineer in the area. Then he started learning about the other aspects of the business. He pestered Patton about oil and gas law--leases, royalties, rights-of-way, and operating agreements.

It wasn't long before Patton had enough money to install a pump, then enough to drill another well, and another, and soon Patton was drilling other wildcat prospects.

From time to time Vince wondered why Patton had picked him, essentially from a crowd, to work for him. Vince didn't buy the logical explanation that Patton had decided that Vince was the best man.

꧁ ꧁ ꧁

In just two years time, Patton's business was doing well, and Vince was enjoying his job. Vince had even quit thinking of ways to cheat Patton. Patton seemed like a "banker-person" that Vince could like.

"You want to help me pick your new boss?" Patton said to Vince at one of their many meetings. Patton had long since stopped working in the field; he was usually busy putting drilling deals together in his office in Rawhide, Colorado or taking flying lessons.

"What's wrong with me?" Vince said. "I read all those production books. I've also read all the books on drilling practices. And you know I understand it."

"The production super will have to deal with engineers and geologists and government people. I don't want to hurt your feelings, but your English is terrible."

Vince could see Patton was looking at his long beard, and scraggly clothes. "Give me two weeks," Vince said, "and I'll be talking better than you."

Patton hesitated. Vince's expression showed his determination. "Make it two months," Patton said, extending his hand, all with an ease that made Vince wonder if Patton was simply using this as an opportunity to get him to change his ways.

Vince knew just the person to help him out, and he had more than tutoring on his mind. Her maiden name was Emily Dill. Her dad was Frank Dill, a big rancher, and she was married to Nelson Bidlow, the Son of another big rancher. She was the only girl who'd talked to Vince when he moved to Rawhide. She always seemed attracted to Vince and he thought he knew why: Emily needed someone to fix. Her mother and grandfather had both been bad alcoholics, and Vince thought she anguished over the fact that they had both died from their affliction, and that she hadn't done enough to change them.

Everyone at Rawhide High had treated Vince like a low-life dummy, but Emily seemed to know better. She was a prim, homespun girl, whose wild side showed in the way she would look at Vince in his rough looking clothes. In the intervening years, Emily had become a schoolteacher.

Vince came to Emily with his hat in hand, head low, and asked for her help. He wanted to learn to speak English, he said. Emily said she'd be glad to help, and they set up a schedule of times Vince was to visit.

When Emily suggested it, Vince shaved his beard and got a haircut. He let her pick out nicer clothes for him.

In three weeks, Vince was talking as well as Patton, and in five weeks, better, and correcting Patton's English.

Emily said Vince was the smartest student she'd ever had-- that he picked up grammar faster than she thought possible. Vince got Emily to loan him every book she had on English grammar. She said it seemed to her like he memorized every word in every book.

When Vince was rewarded with the superintendent's job, Emily suggested they go on a picnic to celebrate his transformation. She had a nice spot all picked out in a deep, tree-lined canyon behind a deserted ranch house that her alcoholic grandfather had lived in.

Vince thought he knew what she was thinking deep down. Emily needed more than someone to fix, Vince thought, she also needed someone who would control her, and Vince liked that idea, because she was a member of the "banker-group," and controlling her would make him feel good.

Vince contemplated with delight the anguish he would put Emily's father and husband through as he made love to her on the blanket she'd brought. Emily moved in with Vince that day, and they were married the day after her divorce was final. Vince insisted it be that way.

🐂 🐂 🐂

"You know what worries me?" Patton said to Vince. It was a couple of months after Vince's wedding, and the two were drinking a beer in the Hiway bar in Manderson. "If the price of oil ever gets too low, I'm out of business, and you're out a job, because our treating costs are too high." Patton had just discovered another pool of heavy oil. Heavy oil wasn't just difficult to treat; it sold for a lot less money.

"Nothing you can do about it," Vince said.

"I got an idea—a way to reduce our high cost of treating *and* increase the money we get for our oil by fifty percent."

"I'm listening," Vince said.

"Ever hear of cracking?" Patton told Vince that tar could be made into gasoline simply by cracking it. Patton had an idea for a machine that would crack his heavy oil on site, make it more valuable and get the water out all at the same time.

"Could you weld up this machine?" Patton said showing Vince the plans.

As Vince studied the plans, he became mesmerized. The design called for a bed of sand. Propane was to be pumped into the sand, mixed with air, then burned. When the sand was hot enough, oil would be pumped in, and the propane shut off. The oil would quickly vaporize.

Just enough air would be pumped in to allow enough oil to burn to keep the sand at the right temperature. The vaporized oil would go to a treater where the water and gases of combustion would be separated. In the sand, the oil that was too heavy to quickly vaporize would become so hot, it would crack and the end-product would be lighter and more valuable, and the treating cost would be far less because it would almost eliminate the need to buy propane, his biggest expense.

When oil cracks, coke, which is nothing but pure carbon, is left behind. At a refinery, the coke clogs the pipes of heat exchangers, fills cracking towers and causes countless other problems. Patton said he figured this machine would solve that problem, because the coke, since it was left behind in the sand, is what he figured would burn.

It seemed too good to be true to Vince. Patton gave Vince the chemical engineering book on cracking he'd been studying. Vince stayed up most of the night studying it. The next day, Vince ordered several more books on the same subject, and paid for them himself.

Vince worked on the machine Patton had dubbed POCUS for six months until Patton said he couldn't afford to spend any more on it. Patton couldn't understand why it never worked.

A year after POCUS failed, Tom Patton had married, and his wife, Belle, was expecting. Patton and his wife had taken a parenting class. Their instructor stressed how important a stimulating environment was to a newborn. Patton pressed the instructor for details, and he was disappointed at the shallowness of her response. He wondered how she knew stimulation was important when she didn't know what it was. He often thought about Vince Longto's intelligence and wondered if he had been brought up in a stimulating environment. He figured he'd never know the answer to that question until the day he talked to a businessman in Ft. Collins.

His name was George Herden, and he was one of Patton's investors. Herden had been born and raised in Ft. Collins. He said he knew about the Chinese who had lived on the Cache la Poudre not far from Brett Longto's old shop. One of the Chinese had married a local cowboy, Herden said. They had three kids, and every one of them was on a scholarship to a name school. When he said that, Patton felt chills go down his spine. Herden promised he'd get the Chinese woman's address.

A week later, Patton had the information. Her name was Haua Stuhlheit and she lived in the foothills of the Rocky Mountains just inside the Wyoming border. Herden also gave Patton her phone number, but said the woman's English was too poor to be understood on the phone.

A month later, when Patton was able to get away, he went to Ft. Collins and spent half a day finding the Chinese woman. The pictures of her three children were displayed prominently. Her oldest son looked good in a military uniform. He was in West Point. The second was also a boy, and he was at Princeton. The third, Carolyn, was present at Patton's visit and it was a good thing because an interpreter was often needed. Carolyn was starting school at Stanford in the fall.

Haua's husband was a cowboy and just like Haua, he didn't have a high school degree.

When Patton told her about Vince Longto, her face brightened.

"Was good baby," Haua said proudly. Patton saw joy in the woman's eyes. He also saw pain.

She told Patton that Vince sometimes spoke English to her but she rarely understood what he said. She told him about the special baby book, and how Vince had been raised just like it said. She even showed it to him, and spent the afternoon telling him what it said. The ancient book had thick pages, and appeared to have been written by hand. The book had been left to Haua in a great woman's will, Carolyn said, interpreting. Then, after a moment's silence, Carolyn said: "This woman was murdered as soon as she returned to China?" Carolyn quit talking when Haua stiffened and gave her daughter a piercing look.

Patton figured the deceased woman was Vince's nanny. It took a good deal of prodding for Patton to get more information. Haua would say no more except that the crime had never been solved. Patton was relieved when Haua asked him not to tell Vince about the murder. Patton couldn't tell him about this visit anyway. Patton had the impression that the woman feared for her own safety.

On his way back to Rawhide, Patton thought about what he'd been told on the subject of infant stimulation and how nothing he'd read so far even remotely compared to what he'd just learned.

8 – Charcharadon Megaladon

"Here it is, big fellow. I'm talking something big. See here--a big color change. Look at this shale--green, tan, even red. Then suddenly the color changes to black."

Tom Patton waved his arm across a cliff face in a steep gully, in the bottom of Hell's Creek. He was in an area ten miles wide, and almost as deep, called Devil's Kitchen. The area was dry lying in the rain shadow of a nearby range of the Rocky Mountains. The ground was dark, carbon-rich, marine shale. On the rare occasion that it was wet, it looked black. Erosion happened so fast topsoil could not survive, and without topsoil the marine shale wouldn't hold even the little bit of water that fell. The ground was bare with the exception of a few widely spaced salt sage bushes, each barely bigger than a softball.

Patton was in a special part of Devil's Kitchen where the sediments stood straight up--not horizontal the way they had originally been deposited.

An occasional sandy zone stood just a little higher than the shale because of its greater resistance to erosion. The sand held moisture that could be utilized by plants. Since it stood straight up, the straight line of its outcrop could be followed across the countryside by the grasses and juniper trees, which grew nowhere else.

Silts, also more resistant to erosion, stood straight up in sheets. Ripple marks were visible on their surfaces. Sometimes the sands and silts resisted erosion long enough to form a cliff face, whose outline on the horizon formed a jagged edge that bobbed up and down like a mini-mountain range.

The erosion in the area created a pattern similar to sandblasted wood. Soft areas were eroded out, with harder areas forming bumps and ridges. Dinosaurs had lived when these rocks were formed.

"Look at this," Tom Patton said to his boy, Billy. "This color change marks the end of the Jurassic and the beginning of the Cretaceous. Look, big guy, you can actually see the beginning of the Cretaceous, and with it, the most prolific burst of life this planet has ever seen. Here's a piece of black marine shale. What do you think?"

A chubby little hand reached out and grabbed the piece of shale. Tom Patton stared into the face of his eight-month-old baby boy as only a proud Father could.

"What the fuck you doing down there?"

Patton instantly recognized Vince Longto's voice, but he was still startled. There wasn't supposed to be anyone within twenty miles. Vince was using the same cowboy twang he'd used before he married Emily.

"Come on down here and tell me what you're up to," Patton said, "and watch your language. We're in company."

Tom Patton was proud of the little bundle he held. The baby boy gave Vince a big smile and said something that had the same cadence, as *hi, how are you.* "He can talk already," Patton said. "Hear him greet you?"

"Ah hell, that baby don't understand nothing," Vince said. Vince slid down the side of the ravine on the bottom of his welder-style coveralls. Loose shale crumbled from the steep sides of the ravine and rolled down like a mini-avalanche in front of Vince. "I know about kids," Vince said when he was at the bottom. "Got nieces and nephews galore. They babble like that for a year before they get to talking."

"He said, 'hi, how are you.' His pronunciation was poor, but he said it."

"Tell me," Vince said with a twinkle in his eye. "What in the world are you doing out here in the middle of nowhere, twenty miles from the nearest house, holding a baby who has mud all over his mouth and carrying on like he has some kind of clue?" Vince slapped his knee and delivered a hearty laugh.

Patton looked at his baby boy. His mouth was covered with mud. The baby had popped the piece of shale into his mouth where, after more than a hundred million years, it turned back into sea floor muck.

"You want to know something really neat?" Patton said.

"Tell me something neat."

"If you show things to a baby, they see better."

"And if they put it in their mouth they might choke and die," Vince said laughing.

Patton sighed. "A baby's fingers are numb stubs. They learn about the world with their mouth."

Vince looked at him with high eyebrows.

"Watch this," Patton said, and looked around until he spied a wolf spider on the steep wall of the dry wash. "Look," Patton said to his boy.

The baby immediately began searching. Quickly he found it and said, "Pider."

"It's a wolf spider," Patton said. "They run around free on the ground--don't use webs." Patton looked up at Vince. "See how well he can see? He can tell it's a spider."

"That don't prove nothing," Vince said with a giggle.

"Ever hear what happens when a child gets musical training before she's six?"

Vince hesitated in thought, then spoke in accent-free English. "If they get music young, their brain's structurally different. Among other things, the corpus callosum's bigger."

"That's right. The important part is it doesn't happen to someone who learns music after they're six. Once you have it, it lasts a lifetime."

"I know what you're gonna say next. Seeing early makes bigger optical pathways, right?"

"Right."

"And hearing different things early on makes bigger talking and hearing pathways?"

Patton gave Vince a suspicious look.

"What?" Vince said innocently.

"You're being agreeable so I can't give my lecture."

"I'm sorry, you're right. I mean, you are my boss." Vince shrugged and smiled, then added in Colorado hick: "So what's all this have to do with saying things a baby can't hope to understand?"

"Lets him hear the words. If he hears them twice, maybe even once, it may be enough to play them to his mind's ear."

"Play it to his what?" Vince said. "Whoever heard of such a thing?"

"Just like a mind's eye. You know, recognizing a word, same as recognizing a spider. Everyone has to hear a completely new word a few times before they recognize it."

"Okay, well, go on," Vince said, showing a glimmer of interest.

"It's the same for a host of other things, like smells--like the smell of shale melting in the mouth--and sights, and motion."

"Motion?" Vince raised an eyebrow. "You thinking you can teach a baby to be athletic?"

"Billy and I were in the park on the merry-go-round when a carload of teenagers pulled up. One of them was that Hansen girl. Paul Hansen's daughter, Gail's her name." Patton had a faraway look.

"Okay, so what's the point?" Vince said, showing disgust.

"First the boys pushed the merry-go-round. They ran and jumped on. Then the girls pushed. Other than the Hansen girl, the girls were nowhere near as coordinated as the boys. The Hansen girl has two older brothers and she grew up running and playing basketball with them." Patton paused. "It proves that with the same practice at an early age, girls can be just as athletic as boys."

"So, what're you telling me here?"

"For those other girls, the opportunity's gone. They're locked into clumsy for the rest of their lives." Patton glanced quickly at Vince, who still looked interested. "It's the same with seeing, and reading. Kids who learn to read after they start school are clumsy readers, just like those girls are clumsy in an athletic way."

"You know, that makes a lot of sense," Vince said. His head cocked to one side. "But I don't believe it," he said with a chortle. "You going to be one of those parents who drives my wife crazy by teaching his kid to read before he starts school?"

Patton took a deep breath. After three years Patton was starting to understand Vince Longto. Patton knew Vince talked to his own baby. In fact, it was from watching Vince that Patton knew how to do it.

"Girls, remember? Clumsy athletes," Patton said in an exaggerated way.

"Okay, late readers, clumsy readers, I got you," Vince said sarcastically.

"Not only that, when you let a baby learn, they're happy. Billy here is always happy. He rarely cries."

"I didn't cry when I was a baby, least that's what my nanny told me. Mom said I cried all the time." Vince turned uneasily. "You hear that?" he said with a curious look. It was a distant rumble.

"What is it?"

"Drag racers at the Rawhide airport." Vince looked down the ravine. "Bring your baby. I want to show you a real special place."

The three walked down the deep ravine. They walked forward in geologic time through the upright sediments, each step covering hundreds of years.

The creek came smack up against a sheer sandstone cliff. It was covered with ripple marks created when it was deposited millions of years ago. It looked like the creek ended at the sandstone slab. Vince was dwarfed by the height of its face.

Vince turned to Patton wearing a reverent look. His voice was low. "See how the creek makes a ninety-degree turn, then goes through this--" Vince hesitated. "I'm not sure what you'd call it. A hall maybe." The creek entered a narrow cut. It was ten-foot wide at the bottom, and it didn't get much wider with height.

"I'd call it a vault, like in a cathedral."

"That fits," Vince said. Vince entered first. He walked several steps, then stopped. The walls on either side were close and cool.

"Okay," Vince said, softly, "now you two sit here." Vince motioned to a little shelf under an overhang facing the sandstone slab. The overhang consisted of tons of low-strength shale. Patton looked at it gingerly.

"If it starts to fall, I'll holler a warning." Vince chuckled. "Just kidding." Vince dug around at their feet in the sand in the creek bottom and pulled out a big triangular object. "Know what this is?"

Patton took it in his hands. It was the length of his hand--glossy, hard looking and almost a perfect triangle. The edges of two sides were serrated like a steak knife.

"I saw a tooth once from a two-thousand pound great white," Patton said. "It looked just the same, except for the size. It was only an inch wide. This thing's huge."

"Charcharadon Megaladon," Vince said with a snarl. "Great white's granddaddy. Look up there on the face of the sandstone."

"All looks the same."

"Way up there, about twenty feet, about a third of the way down from the top."

"The jaws of hell!" Patton said. Two rows of the big teeth protruded from the cliff face. The top row was six feet from the bottom row.

"Big enough to swallow a small car," Vince growled, "and that ain't no bull. And look, see these things?" Vince pointed to a circular structure like a large pipe buried in the sandstone. "This is a piece of its backbone, made from circular pieces of cartilage. Each piece is like one vertebra. All together they make up the vertebral column." Vince pointed to segmented sections rising on the cliff face to the jaws of hell.

"These are only about three-inches across in a regular great white. But these babies are eighteen inches across. When a shark gets fossilized, it's unusual to get anything more than just the teeth."

"That's amazing."

"See this cliff face?" Vince said, slapping it with his hand. "This is the side that was on top when it was deposited. This sand came from a big storm. The fish got buried in the sand. That's how it got fossilized."

"Maybe there are some bones where its stomach used to be?" Patton said.

Vince's face lit up. "Look at this." There was a big flagstone slab lying up against the cliff face. Vince seemed familiar with the slab. "This is where its stomach was," he said.

When Vince rolled the slab away, Tom's eyes got big. He was staring at the skull of a carnivorous dinosaur, its jaw open and twisted.

"Got to be kidding me." Patton's jaw gaped.

"Pretty amazing, huh? See where the shark's teeth are way up there? Its tail is twenty feet below our feet here. This shark was huge." Vince paused, dropped his voice an octave, and continued slowly, "This is the place I was telling you about."

"You mean your Shrine, the place you used to come so you wouldn't kill your brother?" Vince had gotten drunk one night at the Hiway Bar and told Patton about his little brother.

Vince flinched, then continued solemnly. "I can't tell you why I felt that way about my brother. He's nice enough, and not offensive. Rage just seemed to build up in me from nowhere.

"I found this place when I was fifteen, right after I learned to drive. I've been coming here ever since. It's like this shark is a big blotter or something. It sucks the demons out of my head. When I leave, my soul is clean.

"Sometimes I come here and smoke dope just to calm my nerves. Uh--get drunk, I mean. Sorry, I know you're worried about what your baby hears."

"So, what do you think about when you sit here?"

"How minuscule my problems are compared to the problems this fish caused other creatures." Vince was quiet for a moment, and then he looked up at Patton and said in a low voice. "First time I sat down here, it came to me how these guys died." Vince paused and looked at the query on Patton's face, then continued. "Well, I thought up a theory." Vince shrugged. "There must be a million theories. Don't ask me why this one seems so real. Want to hear it?"

"Sure do." Patton looked around at the ground, picked up an object that looked like an animal dropping, gave it a toss, then set his baby down in the sand in the creek bottom.

"You have to go a long way back in time for this story. Ninety-nine million years." Vince's voice was low and distant. "This guy," Vince gestured to the carnosaur, "His name was Cordvoo."

"He had a name?" Patton said, eyebrows popping up.

"It seems so real." Vince stared off then absentmindedly took a small rock from the baby's mouth and handed it to Patton.

"You mean it came to you one day when you were smoking some really fine dope?" Patton said. Patton looked at the rock. Satisfied it was too big for his baby to choke on, he handed it back. "Sandstone," Patton said smiling to his baby, amused at the thought that his eight-month-old now knew more about geology than half the earth's population.

"Could be," Vince said in a distant sounding voice, then looked reverently at the jaws of hell.

Patton was suddenly struck by the feeling that Vince identified with the shark and the dinosaur to the point that they were a part of him.

"Cordvoo was the leader of the pack," Vince said. "Voo is what they called themselves. They were the size of horses but faster and smarter, and more lethal than a giant squid. They had to swim to a distant land. There was no food. Cordvoo got his feathers covered with sap sleeping under a tree. He was careless. He'd been injured in a fight with another pack.

"When he swam out to sea, he was trailing blood. Whitey here swam up and bit him in two, then swallowed the pieces. It was agonizing. That's why Cordvoo's jaw is twisted and his mouth open.

"There was a thousand year storm. The sea got rough, the waves towered. The sea was so shallow the shark's body was dropped against the bottom, not hard at first. Then a series of three waves came. The third was so big it picked up his enormous body, then smashed it hard against the shallow bottom. The force split his liver." Vince smashed one hand into the other. "It was a fatal wound." Vince looked toward the mountain.

"On the distant shore, lightning crashed everywhere. Rain fell in giant drops. Rivulets turned to torrents. Whole hillsides were washed away. Mud and sand and gravel went way out to sea and covered Whitey while he was still fighting for his life. His mouth was open when he was buried. Now it's locked open in everlasting agony. They spent a lifetime living by the sword. It's fitting they died by it." Vince looked at Tom Patton, a smug smile on his face.

The two sat quietly. Patton thought about Vince's childhood, and how he must still bear scars. He was happy that Vince had this place to relieve his pain. Patton glanced at Vince and smiled.

"Why sap?" Patton said, straining to keep a straight face.

"Look here." Vince pointed to a spot about two inches above the dinosaur's skull. "See, amber."

Patton looked at two clear, colorless pebble-sized objects imbedded in the rock face.

"I've been working at excavating this skull for years. I got it where I want it now. I didn't want to remove it, just expose it so I could see more. I also exposed this amber. The story I just told you came to me years before I started digging."

"Before the amber was exposed?"

"It was under two inches of rock. When I uncovered this amber right where I saw the sap in Cordvoo's feathers, it sent a chill down my spine." Vince talked about the deceased dinosaur like he was discussing an old friend. "That's when I knew Whitey here was for real." Vince looked up and gave the jaws a reverent look.

"That's really interesting," Patton said, touching the rock face.

"This place was created just for me," Vince said.

Patton quickly looked at Vince so he could study his face.

Vince shrugged. "It's the feeling I got when I first saw it," Vince said, "And according to the sheepherders who work this area, this here shark was exposed by a huge gully washer in the summer of nineteen forty-nine. Heard it the same way from two of them. I researched rainfall records and there was an enormous rain that summer. As near as I can figure the storm hit the night I was conceived."

Patton looked down in thought. "Look at this pockmark," Patton said, pointing to a spot just above the dinosaur skull. "A piece of amber fell out. It was the size of a big marble."

"I've looked everywhere for it," Vince said. "There was a little water in this draw about five years ago. I figure it was washed on…."

Patton had his hand up in a "stop" signal. "The little guy has something to say," Patton said, then he waited.

"Bood," was his delayed reply.

"Like I was saying--" Vince said. Vince stopped again when he looked at Patton, who was watching his baby and encouraging him with his eyes.

"Where is it?" Patton said. Patton wanted to see what the baby was thinking about. The baby's hand shot into the air and his eyes got wider. Patton followed his gaze. In the sky, an eagle soared.

"You see a bird, big guy?"

"Bood, bood." Little Billy became animated.

"It's an eagle, big guy," Patton said, hugging his baby and giving him a kiss on his baby-soft cheek. "Eagles are raptors, they live off the flesh of other animals. Little mammals, mostly."

The two sat quietly under the overhang.

"I want you to come into the office tomorrow morning," Patton said, "Could you do that?"

"What's up?"

"In the short time we've been together, I've gotten rich. A lot of it's because of you. I'd like to offer you a partnership in the business."

"I'll be there," Vince said enthusiastically.

"There's something else that I need to tell you." Patton's demeanor suggested it was something important.

Vince looked at him in anticipation.

"We'll talk about it tomorrow. For now, let's sit here and let the jaws of hell suck the demons out."

Patton leaned back and wiggled in an effort to get the loose shale to conform to the contours of his back. He looked at the dinosaur, then way up at the jaws, and marveled at how he could almost hear screams of agony.

9 – To Sell a Soul

That evening, Patton told his wife, Belle, about giving Vince a partnership interest.

"Why don't I call Emily," Belle said, "and have her come in, too. Then we can all go out for a nice lunch."

"Better include the kids. Vince doesn't like to go anywhere without his kids if he doesn't have to. He's crazy about his baby girl."

Patton and Belle greeted Vince and Emily at Patton Exploration the next morning.

"I have everything all set up in the conference room," Patton said. "You ladies are welcome to join us." Belle looked at Patton with a frown. She had told him earlier that she wanted to shop, but he didn't want Emily to think she was being excluded.

"Count me in," Emily said, leading the way.

The conference room was lined with graphics. Patton walked to a big map of the Rocky Mountain area. "Green shows our current production," he said. "Red shows planned drilling locations and yellow shows the areas where we have an interest."

"Man talk," Belle said. "Come on Emily—let's get out of here while we still have the chance. We'll never understand what they're talking about, and they'll only make it worse trying to explain." She stepped in front of Emily so close Emily had to step back. She took Emily's arm and led her out of the room.

Patton stared long-faced after them, and thought about how he tried hard to listen to his wife explain things that he had no hope of ever understanding.

"Emily's a ranch girl," Vince said empathetically. "She likes knowing what makes the money come and go."

Patton thought about that for a minute: a woman who cared about what he did.

"You'd think she'd listen for a little while—even if she doesn't understand—for no other reason than to be polite." He didn't like criticizing his wife in front of Vince, but he was hoping Vince'd say something to Emily who'd then talk to Belle.

Patton's glance shifted back to the charts on the wall. "Okay, he said, here's the plan I've devised." Tom handed Vince a sheaf of papers. "The way I have it set up in twenty years you'll own half the company. Once you sign the documents, the company will be called L & P Exploration."

"You have to tell me what's going on here, Tom." Vince was on the edge of his seat. "I mean, what have I done to deserve half your company?"

"You only get half if the company grows substantially."

Vince gave Tom a long hard look. Tom chuckled.

"There's more," Tom said, and began telling Vince his personal reasons for being so generous. As Vince listened, the blood seemed to drain out of his face.

"What is it?" Patton said.

Vince had his hand over his mouth like he had to barf. He stood and headed out the side door.

Before the ladies had a chance to leave, Patton came into the kitchen, his face ashen.

"Seen Vince?" Patton said, his eyes darting around. Patton could see they hadn't, and before they could ask him what was going on, he took a deep breath and returned to his office. Belle followed him in and closed the door.

"What happened?" Belle said, her voice demanding.

"Vince and I started talking--." Patton stared quietly, his brow deeply furrowed. He started to tell her, then realized he couldn't trust her with the information—that in a week the whole town would know. "I know what you're thinking," he looked at Belle and thought about how she regularly reminded him of his alleged insensitivity, "I didn't say anything."

"What did you say?" Belle's gaze was steady.

"It's like he had a seizure or something. A cloud came over his face. It was scary. I can't explain it. Come on, let's see if we can find him."

Tom's secretary said she saw Vince leave in his pickup. Rawhide was a small town. It didn't take them long to find Vince's vehicle behind a bar, but they didn't find him inside. Emily apologized, and said she'd call as soon as she heard.

ᙁ ᙁ ᙁ

Vince Longto bought a bottle of whiskey and rented a room in a cheap motel on skid row over one of the bars. The room reeked of stale smoke, crude oil, and tobacco juice. When he was drunk, he barfed in the sink then stared into the mirror. *The eyes*! They were the same as Patton's and now he knew why. He smashed the mirror with a fist then watched as the trickling blood energized his drab surroundings.

He stumbled into one of the room's dirty corners where he sat with his bottle. It didn't seem to matter how much he drank-- it had little effect.

His skin crawled when he thought about what he'd learned from Patton. He shuddered at how close he'd let him get, and cried when he thought about the secrets he'd told him like pieces of his relationship with Yaping.

When Vince dozed off, nightmares disrupted his sleep. In one, Brett was drunk and yelling, "He's Billy's kid, isn't he." Then Vince heard his mother's laugh echo into the distance. Vince startled back to his bottle. He tried to sort through his feelings, but the demons kept his brain muddled.

He remembered that Tom Patton's father was named Bill— that they'd called him Billy when he was young. Vince's breath was labored and his heart pounded. A vision of little Tommy Patton in his nice middle-class home with his loving father and doting mother caused Vince so much distress it made him heave again and again until bile spilled onto his blood-stained lap. He didn't say it and he didn't think it, but it was there. Tom Patton—not his full-brother, Mike—had stolen his Garden of Eden. It was a place, Vince thought, where every child had a person just like Yaping for the *real* parent.

Vince was disgusted with himself that he hadn't figured out what was going on in Patton's sick mind. Obviously, Patton had felt their father's guilt, and he wanted to soothe it at Vince's expense.

At daybreak, Vince's attention was drawn to a movement. He watched blurry-eyed as a bed bug crept into the open. Another movement at the spot where the bed bug had emerged caught Vince's attention. It was another kind of insect, and its movements were quicker and more coordinated. It had big eyes that were locked onto the little bed bug, and it seemed to move with the confidence of a master. Vince watched captivated as the bed bug ran, but it was too slow. Vince could actually hear the carapace of the little bug crackle as it was crushed in the jaws of its pursuer.

Finally, Vince's mind was clear. He pursed his mouth with determination as he acknowledged his new mission in life. His achievements would far surpass those of Tom Patton, also known as—Vince sneered--William Thomas Patton, *Jr.*

Patton needed to be humiliated and taught his position in life and demeaned and brought down—way down--to a level below Vince's lowest.

Vince had a vague idea how he was going to do it. He knew instinctively that there was something else he had to do first, and it had to do with his Shrine.

Vince rose and glanced at the bug that was still enjoying its meal. He kicked the almost empty bottle of whiskey across the room, and strode into the hall where he put a quarter into the pay phone.

"Charlie," Vince said into the receiver, "I need a favor."

Charlie Nugen owed Vince. The two had gone hunting together several months before. They'd found a bull elk standing at the bottom of a deep ravine. "Don't shoot," Vince had said. "Our horses can't get down there." Charlie reflected for an instant on Vince's words, then squeezed the trigger.

It had a magnificent wrack, and Charlie wanted to keep as much of the forequarters as they could for the taxidermist. The two hauled the hindquarters out first, then, exhausted, they returned for the rest. Halfway up, the hill had become steeper and they were making little progress.

"We're going to have to come back with block and tackle and more help," Vince said panting hard. His legs were shaking from exhaustion.

"What about bears?" Charlie said, grabbing an antler. "You know what this will look like if a bear finds it? Charlie pulled hard, slipped, and the tip of an antler pierced his thigh. Blood spurted.

"It's okay," Charlie had said, pushing Vince away.

Vince could see an artery had been pierced. He knocked Charlie down and screamed into his face: "You have twenty seconds to live, asshole." That got Charlie's attention, and he let Vince apply pressure to the wound to stop the bleeding. Vince split Charlie's pants and put on a tourniquet. "Charlie," Vince said, "I'm going for help. Make sure you don't bleed. If you get tired, you might fall asleep, so make sure the tourniquet's tight."

Vince was back within two hours in a helicopter. He ruined the undercarriage of his pickup racing down the road, but he knew Charlie would either bleed to death or lose his leg if he didn't hurry.

Now, on the phone, Charlie was eager to help in any way. "Come pick me up at my house in your drill-hole truck," Vince said. "Bring those seismograph charges you said you couldn't use."

Charlie had told Vince about a seismograph job he'd done recently for a French company. Charlie had explosives left over when he was finished. The company told him to keep them.

"What's up?" Charlie said.

"It's not illegal." At least no one would know, Vince thought.

Vince was holding a big book when Charlie picked him up. As they drove into the country, Vince studied the book and ran a pencil.

"What's the power of the charges you brought?" Vince said.

"Everything's in French."

"Stop, I'll look." Vince brought a charge into the cab where he studied it, then wrote down some numbers.

"You know French, too?" Charlie said.

Vince didn't answer, he just figured with a pencil. They drove across the badlands until they came to the Shrine.

"I want four holes, here, here, and here," Vince said putting X's in the ground with the toe of a foot. "Tilt your mast twenty-five degrees and drill in this direction." Vince pointed down at an angle toward the deep ravine. He wanted the holes about fifteen feet from and parallel to the crevasse.

Charlie shrugged. "How deep?"

"Forty feet. Want five charges in each hole, all hooked up to primer cord. One on the bottom, then one every five feet. I want the holes filled with cuttings."

Charlie's eyebrows jumped. He looked at the deep cut just a few feet away.

"These are big charges," Charlie said. "Supposed to be in a hole at least fifty feet deep. That's just one." He looked furtively at Vince, who looked back in a threatening way. "Okay," Charlie said, shrugging, and started drilling.

When Charlie was done, Vince marked four spots for three more holes twenty-five feet from the ravine.

The book Vince had been reading was one of the engineering books Patton had bought. This one had a big section on surface mining. The shot Vince had designed was called a "cast" shot. They were used in surface mining operations to move overburden quickly into the pit where coal had just been mined. Too much of a charge, or too shallow a hole, and the force of the charge would go straight up and move little dirt.

"I want to do it," Vince said, when Charlie was ready.

"Just push this plunger," Charlie said.

Without hesitation, Vince did just that. Dust shot a hundred feet into the air. Before rocks were done falling, Vince scrambled onto the rubble. It had worked just like his calculations said it would. The deep ravine was gone, completely filled in by the earth thrown over by the blast.

"We don't owe each other nothing," Vince said in the cab of the truck on the way back.

"Want to keep this quiet?" Charlie said.

Vince stared stone-faced ahead. There were details he still had to work out, and he didn't feel comfortable talking until he knew what they were. He knew Charlie would say nothing. They'd broken laws.

Charlie looked gingerly, and said nothing.

Those were the only words the two exchanged in the two-hour ride back. Vince's mind was working hard. He had several ideas for his grand plan. Regardless of the exact plan he picked,

Vince knew it would be best if Patton considered him to be a friend.

The next day, Vince went to see Patton. Vince was contrite as he was led into Patton's office. He told Patton that his offer was really nice, but it wasn't something he could accept. Vince explained that he'd been thinking about doing something else for some time, that he wasn't comfortable working for someone else, and that he was really sorry.

"What are you going to do?" Patton asked.

"Weld, soon as I got business." Vince's eyes were soft, his expression even and humble.

ᗰᗰ   ᗰᗰ   ᗰᗰ

"How you going to live in the meantime?" Patton said, then stared off and tried to keep his reaction from showing as he contemplated the look he'd seen in Vince's face the last time they'd met. Vince's hatred for Patton had been obvious--yet here he was completely composed and being friendly.

"Make things for Pennell's Gift Shop," Vince said then paused. "Could I buy some scrap from you? I'd pay the going price."

Patton looked out his window at the yard more than a hundred yards away where he stored his excess equipment. "You could have that pump-jack tripod, the one that's bent," Patton said.

"Has to be quarter-inch plate." Vince was looking at Tom Patton's POCUS. The whole thing was made from quarter-inch plate. "You know those Wyoming bucking horses I make?" Vince said with his head down, his face a little long. "*Sally* at Pennell's told me she'd buy a dozen of them for five dollars apiece. I got some other ideas, too." Vince paused. "I'm sure there's a way to get it to work, Tom. You just have to spend more money, that's all."

Patton's gaze narrowed and his mouth pursed slightly. What really bothered him was the thought that Vince was showing him a mask—that underneath there was a whole different person with a different agenda. Patton was anxious to get Longto out of his office. He picked up his phone and gave instructions saying the winch-truck operator should pick up that big hunk of iron in the near corner of the yard and haul it out to

Vince's house. Vince nodded when Tom said that Vince would meet the winch-truck operator in the yard and help load it.

"I shouldn't take up any more of your time," Vince said, and contritely made his way out of Tom Patton's spacious office.

Vince drove to the yard and helped load the machine. Then he led the winch truck to his house in the country. He was animated, as the big machine was unloaded. He had no plans to cut it up. Contrary to his report to Patton, the machine had worked well the first time Vince had tried it, and by the time he was done tinkering, it worked perfectly, better even than Tom Patton's most optimistic appraisal.

Vince had been studying economics and markets, and he was convinced that the price of oil couldn't hold, and that its fall would be dramatic. If the price fell to below twelve dollars, Tom Patton's expenses on his heavy oil would exceed his income and he'd go broke. Vince wanted to have cash on hand and be ready so he could buy Patton's production when that time came.

Vince knew a woman named Mary White who used to work for a company called New York Oil. Mary knew where a lot of gas was located--some, she said in capped wells with pipe still in the hole just waiting to be produced. Vince had been stopping to see her regularly. She gave him a warm and fuzzy feeling.

10 – Mary White

Mary White was cross-eyed as a child. To avoid the pain of rejection, she spent a lot of time in her room reading books. When she was sixteen, the eye was repaired, and from then on, she was very pretty. Nevertheless, she didn't give up her studious and shy ways. But she could be assertive when she needed to be, and her friends knew she was able to win a power struggle with anyone.

She was married right out of high school to an abusive man. She remained steadfastly in love with him through black eyes, loose teeth, and abusive language. Her heart was broken when he left her pregnant, and with lots of bills.

She didn't dwell on her loss. She went to college, and got a degree in accounting in two and a half years.

She was thrilled when she got a job at New York Oil, an oil company in her hometown of Rawhide, Colorado. It was owned by a local rancher who had inherited land in the heart of oil country at about the time he graduated from the Colorado School of Mines as a petroleum geologist.

Mary worked in the accounting department. She was always the first one at work in the morning and the last out at night. She never seemed to notice the time or the fact that other people came and went. Her mother was always available to care for her boy. Mary got to be friends with Bill Spatz, the company's middle-aged head landman. She never thought of him as anything but a friend and if he had illusions about her she never knew about it. She discovered from him that before an oil company can drill, it has to have the legal right, which it usually got by buying an oil and gas lease.

She had male friends, but none she liked romantically. There was one man she was attracted to--a country boy named Vince Longto. He was the production foreman for a small oil company based in Rawhide.

Mary liked to know all the oil people, especially important, knowledgeable ones. Vince Longto wasn't important, but she heard he knew more about production practices than any engineer, and that he learned anything he chose at lightning speed.

They hadn't been talking long when she told him she'd like to start an own oil company. Vince said he'd been thinking about it, too, and doing market studies. The price of oil would crash, he said, but gas producers could do things to protect themselves from falling prices.

🐃 🐃 🐃

It was ten o'clock on a Friday night. Mary was alone in New York's big office building. The occasional strange sound didn't seem to bother her. Suddenly her head popped up, and she looked around. She'd vaguely agreed to meet a man for a drink at nine-thirty, but that wasn't what had caught her attention. She stood and without hesitation walked to the land department. Her eyes got wide when she saw the door to the records section standing wide open. She walked in and started opening file drawers.

Mary's pulse was quick as she went from drawer to drawer. Land, Mary had come to realize, was the most important part of oil and gas exploration. The best geology in the universe wouldn't let a company produce oil and make money until a landman put the deal together.

She searched and studied until three o'clock in the morning. For more than a month she worked weekends and stayed late in order to study the land records. Early on she noticed a curious thing. The company had drilled many gas discoveries, especially in western Montana. Obviously they'd been looking for oil, and when they could find no market for the gas, they had no choice but to abandon the wells. Usually there was a "shut-in" gas clause which allowed the driller to hold a non-producing gas well so long as annual rentals were paid, but the "shut-in" rentals on these abandoned wells hadn't been paid, and therefore the leases had all expired.

Mary discovered that a new natural gas pipeline went through the area. She contacted the pipeline. They were anxious to buy gas, and her research let her understand why. When the price of oil had gone up, users who could had switched to gas, and soon all the excess natural gas was gone. Gas couldn't be imported from overseas like oil. It could only be replaced with new domestic production.

Mary made up a typed and bound report recommending that New York Oil re-purchase the leases. The report told how much gas was tested, how large the reserves were, and whether pipe was left in the hole. In some cases, even tubing was left behind. Finally, the report showed the incredible profits that could be made given the sale prices currently offered by the pipeline.

Mary delayed showing the report to Bill Spatz at New York, but she did mention it to the young man, Vince Longto, at the coffee shop, who seemed very interested. A month went by, and still Mary delayed. Then the rancher-owner died, and the company was sold to a major oil company. Her boss was terminated, and there were other changes. She could keep her job, but she'd have to move to Cody, Wyoming.

Instead, Mary found a job with a local accountant. Her friendship with Vince had grown, and he continued to visit her regularly. He was tall, dark, reasonably good looking, and five years younger than Mary. He walked into her building reeking of the oil field.

She told a friend she thought he radiated sexual energy. She knew he was married, but by the way he talked, it was in name only. She told her friend she wasn't shy with Vince, that she sensed something about him that made her feel a kinship.

Mary looked forward to his visits. She even took the friend's advice and wore clothes that showed her figure. Mary noticed immediate changes in the behavior of the men at the office, but didn't connect it with her new clothes until her friend pointed it out.

She spent hours talking to Vince about the oil and gas business. Mary was amazed at how clearly he saw the importance of the legal aspects concerning the acquisition of drilling rights.

Mary explained how landmen researched county records, and discovered the names of the mineral owners, then negotiated and purchased an oil and gas lease. The mineral owner retained a royalty, usually one-eighth of the gross sales. All the rights of the prospective oil or gas pool should be under lease, and since an oil pool typically covered several square miles, and mineral rights were often split up into fractions, there were usually many mineral owners. Other companies purchased leases too, so part of being a landman included putting deals together with other oil companies.

Vince was often struck dumb when he came in to see her and unable to do much but stand and look at her admiringly. Mary liked it once when he gave her a bunch of lilacs he'd picked on the way in. She gushed and told him how nice he was. After that, he brought a rose when he stopped.

"Another rose?" she said to Vince when he dropped in.

Vince stood and stared.

"Have a seat," Marry said. "Hear you quit your job." Mary looked out the window. "It's such a pretty morning. I love springtime." She replaced the last rose he'd given her with the new one. Then she stepped around her desk and stood next to him. She pressed her hip into his shoulder and rubbed his neck and back--the same as she'd done many times before.

This time Vince's hand slid up her leg and came to rest on the outside of her thigh. Mary pulled his hand up to her buttocks all the while carrying on a normal conversation.

As Vince rubbed, his hand shook. Mary took his head in her hands, looked at him with a little smile, and said, "Stand up, then I can rub your back." Mary looked at the open door, and saw another accountant standing there, gawking. "Hi," Mary said.

The accountant looked at them, started to scurry away, stopped, spun around, and bumped into the wall before getting their door closed on the second try.

"It feels good rubbing your back," Mary said, as she slid her hands onto his buttocks and up again. She wore a little smile, the same one she wore when she hugged her boy. She could see that Vince was very appreciative.

Vince put his head on her shoulder and cried.

"It's okay," Mary said, as she undid his pants, and let them fall. He was erect. She rubbed him through his underwear.

"I know what you need," Mary said. With his pants around his ankles she led him to a chair covered with papers, slid his underwear down, and had him sit, then mounted him.

When he was finished, she had him stand, pulled up his pants and buckled them. She made sure his shirt was tucked in just right, his belt, shirt and pants even. "Now you're all fixed up," Mary said, like she'd just gotten him bundled up to go into the cold. Then she sat back down at her desk, and rummaged through the papers.

"I have an idea," Vince said after a pause. "I'm going into the oil business. You could come to work for me. You know where some gas is."

Mary sighed deeply. "It takes money to start an oil company," she said.

"Gas," Vince said. "Prices are rising." Mary's expression didn't change. "My wife has money. Why do you think I've stuck it out with her? These gas wells you know about, maybe we can buy options at a reduced price?"

Mary looked out the window. "Finding a market for the gas is the biggest problem. Gas pipelines are privately owned. That should change one day, but for now, it means they buy gas from whomever they want."

Mary knew they had an uncommon window of opportunity. She'd heard that the pipeline owner, Yellowstone Basin Utilities, needed gas. A hard winter would find it short.

It was Mary's dream also to be an oil and gas producer, and she thought this was one person who could pull it off. Slowly her eyes met Vince's: "You have to give me a piece of the business."

"I promise," Vince said, with total sincerity.

11 – Getting by on Nothing

Vince's wife didn't make much as a schoolteacher. Every month, she gave her check to Vince, who controlled the way the money was spent. She wasn't happy that Vince had quit his job with Tom Patton, and she refused to approach her father for a loan. Vince had five thousand dollars on hand. He knew it wasn't enough and decided to talk to Frank Dill himself.

Vince was at the Dill Ranch before sunrise. It was a cool spring morning in 1978. Vince knew Frank would be out soon. His ewes were lambing and he was probably short handed. For three years, Vince had been going to the Methodist church every Sunday where Frank was a deacon. He was beginning to treat Vince better, although Vince still felt like a lower life form in his presence. Vince had helped him recently get ten thousand dollars more for an oil lease on his ranch than Frank thought possible. That's what Vince thought he'd propose to borrow.

Vince became alert when Frank stepped out of his house and into a pretty sunrise. Frank glanced up and saw Vince sitting in his pickup in the yard. Vince thought his reaction was neutral. Frank immediately began walking to Vince, who watched his demeanor closely. It stayed neutral as he walked and even as he greeted Vince.

"Hear you quit Tom Patton," Frank said looking at the sunrise.

Vince thought it was a good start. Vince had his speech planned, but Frank spoke first.

"I'll loan you ten thousand," Frank said, finally looking at Vince with a cold stare. "Might even go twenty."

Vince was startled. It meant Emily had alerted Frank to the purpose of his visit.

"There's only one condition," Frank said. "Emily's my only child, and you will agree never to hurt her the way she hurt Nelson Bidlow."

Vince nodded his head and began to speak, but Frank put up a hand and his eyes narrowed. He pulled his big coat back revealing a large pistol on his hip. In a flash he drew the pistol and fired. The concussion hit Vince with a thud and the report was so loud it made his ears ring. A magpie dropped from a nearby cottonwood tree. Vince was stunned. Magpies were smart. Vince had been trying without success to shoot one since he was twelve years old.

"You violate that condition," Frank said, "you end up just like this here maggot-eating bird."

The Magpie was flapping its wings and trying to gain flight. Frank took careful aim and fired again. Feathers flew and the magpie's body lurched.

"You know I'd never hurt Emily," Vince said, staring at the tangled heap of black and white.

"You saying we have a deal?" Frank said, holstering his pistol, turning his gaze to Vince.

"Deal," Vince said, swallowing hard.

ᴆ ᴆ ᴆ

Vince told Mary that they couldn't pay themselves a salary or even expenses until money started coming in. Mary had some savings, she said.

Mary got right to work and picked an easy looking shut-in gas well close to Yellowstone Basin Utility's new pipeline, and went to Montana to see the rancher. The ranch had been in his family for a hundred years and the minerals were all his. He was ready to lease his 5,000 acre ranch, he said, for ten dollars an acre plus a dollar an acre per year thereafter for ten years, which of course was way more money than Vince and Mary had.

She told the rancher that the problem with gas was finding a market and the only market for the rancher's gas was Yellowstone Basin Utility's natural gas pipeline. If Yellowstone didn't buy the gas, it couldn't be sold. She said she had friends at Yellowstone who had promised to buy her gas if she had a contract with the rancher. As soon as the rancher signed a lease, Mary said, her oil and gas company would get production on his land. That's where he would make the most money she explained, by getting paid for production. She asked him to forego the big lease payment in exchange for an agreement to drill. She showed him the lease she'd prepared and pointed out the "drilling guarantee" clause, which said: "This lease is void unless, before the passage of one year, gas is being produced and sold." Mary studied the rancher as he read the clause. It was obvious he didn't know he had a well on his property that was ready to produce and therefore he was under the impression that Vince and Mary would have to drill a fresh hole. Mary put on the honest, trustworthy face that Vince had showed her, smiled at the rancher and rubbed his shoulder as any good friend would. He signed.

Vince was ecstatic. "We can get more than the two-eighty the utility told you on the phone," he said to Mary. "The last thing they want to do is search for gas and beg small producers to sell to them. Their status as a monopoly makes them think they don't have to work for a living. If we can satisfy all their needs for the coming winter, they'll want to deal with us. But before we deal with them, we need to know the answers to a fistful of questions.

"What if we discover more gas in the same area? Since Yellowstone has the only market, we need an agreement with them that they will give us a market for it, too.

"What if the utility isn't their own boss? Maybe they're owned by an oil company who can make the utility do anything the parent company wants, which means the utility would cut us off if it could, and start buying from their parent company if the parent company finds more gas."

While Mary researched, Vince went to Montana to work on the well. It had been fully completed and tested. It hadn't been plugged. It even had tubing in place, which would allow the well to be produced immediately.

When Vince arrived at the well, the first thing he noticed was a ten thousand-pound per square-inch heavy-duty ball valve coming off the side of the tubing. The valve had a bull plug in it.

Vince used a thirty-six inch aluminum pipe wrench to remove the bull-plug. He looked at the chrome-plated ball. It was shiny, and the Teflon seat appeared to be in good condition. He grabbed the valve handle and with a quick motion, turned it ninety degrees.

He knew nothing about gas. There were always mistakes when something new was being learned. He knew that much.

It was a deep well. There were seven thousand pounds of pressure at the surface, and it exploded into the surrounding air like a stick of dynamite. Vince was instantly knocked to the ground. Since new, pressurized gas continuously became available, it was an unrelenting explosion.

Vince lay on the ground, afraid to move. The sound was beyond his experience. He felt the shock waves on his body from the expanding gas. They stung his exposed skin, and his body vibrated so much it moved across the ground. His hair stood straight up from the static electricity generated by the agitated dust.

The valve was pointed at a forty-five degree angle to the ground, which was being quickly eroded away by the blast of high-pressure gas. A plume of dust billowed hundreds of feet into the sky. Little twisters in the agitated air kicked dirt into Vince's face.

His immediate thought was to get the valve closed to avoid the humiliation his mistake would cause. Without thinking, he jumped up and groped for the valve. He turned something. His ears were so traumatized, he wasn't sure if he turned it off. He couldn't see much, either. He figured it had to be closed. He could no longer feel the ground shake and his skin had quit stinging.

He stood there shaking, unable to move as he realized he could have lost his hand if he'd stuck it into the blast, or his life if he'd walked into it. If the gas had ignited, he would have been cooked. He was only alive by luck.

It was just as Mary White had said. All he had to do was open a valve and gas would come out. He had opened countless similar valves working for Tom Patton. That area had very little gas.

When the dust settled, he stared at the innocuous-looking pipe. A fit of rage came over him, as he thought about how

Mary hadn't said the damn thing would turn into the booster rocket of a space ship.

The next day, Vince hooked up a meter and tested the well on a flare. On the first day, it produced four million cubic feet of gas. After that, it produced two hundred thousand cubic feet a day, but Vince wrote down a million. A gas well rarely maintains its initial production. He'd be able to bullshit his way through if he was ever called on the point.

Vince called Mary. "This baby'll produce a million MCF a day," Vince said enthusiastically.

"But it'll only sustain two hundred thousand," Mary said evenly. "I have another in the works. I'm going up to see them tomorrow. In the meantime I want you to visit an old oil field thirty miles north of where you are now. There are eight owners in the field, all little operators. There's thirty wells and each makes about a hundred thousand MCF of gas a day, which is flared." Mary paused.

Vince knew where she was going. The little owners had probably tried many times in the past to sell their gas. Vince could sign up the little operators and buy their gas for little to nothing, build a gathering system, then sell it for top dollar.

"How close is Yellowstone's gas line?"

"Two miles," Mary said.

Within an hour, Vince was talking to one of the small operators, who said there was no market for gas in the area--that he and a couple other producers had talked to Yellowstone a couple years ago and they didn't need it. Vince didn't let on that he knew the situation was now different.

Vince talked to the operator enthusiastically about his plan to spend millions on a gathering system. Vince told him that since he'd be building a long pipeline to a distant market and spending a lot on the gathering system, that he'd only be able to pay the operator a small amount for his gas. Vince had the actual cost of the gathering system figured at a hundred and fifty thousand.

"I'd be buying gas a month after you sign," Vince told the operator.

In less than twenty days, Vince had all the little operators in the area signed up. It only cost him his time. He'd been able to find an appropriate contract in one of the landman books that

Bill Spatz at New York Oil had given to Mary. Vince made changes to the contract that he thought would be of later benefit. The contract provided that if Vince could bring in a pipeline and start buying their gas within one year, he'd have exclusive right to buy it for as long as there was production.

The price was fixed at ninety cents per thousand cubic feet, unless that caused Vince economic hardship, in which case it could be lowered. It could also be raised, but Vince had worded the provision so cleverly that the latter was unlikely ever to happen.

Mary found several more cased wells. Half of the ranchers went along with the option agreement, and she signed them up. The ranchers on the remaining wells assured Mary they'd lease for two dollars an acre. She did all the paperwork on these wells so that the producing rights could be secured as quickly as they had the money.

Each well would cost about ten thousand dollars to put on line, which was about a twentieth the cost of drilling and completing one. When Vince finally had a big package to sell, he called Yellowstone Basin Utilities. They had done their research.

Mary had discovered that a larger oil and gas company owned the utility, and the utility bought almost all its gas from this parent company. Most of this gas was purchased for far more than its fair market value. The trick was simple. They put a fixed price provision in the contract. If the price came down, the company showed the regulators the fixed price provision, and said it couldn't be changed. If the price went up, the contract was renegotiated. The new contract had the same fixed price provision to guard against the next round of low prices. Consumers rarely paid a fair price because it was always fixed at an historic high price.

"A utility's a quasi-public company," Vince's honest Montana lawyer/law professor said. "In return for the grant of a monopoly, which includes the assurance that the company will never fail, it must treat its customers in a fair and decent way. It can't cheat them by charging too much. It can't cheat them by buying raw material from its parent non-utility company at an inflated price, which is any price that is higher than the fair-market price."

"How do they figure fair-market price if they buy from themselves?" Vince said.

"Simple," the lawyer said. "Just answer the question, 'How much would the company sell the gas for if it didn't own the utility?'"

"So, with gas, if other people are selling it in the same area for a dollar, and the parent company's selling to its own utility for four dollars, that's wrong?"

"It would be a fraud on each and every customer they have. They might just as well hire burglars to steal money from their customers. What gives the utility the right to sell to their own captured utility at a price they couldn't get on the open market?"

"I like your choice of words," Vince said. Vince knew the professor lived in a make-believe world. He didn't understand that a regulated industry quickly captures the regulators, and has its own way.

Vince and Mary discussed strategy. They were concerned about the $150,000 they needed so they could lay a gathering system to the oil wells. Vince hoped they could get a signing bonus to cover this cost, but everyone Vince had talked to said such a thing wasn't customary. They were also concerned that any deal they made would be short lived.

"You know that as soon as their parent company finds more gas," Vince said, "they'll turn our gas off so they can buy from their parent at a price greater than the parent could get on the open market."

"And," Mary said, "to get rid of us, they only need one good market-out provision."

Vince said the negotiation would be lengthy. He knew that the more time the utility spent, the more they would be invested which would make them less willing to give up. In addition, if its negotiators were tied up talking to Vince, it would have no time to deal with another producer. "It ain't like reading a novel," Vince told Mary with a chuckle, "where you can skim over a boring part."

The first day, Vince and Mary met with the utility's Vice President; a man named Sam Castlebaum. That evening they took him to dinner.

Vince tapped their new company's bank account for the first time and hired a limousine. He figured the extravagance would reduce the chance that the pipeline company would look beyond the leases and contracts Vince and Mary had gotten. Vince had the limo driver deliver Castlebaum to the Bull's Eye, a steak house on the ridge above Billings. They were given a private table in a glass-enclosed area on the balcony overlooking Billings and the Yellowstone River. Vince instructed the cocktail waitress that their meeting was so private she couldn't come in. Mary would have to get the drinks. That way Mary could make sure that Vince's drinks were weak and Castlebaum's strong.

"Where'd you work before?" Vince said to Castlebaum.

"Exxon."

"Know Sal Peters?"

Castlebaum shifted uneasily. Vince glanced at Mary. Her research included personal details. She'd found out from a secretary at Exxon that Peters had been caught selling company secrets. His wife had been a friend with Castlebaum's wife, and the couples visited each other's houses frequently.

"Heard he wasn't the only one selling secrets," Vince said, "That he took the fall in a pre-arranged deal."

Castlebaum looked at Vince through squinty eyes.

"What a nightmare," Vince said, satisfied with the effect he was having on this good company man. "You think they'll ever catch the rest of them?"

"He did it," Castlebaum said pointedly, "and they caught him." One little sully on Castlebaum's name could spell disaster for his career. Vince was showing his ability to provide the blemish.

"What a beautiful view," Mary said, looking at the lights below.

Vince gave her a satisfied glance. "Let's make this deal," Vince said to Castlebaum. "You know it's a good deal."

"Sure," Mary said, grabbing Castlebaum's hand and pulling it to her so that it rested in her bosom. She rubbed his arm and shoulder. "Right thing to do."

"I'm sure we can do something," Castlebaum said, trying to pull his hand away without being forceful. "Let's meet in my office at ten in the morning." He stood and positioned a chair between himself and Mary. "We'll do something."

When they met again, Castlebaum had a contract ready. The price was three dollars and sixty cents per thousand cubic feet. He held out a pen for Vince to sign.

"I'm sure this is fine," Vince said, "but our lawyer will have to look at it. Why don't we meet again at one o'clock?"

"Fine," Castlebaum said with a slight edge in his voice. Vince figured Castlebaum still thought he was dealing with an amateur.

Back in their room, Vince and Mary studied the contract. It was for five years. There were "market-out" provisions everywhere, some obvious, some subtle. One said the utility could cancel the contract completely if the fair market price of gas fell to below two dollars. Another said the utility could impose new standards on the quality of the gas, and cancel completely if the new standards weren't met within thirty days.

"Call Castlebaum," Vince said. "Tell him our lawyer doesn't have the time this afternoon to look at the contract. We'll have to meet in the morning. Invite him to dinner tonight. Make him say yes. We need to get him invested before I lower the boom. Tell him our lawyer said we had to get a signing bonus, that we'd repay it from fifty percent of sales."

This scenario repeated itself for days. Vince was almost ready to sign except he needed to check one more detail. Castlebaum seemed to be getting desperate.

The big boys must have been watching, because on the fifth day, Castlebaum's boss joined the negotiations. The sticking points were the market-out provisions, the term, and the minimum take provisions. Vince wanted them to take sixty percent of his maximum production for six months of the warmer months and one hundred percent for the remaining six months. They agreed. They also agreed to a $50,000 signing bonus, fully repayable from fifty percent of sales.

Finally Castlebaum assured Vince there were no more market-out provisions, but a subtle one lingered. Vince played along, letting them think he didn't notice.

A final meeting was set up at the Bull's Eye where everything would be signed. Vince looked happy and eager.

Suddenly his expression changed. "Just a minute," Vince said. "I have to check on something."

He looked at the executives and began turning pages. The executives' faces grew red as Vince read out loud the market-out provision.

"This isn't supposed to be here," Vince said, his jaw jutting out. Vince stared harshly at the executives. It was going just as he and Mary had planned. He knew they wouldn't sign a one-sided contract if they had time to think about it.

"You haven't shown good-faith," Vince said, and slumped back in his chair like the negotiations were over. No one talked. "Tell you what," Vince said, "we'll strike this provision, and to repair your good faith, we'll change this signing bonus number."

Vince struck the offending phrase and changed the signing bonus to $200,000, then held the pen up for Castlebaum's boss, who stared at it without moving.

Mary acted like she was trying to break the tension, but really she added to it. She walked over to Castlebaum's boss, began rubbing his back, and said in her own inimitably motherly way, "It's okay, just go ahead and sign right here." Mary was standing where the man couldn't move without bumping into her groin.

He sat there like a statue. His ears glowed red. Mary and Vince exchanged knowing glances. Unless he had another source for this winter's gas, he had to take this deal. They could both see in his body language that he had no other source. He signed.

"Now, initial this change," Mary said, warmly.

He initialed.

Finally, Mary initialed and signed. She was the president of the corporation that was selling all the gas. All the stock was in Vince's name. It had to be that way for now, Vince had explained, because of the loan from his father-in-law. As soon as that was cleared up, Mary would get half.

The contract was all that Vince wanted. The remaining market-out provisions were not burdensome. Only an act of God or severe economic depression would allow them to avoid buying Vince's gas. The contract endured so long as Vince had production and the utility had a market. The price could never be changed. In addition, they had to buy his future production.

Vince and Mary went right to work. With the signing bonus, Mary put together the deals on the remaining wells, and Vince got the gathering system into place. Within a month they were in production, and soon they had their first monthly check: $212,000, *after* the entire signing bonus had been deducted.

Vince was happy. He flew Mary to New Orleans for the weekend. He bought her a new dress, and then they went out and partied. He promised Mary he'd divorce Emily, then she'd own half of everything because she deserved it.

Vince saw a way to make more. A contract provision allowed him to cut the price on the gas he was getting from the little oil wells by half if he could show a hardship. By including the expense of the cost of building the gathering system, Vince showed a small loss for the year, although he'd only gathered gas for the last three months.

Any accountant knew this expense was not legitimate. The gathering facility would last for years and its cost should have been capitalized, then depreciated gradually. Unfortunately for the little oil operators who had signed on to sell Vince their gas, Vince had it set up so that if they didn't object in writing in twenty days, the change went through automatically. Vince knew what to do to keep the little operators from making a formal objection in the twenty-day period. When an operator complained on the phone, Vince wasn't pleasant. He raised his voice and told him he'd have to sue, and pointed out the contract provision that the operator would have to pay Vince's attorney's fees if the operator lost the suit. The operator backed off.

A year later, when the new wells were completed, their net income in Montana was four million dollars a year. Once it was set up, it didn't take much management.

Vince's mother even started claiming Vince. She bragged on him and told everyone how she'd saved him from himself by being extra tough on him when he'd needed it. Vince heard her spiel once. It didn't seem to have any emotional effect. He felt disconnected from her, like she didn't really matter.

Vince was proud of his accomplishments in Montana. He'd cheated Yellowstone by fraudulently inducing them to buy one hundred percent of his gas year around by lying to them about his production potential. He'd cheated New York Oil by using stolen information worth millions of dollars. Finally, he was cheating Mary out of her fair share of the booty.

Vince didn't feel guilty about cheating Mary. She had a quality he found irritating. No matter what, she liked him. He couldn't help thinking that Mary was intentionally deceiving him, which caused Vince to be uneasy about trusting her. Vince knew Mary didn't really like him because deep down he knew he wasn't worthy of a person like her. His mother had told him as much from the time he was born. It was a personality trait that had formed even before he could remember, and as a consequence, he wasn't aware of the reason for this bizarre behavior.

12 – Nickel Gas

Back in Rawhide, Vince put together and drilled ten wildcat prospects. Two were discoveries, which was a respectable success rate. They were called Sheep Mountain and Enigma. Vince didn't spend his own money; he raised it from investors.

Sheep Mountain was heavy oil. It would have been marginally profitable to produce; except Vince had Tom Patton's POCUS which would crack the oil on site and make the field very profitable.

Enigma was a gas discovery and there appeared to be room for several more wells. But Yellowstone Basin Utilities was the only pipeline in the area, and they said that they no longer needed gas.

Enigma wasn't far from Rawhide, which was being served by Rawhide Gas, a small natural gas utility. Vince wondered if the little utility would buy the gas and told Mary to find out what she could. Mary called the president of the little utility who said they were already under contract to buy gas.

"Can you get out of that contract?" Mary said. The president of the little utility was a man named Carl Russell. "Then you could buy from us."

"The contract," Russell said, "is for gas from Green Creek. It's a two-well gas field about twenty miles north of Rawhide. I don't think we'll switch." Russell chortled softly, "Because we buy it for a nickel."

"You mean five cents per thousand cubic feet?" Mary said incredulously, thinking for the first time that her gas bills never exceeded ten dollars, even in the coldest months.

"That's right," Russell said. "The well's on land we own, so we even get one eighth of that back in the form of royalty. We've got the lowest natural gas utility rates in the nation, and we're proud of that."

Mary had been around Vince Longto too long, because she thought Russell was a fool. She found out from Russell that the field had recently sold to Conoco.

"Sure we'd like to sell," the man at Conoco said. "We've tried for years to sell the lease to Rawhide Gas, the little utility who owns the land and buys all its production. But they keep saying they aren't in the production business. When I talked to their president, he said they didn't know what kind of production reports to file."

Mary couldn't believe what she was hearing. In fact a clerk at Rawhide Gas had been filing all the necessary reports on behalf of Conoco and its predecessor for more than thirty years.

"How much?" Mary said.

"Fifty thousand dollars and it's yours."

"Isn't that a little high for a field that nets eight thousand dollars a year?"

"But if something happened to the existing contract, it'd make millions."

Before Mary was done explaining the situation to Vince, he was on the phone making reservations for her to fly to Denver. "Tell them you were in Denver on other business," Vince said, "and just dropped in. Write a check right there."

"Why don't you come with me?" Mary said, as she rubbed his back.

"Guess I could. We could stay at the Brown Palace. Change those flight reservations for two on Sunday afternoon. That way we can all go to church in the morning." Vince liked going to church with his family.

That Sunday morning, Vince made love to his wife, Emily, still as pretty as the day they had met. Later, Vince and Emily sat with their two children in church, and saved space for Mary White--who was always a little late--and her boy at the same pew. Vince liked this arrangement. After church, Vince and Mary were on their way to Denver.

"Why do you bother getting two rooms?" Mary said as they checked into their rooms in Denver. She'd asked the same question before.

"You never know what might come up," Vince said.

Vince needed a place where he could make private phone calls. Vince had been seeing someone else. Her name was Jean Butzsaw. She was the Daughter of an oilman, and she worked as a clerk at a small oil company in Denver.

The next day, the fifth of October, Mary went to Conoco and bought the Green Creek gas field without a hitch. For the next two months, Vince and Mary developed the details of their plan.

"We have to pressure-test the wells at Green Creek," Vince said to Mary one crisp, clear December morning as he put down the newspaper. Pressure testing required that the well be shut in. He'd also just read about an arctic cold front that was descending on their state. It was supposed to be ten below zero in the morning.

Mary smiled. It was part of their plan. Their goals were to get more money from the gas wells at Green Creek, and find a market for their gas at Enigma. Their plan was simple--weaken the utility by shutting off its low-cost gas, then start buying its stock. When the officers realized Vince would soon be their boss, they'd renegotiate the contract on the gas from Green Dome, and start buying gas from Enigma. Vince and Mary would make millions.

Mary had someone lined up to give them inside information on the little utility. It was Motley, a tall, lanky Mormon kid. The information from Motley would come in handy. They'd know which of their actions were causing the most distress. They'd know how close the opposition was to cracking.

"Better give old Russell a call," Vince said to Mary.

Russell had started out as a meter reader working summers for Rawhide Gas while he went to college. He knew nothing about natural gas production, only its distribution.

"I'll send Mike out there right now to shut the well in," Vince said. Vince knew that as soon as the pressure in the Rawhide system dropped, gas from Yellowstone would automatically take its place.

It took some time before Mary's message soaked in. When it finally did, Russell was frantic. "You can't do that, not now," Russell said. "We're going to need a lot of gas tonight. Cold's coming."

Mary wasn't flustered. "I'd let you talk to Vince, but he isn't here right now." She was patient, even empathetic. "He just bought this well," Mary said. "It hasn't been pressure-tested in years. Everyone does it. It's good gas field practice."

"In the middle of the winter?" Russell screamed. "Where will we get the gas?"

"You have an arrangement with Yellowstone."

"You know how much gas costs from Yellowstone?" Russell said. Mary knew. Getting gas when it was really cold used pipeline capacity that was rarely used. That let Yellowstone charge a lot extra—one hundred and thirty times more than the nickel the utility had expected to pay.

Vince grabbed the receiver from Mary. "Listen you little asshole. I've heard about enough of your bullshit. Now if you can't be nice to my partner, you can cram it up your ass, or maybe I'll come there and do it for you. Now shut the fuck up." Vince slammed down the receiver. He looked at Mary with a gleam in his eye and a little smile on his lips. Mary walked to the window and looked out with a long face. Vince walked up to her, and put his arms around her.

"Those guys at Rawhide," Vince said, "they put on nice faces, act nice, and say nice things, but you know they're just like bankers, they spend their days and nights thinking how they're going to screw us. The difference between them and us is simple. We're honest and they aren't."

Mary smiled at him and pulled his arms tighter around her. Frost was forming on the window.

The next day, Vince went to see Russell. Vince greeted him warmly and shook his hand with a firm, sincere grip. "Nice office," Vince said, thinking it had to be the most impressive one in Rawhide.

"Sorry about the pressure test, but you know the contract allows it." Vince and Mary had considered this point carefully. They didn't want to get sued by the utility for breach of contract. "You know, Carl, a nickel for a thousand cubic feet of gas just isn't right. You got us locked into this price--forever. No one could make money producing for a nickel." Russell wasn't buying any of it, and from his expression Vince figured he had to be careful to keep from getting thrown out of his office.

"Saw your boy play basketball last night," Vince said. "You must have worked with him. You have good reason to be proud. I hear he's smart, too." Vince glanced up at Russell. He still looked tense, but Vince figured he was no longer at risk of getting thrown out. "I'm not a bad guy," Vince said, "Neither's my partner, Mary. All we want's a fair price. If I were a farmer, the Federal Government would be in here right now talking to you on my behalf, maybe even passing laws saying what you're doing's illegal." Vince gave Russell a sincere look. "You know that's true."

Russell cracked the smallest of smiles. When Vince excused himself, he knew he was in for a long battle.

The wells at Green Creek stayed shut in for several months. When one excuse was used up, Vince found another. He was a genius at finding loopholes in the contract.

Russell fought back. At Russell's behest, the Interior Department got involved. The Federal Government owned a small piece of land in the unit. Vince was ordered to produce the wells or lose the federal lease. Vince's lawyer assured him that he only needed to produce the well for a couple hours each month to hold the lease.

The little utility got weak very quickly. Their rates were established for the nickel gas. At first they didn't even try to get the rates changed. Apparently they thought it would soon be over and they'd start paying a nickel again. Soon the utility's stock was severely depressed.

Meanwhile, the investors at Sheep Mountain and Enigma were complaining about the large, annual assessments for maintenance. Vince told them they better get used to it, because there was no possibility of selling gas at any time in the near future, and the oil at Sheep Mountain was too heavy to be produced profitably.

Vince took pity on them, he said, and gave the investors at Enigma thirty cents on every dollar they'd invested.

At the heavy oil field, Vince paid the investors fifty cents on every dollar. He could have gotten it for less, he thought, but he was anxious to hook up Tom Patton's POCUS. It would raise the oil's value by cracking it and reduce the cost of treating, and turn the oil field from a loser into a real moneymaker.

13 – Making them crack

Vince searched for weaknesses. He did background checks on all the directors of the little utility, but they were all clean. Finally he found something—oil theft.

The Green Creek gas field had two gas wells. The utility was pumping the field, which meant it took care of the field's daily needs. In addition to methane, the well produced other heavier gases, including propane and butane. It even produced some pentane, which is a lighter component of gasoline, and is a liquid at room temperature. In the summer, the pentane stayed gaseous, and went down the pipeline. In cool weather, it condensed on location, and was separated before it went down the pipeline. The liquids were called condensate, and there wasn't much. In a year's time, less than a hundred barrels collected in a tank on the location. The condensate could be used to run a car if a lead additive was used to raise its octane. Goldfarb, the original driller, had told the people at Rawhide Gas that since the condensate had come out of the well as a gas, that it had been metered and therefore paid for by the utility.

Every spring, Rawhide Gas put the condensate into the pipeline where it swelled the rubber connectors between joints of pipe so it didn't leak. In the warm weather, the condensate didn't hurt anything because before it got to town, it became vapor again and burned just like any other gas.

Conoco had known about the condensate, too. The man at Conoco told Mary the same thing, that since the condensate was a gas when it came out of the hole, it had already been metered and paid for.

Vince told Mary that since Russell and his directors were all from cowboy stock, they wouldn't understand that the condensate was gaseous when it was produced. They knew as much about oil and gas as a city slicker knew about cows. Vince began talking to lawyers about oil theft. Vince had difficulty, but he finally found the right man.

The lawyer was short and round. He was bald and he had a greasy look. He had a fat, red face, and lips so thin they were barely visible. When he smiled, his mouth got crooked, and a bump formed on the line of his upper lip so a small part of his lip could be seen. It looked deep red, almost diseased.

His name was Jim Wartsall, but everyone called him Poly. No one knew why. Most thought it was from his being Roly-Poly. Vince met with Poly in his office on Main Street.

"We need to sue these guys," Vince said. "I'm willing to spend ten, twenty, thirty thousand dollars--whatever it takes. I have the money. I'm the largest natural gas producer in all Montana." At least Vince was the largest producer in a certain county in Montana.

"They're stealing condensate, huh?" Poly said. "We could say they endangered the lease by not paying royalties on the condensate. If you don't pay royalties, the lease can be terminated, right?"

"That's great," Vince said, enthusiastically. "That lease is worth millions."

"Then we'll sue for millions," Wartsall said, smiling.

The lease was only worth fifty thousand dollars to Vince, the supposed aggrieved party, because that's what he'd just paid for it. But because of the nickel provision, if the utility lost the lease, it would cost the utility millions to replace the gas somewhere else. In other words, Vince's suit would be seeking damages from the utility that it might cause to itself.

"Then," Poly said, "we can sue for stolen condensate for the last thirty years. Since no one knows exactly how much condensate the well produced, we can multiply the amount you gave me times twenty, and no one will be the wiser."

"But I've only owned the lease for a couple months," Vince said.

Poly leaned closer and smiled. Vince leaned closer, too. Vince was starting to like this little fat man.

"Mind if I smoke?" Poly said, not waiting for an answer.

It was a low-tar cigarette, the kind with holes in the filter. Poly neatly defeated the purpose of the holes by popping the entire filter into his mouth. He inhaled deeply, leaned forward again and continued.

"We can sue in the name of the oil field. It would be the Green Creek Field versus Rawhide Gas. That won't hold up in the long run because the field itself isn't a legal entity. We would also sue all the directors. It'll work long enough for you to get some press coverage. Oil theft's hot. The papers'll jump on it."

"That sounds great," Vince said. "When can you have the suit ready?"

"Morning soon enough?"

"Don't sue before I tell you," Vince said. "I have to set the scene."

Vince called the pumper, the utility man who cared for the well. He was a man named Lonnie Freeman, who was also a director of the utility.

"Hi," Vince said. "Mind if I come out and look at Green Creek tomorrow? I'd just like to look around."

"I'll be there at nine in the morning." Lonnie sounded nervous on the phone. Mary knew him. She said he was always scared of something. He was nearing retirement and looking forward to it. He had a big pension with Rawhide Gas that would let him spend all the time he wanted with his grandkids, which is what Mary said he loved to do. He was a fisherman, and he had five Grandsons, all budding fishermen who loved to go fishing with Grandpa. He also had five little Granddaughters who were so pretty when they went to church all dressed up. Lonnie was having chest pains, and he was supposed to stay away from stressful situations.

The next day was a warm spring day at the Green Creek Gas Field. The air was so crisp and clear, snow-capped mountains almost a hundred miles away stood out clearly. Meadowlarks sang, butterflies danced. A Hereford bull bellowed in the distance.

Vince and Lonnie walked around until Vince seemed satisfied. "Looks good," Vince said. Lonnie looked relieved.

"Hey," Vince said, climbing into his pickup. "This well make any condensate?"

"Maybe a hundred barrels a year. We put it in that little tank over there."

The tank was fifteen feet high—small for the oil patch. "What's that thing hanging up on the side of it?"

Lonnie shrugged.

"Looks like a small neoprene hose with the kind of spigot you see at a filling station," Vince said, innocently.

When Lonnie saw what Vince was talking about, he laughed and guffawed. "Well," Lonnie said, between chuckles. "That's what it is. I fill up my truck every time I come out here. If we have any left over in the spring, we run it down the pipeline." Lonnie's smile went away when he looked at Vince's face.

"You mean you're stealing oil!" Vince's voice boomed. Vince jumped out of his pickup and put his face into Lonnie's who was visibly shaken. "You lousy thief! I only sell you gas. That makes it *my* condensate. You're going to jail. No pension for you."

Vince had practiced, and he had more to deliver, but he started worrying that Lonnie might not survive the full harangue. Lonnie was holding his chest and gasping. Vince needed Lonnie for his vote on the board and to put a scare into the others. He cut it short.

"Tell that no-good, thieving president of yours he's going to jail, too," Vince said, this time a lot more softly.

Lonnie leaned against his car, gasping and mumbling something about not meaning any harm.

Vince stomped back to his pickup. Before he left, he stopped once more to admire the scene. He liked watching butterflies flit over wildflowers with snow-capped mountains rising behind them in the distance.

Vince waited until he got news from Motley that Lonnie had talked to Carl Russell. Then he called and screamed at Russell in the same way he'd yelled at Lonnie. He told Russell his reputation was through, that he was nothing but a no-account thief. When the papers got through with him he'd be run out of town. Russell showed no emotion, but Vince knew the harangue would take its toll.

Vince had one more thing to accomplish before he sued. There was a director of Rawhide Gas named Bill Kincaid who lived in Denver. Kincaid was the largest owner of the little utility's stock. Kincaid also owned a large stockbrokerage house in Denver. Vince hired an agent to try to buy Kincaid's stock, but Kincaid wouldn't sell.

As soon as Vince filed suit, he contacted the local papers, but they would print nothing bad about the little utility or its directors.

In Denver, Vince had better luck, because the *Herald* ran the story with a big headline saying Kincaid was being sued for millions for oil theft.

Two days later, Motley reported that Kincaid was frantic, that he wanted the problem fixed. There was an emergency session of the directors, but nothing was resolved. Shortly thereafter, Vince's agent got a call from Kincaid saying he wanted to sell. Within a week, Vince owned Kincaid's stock. He waited to put his name on the certificate.

Vince took Russell to coffee. "Have a look at this," Vince said, showing Russell the endorsed stock certificate. Vince didn't let the certificate out of his hands for fear Russell would show it to someone else or even steal it. Russell was a decorated World War II army officer, and Vince knew he was capable of almost anything. As soon as Russell's face showed that he fully understood, Vince folded the certificate and stuck it in his pocket.

"Sugar?" Vince said with a little smile, pushing the sugar dispenser in Russell's direction. Russell shifted uneasily. "It means," Vince said, "that your fate is in my hands." When Russell began to talk, Vince rose a hand and silenced him. "I had Mary check into pension plans," Vince said. Mary had discovered that some pension plans at Rawhide Gas had a provision that allowed the plan to be suspended, sometimes even canceled. "And it seems to me that you're on thin ground here, I mean your actions are contrary to the best interests of the utility. That allows for your firing, and a suspension of your pension, possibly even cancellation if your actions are found to be willful. In any event, you have to pay your own attorney fees. A full blown trial would run seventy-five thousand dollars."

Vince watched again as Russell shifted, and tried to think of something to say.

"Cream?" Vince said, sliding the cream dispenser in Russell's direction. Russell's mouth pursed slightly.

"Listen," Vince said, in an empathetic voice as he stood, and patted Russell on the shoulder, "nothing's going to happen to your job or your pension. I like you, Carl; you're my kind of man. Stop worrying. When I'm in charge you'll still be running this gas company exactly the same as you are right now." When Vince departed, Russell was so deep in thought; he didn't bid Vince farewell.

The next day, Vince had Mary call Lonnie Freeman and had her tell Lonnie to put pressure on Russell, too, and to remind Lonnie that his pension was in jeopardy.

Motley kept them up to date and reported that Russell had called another meeting—that he went around to all the directors before the meeting, and told them they should make a deal with Longto, that a nickel was absurd. Their finances were in shambles. It would get them out of a hot spot on the cost of gas, and out of the lawsuit. They could start buying gas for $3.80 instead of the $4.50 they'd been paying Yellowstone.

At first, Russell couldn't get a majority. Finally, in a secret meeting, the directors agreed to the deal with Longto.

The phony lawsuit was dismissed when the nickel contract was changed, and Rawhide Gas paid fifty dollars for five barrels of condensate, the amount taken since Vince had become the owner. Vince insisted on being paid. That way he could show the suit wasn't frivolous. Vince had won. It didn't bother him that fifty dollars was a long way from millions.

Shortly after the lawsuit was settled, Vince submitted the endorsed stock certificate for transfer to his name. It gave him a controlling interest in the utility. It didn't take Vince long to acquire most of the remaining shares of the utility. It had taken three years to do it, one year less than Mary had predicted.

Soon the Federal government and the State of Colorado were demanding that Rawhide Gas pay almost a half a million dollars for royalties and taxes on the stolen condensate. Now that Vince was the owner, he'd have to pay. Instead, Vince launched an investigation. This time, Vince discovered and reported the truth, that no condensate had been stolen.

When the dealing was done, Vince relaxed, and marveled at how good it felt. Relaxing and feeling good was something new to Vince, and at first he liked it. He felt smart, and he felt like a good person. He was now the owner of *Rawhide Gas*. He had known about Rawhide Gas when he was still in Ft. Collins from advertisements he'd seen. It seemed like such a good company then. It was a company a person could trust and depend upon, and now that he was the owner, didn't all that accrue to him as well?

A month later, Vince's mood turned sour when Mary brought some bad news. "Ever hear of the Natural Gas Policy Act?" Mary said. "Look at this."

Vince studied the mumbo jumbo of the regulation for a minute, then looked at Mary for help.

"Says you can't change the price of intrastate natural gas that was under contract in November of nineteen-seventy-eight. If the federal regulators find out about it, they'll force you to buy the gas for a nickel and reimburse all overcharges."

"But Green Creek didn't produce after November of seventy-eight," Vince said. "We'll say there was no contract."

"Except the contract is on file with the PUC, and you made two small sales to keep the BLM from canceling the small Federal portion of the unit."

Vince gave Mary a piercing glare and grabbed the regulations from her. A minute later, he was on the phone to the law professor in Montana. When he hung up the phone, his face was white.

Vince realized that in just a few short months, the payback bill would be enormous. In a year, it could easily break him. He consulted every top-notch lawyer on the subject he could find. All said he had a big problem. One lawyer, who knew something about the way Vince had acquired the utility, told Vince that the Natural Gas Policy Act was the least of his problems.

"That lawsuit you filed was phony," the lawyer said. "Coercion with a phony lawsuit is called fraud."

The lawyer went on to say Vince could lose the utility, *and* all the monies he'd earned from charging almost four dollars per thousand for his gas from Green Creek instead of five cents.

This news was even harder on Vince, and for a little while he felt devastated.

The idea of fraud resounded in Vince's mind like a twenty-one gun salute from a battery of old canons. He'd lose all the respect he'd gained; he'd be penniless, totally humiliated, not smart, and definitely not loved. It was a fear as powerful as any Vince had experienced--greater, it seemed, than even his real fear of death.

Vince was still searching for a solution when Mary came into his office. "Look at this," Mary said, and placed a letter in front of him on Rawhide Gas' old stationery. It was dated October 1, 1978, and said: The Green Creek gas contract is hereby suspended, pending renegotiations.

"No contract in October means the gas isn't subject to the Natural Gas Policy Act. It's that simple," she said.

"But we had sales in November and December," Vince said.

"Must not have made the sales pursuant to the nickel contract," Mary said with a shrug.

"Even though we sold it for a nickel?"

"As long as your good press holds out, you should get away with it," Mary said with a shrewd smile.

Vince called Russell into his office. "Sign this," Vince said. Russell read it, then quickly signed it and left Vince's office. Vince wasn't surprised at the ease with which Russell signed. Russell was a good soldier, and Vince had established himself as the power.

But the biggest problem, the fraud of the phony lawsuit, remained. Vince knew Mary was right that he'd have a far better chance of repelling a fraud attack if the public believed that he was too good a person to be guilty of such a thing. A jury is picked from the public, and also influenced by what everyone thinks, and Vince was very aware of the power of bias. Any good lawyer would carefully consider existing bias before bringing a suit alleging fraud.

Vince decided to triple the utility's advertising efforts, and hire a publicist. The ads would focus on the high integrity of Rawhide Gas. Each ad would have a picture of Vince, and each would be carefully designed to increase his respect in the public's eye.

Vince started buying stock in newspapers wherever he could, and he cultivated a friendship with the publisher of the local paper. He thought about how he could impress the local publisher, and others, like Public Utilities Commissioners.

He wished he had a big mansion where he could bring them for dinner. A big airplane would also be good. He could use it to take important people to Denver Broncos football games—or Northern Colorado's favorite: Wyoming versus Colorado State.

Vince looked at the courts in the state and saw that the judges were an independent bunch. Vince had Mary research. She discovered that the Missouri Plan, where judges were subject to recall by the people, had recently been implemented in Colorado, and was under consideration in Wyoming. He knew that with time, the Missouri Plan would cause judges to be responsive to public opinion, which would allow him to influence judges by controlling the opinion of the public.

When the Methodist church called and asked if Vince would buy a modest piano, Vince saw another opportunity to influence public opinion. He bought a grand piano, and made a big deal of its presentation to the parish. From then on, he looked for high-profile places he could make charitable contributions. Actually, Rawhide Gas made the contributions. No one cared. Everyone thought that Vince and Rawhide Gas were the same. No one thought that if the gift came from Rawhide Gas, that the whole community would end up paying for it in the form of higher gas prices.

Vince knew he was in for the long haul, because the statute of limitations would not start to run until the fraud was discovered.

꩜ ꩜ ꩜

Mary White had no reason to rejoice. The day they took over Rawhide Gas, Vince stopped referring to her as his partner. Vince still showed affection toward Mary, but she knew he was spending more and more time in Denver with his new mistress, Jean Butzsaw.

Mary had worked twelve hours a day, six to seven days a week for years in order to build Vince's and her empire. They had paid themselves almost nothing during most of the period. Vince said it would give them more later on.

In disgust at Vince's affair with Butzsaw, Mary began dating. The man she chose was one of Vince's best friends from his single years. She told Vince she was going to marry him unless Vince gave her a fair share of the company. They fought, but Vince wouldn't budge. In her rage, Mary took a check for two hundred and fifty thousand dollars. It was from Yellowstone Basin Utilities, a rebate to Rawhide Gas for an overcharge.

Mary had no trouble cashing the check and depositing it in her own account. The bank was used to her signature on huge checks, and she was either president or vice president of all Vince's corporations. Things were okay for a couple of weeks. When Vince spent that weekend in Denver, they fought again.

The next day, Mary eloped with Vince's old friend.

The pain Vince suffered when he heard that Mary had left him was intense. Vince needed her kind of love. He relived again the years of pain he'd endured because Yaping had left him.

On his second day of mourning, Vince realized a simple fact: He wasn't powerless. He grabbed an engineer and two accountants, and flew to every big city in the area. Vince had them fan out and search at every motel. He searched for ten days before he gave up.

Vince went home a broken man. He felt betrayed. The money didn't matter. Mary had left him. Vince decided Mary White wouldn't get away with it. He put Poly Wartsall to work and got charges of embezzlement filed. He knew the little bulldog would create all kinds of fits for her.

Wartsall got the county attorney to file charges and throw Mary in jail. For her part, Mary sued for a part of the company.

It ended in a strange settlement. Wartsall and Mary's attorney talked to Fruitman, the county attorney, and got him to join the negotiations. It ended in a combination civil/criminal settlement. Mary settled the civil suit for an undisclosed amount. She pleaded guilty to embezzlement, but the guilty plea was to be suspended and expunged after a year.

Just as Vince had planned, Wartsall saw to it the final requirement was never met. The charge wasn't dropped, and Mary ended up with a felony conviction on her record. Vince hired Jean Butzsaw, his mistress from Denver, to replace Mary White. Within two months, Butzsaw was running the show, and Vince was happy to let her do it.

ۿۿۿ

"It's stupid the way you're running this place," Butzsaw said, busting into his office. "Presidents of natural gas utilities get a hundred and twenty thousand a year."

Vince looked out his window, smirked, then nodded toward the utility building a block away. "I should pay Russell more?"

"You! And me, too. No reason our offices can't be down there." Butzsaw pointed at the utility building.

"Yeah," Vince said, catching on, "and I've been wanting a big Caterpillar for building drilling locations. Hell, the utility could buy it and lease it back for little or nothing."

"When the utility remembered to charge it out," Butzsaw said with a wicked smile. "I'm telling you this because I want to make more money. Make me VP, and pay me eighty from the utility and forty from the oil company."

"Do it," Vince said, and returned his attention to the scattered papers on his desk.

A week later, Vince was President of Rawhide Gas, and Butzsaw moved him into Russell's office. Jean Butzsaw became its Vice President. Vince paid himself $80,000 a year and Butzsaw the same, even though Russell continued managing the utility, same as he always had.

Vince had the utility hire an engineer and paid him $50,000 a year. The engineer was used by Vince's exploration companies, and rarely by the utility. Finally, Vince had the utility buy lots of equipment that his non-utility business could use including a D-9 Caterpillar for use in building drilling locations. As the utility got more and more assets, it was entitled to higher profits by the PUC rules.

Vince got so cocky, he used utility equipment and employees to help build his brand new multi-million dollar home.

ۿۿۿ

As the years slipped by, Vince built his empire. The richer he got, the more he felt a pull from the east.

In May of 1984, Vince went into Butzsaw's office. Vince had been distant for a couple months.

Vince looked around for a minute, then looked at Butzsaw and said, "This place runs okay without me. The hardest thing you have to do is take the money to the bank, and you've got three accountants to help you do that. I'm going to Russia for awhile."

"Where?" Butzsaw said with an incredulous look.

Vince glanced quickly at Butzsaw. He couldn't imagine she hadn't noticed his elaborate preparations. "While I'm gone," Vince said, "I'd like you to pick up a couple more natural gas utilities. Give the one in Cody, Wyoming a close look, would you? They're buying their natural gas for a dollar fifty-eight a thousand. Compared to the four-fifty we're charging our own utility just south of them, that's really cheap. Makes us look bad. Who do they think they are anyway? Assholes?"

14 – Sharks, Boys, and Flying

"Hey big guy," Tom Patton said to his nine year-old boy. It was a Saturday morning in Denver. "You want to take the plane to Rawhide and see the skeleton of a shark that was big enough to swallow a car?"

"Wow, okay." Billy jumped up and down. "Is it Charcharadon Megaladon?"

"Sure is," Patton said, smiling warmly. "It's near Rawhide. You can fly once we get into the air. I'll even let you drive the pickup a little bit when we get into the country."

Patton kept a pickup at the airport in Rawhide. There hadn't been drag races at the airport there on Sunday in years.

It was an hour's flight to Rawhide, and another hour and a half drive to the site. Patton had started letting Billy fly when he was seven. At nine, Billy was good enough to land, but he was so short, he couldn't reach the rudder pedals and see out the window at the same time. Billy didn't like it, but it was fine with Patton because it gave him an excuse to land the plane himself.

Patton loved these outings with his bright-eyed boy. When Billy was younger, Patton had tried to get his wife, Belle, involved in camping and hiking so they could be together, but she wouldn't get interested. Unlike Patton, who was born and raised in Rawhide, Belle was raised in a city and couldn't get used to a small Colorado town.

In an attempt to keep his family together, Patton had moved his office to Denver. He was devastated when his marriage failed, and Billy was left without a family, or a chance to have a normal life with brothers and sisters.

Patton thought there would still be hope for a good family relationship with another woman. At thirty-three, he was still attractive, and there were scores of women who would have him. This time, he was determined to find the right one, one who enjoyed the things he enjoyed, one he could talk to and smile with and be happy all the time.

He wasn't intent on finding a pretty wife, just one he really liked doing things with. On the other hand, pretty would be nice. He couldn't help thinking about the young girl at the Pump--Sue Hansen was her name. She was the prettiest woman he'd ever seen. Too bad she was so young, he thought. For an instant, he allowed himself to dream about a time when she would be older. Patton cleared his throat and pushed the thought away. She didn't even know he existed, he thought, and she certainly had no interest in a man his age.

The loneliness wasn't bad when he was with his boy, or buried in his work. But sometimes, late at night, after several drinks, he allowed his mind to dwell on the fact that he had everything but a happy family.

At Rawhide, Patton and his boy jumped into his old pickup, and drove deep into the desert to Devil's Kitchen. They stopped at a bridge across Hell's Creek that Vince Longto had built, and walked more than a quarter of a mile down the sandy bottom of the dry wash.

"It's right over there," Patton said, with a curious look, then his face grew long as he studied the situation. The vault to Vince's shrine was gone, filled with rubble.

"Underneath all that dirt?" Billy said, his exuberance faded. "How's the stream run, Dad?" The streambed came to a dead end at the pile of rubble.

"We're in the rain shadow of that mountain over there, so it rarely rains here." Patton pointed to a snowcapped mountain. It appeared, in the clear air, to be a stone's throw away.

"So when are we going to get to see the shark?"

"One day there'll be a big gully washer, and all this will be washed out. We'll have to come back every couple years."

"What happened, Dad?"

"Vince Longto drilled for oil nearby. Before he drilled he probably buried the shark. Last thing old Vince needed were environmentalists shutting him down because of old bones in the area."

"Where's the oil well?"

"Turned out to be gas, and one's right over there, about two hundred-yards away."

Billy strained to see.

"It looks like a lone fence post."

"That's the thing that made Vince Longto rich?" Billy said.

"That and a bunch more like it."

"Where's the rest?"

"They're about a quarter mile apart and run east and west for about two miles. We could go look at them, but they all look pretty much the same. Vince sure did the right thing when he went with gas. Talk about low maintenance. I had a pipe break once and oil went into the desert. It cost me seventy-five thousand dollars to clean it up. If a pipe breaks on one of Vince's gas wells, it spews gas until one of his field hands comes out and shuts a valve. A little later a crew comes out and fixes it. There isn't a mess to clean up, because it all went into the air. It's even sweet gas, so there's no danger of anyone being poisoned. But that's if a pipe breaks. They almost never do."

"Where's Vince drilling now?" Billy said.

Patton chuckled. "I heard he went to Russia about six months ago. Everybody in Rawhide's wondering if he'll make it back." Patton smiled at his boy. "Hey," Patton said to get Billy's attention. The boy had his head in a bush. "Want to walk up the creek or down?"

"Down. Heard being up the creek is a bad thing."

Patton smiled, and picked his boy up, gave him a big kiss on his soft little cheek, and squeezed his muscular body.

When they were ready to return, Billy said: "Hey, let's look for arrowheads on the way back."

"Vince probably had them all picked up."

"Why would he do that?"

"Same reason he buried the shark. Vince had an operation on public land shut down once because a government archaeologist found an arrowhead. After that, Vince scoured the areas where he drilled and removed the arrowheads and other things that might cause a problem."

"But an arrowhead might mean there was a village here."

"That's what people think who grew up in an apartment in a city. Vince said Indians and the people who came before them lived here for twenty thousand years. They used spears to kill stuff. You know what happened when they threw a spear and missed?"

"Spear hit the ground."

"And maybe the point broke. Same goes for an arrow with a flint tip. So finding a piece of an arrowhead or a spear point doesn't mean much, except sometime in the last twenty thousand years someone might have been hunting in this area. Everyone already knew that."

"But Dad, people can't hurt fossils and stuff."

"That fossil was doing fine until about thirty years ago when the sun shined on it for the first time, and rain fell on it, and wind blew, and every so often in a wet year Hell's Creek would wash some of it away. Vince told the local high school science teacher. When nothing happened, he told the curator of the museum of the Dinosaur National Monument, and then at CU in Boulder and at UW in Laramie. Still nothing happened, so he decided to dig it up himself. When he asked permission, he ended up getting the run-around for years until finally he gave up."

"Why couldn't he get permission to do it, Dad?"

"Because the self-centered professors got laws passed that keep private collectors out of the business. They told everyone it had to be preserved for science. That means this fabulous fossil was rotting in the sun, getting destroyed by oxygen and ultraviolet rays and wind and frost, just like thousands of others all over the world, because the professors don't have money to excavate."

"Covering it all up with dirt will make it last longer?"

Patton took his boy's hand. "That's what I'm saying, big guy. Vince Longto's one man who knows something about the environment from books and from living it. He knows about the sweat, the cold, the poisons, and the stings." Patton pinched his little boy in the tummy.

Billy giggled and twisted to get free.

"And he knows about death. If there's one thing book learning misses, it's knowing about death."

"Because if something dies its genetic code dies with it."

Patton smiled and nodded. "At first, Vince was all for environmentalism. He was tired of farming practices that let nasty chemicals seep into river systems."

"What did Vince care?"

"Vince loved to go down to the river at night and gig frogs, then eat them up with a clam chowder made from real fresh-water clams and crawfish. Sometimes he'd have a big feast and call it his 'Rocky Mountain Unsea Delight.'"

"I went to one of those. It was neat. I ate a rattle snake, and crawfish."

"How'd you like the 'possum?"

"Dad, there aren't any 'possum around here."

"Then I don't know what he was serving up."

"I heard he eats puppies."

"Where'd you hear that? Never mind." Patton ruffled his boy's hair. "Vince had every kind of wild mushroom imaginable," Patton continued. "If you didn't eat the mushrooms, you didn't get invited back. He guaranteed none were poisonous."

"I remember the witch's butter," Billy said.

Patton looked like he was going to gag. Witch's butter was a slime fungus with a deep purple color. "Anyway," Patton said, "in the spring, he'd have fillet of walleye and eel. Vince loved the frogs' legs the best. When the frogs disappeared, Vince figured it was farmer's chemicals. Amphibians soak up everything through their skin." Patton looked to the sky, and noticed the position of the sun. "We better hurry up and get out of here, big guy. If I get you home late again, your mom will blow a cork."

"Dad?" Billy said, taking his dad's hand.

"Yeah, big guy?" Patton said, with a little smile.

"I like you."

"I like you too, big fella."

15 – Sue Hansen

Sue Hansen worked for her Italian grandpa at his restaurant in Rawhide called The Pump and Derrick. "The Pump" for short. There was an oil derrick on the roof of the building along with a small oil well pump that went up and down with an occasional squeak. There were two horseshoe counter positions near the kitchen door, where the regulars drank coffee.

Photos of ranching scenes lined both sides of the narrow dining hall. Sue's grandfather, Tony, said they made his rancher customers feel welcome. Tony wanted to keep the ranchers coming, he said, because one-day oil would die.

Grandpa Tony had strong feelings about the way kids should be raised. "Bring them up in the restaurant," he said gruffly in his Italian accent, "that way they'll know the business, and they'll know something about life, too." He gave this lecture with a mean look on his face. "It isn't something you can learn in school," he'd add.

In Rawhide, restaurants came and went, Tony explained. The ones that stayed were the ones owned and operated by someone who had grown up in the business.

Sue was Tony's favorite grandchild. When she was a little girl, she came in to see her grandpa regularly. She sat on his lap as he sucked on an old cigar. Tony told Sue about people, how to find the phonies, liars, and cheats, and good, honest people, as well. Talking about people was something the two still had in common.

At first, Sue's Danish dad wouldn't let his kids work. But the Italians had put pressure on Sue's dad until he relented with Sue's older brother, and when that seemed to work out okay, he relented with Sue. When she was nine her father put her to work in his veterinarian clinic that was attached to the house.

Sue loved the work and soon she was doing simple surgical operations by herself. When she was twelve, her father retired from active veterinarian work, and she went to work for her grandpa, Tony.

Grandpa Tony only hired shapely waitresses with nice smiles. Sue had a pretty smile, but she wasn't shapely. Tony made an exception for Sue, because she was smart, he said, and she paid attention.

She started busing tables. When she turned thirteen, roughnecks began paying attention. When she was fifteen and waitressing, everyone was paying attention. Sue had gray eyes that sparkled and pretty white teeth that complimented her clear complexion. But it was Sue's personality that made her especially memorable. It wasn't long before she had so much savvy that Grandpa Tony had her watch things when he was gone.

☒ ☒ ☒

It was on a Saturday evening, when Sue, seventeen years of age, approached a table of six especially rowdy-looking roughnecks.

"Well, hello, Honey," the self-appointed leader said. "Get a load of this boys." He punched the man next to him, who was already ogling Sue from head to toe.

The leader wore a tight T-shirt that showed ample muscles. The sleeve of his left arm was folded up high to hold a pack of Marlboros. His shoulder muscle was big and round and sported the tattoo of a dragon breathing fire upon a naked woman. His hands were scarred--fingernails dirty.

"God, my eyes go screwy trying to follow all those curves," he said, gawking, showing big, gapped teeth.

Sue smiled sweetly. She'd been around these kinds of men for years. They just had a different way of acting, her friend, Rosita had said. If you're nice to them, they'll be nice to you. Rosita was referring to tips. Sue liked the tips, but she also liked being nice.

"You know what I really like about you?" the leader said to Sue, "There ain't no part missing. Look boys, it's all there." He formed an hourglass in the air in front of her.

Sue wore a white dress, not too tight, but snug enough so it didn't take much imagination to know what was underneath. Sue put her hand on the lead roughneck's shoulder, leaned toward him, smiled, and said; "Too bad I'm only seventeen, huh?" Sometimes she would press her hip against a shoulder, but this time she just came close enough so he could feel her warmth.

"We'll go to jail for you," the roughneck said, a look of defiance on his face. "Won't we, boys?" They all agreed.

"You boys are out of luck," Sue said, "because I'm saving myself for my wedding night."

At that, the slowest-looking one got serious. "We understand," he said. "And that means you guys lay off." His little speech cooled them off. He was the biggest one.

"What'll it be, boys?" Sue said, ready to take their orders, assured of a good tip.

These men didn't cause Sue any fear. Every summer since she was ten, Sue had spent time in Denver with relatives where she attended karate camp with her far less athletic cousins. During the winters in Rawhide, she practiced every day for five minutes.

Sue got a black belt the summer she was fifteen, one of the youngest girls to do that. Although she liked it and she was proud, it remained her secret. If she were pressed, she'd admit to having taken lessons, but she always dodged the question about her black belt.

When she was sixteen, Sue had an opportunity to confirm her karate skills. A roughneck had been waiting by her car in the darkness of the deserted parking lot. She recognized him right away. The roughneck was a domineering type with acne. His hair reached the middle of his back. He wore it in a ponytail, tied off with a piece of leather. The roughneck had an unruly mustache that was stained darker near the corners of his mouth. He seemed a little wobbly standing between his car and hers. He didn't see her coming at first. Sue hesitated, then continued towards him.

When Sue saw the look on his face, her heart pounded against her chest. Only last week, a beautiful girl had disappeared driving from Rawhide to Boulder. Her dad told her what he thought might have happened. The scene was familiar. Sue was too close to turn back.

"Come on, Honey, we're going for a drive," he said, slurring his words, his alcoholic breath wafting in the breeze.

Sue stayed back. "No thank you."

"Man, this is sure a pretty car," he said, looking her up and down as he patted the hood. Sue heard the rivets in his jeans rub against the finish. "This baby's got a stick. You know what to do with a stick?"

"Rulon, I'm a schoolgirl," Sue said. "You need to get in your car and let me go, okay?"

"Come on and jump in," he said, opening her car door for her.

The cars were too close. She wasn't getting near him in close quarters. "You're going to get me in trouble with my boyfriend."

"Come on," Rulon said, his bad disposition showing. When it was obvious she wasn't coming, he hissed, "I said, come on."

Rulon lunged at her and grabbed her collar. She tossed her purse under her car and raised her hands to eye level. It was a fighting stance, but she made it look like she was cowering. She walked with him as he pulled on her collar, a meek look on her face. Slowly she reached across and took his hand. Rulon smiled, then looked toward the direction of their travel.

What happened next must have looked like a blur. To Sue, it happened in slow motion.

She squeezed his hand tightly, and stepped back. The move surprised him and pulled him off balance. Her hip twisted hard to the right, then her torso followed as she punched the back of his elbow with the palm of her free hand. She heard a loud snap as his elbow hyper-extended. She stepped free.

Rulon still had the angry look on his face. It didn't look like he was a fighter, because his nose floated out in front and his arms were at his sides. Sue grabbed his shirt with both hands at his shoulders and turned him into place. He was taking no effective steps to protect himself. As she drew back to strike, she heard the words of her *Sensei*: "Always hit your target."

The karate chop landed perfectly on the end of his nose, flattening it, and standing him up. The angry look was gone. Sue put both hands on his right shoulder. She pulled down with all her strength and doubled him over in order to bury a knee in his solar plexus. The blow knocked his wind out. He bayed like a bloodhound as he tried to get air back into his lungs. She knew the sound. So far so good, she thought. She was still afraid he might hurt her.

She squatted low and located the right spot on his shoulders, took careful aim; then with both hands cupped slightly to protect them from breaking, she began her lunge. Again, she heard the voice of her *Sensei:* "The collar bone is easy to break if you hit it in the right place with full force not just with your arms, but with your whole body. It's important you succeed. A broken collarbone will stop any attack."

Thud. She caught both collarbones fully exposed. She felt one buckle. She stepped back, still in a fighting stance, and watched.

The man stood with blood pouring from his nose. "You bitch. I'll kill you," he said, and started toward her. His arms looked useless at his sides. Sue knew it was over, but now she was mad. This time she located his jaw, stepped forward, raised her right leg high, chambered, and, as they moved toward one another, and with the full strength of a strong thigh muscle, she struck him on his chin with the ball of her foot.

She heard his jaw crackle, and she saw his head snap back. As he lost his footing his whole body seemed to sail into the air in a sweeping arc. It hit the ground, collapsed upon itself, and then quivered briefly. Parts stuck out at strange angles.

For a minute there was no movement. Then he grunted, rolled over and tried to pick himself up. His arms failed him, and he fell forward. His mouth hit the concrete and made a crunching, grinding sound. A tooth skittered away. He lay there moaning, then vomiting.

Sue felt shock. She'd never hit anyone who wasn't wearing thick layers of protective gear. The blood and the gore didn't bother her. She'd worked around that on a regular basis in her dad's veterinarian clinic.

"You all right?" Sue said.

"You bitch," he replied, then he hesitated. "You bitch," he said, again. He tried to get up, but fell back.

"I'm sorry, Rulon," Sue said, "but you can't do that to a girl. You have to make a date first." Sue picked up her purse and jumped into her car.

She watched at the edge of the parking lot. When Rulon got into his car, she drove on.

A few days later, Sue heard a lawyer talking about Rulon's case in the restaurant. Rulon had told them at the hospital that he hurt himself on the job. The hospital spent more than ten thousand dollars fixing him up before they discovered Workers' Compensation wouldn't pay. He must have left town because she never saw him again. She told no one about the incident.

"You need a man," Rosy now said, when Sue returned to the kitchen. Apparently Rosy had been watching as Sue took the roughnecks order, "Then those animals will leave you alone." Sue looked at Rosy.

"Good men can be fun." Rosy said becoming animated and looking at Sue. "The right man can really be fun, if you know what I mean?"

Sue blushed. Rosy was pretty. She had long, dark hair, brown eyes, round, happy cheeks, and a quick smile with lots of white teeth. She was five-foot four with a body that drew stares from the working men. With the oil boom on, and twenty men for every woman, Rosy was picky. Only tool-pushers and drilling supers for her, she told Sue.

"But how do you expect a man to give you a second look wearing a gunny sack?" Rosy said, her own dresses revealing every detail.

"The only men who ask me out are roughnecks," Sue said. "My dad would kill me if I went out with a roughneck."

"A woman doesn't go out with the men who ask her out. She picks the man she wants, then gets him."

"What's that mean?"

"Make him want you. It'll be easier than you can possibly imagine. You got long legs, and you know how to use them, and *buenas tetas*," Rosy said, almost blushing, jostling her breasts and nodding to Sue's. "And nice skin. But the part men'll like best's your mouth."

"How come?" Sue said.

Rosy looked around, then in a low voice said, "When you see a man looking at your mouth, and he's smiling, he's imagining how good it would feel wrapped around his penis." Rosy gave out a horselaugh, slapped Sue on the bottom, and left her standing there stunned.

The next time they were in the kitchen together, Rosy said, "I got the man for you. He owns an oil company."

"You mean like a filling station?"

"No, dummy. He owns oil wells. And he drills oil wells. Tool-pushers work for him. Pumpers work for him. You know, Tom Patton."

Sue looked away with big eyes. She knew him all right. She liked to watch him when he wasn't looking. He had a young man's body, but an air of confidence that older men carried. Everyone in the restaurant looked up to him, even company men who rarely looked at anyone.

"How old is he?" Sue said, her breath a little short.

"What matters is how he looks."

"He isn't married?"

"His ex was a gold digger. First she made him move to Denver, then she divorced him. I heard she couldn't stand it, that he was traveling all the time. She thought he was having affairs."

"Was he?"

"Never heard of none."

"So what makes you think he'll like me?" Sue said, looking out the kitchen window at Tom Patton. She liked what she saw. Sue wandered if Patton knew of her existence. When she waited on him he always left her a nice tip, and he was always a gentleman.

"Tom Patton sends a pretty woman packing every month," Rosy said. "Some as pretty as you. But he'll find you special because what he's looking for is smart." Rosy left with an order.

The next time they met in the kitchen, Sue talked first. "You got a twenty-dollar tip."

"Someone left me a twenty-dollar tip?" Rosy said, looking in the dining room.

"The guy at the cash register."

Rosy's eyes got big. "The one with the nice butt?"

"I don't know," Sue said, embarrassed.

"Don't know?" Rosy said. "There's two butts out there. One's dynamite--one's flabby. You saying you can't tell the difference?"

Sue gave her a blank stare.

"How old did you say you were?" Rosy said.

"Seventeen."

"You could pass for thirty if you dressed right. All I can say is somebody better be wising you up pretty quick."

"How about you?" Sue said.

"First things first. Which one of those boys left the big tip?"

Sue glanced into the dining room, "Not the one with the nice butt," she said, giving her friend a smug smile.

"Damn," Rosy said.

"Wait a minute, that's him," Rosy said. "The nice butt's Tom Patton. Now there's one hunk of a man."

"What about him being old?" Sue said.

"Looks like to me every single part works just fine. And if what I hear's true," Rosita's eyes sparkled as she held up her hands and demonstrated size with perfect clarity, "it really works well."

Sue looked dumbfounded.

"Honey, old is good," Rosy said, with a dramatic flair. "Old knows how to keep from getting a young girl pregnant." Rosy patted Sue on the tummy. Rosy paused, lowered her voice, and with a knowing look said slowly, "Old knows how to make a young girl happy. Besides, you're not going to marry him. At your age, it's just for fun."

Sue looked away in contemplation, a little smile on her face. Fun would be good, she thought. She had already decided that she wanted an older man. When she was twelve, she was taller than her teachers. When she was fifteen, she looked as good as any model. Her male contemporaries were clueless, penniless, geeky-looking weirdoes. Some day they might be okay, but that day hadn't come.

Rosy told her what she knew about Patton. He lived in Denver, but he was in Rawhide so much he kept an apartment there. When he was drilling a well, he was there for two weeks at a time. He flew back and forth in his own plane.

Rosy stared off studiously for a minute, then said, "Get on out there and cashier. Let's see how that oilman likes looking at a pretty woman. Get your mouth out there where he can't miss it."

Sue giggled and wondered for an instant how to display a mouth.

"Don't tell him how old you are," Rosy said.

Sue stopped. "Why not?"

"Think he's going to sleep with you if he knows you're not eighteen? Come on, girl."

"Think he would?"

"Damn right he would." Rosy paused. "I'll tell him you're eighteen. Now get out there before your grandpa fires us both." Sue took a deep breath and went through the kitchen doors. She tried to ignore the butterflies in her stomach.

"Hi, Sue," Tom Patton said, with a warm smile, obviously flirting.

Sue liked him right off. "How'd you know my name?" Sue looked right at him.

"I'm not going to know the name of the prettiest girl in the whole state of Colorado? I take that as an insult." He smiled and looked at her. Sue couldn't help becoming self-conscious as his gaze settled on her mouth. She put her hand to her face, then stood that way wondering what to do.

"My change, please," the other patron said, clearly irritated, glancing between her and Patton.

"Sure," Sue said, counting his change. "Thank you, come again."

When she took Patton's check, his hand lightly brushed hers. It was a gentle touch, and it made her feel at once at ease and more tense. She looked up. He had a nice face. Most men looked around and fidgeted when she looked at them. He took his change with both hands and almost held her hand for a second. They felt warm and strong.

"Have to get out to the airport and get my plane fueled up before everyone goes home. I'm headed to Denver. See you Monday." He was obviously delighted with the conversation.

"Okay," Sue said, excitedly.

Patton smiled back and took one more long look.

"Sure you're coming back on Monday?" Sue said.

"Monday morning, early," Patton said, apparently happy to have an excuse not to leave. "We're completing a well."

"Could I come?" Sue said, with big eyes, worried he'd see her heaving chest.

Patton gave her a studious look.

"I mean," Sue said, "I have relatives in Denver I haven't seen for a while, and I've been looking for a way to get over to see them." When Patton suddenly looked nervous, Sue relaxed, realizing Rosy was right--he was just another man. "My relatives will pick me up at the airport," Sue said, now calm enough to touch his sleeve gently. "I won't be any trouble."

Patton shrugged. Sue could see him struggling for calm. "Guess it wouldn't hurt. I'll call your mom and make sure it's all right."

"You know my mom?"

"I grew up around here."

"Why do you want to call her?"

"I imagine your mom will want to know that I'll be careful flying her precious daughter over to Denver."

Sue hesitated, wondering if he knew her age. "Let me call her first. Give me fifteen minutes."

"I'll meet you at the airport at six o'clock, at hangar number eight."

When he departed, Sue went to the phone in the kitchen.

"He wants you," Rosy said, in a dramatic voice. "Is your heart pounding? Mine is, just watching. He stood by the door and watched you walk all the way to the kitchen. I swear it."

Sue smiled a smug smile. Rosy wasn't telling her a thing she didn't already know. Sue turned and talked to her mom.

"Is this a date?" Sue's mom said.

"It's a ride, Mom. He seems really nice."

"Okay, but I'd watch that Tom Patton. He might decide to get a little extra nice."

Sue grabbed a quick breath at her mother's suggestion, then smiled a salacious little smile. "Thanks, Mom. I'll be back by nine o'clock Monday morning. Now listen, he's going to call you. Be careful what you say. I mean, I want to see everybody in Denver and if you say the wrong thing, he won't take me. So don't tell him anything you don't need to, okay?"

"You mean," Mrs. Hansen said, sarcastically, "like you're being seventeen?"

Sue's mother paused for a couple seconds. Sue swallowed nervously. Her mother loved to let tension hang.

"I won't tell him," her mother finally said. Sue knew her mother still had enough of the old Italian culture in her, so she didn't think that seventeen was too young.

Sue couldn't help wondering what would happen. She wondered if she should seduce him quickly before he found out her age.

☞ ☞ ☞

Any reservations Patton had had about taking Sue Hansen to Denver disappeared when she showed up at the airport. She was almost his height in mid-heeled pumps. She was wearing a skirt and a sweater. Her image was sexy but elegant. Her pretty brunette hair was down, looking silky and smooth. When he took her bags, he caught her fragrance and it made him clumsy as he finished his preparations for their departure.

Patton enjoyed the flight to Denver more than he imagined possible. There wasn't anything he couldn't talk to her about. "Why do you know so much about animals?" Patton asked. Patton had been reading books about animal behavior, and Sue was way ahead of him.

Sue shrugged. "My dad's a veterinarian. When Mom's side of my family finally convinced him that it was okay for my brother to work in Grandpa's restaurant, he had a change of heart about kids doing things young. He made me his surgical assistant. When I was eleven, I could do many surgical procedures by myself."

"And you're well read," Patton said. "I'll bet you started reading before you started school."

"How'd you know?"

"I know it works. My little boy started reading when he was four. Now he's ten, and he reads everything, often faster than I do. Every good reader I've ever met learned how to read, or almost how to read, before they started school. So, how'd you learn?"

"When I was three, my seven-year-old brother was reading poorly, so my mom tutored him. She showed him flash cards and read to him. I watched. When I was four, I knew all the

cards, and my mom ran me out of the room so my brother
would have to answer."

"Bingo. I'm writing all that down when we get to Denver.
That's another case study that proves my theory."

Patton's gaze remained in Sue's eyes. He didn't want to stare,
but her eyes were attractive and sexy, yet innocent, and she had
the prettiest smile he'd ever seen. When they landed at Denver,
Patton told Sue he'd keep her company while she waited for her
relatives.

"Have you ever been to the Denver Zoo?" Sue said with
bright eyes. They were standing in the lobby of the small
general aviation terminal. "It's one of the best around."

Patton looked at Sue and tried to maintain a serious
expression as he imagined how she'd look with no clothes. She
had full breasts, a narrow waist, and long, graceful legs. Patton
closed his eyes, took a deep breath, and remembered that his
father had set out to teach him one thing in life--never sleep
with a woman he couldn't marry. He thought Sue was too young
for that. He was relieved when Sue's relatives arrived and
interrupted their conversation.

That night, Patton couldn't get Sue's fragrance out of his
mind. He tossed and turned as he relived their conversations.
He thought it was wonderful the way her mother had sent her to
Italy when she was eight to learn about the country, and her
Italian culture.

She seemed to like him, he thought, and he found himself
wondering if they could be friends. He vaguely thought about a
day years away when they might be able to be more.

The next morning, Patton called a friend in Jackson,
Wyoming, and asked if he was still invited to a barbecue at the
Jackson Country Club. The friend said he was.

Patton took a nervous breath and called Sue. "Mind if we go
back a little early?" Patton said. "I need to stop in Jackson on
business."

Sue met him at the airport at ten. Patton was startled when
he looked at her bright eyes because they were prettier than he'd
remembered. They talked all the way.

Patton swooped low over the red desert north of
Rocksprings and pointed out a heard of mustangs. The Grand
Teton Mountains towered above them as they landed at the

Jackson airport, taxied to a parking spot, and then walked to the terminal.

"Business is on hold," Patton reported to Sue after making a phone call. "The man I need to visit is going to a barbecue at the Jackson Country Club."

Patton looked at Sue, who looked back with a smile in her eyes. He fought off the urge to take her hand.

"My friend said if I brought a date, I could go," Patton said a little nervously.

Sue smiled at him with big, happy eyes.

"But it wouldn't really be a date," Patton said.

"Not really," Sue said with a sweet smile.

"On the other hand, everybody will *think* you're my date."

"I'll tell everyone I'm twenty-one," Sue said.

Patton was relieved when she caught on so quickly.

"But I don't have anything to wear," Sue said, gesturing to her small travel bag.

"We have plenty of time," Patton said, "Jackson's a great town to shop in." The two shopped until mid-afternoon. Patton liked seeing her in several different outfits.

Sue wore a white short-suit with a low-cut vest. Her bare arms looked healthy with well-toned muscles. The gold necklace she wore looked good against her tanned skin.

Before dinner, guests gathered by the pool. Sue gave Patton a smug smile when he frowned as she ordered a cocktail. Blue birds and goldfinches flitted in the grass and nearby bushes.

Sue introduced Patton to a potential investor from Connecticut named Don Comstock, with whom she'd struck up a conversation. Comstock told Patton he was eager to look at anything Patton had, because he liked investing with men whose resources allowed them to date a woman like Sue.

ᛞᛞ ᛞᛞ ᛞᛞ

When they were back at Rawhide, Patton was clumsy again as he unloaded their baggage.

"Thank you for everything," Sue said, walking up to him. She put a hand on his arm and looked at him square in the face.

What a beautiful face, Patton thought, as he fought the urge to kiss her. "I'll carry your bags to your car," he said, gathering them. He thought Sue's look suggested that he was a chump for not kissing her. He glanced at her quickly, and wondered if he still could, then steeled his will and reminded himself about his promise to his father.

For the next couple of weeks, Patton had no reason to go to Rawhide. He'd planned to start a well on a Thursday, and when it was delayed, he went to Rawhide anyway. He thought again about the possibility of being friends with Sue.

Sue wasn't around when he arrived. He told Rosy to tell her that if she wanted a ride to Denver, he was going that weekend.

The next day he was at the Pump, long-faced. Sue was nowhere around, and neither was Rosy. Just as he was getting ready to leave, Sue walked in.

"Hear you're going to Denver this weekend," She said.

"Sure am." Patton's face was beaming.

"That was a fun time we had in Jackson."

Patton nodded.

Sue didn't say a thing. Patton waited as long as he could, then said, "So, what're you doing this weekend?"

"Hadn't really thought about it. You?"

"We had a rig moving onto a location, but it's been held up so I have to come back Monday."

"Looks like neither of us are busy." Sue looked at him.

Patton hesitated. "Hell, you might as well go to Denver and visit your relatives."

"I could stay overnight with them, but they're really busy. They have a new restaurant. I wouldn't have anything to do." She looked at Patton with big eyes.

When he looked into her eyes, a wave of affection swept over him. He'd never met a girl as quick. He reached out with a hand and she didn't hesitate taking it. It felt good, and she looked incredibly beautiful standing there, poised and confident.

"You could go to the zoo with me," he said.

"That would be nice, but what would I do in the evening?"

Patton took a deep breath, and gave her hand an affectionate squeeze. "You can't tell anybody we went on a date."

"I guess I could make one concession," Sue said, smiling. "When're we leaving?"

"As soon as you're ready."

"I'm ready. Hangar eight?"

"What about calling your relatives, and asking your mom?"

"Already took care of that," Sue said.

Another wave of affection swept over Patton followed quickly by pangs of fear as he wondered what he was getting himself into.

ᵈᵘ ᵈᵘ ᵈᵘ

Sue looked good at the zoo. Her figure was perfect for the cut-off jeans she was wearing.

The elephant's enclosure was under construction, and as a consequence, Patton was able to feed popcorn to a big bull African elephant across a temporary fence. He teased the elephant by placing one piece of popcorn at a time in its trunk. Patton caught a movement, looked up, and saw the elephant's trunk up high. It was coming down fast and ruffled his hair without touching him as it raced past and loudly knocked the popcorn out of his hands. The elephant curled its trunk around the popcorn, cardboard and all, stuck it in its mouth, and after a couple of chomps, swallowed.

Sue convulsed in laughter.

Patton stared at her, wishing he had the courage to grab her, wrestle her to the ground and kiss her. When he realized he was staring, he took her hand. "Have you ever eaten at the Brown Palace?" he said.

"The Dove's a nice place, and they have a disco where we could dance."

"Except you have to be twenty-one to get in."

"I went in last year." Sue giggled at Patton. "My cousin lined me up with a man who was twenty-two."

Patton looked with a furrowed brow, then tried to think about something else as he realized he was seized with jealousy.

"Tell you what," Sue said. "When you see me, you decide if they're going to ask for ID."

Patton shook his head. "They'll ask," he said, "and we'll both be embarrassed."

"No we won't," Sue said, pulling out an ID. "It's my cousin's."

Patton thought about the several laws he'd be breaking. He looked again into her pretty eyes, and then at her beautiful smile. When he let his eyes drift over her body, he took a deep breath and decided to take the chance.

That evening, Sue wore a shiny, silver dress, which clung to her figure. The bodice was snug with spaghetti straps over her shoulders. Her hair was long in the back and swept up from her face in the front. She wore no jewelry, and didn't need any, because her bright eyes gave plenty of dazzle.

The last dance was slow. Sue stepped up close. Patton felt her warm curvaceous body rubbing against his. Her fragrance was going straight to his brain. He'd had a few drinks, and his desire was out of hand. She was mature and lovely, and he was thinking how wonderful it would be to make love to her until daybreak.

A wave of guilt hammered him and commanded him to think. He couldn't marry her--she was too young. He eased away from her sensuous body.

"You know," Sue said, "I'm not exactly a virgin."

Patton couldn't help himself. He took her head in his hands and kissed her. It lasted long after the song was over. He was burning up with desire as they walked to the parking lot. As soon as they were in the car, they began necking. "I can't sleep with you," he said, his breath coming in spurts as he broke away from a kiss. He gained his composure, and told her about his promise to his dad.

"All that may be true," Sue said, "But I can't let you go home the way you are."

He gave her a curious look.

"I saw you walking funny at the zoo."

Patton started to talk, then thought better of it.

"And you've been ready for love for two hours out of the last four."

Patton looked away, wondering if she also knew how embarrassed he was.

"Don't be embarrassed. It's just life. It's how I know you like me."

Sue kissed him. Her mouth was warm and wet, and he wondered how she knew how to kiss so well. He didn't stop her when she unzipped his pants, and quickly relieved a month's worth of sexual tension. Patton was finally able to relax, very relieved that he didn't have to drive home with the pain of unfulfilled desire.

Patton knew if he wanted to keep seeing her, he'd have to satisfy her, too. Slowly, he caressed her body. It felt even better than he'd imagined. He took his time massaging her to climax, and as her beautiful face contorted in ecstasy, he watched carefully. It was an image he wanted to take with him.

Afterward they sat in the parking lot and talked for hours. They didn't leave until a policeman began driving around the nightclub, shining his spotlight around.

ᛗ ᛗ ᛗ

"Haven't you gotten that lovesick puppy in bed yet?" Rosy said to Sue a few weeks later. "I don't know why he bothers to order food. He can't eat it when he never takes his eyes off you. He must leave here and go somewhere else and eat, that's all I can figure. You aren't holding out on me, are you?"

"Says we have to wait 'til I'm eighteen."

"Your secret's good with me," Rosy said.

The only other person Sue told was her mother. Mrs. Hansen had successfully raised five kids, and she wasn't worried about Sue.

"Dating an older man won't hurt a thing, especially when a girl is as good-looking as you are," Sue's mother said. "Besides, it looks like his intentions are honorable."

They dated as often as they could. Patton made special flights into Rawhide, where he picked her up at the airport and took her to another town. Sue knew what he was doing. She didn't have the heart to tell him that everyone already knew.

Several times they flew to Denver for a movie. Another time to Devil's Tower, Wyoming, where they hiked in the beautiful mixed forest. Once they flew to the Jackson, Wyoming airport, rented a car, then drove to Jenny Lake where a launch carried them to a pier located directly under the Grand Teton. They hiked up the trail in the valley, which passed under the spire of the Grand Teton. It was the most majestic view imaginable. The Grand Teton rose almost straight up for a mile and a half. The sky was deep blue, the clouds crisp and white. As the clouds passed the spire of the Grand Teton, it appeared to move like a boat sailing on the ocean. It was a dizzying sight. It was as good a place as any to tell her, Patton thought, and when they were both lying, satisfied, staring at the spire of the big mountain, he began.

"Sue," he said, "my father had a child out of wedlock." Sue looked in anticipation. It's all he'd planned on saying. He placed his hands on her beautiful face and stared into her eyes. He knew he loved her. Every time he was with her he felt the same way, and now, there was a psychic flow between them that made him open his mouth and say, "And that child was Vince Longto."

Sue must have seen the pain, because she rose, hugged, and then kissed him warmly. He thought he should feel guilt for telling her, but all he felt was good, that the union between them had been strengthened, and he wished—as he had a hundred times before—that he could make love to her.

"We were conceived in the same week," he said. He told her about the meeting where he'd offered Vince a partnership.

"Have you ever put salt on a snail?" Patton said.

"I was a tomboy remember?"

"That's what happened to Vince when I told him. Before my eyes he melted and an entirely different person appeared." Patton looked away, closed his eyes for a moment and took a deep breath.

"My dad began preaching to me when I was a baby that a man should never sleep with a woman he couldn't marry."

When Sue began to talk, he silenced her with a gesture. "Sure, we could get married in a few years," he said, "but if you got pregnant, it wouldn't be right, and while we could get married now, that wouldn't be right either."

Sue seemed devastated by the news, which caused Patton so much anxiety, he found himself promising her that they would only have to wait until her eighteenth birthday.

Later, when Patton reflected that her birthday wasn't far, and that she'd still be in high school, he worried that he wouldn't be able to go through with it. He also worried that he would lose her if he didn't.

It was only a few months later, when Sue broached the subject again. Patton was in Rawhide more to see her than anything. "What are you going to get me for my birthday?" Sue said, as she set a bowl of chili in front of him. It was the second day of January 1986.

"So, how old are you going to be?" he said, sorry at once he'd picked these words.

"You know exactly how old I'm going to be," Sue said, both blushing, and showing frustration.

"How about a ride in my airplane?"

"You won't need your airplane when I take you for a ride," Sue said, recovering quickly.

Patton felt butterflies in his gut, which disappeared when he looked deep into her beautiful gray eyes, and thought about the fact that while she was young, she was definitely his equal. "I'll meet you at the hangar when you get off work. We'll make plans."

At the airport, they made plans to go skiing in Salt Lake City in February. Sue said her cousin in Denver would cover for her.

Patton stood with his back against the wing as they kissed and petted until it looked like he wouldn't be able to quit.

"Oh, no," Sue said, stepping back. "You have to wait. And it serves you right, too, for making me wait so long."

When they kissed again and embraced, Patton wished he didn't have to let go. But in the air on the way back, he became anxious again, and wondered if he was doing the right thing.

16--Russia

"The concept of communism is a good one," Yaping had explained to young Vince. "But in practice, it can't work. In the free market system, reality is created by failure. In communism a business can't fail. As a result, business practices gradually change until they become absurd. When communism owns all businesses as it does in the Russia, communism must fail."

At the time, Vince wasn't sure what Yaping was talking about. When he was older, he was always interested in communism and monopolies, and he seemed to have a grasp of the critical issues. When the money began rolling in, Vince's interest in Russia became more than passive.

He hired consultants, and discovered as much as he could about Russia's oil fields. He was surprised at how much information the consultants found. Although nothing was concrete, the information included locations of fields, some information on reserves and potential, and delivery systems. He found a photo geologist in Denver named Don Anderson who obtained Landsat satellite images of large portions of Russia. Anderson identified dozens of apparently undrilled, enormous structures in roadless areas.

Vince's research didn't show the incredible inefficiency Yaping had predicted, but Vince could see that the Communists themselves had almost total control over the information that came from Russia. He figured that the inefficiency existed and that there would be a bonanza of passed-up oil production. There might be huge domes just waiting for a drill bit.

Russians were hurting economically, and it was getting worse. Vince figured the Russians would have to change economic systems, and when they did, sooner or later exploration in Russia would be given over to the free enterprise system. Vince figured the man who was there and ready when it happened would be super rich. He decided his first step was to learn the language, the customs, and the system.

Getting into a University in Russia wasn't easy, especially since Vince had been a total academic failure. Vince created, for his Russian University applications, both a new high school and a college and got mailboxes where he could receive requests for transcripts on their "students." It worked smoothly.

When he finally got to Russia, he found the difficulties he'd heard about, and he loved every bit of it. He had to learn an entirely new set of rules for overcoming bureaucratic problems, and for every problem he overcame, he felt a rush of pleasure. He learned ways to offer bribes so that he couldn't be accused of bribery. He learned ways to make friends with unfriendly people.

He also loved learning the language. He was determined to speak Russian without an accent, and spent his evenings practicing pronunciation. Vince was to study Russian for a year, then take regular university courses. But within six months, He had learned everything the language school could offer. Vince began cutting classes in order to find out about the Russian oil business. He got nowhere, and after months of futility he became depressed and the demons in his mind became powerful. He started having the same nightmare he'd had as an adolescent.

He tried to enroll in meaningful science courses, but got nowhere. Despondent, he made arrangements to go home. At least, he thought, he'd learned the language and customs. He'd be ready when Russia changed.

A couple days before his planned departure date, he noticed something that caused his spirits to rise. Vince was sitting on a park bench, absentmindedly staring in the direction of a man who appeared to be unemployed and also unemployable. Vince had seen the man several times before.

The man had a butane cigarette lighter in his hand. As the man stared off with his normal dumb look, the butane lighter climbed in his hand until it teetered on his index finger. Slowly the man's second finger raised to a point above the lighter, grasped it, and then quickly spun it around. The man's ring finger just as quickly reached and grasped it and spun it, the little finger did the same and spun the lighter into the man's palm. The trick was quick and beautiful and deft, and instantly raised the question in Vince's mind that the man had been faking his stupidity. Vince realized that he'd seen this man more than mere chance should allow, and he wondered why he never thought it odd that the man could possess a butane lighter which in Russia was quite valuable.

Vince paid closer attention, and quickly he was noticing at least one other, similar looking man. He was sure the men were spying on him, and he was astounded at the effort put forth just to find out what he was doing. He figured his snooping had brought on a full-blown KGB investigation. Vince had heard that the KGB used honey traps for getting information. He wished it was true, and found himself daydreaming about the time the buxom blond showed up.

He also found himself daydreaming about a trip to the Gulag, and wished he could get out of the country sooner.

Vince returned to his room, and quickly returned to his depressed state. He was lying on his bunk. His heart was pummeling his sternum, and he was breathing hard. Vince looked with disgust and hostility at his roommate, a kid from Siberia, who was studying--always studying. Vince contemplated throwing a shoe at him to get his attention so he could tell him he needed a shower. Vince started to slip a shoe off for that purpose when a soft knock came at the door.

It was the first time that had happened. Vince stared, and visualized the pressure waves of the sound as they came to him from the door. If he liked, he thought, he could assign each pressure wave a different color. When his roommate stood, Vince sat him back down and went to the door. He was sure it was a woman's knock, and since his roommate stunk too badly even for Russian women, it had to be for him.

She was at least five foot ten, a brunette with deep blue eyes. She shaved her legs, and best of all, she had a body that wouldn't quit. Vince was ecstatic. He figured she was the spy he'd been waiting for. He would have a way to communicate with top communists, but for the moment, he had other thoughts. He desperately needed a woman.

"Come in," Vince said in English, as he looked at his surprised roommate and indicated he should leave. When the roommate hesitated, Vince handed him a twenty-dollar bill. The roommate stared for a second, then ran out the door.

Vince closed the door, went to his closet, and threw it open for the girl to see. It was full of blue jeans. It was like having a chest full of jewels.

"I have something for you," Vince said as he pulled out a pair of jeans. "You can wear these to dinner. I'm a westerner, I can get into The Toaster." It was an exclusive nightclub where only western money could be spent.

The woman smiled deeply, but didn't speak. Vince realized he'd put her off-balance with his presumptive approach. A painful thought flashed through his mind. She wouldn't make love to him if he didn't play along. She had to feel like she was seducing him. Vince quickly decided to make her job as easy as he could.

"My name's Vince," he said, switching to Russian, and extending a hand. "For a minute, I thought you were sent by a friend to pick up some jeans."

"Natalia." She flashed a girl-next-door smile. "I saw you on campus. You look like someone I'd like to know."

Vince smiled casually. In his mind, he was rubbing his hands together.

ɪɜ ɪɜ ɪɜ

Natalia turned out to be incredible in bed, and Vince couldn't help wondering if she'd taken "Love" courses at KGB school. Vince showered her with western gifts, took her on a trip to the Crimea, and to fancy nightclubs. He knew her superiors would get most of the gifts, which was good, because they wouldn't want to cut off the flow by putting him in jail. He chuckled to himself when he thought about it all being tax deductible.

Vince thought he could tell when they were near a listening device, because Natalia acted differently. When they went to the school cafeteria, there was one table that was always available and Natalia insisted they sit at it. Vince imagined it was wired to a big speaker on the desk of the local director of the KGB.

One quiet afternoon, Vince and Natalia were drinking coffee at the wired table. Natalia was waiting for him to speak.

"Russia," Vince said, "is the world's largest producer of oil. I'm a millionaire oilman, and I'd like to give to the fine Russian people my oil expertise. I can find lots of oil for Mother Russia."

Natalia looked at Vince with big blue eyes. Vince thought she didn't believe a word. He reached into his shirt pocket and pulled out a piece of film. "Microfilm," Vince said. "It tells who I am. There are photos of my oil and gas fields. There are photos of legal documents showing that I'm the owner. There's a financial statement showing how much money I'm worth."

Natalia shifted uneasily. "Why me?" she said.

"I'm growing fond of you. I want you to know all about me." Vince shifted casually. "For now, I need good people to help me. What I'd really like is a good KGB agent. I'd pay him a thousand dollars a month to work for me on his off-duty time. If I succeed in getting drilling concessions, I would hire him full time and teach him about the oil business. If the free enterprise system comes to Russia, the people I hire will be among the most wealthy men in Russia."

"How will you hire KGB?" Natalia said with a little smile.

"I was hoping a good KGB agent would come to me."

"Good luck."

Vince and Natalia exchanged sly smiles.

ꙮ ꙮ ꙮ

A week later, one of the "homeless" approached Vince, handed him a note, then departed. Vince was to meet the man later that evening. Vince was pleased with their selection. He was a big man with black hair, a heavy beard on white skin, and an oversized Roman nose. His name was Uri Novotny.

Vince told Novotny what he wanted, and who he wanted to meet. He also told him that Natalia was to stay on his case.

Novotny, with help from Natalia, introduced Vince to the Daughter of the Minister of Oil Refining and Production for the Russian Republic. Vince began seeing her, and thereby came to know her father. Vince gained the Minister's trust, and soon he was touring oil provinces, and discovering what he had suspected. Their production and exploration practices were as poor as anything he could imagine. On a visit to a large oil field, he asked the manager of the Production Province how deep their production was.

"From three hundred to five hundred meters," the manager said.

"What age are the producing zones?"

"Tertiary."

Vince knew these sediments were the shallowest ones that could have production. "Are there older horizons?" Vince said. Older horizons would lie below the existing production. Older sediments don't always exist, because deposition may not have occurred in those times, or they may have been eroded away eons ago. Vince was anxious to hear the answer to the question, because exploration into deeper zones, lying below existing production, was far less risky for the simple reason the shallow production usually confirms the existence of a deeper oil trap.

"There are no older sediments," the manager said.

Vince thought he knew better. He'd just visited adjacent regions where there was older and deeper Cretaceous and Paleozoic production. He'd studied the formations as they drove toward the oil field. He'd watched the older sediments plunge below the younger ones. There could be an incredible bonanza just a little deeper.

In addition to passed-up production, there were enormous structures in the area that had never been drilled. The photogeology Vince had obtained allowed him to identify these structures.

Vince talked to his friend, the Minister of Oil Refining and Production, about the advantages of giving a concession. Vince told him how hard money would begin to flow to Russia.

Vince lavished the Minister and his family with western gifts. If the Russian economy became free, Vince promised he'd make the Minister a full partner in the Russian enterprises.

Vince worked out the details of a pilot program with the minister. When they were finished, he was given an audience with Boris Yeltsin, the president of the Russian Republic. Yeltsin thought it would be an excellent way to test the waters and approved the plan in every detail except one. The Russian experts assured everyone there was no more oil to be found in the concessions Vince wanted. It would all be for naught. They better have some money to cover their trouble. Vince had to pay one hundred thousand dollars.

Vince was prepared to pay ten million. Nevertheless, he talked them down to ninety thousand. To accept their price would raise suspicions. Vince Longto would get the first private enterprise concession given in Russia in more than fifty years.

Vince had seen the way Russia operated. It was a system of graft upon graft, where people went to jail for falling out of favor, not for doing anything any differently than anyone else. He knew he had to establish himself as powerful.

Russia was already falling into anarchy. Vince figured it would get worse. In addition to Uri Novotny, Vince hired five top executives, all ex-KGB agents. These agents were well educated. They spoke English and one or two other languages. Two spoke Chinese. What's more, they were trained executives and knew how to organize and motivate people to do a job. Vince knew it would be far less difficult to train these people in technical matters than to train technical people to be executives. That wasn't true in the United States, but in Russia, college grads were much better educated because those bound for college had been challenged in their earlier education and therefore had a far better grasp of the fundamentals.

Vince supervised, hands-on, the building of a good drilling rig. His ex-KGB agents were able to get through the red tape to import the necessities, like good drilling bits, high-pressure hoses, and blowout preventers.

Vince's first discovery was in the middle of the oil field, which had shallow production. The discovery was in Cretaceous rocks. He found four producing horizons, all sand.

The well had an initial production rate of seven hundred and fifty barrels of oil a day. The oil pool could be large enough to accommodate a thousand wells. Only additionally drilling would define its exact size.

Vince skidded his rig a short distance and drilled another, this time deeper to the Paleozoic. It produced from a dolomite zone at an initial rate of 1,500 barrels per day.

Next he went to an adjacent oil field. He found no Cretaceous production there, but when he went deeper, he found production in the same dolomite zone in the Paleozoic.

Vince was in an euphoric daze until he discovered that the hard part was still ahead.

When he tried hooking all this oil up to the existing pipeline, he was told there was no room. Bewildered, he put Novotny to work solving this problem, and went off for what he called the "elephant hunt."

Vince drilled several wildcat wells on the undrilled structures he'd found using satellite photos, and one resulted in a good-looking strike. It came in flowing two thousand barrels a day. The structure was huge, and if full of oil to the spill-point would accommodate thousands of wells. Vince needed a pipeline for the wildcat discovery. It was too remote to be trucked profitably.

Meanwhile, Novotny was getting nowhere getting Vince's oil to market. Vince was told there was not enough room in the existing pipelines for his oil, and his discovery did not warrant the construction of a new pipeline. After months of wrangling, Vince was allowed to ship one hundred barrels a day, barely enough to pay his expenses.

Vince summoned Uri Novotny. The two walked into the city of Moscow, and down a large boulevard with few cars. Vince frisked Novotny for a listening device, then began. "We know there's room for more than a hundred barrels per day on that pipeline," Vince said. "The shallower production is more than twenty years old, and it's been declining for more than ten years. What's going on?"

"There are those in the Office of Oil Refining and Production who will look bad if your enormous discoveries become common knowledge. It appears the bureaucrats have been instructed to cover you up. There's nothing we can do."

"I hired you to solve these kinds of problems," Vince said. Just a week before, Vince had fired a man in front of Novotny, and he'd used the same inflection in his voice.

"We could kill the bureaucrat who's obstructing us," Novotny said calmly.

Vince frowned and looked around. "Where's your intelligence? Motive is evidence of guilt, and you have a motive to kill this bureaucrat. And where's your humanity?"

Novotny looked less calm.

"I hear she's good looking," Vince said with a cunning smile. "And she has an Uncle who's dying of brain cancer." Vince was suggesting Novotny have the Uncle murdered, but he didn't dare give a better hint. Vince looked at him and thought he understood.

"I'll be back from the States in six months," Vince said. "If this problem isn't solved when I get back, we'll be making some changes."

17 – Going Broke

Tom Patton thought about his upcoming ski trip with Sue Hansen as he flew back to Denver. She was perfect in every way, he thought. If only she were older.

When he arrived at his condo, he was surprised to see that he had several messages from his banker. He wondered how his banker had gotten his personal number as he listened to his messages. The banker said Saudi Arabia had dramatically increased its production and he was worried the price of oil would slip below Patton's cost of production. Patton told the banker he'd be able to cut expenses enough to stay profitable, so long as the price didn't go below ten dollars. He thought his banker was convinced, but the next day, he got a notice calling his line of credit. He had fourteen days to come up with the money.

Patton's first thought was to sell. He'd come away with close to a million dollars. On the other hand, maybe he could hang on. Most experts said the price would be back in five years. If the price came back and stayed at thirty dollars for ten years, he'd be worth ten million dollars, just on his existing reserves. But that was remote and if he couldn't last and he had to sell when the price was low, he may not get enough to cover his debts.

Selling quickly was clearly the best choice. But he was an oilman when Sue picked him, so that must have been one of the things she liked about him. Maybe he'd even lose her if he sold out, he thought.

Patton decided to stay. In the morning, he liquidated all his cash securities. Then he made arrangements to sell his airplane and his sports car.

He felt shorter as he walked from the auction where he sold his airplane. He was still two hundred thousand dollars short so he sold his sport car, then his condo, and came to within twenty thousand. He didn't have room for everything in the new apartment he rented, so he had a big garage sale. With the sale of every piece of property that was dear to him, his esteem fell just a little more.

Patton wanted to see Sue, and thought about how wonderful it would be to make love to her for the first time. It also scared him. For one thing, he didn't want her seeing him this way, looking almost penniless. As a rich oilman, their age difference didn't seem so great. Now that he'd been humbled, it seemed insurmountable. He got nervous when he thought about an airline trip with Sue where they were sure to run into someone they knew. He waited until the last minute to call. He told her he'd be up soon to see her, but he knew it would be a while. He knew the future would be rough. He also knew he'd survive. He set a four-year goal to get his affairs in order. It would be in time for Sue's emergence from college, he told himself. He knew that once she was out of college, everything would be fine between them. She said she'd gotten accepted at a couple of name schools, but she was planning to go to school in Boulder, which was close to Denver. When things were settled, they'd get together again. He figured he could handle dating a college girl.

Several months later when the price of oil was bumping the ten-dollar mark and Patton started losing money monthly, he realized he'd have to move to Rawhide. He figured he could cut expenses by supervising his own production. He could even bring in money by practicing law. He had finished his degree in Denver, and he'd even become a member of the Colorado and the Wyoming Bar.

He pleaded with his former wife until she agreed to let Billy go to school in Rawhide.

A couple months after the crash in oil prices, Vince approached Sue Hansen's mother. He knew more than most

about Sue and Tom Patton. He was home for a month from
Russia, he told her. Vince talked to her about coming to work
for him at Rawhide Gas, and made her a generous offer that she
accepted. When Ms. Hansen was settled in at Rawhide Gas,
Vince came to see her again.

"Hear you have a smart little girl," Vince said to Sue's
mother.

"National Merit finalist, but she isn't a little girl."

"What's she going to study?"

"Science, I suppose."

"Why don't you have her apply for the Rawhide Gas
Scholarship?"

"Didn't know there was such a thing." Mrs. Hansen
brightened, "She's been accepted at two very expensive
schools—more than we can afford—would it cover that?"

"You bet," Vince said with unusual enthusiasm. "We're
going to need another landman in a few years. She could go to
work right here. A landman with a background in science goes
the furthest in this business." Vince smiled a smug, satisfied
smile.

The scholarship wouldn't cost Vince a penny. He'd pass the
cost on to the people of Rawhide in the form of higher gas
costs. Sue would graduate from college at the same time as his
daughter graduated from high school--in the spring of 1990. His
daughter would quietly "win" the scholarship. That would save
him a hundred thousand dollars.

Sue had been accepted at Stanford and Harvard. Her family
couldn't afford either without the scholarship.

꿈 꿈 꿈

It was June when Patton got back to Rawhide. He went
straight to the Pump. He thought Rosy's initial look showed
disgust.

"You're out of luck," Rosita said. "Sue's in Arkansas
working for Vince Longto for the summer. Vince gave her
some kind of a scholarship. It included summer jobs. She
thought he meant working here in Rawhide, but I guess she was
wrong." Rosy went about waitressing. "I hear you moved to
town," Rosy said, the next time she was near Patton's table.

"Why don't you come down to the Sportsman tonight? They have a band."

Tom Patton was far away. "Thanks," he said with a start. "Sounds like a great idea."

But Patton had other things to do with his spare time. He and his boy were building an airplane, a beautiful three-seater called a Cozy. The plane's exterior was perfectly smooth, and very aerodynamic. Her main wing was in the rear and swept back. In front was a smaller wing called a canard. With the engine in the rear, she looked like a little jet.

The major work took inexpensive materials. When he was almost finished, he'd have to spend a lot of money on the engine and radios. He figured his law practice, combined with the little bit of money he was still getting from his oil business, would take care of it.

As time slipped by, Patton wondered why Sue hadn't written. His office manager was a good friend of his ex-wife. He wondered if she'd keep Sue's mail from him. His ex had asked him sarcastically about Sue. He was being a fool, she'd told him. The rumors in Rawhide were embarrassing.

As his financial situation worsened, and time passed without a letter, he began to feel that his dream of getting back together with Sue might never happen. And as that thought became more likely to him, he found himself wishing with continually greater urgency that he'd made love to her at least once.

When Patton's oil business finally failed, the transition was smooth. His law business was going well enough by then to pay for his modest existence. But in another way, he was rich again, because he was able to spend more time with his boy. They went hunting, fishing, and backpacking together.

☒ ☒ ☒

Several years later, Tom and Billy Patton found themselves in the badlands exploring Hell's Creek. Fourteen year-old, Billy, was ahead of his dad in the deep ravine.

The geologic bedding was flat where they were, not straight up like it was at the shark site. The creek cut through thick sandstone layers of the late Cretaceous Fort Union Formation. Cliffs rose two to three hundred feet on either side. They were beyond the Devil's Kitchen area, and more than five miles from the shark higher up on Hell's Creek.

"Look," Billy said, "coyote and raccoon tracks, all mixed up with blood. The coyote must have caught the coon away from trees. This blood's still red. Must've happened early this morning."

"A deer and her fawn walked through here before the scuffle," Patton said. "See this track sitting on top of the deer track?"

Water birch and thin-leafed cottonwood grew in the bottom of the dry wash. Juniper grew on the several terraces on the way to the top of the cliffs along with an occasional ponderosa and limber pine.

A hawk looked down from a huge nest in the cliffs above. Little songbirds jumped back and forth between the sticks on the side of the big nest.

"Suppose a gully washer's exposed the shark?" Billy said.

"Doesn't look like there's been any water in this dry wash lately. But one-day the rains will come, and this little creek will be a river of mud and foamy white water.

"Look at this," Patton said pointing to a pebble about an inch in diameter sitting half-covered in the sand at their feet. He wouldn't have seen it except it was sitting in a beam of sunlight, which passed neatly though cliffs, trees, and bushes. Patton resisted the urge to grab it himself, and waited for Billy to come along.

"What is it?" Billy said, collecting it. "Some kind of mineral? There's no crystalline structure, so it should be a fossil. What do you think?"

"Fossil could be right," Patton said.

"Feel how light it is. Definitely isn't a normal rock. Maybe it's amber. Where do you suppose it came from?"

"That could be a problem. We're here in the Upper Cretaceous. Looks like it washed down from higher up. This dry wash goes into older sediments, and they're all marine. Amber couldn't be from a marine sediment."

"Doesn't it start in the mountains?"

"No. It starts just a little beyond Vince Longto's Enigma Gas Field."

"Where the shark is?"

Patton spun around.

"What is it?" Billy said.

"Remember me telling you about the amber at Vince's Shrine? When I was there with you when you were a baby, there was a piece about this size missing. Maybe this is it?"

"Looks like there's something in it. Maybe an insect? An insect in amber. I could polish it up and make a ring. I've got the gold and the kiln for melting it. Hey, mind if I take the plane and fly over to Boulder tomorrow? I'd really like to go to the science library and see if I can figure out what insect this is. It looks like a modern black fly. You know, the kind that eats flesh."

Patton was barely listening. He was thinking about the jaws of hell, and the carnosaur skull, and how Vince had used them to cleanse his soul, and if Vince had buried them, how he was getting along without them. A breeze came up and Patton felt a chill in the cool spring air as he thought about the real reason Vince visited his shrine--to allow him to control his irrational urge to kill his brother.

🐚 🐚 🐚

When they got home, Billy went to work on his piece of amber. First, he picked a side to be the bottom and filed it down flat. Then he ground it down to the size of a large thumbnail, always careful not to grind too close to the precious little insect. He had an idea he might be able to shape the overlying amber into a lens to magnify the little insect inside. Once all the cracks were out, he shaped it like a mushroom cap with the insect in the middle.

Using sealing wax, he made a mold of a magnifying lens. He chucked the mold of the magnifying lens into a drill bit, then began polishing the amber with the mold, using successively finer abrasive, and finally using the finest rouge. When he was finished, it was perfectly glossy and the shape of the amber was the same as the little magnifying lens.

It was beautiful. The little bug stood out boldly, many times bigger than its actual size. Its beady little eyes stared at the viewer as if it were still alive, looking for a meal with jaws that were strangely distorted, almost the way one would expect for a meat-chomping machine.

The amber was so finely polished it was virtually invisible. It was hard to imagine the little monster was a thousand times older than mankind.

Under the microscope, Billy could see a small tear in the little insect's abdomen; right next to where he thought its stomach was located. A small dot of bright red material was clustered near the tear. Billy's excitement grew. This had to be stomach contents. Just what he was looking for, actual flesh. Why was it red? Did that indicate oxygen, maybe blood? And if it was blood, how could it still be bright red, looking as fresh as the day it was eaten?

He put his microscope on the highest power possible. He got a remarkably clear image, an image of what looked like a red blood cell with a nucleus. He knew the red blood cells of mammals had no nuclei, but those of birds did, and therefore, probably dinosaurs. Since dinosaurs outnumbered birds in the Cretaceous, Billy figured he was looking at flesh from a dinosaur.

"Time to eat," Tom Patton called to his boy.

"Dad," Billy said, slowly. "I'm looking at the blood of a dinosaur."

"That sounds good, big guy," his dad drawled, looking serious as he approached Billy.

"Look in this microscope," Billy said, putting it on low power. "See the red spot next to the little guy's abdomen? Looks like stomach contents."

Patton bent over the microscope, and quickly recoiled when the jaws of the little insect filled his view. They were open, jagged, and twisted in agony, just like the dinosaur and the shark. The thought entered Patton's mind for the first time that they were all twisted like Vince Longto's soul. Patton suddenly wanted to grab the piece of amber and destroy it. His little boy was going to make a ring out of this piece of Vince Longto and the thought was nauseating.

"Look at this picture," Billy said, tugging on his father's sleeve to get his attention. "Now look at the red spot on high power." Billy set up the microscope for his dad. "Does it look similar?"

"Sure does," Patton said, gaining his composure. "Looks like they are both red blood cells, and they both have nuclei."

"Know what that means?" Billy asked.

"Our little friend ate a piece of bird just before he got caught in sap?"

"Maybe, but birds have thick feathers, and flying bugs like this little guy would have a hard time getting in to take a bite. Besides, he might just get eaten in the process. I think it's the blood cell of a dinosaur."

"Maybe we're rich?" Patton said, with a straight face. "You sure got this polished up nice."

"Think we could go to Boulder tomorrow?" Billy said, wide-eyed, holding a deep breath.

"No!" Patton said sharply.

"Billy sat back and looked at his dad.

"I'm sorry. There's something bothering me. How about the University of Wyoming at Laramie? We know our way around there. I have some things I need to do in Cheyenne. But I have to check my calendar first."

Billy jumped from his chair. In his excitement, he almost knocked the microscope off the bench. Patton had gone to school at Wyoming just like his father, and he and Billy had spent time on the UW campus, especially on game days.

"But it's no deal if you don't come upstairs now. You have to go to bed early tonight. We'll be in the air by six." The two went upstairs and sat at the dinner table.

"Dad, you think you'll ever get married again?" Billy said.

Patton figured his boy had seen the pain on his face the amber had caused, and thought it was loneliness. Billy had pointed out two or three nice women he'd like to have as a stepmother. But none of them appealed to Patton. He closed his eyes and the image of Sue's face in ecstasy flashed into his mind. For an instant, he liked looking. He tried to force the vision away before the pain hit, but he was too slow.

"What's wrong?" Billy said.

"We'll probably have to file an instrument flight plan so we can fly though clouds," Patton said, doing his best to make his face neutral, "so why don't you get the flight plan ready and file it tonight."

Billy was virtually a full-fledged pilot. He'd passed all the right tests, both flying and written, to be a commercial pilot. He was just waiting until his sixteenth birthday to get his ticket.

Patton had his boy fly every chance he could. The more hours a pilot had, the safer he was.

When they left, they discovered that it was a good thing they filed to go down on instruments because the tops of the mountains on the way to Laramie extended into clouds. Ice in clouds was always a concern in the springtime, but the homebuilt plane they were flying had so much extra power and climbed so fast Patton rarely worried about it.

"Tell me again how Vince got rich?" Billy said, as he turned to line up for the runway at Laramie.

"What kind of a cross-wind do you have?" They were on a ten-mile final approach for Laramie.

"Twenty knots."

"You mean a twenty knot wind."

"Twenty knot cross-wind component. The wind's forty knots gusting to forty-five."

"Forty-five knots!" Patton said.

"It's no problem." And he was right because Billy was to an airplane like a farm boy was to a tractor.

18 – A Blond Hit Man

Maxime Efremov grew up in the Ural Mountain area of Russia. He was tall and blond with powerful, steel blue eyes.

He'd been a jet fighter pilot in Afghanistan. He enjoyed flying, but the actual combat had left him with a hollow feeling. When he fired into a target, like a house, he couldn't see his bullets pierce the bodies of those inside. He was certain he was doing nothing but spoiling their day, that those inside had moved quickly into trap doors in the floor of their house.

His bombs were behind him when they detonated, but even if he could see them explode, he figured the enemy was too smart to let them rip away arms and legs. Efremov felt best when he was in full control of others, and to that end, he decided that the KGB was where he belonged. His third application for a transfer was accepted.

Efremov's first assignment had been to a luxury resort in the Crimean Peninsula on the Black Sea. His job was to spy on the high communists who used the resort.

The idea was to identify secret pieces of paper on the "suspect," such as the formula for a code. It was common for a high communist to encode important material and to write letters in code. The code had often been kept on their person.

Since this approach bore little fruit, and since the tactics-- at least concerning the high communists--had fallen out of favor in what was the final hour of the USSR, the KGB officers mainly used the spy holes for photographing high officials in intimate moments with themselves or their lovers. Such information could be sold at a handsome profit to the right person, usually a rival, who might use it to ensure or deny a promotion, even blackmail. Efremov wanted to use the photos himself.

Efremov's first victim was a man who managed a large factory in the Ukraine. The man had a bright career. Efremov figured he could use that to his advantage.

To get in to see him, Efremov had to show his KGB identification. He knew it was risky. His superiors would not be happy if they knew.

The plant manager's secretary guided Efremov into the expansive office. The manager looked cocky and in control. He was busy at his desk and didn't bother to look up. Apparently the fact that Efremov was KGB had done little to diminish his confidence. Efremov had already decided that he hated the man and now the man's arrogance made his hatred real.

"To what do I owe the pleasure of your visit?" the man finally said, glancing up, then quickly away.

Efremov continued glowering. The pictures he held showed the man with a boy.

"I'm a busy man," he said with obvious disdain, "State your business."

Efremov continued glowering. He had one hand inside the large envelope that sat on his lap; his fingers embraced the top photo. When the man pushed the button on his intercom, and began to speak, Efremov stood and threw the photo at him. It hit him on the chest. Efremov continued to glower.

"What do you want?" the man said, still appearing unflustered as he recognized the photo, but finally directing his gaze to Efremov.

Efremov wanted money, but he really wanted to control the man's soul. He'd imagined the man melting before him as he looked at the photo. But when the man didn't, Efremov was glad he'd come with more ammunition.

Slowly he pulled another photo from the envelope and slipped it below the man's nose.

"I want this," Efremov said coldly.

It was a picture of the man's teenage daughter, stretched out naked under ultraviolet tanning lights. The man exploded in rage, and stepped from his desk. Efremov knew the man's history. He'd been a lieutenant in the army, and wrestled on the army's wrestling team. Efremov knew better than to let the man get close to him. He also knew he would have no trouble with him, and as he approached, Efremov's hand, fingers straight and ridged, shot out and hit the man in his throat.

When the man stepped back, trying to take a breath, Efremov side-kicked him in his knee, which popped, then buckled. As the man went down, Efremov punched him in the nose with his open palm. The man reached in his jacket, possibly for a gun. Efremov grabbed the reaching hand and twisted it just right, laying the man back in pain. Blood poured from his nose. He was breathing with difficulty.

"I am a nice man," Efremov said, "Your daughter is no virgin. She will only feel pain when I leave her. On the other hand, the pain she will feel if I have to show her these photos will last her a lifetime. I'll be by this evening to pick her up, and for my first monthly payment. Don't worry, it will be affordable."

Efremov stood, figuring the danger that the man would use his handgun had passed, and threw a smaller envelope on the man's chest. "Everything you need to know is in there." Efremov turned and departed. He smiled sweetly to the secretary on his way out.

☒☒ ☒☒ ☒☒

Efremov had a reasonably large clientele when he was called onto the lustrous granite floor at the KGB office. They were harder on him than he thought they would be. He lost his job. He could avoid prison, but only if he ceased his blackmailing activities.

A month later, Efremov was still wondering what he would do when he was approached by another ex-KGB Officer who said he worked for an American oil company, and that his boss wanted to see him in Moscow.

Efremov wondered if it was some kind of joke when he saw the poor-looking offices of the so-called rich American oilman. He was led into the small office of the man he was told was the head Russian. His name was Uri Novotny.

"I was also raised under the white caps of the Ural Mountains," Novotny said even before introductions had been made. "Americans are different," Novotny said, indicating his surroundings. "They are most interested in making money, and since people make them money, they are most generous with salaries. We are paid twenty times what we made in the best of Russian jobs."

Novotny told Efremov that it took twenty men two weeks to find him. But he could afford it, Novotny explained, because his American boss had approved a large budget.

"I have a small job for you," Novotny told Efremov when they finally got down to business. "I think you will find it enjoyable. And if you succeed, you'll be richly rewarded."

Efremov explained the circumstances and told him about the bureaucrat. She was a woman, he said, blond, with short hair, about five-foot, seven inches tall, rapidly approaching middle age. Efremov was interested in the money he'd earn. He was also intrigued by the job.

Two weeks later, Efremov met her at her uncle's funeral. He'd been found dead on a park bench, his neck broken. Efremov could see she still considered herself sexually attractive from the clothes she wore, in spite of her overweight condition.

"Excuse me Krivenko," Efremov said as he approached, hat in hand. "Your uncle asked me to give you this."

When the woman looked at him with a question on her face, Efremov continued, "Your uncle and I were close. We were both unemployed, and we spent time together in the park."

"Why didn't he bring it to me himself?"

"He always told me how disappointed he was that he didn't get to see you more." Efremov was satisfied with the apparent guilt he'd inflicted. "He said he had little time to live. He made me promise I'd spend some time talking to you on his behalf, time he wanted to spend himself."

Natasha Krivenko looked harshly into Efremov's eyes. Then, apparently seeing his guileless expression, her look softened. "There's an Inn nearby. We could stop for a drink," Natasha said.

Efremov smiled demurely.

The next time Efremov and Natasha met, she shared the contents of the letter with him. She was baffled by it. It was typed, unsigned, and it asked her to be fair and impartial, that life was too short for anything less.

Efremov said he'd seen men talking to her uncle in the days before his death. Maybe, he suggested, they had something to do with his death. Maybe the letter was from them.

"But you said he gave it to you," Natasha said.

"He mailed it to me," Efremov said. "I received it in a larger envelope with a note, also typed and unsigned."

Natasha looked at him with big eyes, her trust evident.

"Perhaps someone thinks you're treating them unfairly," Efremov said.

Natasha confided that she was unfairly blocking the transportation of oil in a pipeline, but it was not her doing. The committee of three had decided that the American's oil would not be shipped. She could do nothing.

"Talk to them," Efremov said, sincerely concerned.

Several days later, she reported back to Efremov that the committee chairman said she was imagining things.

A week later, the Uncle of the committee chairman was found dead in his room at an insane asylum. He had been bound to a chair. His mouth was taped. His intestines had apparently been pulled from his body as he watched.

From then on, the bureaucrats were on the side of the young American. Vince was allocated 100,000 barrels a day, all the way to port. The money from the sales went straight to his bank in Denver.

To ship more, another pipeline was required. Vince wanted his own, but there was no legislation that allowed such a thing. He put his executives to work on the problem. It was not easy, given the turmoil in Russia.

More than a year later, when communism in Russia fell, the legislation concerning a private pipeline still hadn't been approved. Vince returned to Russia and found the anarchy he expected. He hired more former KGB. One-day, he thought, he would have trouble with his employees, but until then, they were his avenue to billions of dollars.

Before he returned to America, he was introduced to a man named Maxime Efremov, whom, Vince was told, was a former fighter pilot. Efremov's ancestors were Jewish, and because of the prejudice against Jews in Russia, he wanted to come to the United States. Efremov spoke English and Chinese perfectly. If he had a job, his immigration to the States would be approved.

Vince said he needed a good pilot. And he liked the idea that his new pilot could speak Chinese.

19 – Rex Widehead

Several geeky looking science-type students stared at Billy as he walked into the University of Wyoming science library. Billy was familiar with the looks he was getting. He figured he'd proceed like he knew exactly what he was doing. Soon he'd be ignored.

Billy's research showed that his little fly was in the biting fly family. They had chewing mouthparts and used them to bite off and eat pieces of flesh. Their mouthparts were not strong enough to chew into a dinosaur's tough scales. Billy figured the fly must have found soft tissue somewhere, maybe around the eyes.

Billy knew from raising wild birds that information on birds was harder to come by. As Billy worked and studied, he noticed an old man with long white hair and a straggly beard sitting at the table next to him.

"Excuse me," Billy said. "That a dinosaur work you're looking at?"

"Yes, it is," the man said. His craggy face softened as it formed a friendly smile.

Billy and the man talked about dinosaurs. Billy discovered that the man was Rex Widehead. To Billy he was one of the world's great celebrities. Widehead wrote books and drew incredible works of art that brought dinosaurs to life.

When Patton came back, he looked through the library until he caught a familiar sight. He could only see bits and pieces of color and movement through rows of books, but he knew immediately what he was seeing. His boy was animated, and talking to someone. When Patton was closer and saw Widehead listening and interested, Patton was proud, because it was apparent that his boy was talking man to "man" with one of the world's most famous paleontologists.

"Know who this is?" Billy said, when he saw his dad.

"Rex Widehead," Patton said, with little hesitation, extending his hand to the older gentleman.

"Beautiful the way your boy polished and molded the amber," Widehead said.

Patton smiled and nodded.

"Mr. Patton," Widehead said, "would you mind joining me in my office?" Widehead stood and indicated the direction. Patton smiled and wondered what was going on as he headed in the direction Widehead had indicated.

The office was more of a mini-lab with a big workbench on one side. It looked like there were a couple projects on it. Patton saw big rocks and assumed they contained bones. One was under a magnifying lens with delicate-looking tools lying around. There was a thick layer of dust near the rock.

On three sides, bookshelves went to the ceiling. They were full of books except one row at shoulder height. It was full of specimens of bones and jars with specimens with flesh in clear fluid.

Widehead opened a drawer in his desk and began fooling with a pipe. He lit it, then looked at Patton.

"More than twenty years ago, a boy of maybe fifteen years came to see me from Rawhide. I was amazed to discover that his knowledge of paleontology exceeded that of some of my graduate students. I thought that was a once-in-a-lifetime experience, but now, here's a second boy from the same town, who's just as knowledgeable. I find that most difficult to believe.

"I wanted to find out more about the first boy. His name was Longto. His high school principal told me he wasn't doing well. I found a scholarship for him here at UW, and called back only to discover he'd dropped out. Such a pity. They didn't even know, or more likely they didn't care, that they had a genius in their midst."

Patton listened and cocked his head, wondering where Widehead was going.

"My father was a mechanic," Widehead said. "When he fixed a car, if he didn't do it right, it came back. If he made too many mistakes, he went out of business. That's reality. Public schools have no access to reality. What's more, they do everything to cut themselves off from it. By creating their own reality, they always succeed.

"Getting back to your boy, would you share with me your ideas concerning the genesis of his intellect?"

Patton shifted in his seat, reflected for a moment, then began.

"The first boy you mentioned worked for me for several years, and it was from that experience that I discovered the importance of the first six years of life. Vince Longto's ability to learn other languages and everything else was unbelievable."

Patton explained about Vince's Nanny, and his meeting with Haua, and how Vince had learned three languages before beginning school, and how he'd learned math from an abacus before he could walk.

"Before then," Patton said, "I was a firm believer that intellect was one hundred percent hereditary. I can tell you, Vince Longto's a whole lot smarter than his parents."

"And you think it was his environment," Widehead said.

"If a baby's raised in a closet, he'll have no intelligence," Patton said. "He won't be able to talk, see well, or move in a coordinated way."

"I've read the studies," Widehead said fidgeting.

"When I read that if a baby is in a closet for a year, his intelligence will be stunted, I realized a simple truth. Most babies are in the "nice" equivalent of a closet for a large part of their infancy. They're first placed in a crib where sometimes they're left for hours. Then they're left in a playpen where Mother doesn't talk to them. My idea was to make sure my baby spent no time in a closet. I duplicated Vince Longto's experience in infancy as closely as I could with my boy."

"Tell me about it, please."

"From the start, I talked to him as if he were an adult. Then, I did ten-minute sessions with him three times a day.

The idea was to stimulate all of the avenues into the brain. There are six--seeing, hearing, feeling, tasting, smelling, and the last one, not usually on this list, is motion."

"The seeing, I take it, consisted of showing him things, at first bold black-and-white pictures," Widehead said.

"That's right."

"Followed by more subtle material, including written material."

"Right!" Patton said.

"Do you think that's why he's such a good reader?"

"Most definitely, because seeing complicated shapes like letters early on makes larger optic pathways so more data can be handled."

"I noticed he can do calculations swiftly in his head," Widehead said. "Same as the other boy I mentioned. Can you explain that?"

"When he was a baby, I showed him red dots on eleven by eleven cards."

"Yes, I've heard about that," Widehead said. "You show them the card and tell them the number. It must create a foundation in the brain that facilitates later development." Widehead puffed on his pipe. "The Longto boy had a chip on his shoulder. Your boy, on the other hand, seems well adjusted."

Patton talked about the importance of listening to what a baby says and how it contributes to their self-esteem. He explained about the life strategy program he'd done. He'd read Billy stories when he was two. The first was called, "Who Am I?" It explained that Billy was the one who saw the clouds in the sky and heard the pretty music play. It showed him he was an independent entity in the world, not tied to others, able to function independently.

Other stories taught Billy basic social truths. The most important of these was that his actions, even when he was a baby, affected the feelings of others. Patton had always felt that some people never understood this, and went through their life hurting others.

Another story taught Billy that he was responsible for his own actions that he could decide to be happy, or he could decide to be sad, and he could decide on his own. He didn't have to do what his friends did. When he was older and his friends pushed him to use drugs, he'd be able to decline. He wouldn't have to rely on someone else. He could act independently.

"The main difference in the way the two boys were raised," Patton said, "was that Vince Longto was abused by his mother." Patton paused, put on a serious face and looked at Widehead. "Vince and I were having a beer once when we ran into her. When she and Vince argued, I heard her say she wished she'd let him die when she'd had the chance. She was wearing a vicious face."

The professor stiffened, and his eyes closed momentarily.

After a pause, Patton continued. "As babies, neither was *pushed*. In other words, no attempt was made to impart knowledge." Patton noticed a subtle reaction from the professor, and decided to explain the point in more detail. "I mean they were never *required* to learn anything, nor were they tested. Instead, their interests were followed, and material was presented, at their request."

Widehead stuck a finger in his ear, wiggled it, and then looked at Patton. "A request from a month-old infant?"

Patton closed his eyes and smiled fondly as he remembered his own baby and how, from the first week, he'd made his likes and dislikes known. "It's in their eyes," Patton said. "If you show them something that they like, they look intensely. If they're tired of it, they don't look at all."

Widehead stared off for a moment, then nodded and looked back at Patton. "Well," he said, hammering the contents of his pipe into his open palm, "Could we meet again?"

"I'd enjoy that."

"Maybe Billy could start college a little early. He seems to be ready."

"But he's fourteen, and he loves football, wrestling and diving. His grandfather was a football player, and he has high hopes for Billy." Patton thought about his own father's disappointment when he didn't turn out to be a football player. "And for me, I'd like to see him go through school like a normal boy."

"Would his grandfather be William Patton?" Widehead's eyes were a little wide.

"Sure would be," Patton said proudly. "Know him?"

"Had him in geology when I was a grad assistant. Hell of a football player. Good scientist, too."

Widehead paused in thought. "UW has video courses." Widehead went on to propose that Billy enroll, take video courses, and still attend high school. Tom Patton loved the idea of letting his boy learn at his own pace. From first grade on, school had been little more for Billy than a place to make friends.

Patton hoped it would be a simple thing to walk into his boy's school, explain the situation, and then watch them make special arrangements. Right off, the assistant principal infuriated him by laughing derisively at his idea, and that was only the beginning. After months of wrangling, Patton threatened a lawsuit. He was amazed when the threat barely got their attention. It was help from Widehead and the help that Widehead recruited at the University of Colorado's Paleontology Department that finally convinced them to cooperate.

PART TWO:

BILLY

20 – The Reporter

Vince Longto frowned and set his book down. He glanced at the road leading up the hill to his new house. He liked watching the road. If someone wanted to come to his house, they had to come down this road. He looked at the white caps of the distant mountains and tried to focus on the fact that he'd done most of what he'd set out to do. He was a billionaire, he lived in the biggest mansion in Colorado, and he was the smartest person anyone knew.

Butzsaw, and before her, Mary White, had hired efficient people, and everything was running smoothly. There were no big problems for Vince to solve, nor anything pressing that he needed to learn. Vince looked in disgust at his swollen belly, then absentmindedly felt the bald spot on the back of his head. He'd tried jogging for a month, but it didn't seem to do any good, and it was time-consuming. But the worst part was that it let his mind wander.

Vince felt disgust as he contemplated the simple truth: A billion dollars did nothing to keep the demons at bay. If anything, his condition was worse. Even during waking hours, he still had to fight for control.

He'd been getting counseling in Denver. The psychologist said he'd tried to win his mother's love by getting rich and being smart. He'd been obsessed with killing his brother to eliminate his brother's competition for his mother's love. When Vince finally achieved most of his goals, and his condition didn't change, he felt cheated and since he no longer had a solution he could work toward, he felt intense frustration.

Vince thought it was all a bunch of fucking bullshit. His mother loved him. She bragged on him and told everyone how smart he was. How could a Mother's love be important to a baby who knew nothing? And his brother Mike was an ass with no brain. Vince wondered again how he could ever have been jealous of him.

Vince's breath was labored, his heart hammered, and his chest ached. A doctor told him it was angina--that he needed to learn to relax. Vince put his hands in his lap, pressed his thumbs together and chanted his mantra. Sometimes it seemed to help.

Suddenly he stopped chanting, and looked around the room as he thought about how much he hated Tom Patton, and how good he would feel if Patton were dead. For an instant, as Vince's mind dwelled on Patton's demise Vince felt better, even good. Perhaps Patton could die in a humiliating way. He'd seen Patton with his boy earlier that day. Patton had seemed so proud of that boy who was on his way to college.

The phone rang. Vince was mad that someone was disturbing him. He snatched up the receiver.

"Mr. Longto," the caller said, when Vince said nothing, "this is Rich Anderson. I'm a reporter for the *Colorado Herald*. I'm doing a special edition feature on the most successful men in Wyoming and Colorado."

"How can I help you, Mr. Anderson?" Vince said. Vince knew the name. The reporter had been calling him at the office for a week.

"I'd like to include you in my interview program."

"How much time do you need?"

"Eight hours, maybe more."

"I appreciate your calling, but I could never fit that kind of time into my schedule." With barely a pause, Vince added, "How many people did you plan to interview?"

"Just three."

"Who might they be?"

"Fred Peña the politician; Gerry Spence, the lawyer; and you. I have Dave Hamilton, the oilman, penciled in if you aren't available."

Longto wondered if the newsman was clever enough to use Hamilton as bate--that he knew how much Longto disliked him, a cocky small-timer worth thirty million if he were lucky.

"The time, Mr. Anderson, is such a factor. You must be aware my operations are worldwide, and the *Herald* covers such a small area."

"Perhaps I could do it in a way that didn't take time from your business. Maybe I could go with you on a business trip?"

"I just don't know."

"The *Herald* has the largest circulation of any paper in the State of Colorado. The article may help the value of your stock."

"I'm the sole stockholder of all my corporations. Tell you what, give my assistant Vicki a call in the morning and see if she can fit you in on one of my upcoming trips. Thank you, Mr. Anderson."

Vince hung up, then quickly dialed his office and left a message with his administrative assistant. His pounding heart was already starting to settle down.

"Vicki," he said to the machine that was specially designed to handle his long messages, "schedule a tour of my facilities next weekend beginning on Friday. Notify all the division chiefs. Tell them there's someone I need to impress. We'll go over to Denver first and look at the international boys. Then to Utah, where we'll overnight. We may go to Montana, New Mexico, maybe even Arkansas if we decide to take the time.

"When the reporter calls--Anderson's his name--make it sound like this trip has been planned for a while, that you can't fit him on the flight. Then call him right back later and tell him you talked to me and you couldn't believe that I said you could go because I was so busy and the *Herald* is such an insignificant paper. Schedule Sue, yourself, and Jean for the trip. We'll stay at the Hilton in Salt Lake the first night.

Jean and I will stay in the penthouse suite. Get a nice room for you and Sue. Put the reporter somewhere far away, and make sure he accepts our offer for a free room. Make dinner reservations at that Japanese place at Trolley Square. We may have to stay an extra night, so make similar reservations in Little Rock.

"And Vicki, why don't you set aside the hot tub, sauna, and swimming pool at the Hilton for a private party beginning at nine o'clock. The pool usually closes at about ten, so they won't mind. Sue's just back from Russia and we need to get her broken in, so get with me beforehand and we'll go over the details. She might turn out to be tougher than the reporter. We need a big screen TV and a VCR, and some appropriate movies. Don't forget champagne and hors d'oeuvres. Use your imagination." Vince paused, "Hell, why don't you get yourself and Sue each a nice room all by yourselves."

Vince Longto was tight with his money. Giving each of these girls a private room was an unusual extravagance.

Vince put down the receiver and looked at his watch. Jean would be calling in thirty minutes. She was busy at her church. For the moment, he went back to his reading-- Chinese poetry. What beautiful script, Vince thought. He'd worked hard on his own calligraphy, and he knew the work of a real artist.

Vince was confident that Vicki would handle his instructions just right, especially the misleading of the reporter. She was used to lying for Vince. All Vince's insiders could lie convincingly. There were three others: the lawyer, Poly Wartsall, Butzsaw, and Vince's pilot, Danny Trooper.

Insiders knew about the fraud and corruption on a need-to-know basis. United their story could cause a lot of trouble. It was a firm rule, established early by Vince that they not talk or even socialize together or with another important individual in his organizations without Vince's prior approval. The four insiders weren't the most important people in the organization, nor the highest paid, but they had considerable influence, and he often used them to communicate with his several division chiefs.

Vince paused for a moment from his reading to look out the expansive picture windows of his mansion and enjoy the view of the mountains, high and snow-capped. He loved the Rockies. The things in them were wild and free.

His phone rang. It was Butzsaw.

"How you doin' *Butt*aahh." Vince emphasized the first syllable and said the second as if he were emoting satisfaction.

"Not bad, *Long*ooooh," Jean said, mirroring Vince's upbeat tone. Vince had been dour since their last trip together, several months ago.

They felt at ease saying anything they wanted because the phones they were using had sophisticated scramblers.

"Done with your Bible stuff already?"

Butzsaw was active in her church, the *Church of Born Again Believers in Christ Almighty,* or BABCA to her. She regularly conducted revival meetings.

"I got away early when I heard about the trip," Butzsaw said.

"News travels fast," Vince said, sounding irritated.

"You can't keep a secret from me." Butzsaw had a sinister tone in her voice.

"You bitch," Vince yelled into the receiver. "What the fuck's going on? You been talking to Vicki?"

"That rule doesn't apply to me, prick face, so shut your filthy mouth."

"You cunt, who do you think you are?"

"I'm the one who can put you away you oozing asshole."

"You fucking whore," Vince was screaming out of control.

Vince dropped the receiver and looked around with an annoyed look. His wife, Emily, who was entertaining in the parlor, had turned up the music. Vince stomped into the parlor. "What the fuck's with the noise?" Vince screamed.

Vince yanked the wires out of the stereo and stomped back. His daughter stood in the doorway to his study. Her eyes showed determination.

"You get back down that hall and apologize to my mother," she said.

"You aren't too old to be spanked," Vince said, taken back by his daughter's show of force.

"You touch this sweet little ass," his daughter said, turning and bending just enough to reveal her pretty bottom, "and you'll go to jail as a sex offender."

Vince hesitated.

"You know I'll do it, now get down that hall."

The two stared at each other. When Vince sighed, she said with less emotion, "If you do a good job, I'll give you a hug. Now go." She pointed down the hall.

Vince loved his little girl. He'd hoped she'd be able, some day, to take over his business. His boy, from the time he was born, reminded him of his brother. So he'd taken his daughter under his wing. He took her on business trips where she listened to him negotiate tough deals. They talked about the strategy afterwards.

Seeing her now being assertive and sizing up her power with clarity, caused Vince to choke up. He stared at her, and when he started to cry, he spun on a heel and headed down the hall. His apology was sincere. He even fixed the stereo.

"You did good, Daddy," his daughter told him, as she hugged him tightly.

When Vince felt her full breasts against him, he started to cry. He knew it was just a matter of time before a man would try to take her away.

"You still have someone on hold," she said. She kissed his cheek and departed.

Vince closed the door to the study, stood pensively for a minute, then returned to his phone call.

"Okay, Jean," Vince said, the emotion gone, fully expecting Butzsaw to be waiting in spite of the long hold. "You have work to do." Vince briefed Butzsaw. He wanted good publicity, but he needed protection from muckraking. "Go to Denver and see the paper's publisher and owner," Vince said, "You know them, don't you?"

"Peoples, the publisher, is friends with my dad."

"Tell them we won't put up with muckraking. Make them agree to that. When this Anderson fellow, the reporter, starts getting wise, we'll have a jump on him. As soon as he gets on the plane, I want you to give him the low-down."

"Sounds like a good plan to me."

"We're in business," Vince said and hung up.

Monday afternoon Vicki came to Vince's office and played the conversation she'd recorded earlier with the reporter.

"Don't you suppose Mr. Longto could land in Denver and pick me up?" the reporter had asked Vicki.

"Mr. Longto's far too busy for that," Vicki replied in a snotty voice.

Rich complained that it was a several-hour drive from Denver, and the jet was leaving at six in the morning.

"Mr. Anderson, your time is worth far less than one percent of Mr. Longto's. How could you suggest that he take the time to stop when it'll only take you a few hours to drive?"

Vince looked forward to the trip with the reporter for the rest of the week. He spent hours planning with Jean and Vicki and his pilot, Danny Trooper.

On Friday, Vince and his entourage were in his airplane ready to go at six in the morning.

"That dumb shit reporter isn't here yet," Vince said. He was sitting in the cockpit in the left seat of his business jet. Danny Trooper, his pilot, was in the right seat.

"There're lights coming," Trooper said, pointing to the only road that led to the airport.

"Taxi slow," Vince said.

Vince watched as the vehicle lights approached. A man got out and ran into the executive terminal. Vince could see him talking to Claude, the base operator. Claude shook his head, then went into the radio room.

"Citation-One-Six-Five-Victor-Lima," Claude said over the radio, "Vince, there's a fella here who says he's supposed to be riding with you."

Vince gave his pilot a shady smile and told him to tell Claude to send him out on a run if he wanted to go. Claude left his mike open as he instructed the reporter. "Their pilot says if you run, they'll let you jump in. You better git. He's opening the hatch. I doubt that offer will last more than about fifteen seconds."

Danny Trooper stood at the door and waved to Rich to run, but he walked with a defiant look on his face. As Rich approached, Sue stepped out, wearing a conservative blue suit. Vince watched the reporter become alert when he saw Sue Hansen.

Sue was nice to the reporter, and her politeness obviously irritated Butzsaw. Rich greeted Vicki, who was sitting near the hatch. Vicki snubbed him. Rich climbed past her and went into the rear cabin where Butzsaw sat alone.

Vince noticed that the reporter had a determined look as he climbed aboard. He imagined the scenarios running through his sick head. The guy probably thought that the public had paid for Sue's Ivy League scholarship through higher utility rates—that she was Longto's newest mistress; and the public was now paying for Longto's daughter's high-classed education.

The son of a bitch, Vince thought, then he smiled as he considered the joy he would experience when he twisted the man's mind.

21--Rawhide

"Cozy One Four Niner Charlie Zulu, cleared for departure."

"Cozy Niner Charlie Zulu's rolling," Billy Patton said, adding full power for his takeoff roll. Billy was seventeen years old, a strapping, powerful-looking boy with a quick smile and a quicker wit.

Billy and Tom Patton were in the airplane they'd built, on their way to Cheyenne, Wyoming, where Patton was trying a case in Federal Court. Patton needed Billy to do some investigating.

"Tell me again how Vince got rich?" Billy said, after they were in the air and on course.

"Not as pretty as people think. Never ceases to amaze me how people close their eyes to his cheating."

"How do you know he cheated?"

Tom Patton clenched his jaw as he experienced the emotional pain that Vince Longto caused him. Patton considered the fact that he and his father together had played a big roll in creating Vince Longto. Patton glanced quickly at his boy. It didn't appear Billy had noticed his discomfort. "I know it from what Mary White told me," he said.

"Why'd you hire someone right out of prison?"

"Maybe Longto's the crook?" Patton said, still thinking.

"Why isn't Vince in jail?"

"Crooked lawyers, but mostly good press."

"But Vince seems like such a nice guy," Billy said.

Patton laughed nervously and chastised himself for Billy's attitude. "See what good press does for you?" Patton said, maybe, he thought, a little too derisively. "Drives me nuts. A bad guy steals a thousand dollars, and everyone is more than willing to spend a hundred thousand dollars keeping him in prison for three years. But when Vince Longto steals fifty million, no one cares."

"Sounds like bullshit to me," Billy said with a straight face.

Patton's mouth pursed in a half-smile. He'd tried to indict Vince in Billy's eyes without evidence, and Billy had smelled it out. He always gave his boy the facts he needed, and he knew this case should be no different. His father had told him about Vince Longto when Patton had graduated from college. That was probably good for Billy, too, Patton thought. But there was still plenty he could tell him. Patton gave his boy his most sincere look, then explained in detail the nickel gas story.

"Mary White told you all this?" Billy said.

Patton nodded. "Most of it just a couple weeks ago. She was angry when she visited. She'd had a good job as an auditor with the state tax people. She thought Vince got her fired because he was scared to death she'd audit him. She said she thought she'd have to work as a maid."

"Doesn't sound like that big a deal to me," Billy said.

Patton closed his eyes and took a deep breath. Billy was as smart as they come. It's no wonder no one bothered to go after Vince—no one understood how badly Vince was defrauding the community.

"Vince bought a gas field for fifty thousand dollars," Patton said. "Normally, a field like that would sell for a million or more, but Vince paid very little because the gas was locked in at a nickel. Vince wanted the provision changed. So he pulled out his thirty-eight magnum, put it to the head of the corporation, the little utility which bought the gas, and made demands—about as close to armed robbery as one can get."

"Because," Billy said, "a corporation has no blood or bones—nothing physical that a bullet could hurt. So he hurt the utility in the only way possible, with money, by shutting off their lawful access to cheap gas which made them pay—

what'd you say, six bucks—which was a hundred and twenty times more than they'd budgeted."

"Now you're catching on. The little public utility was buying gas for a nickel under the terms of a valid contract where both parties were treated fairly. That contract was its life's blood."

"Until Vampire Vince drained it."

Patton laughed.

"But why has no one stopped him."

Patton shrugged, delighted that his boy was on board, but worried about Billy's insatiable curiosity.

"How'd Mary White go to jail?" Billy said. "It was her word against his."

"Who'd believe her? She was in jail. Vince was the power, a multimillionaire who owned Rawhide Gas that paid his attorney fees. No one knew, believed or cared that Mary had played a big role in making Vince rich. It was always Vince's picture in the good-guy ads, never Mary White's.

"Vince's crooked lawyer, Wartsall, got Mary White's bank to put a freeze on her bank accounts. The banks did it, even though it's illegal because Vince was such a big customer and because Wartsall's firm represented the bank. That way she didn't have money to hire a good lawyer.

"Even though the Mary White problem had little to do with the utility, it picked up the tab for all the legal expenses, which means all the people of Rawhide paid Vince's tab to screw Mary White." Patton looked away.

"You know what the problem is with your story?" Billy said.

"Mary White?" Patton sighed, wondering how much more he dared tell his boy.

Billy nodded.

"Why you so worried about Mary White?"

"For one thing, I don't hear you saying you're going after Longto." The words hit Patton hard. In fact, Tom Patton had been involved in an effort to go after Longto. A Wyoming oilman named Jack Delaney had approached Patton. Patton had been active in that area of Wyoming, and was spending a lot of time there. Delaney had an employee who had gotten drunk at a bar and drove into a main gas line belonging to a small utility owned by Vince Longto.

The line was ruptured, and then the employee failed to report it. Gas spilled for two days. The utility sent Delaney a bill for $20,000 for 5000 MCF of gas.

"That's four dollars a thousand," Patton had told Delaney. "Gas hasn't been dear for years now. I got a friend with wells in that area on the same transportation system. Last time I talked to him, he was getting seventy cents--that is, when they let him produce, which was almost never. I know he'd sell to you."

"You mean replace Vince's gas?" Delaney said.

"Why not?" Patton said. "It'll cost you," Patton pulled out a pocket calculator and pushed buttons, "Three thousand, five hundred dollars."

A week later, Delaney visited Patton again and told him the utility wouldn't do it. Delaney had investigated and discovered that Vince Longto was selling the gas to his own utility. Replacement gas would cost a bundle in Vince's own lost production. But what it really meant was that Vince Longto was cheating a large portion of Wyoming's population out of several million dollars a year by selling gas to his own utility at a far greater price than he could get if he didn't own a utility.

Delaney went on to say that he'd been busy forming a consumer group. He planned to raise money, hire a lawyer, and then go after Longto before the Wyoming Public Service Commission. He had two Wyoming oilmen lined up to be directors and he only needed one more. Both directors had contributed $10,000 apiece, and Patton would be expected to do the same.

Patton deferred, but Delaney insisted, saying he knew Patton had gone to law school, and that he'd passed the Bar. It made him indispensable. Patton agreed to come on board if they would hire an attorney by the name of Dave Daniels. He was smart, Patton said, and he'd just returned to his home in Wyoming. He'd spent the last several years as an oil company executive in Texas, but returned to Wyoming when he couldn't get used to Texans. Patton liked Daniels. They'd gone to school together at the University of Wyoming.

Patton figured it would be a way for Daniels to make a name in Wyoming and get his law business going.

A week after the complaint was filed; Vince was home from Russia. Vince ignored the oilmen directors and instead made it appear that it was all Daniels' doing. Vince got it printed in the local paper that Daniels was a crackpot. He put a letter in the monthly invoice to all his natural gas utility customers which said that the Wyoming Public Service Commission had already ruled on all his contracts, and that Daniels, an amateur, was saying that he knew more about the natural gas business than the professionals at the Public Service Commission.

In fact, Daniels, Patton and the other two oilmen knew magnitudes more about the oil and gas industry. No commissioner on the Wyoming PSC, nor any staff member, had solid knowledge about the oil and gas industry.

Patton went to Wyoming for the hearing and was shocked when immediately the chairman, Commissioner Smyth, came out hostile to Daniels. Patton thought he acted like a ten-year-old, ranting and strutting.

The next morning's newspaper made Daniels, not Smyth, look like an idiot. Patton studied the article, but while it appeared to be unfair, he couldn't see any falsehoods. He put the article down with a sigh, thinking he'd made a big mistake recommending Daniels.

The hearing lasted two more days, and each day there was an article in the local paper that made Daniels look stupider. No one was surprised when Vince won, given their lawyer's incompetent performance.

A month later, on a trip to Wyoming, Patton visited Daniels, who said that all his good clients had left him, that his savings would be used up soon, and he didn't know what he'd do after that. He showed Patton the transcript of the hearings and asked Patton to compare it to the articles.

Patton was absolutely amazed at how cleverly the paper had used tiny distortions of fact to arrive at enormous differences in meaning. It was obvious that someone very clever had manipulated the facts with one goal in mind, and that was to destroy Daniels. But what motive did the paper have?

Daniels said he had some information and called into his office a tall and pretty blond typist who said she'd worked at the newspaper during the hearings. She said that every day in the two weeks before the hearings and right through the hearings she'd noticed either Vince or Butzsaw talking to the paper's publisher.

Patton discovered that the hearing had been conducted in the meeting room of the local Elks club and that Vince owned the building. Patton went to the Elks club for lunch and talked to the woman who'd cleaned the hearing room. He discovered that Vince had stayed late after each hearing and participated in a meeting with Butzsaw, the reporter, and Jim Wayne, Vince's local lawyer. Daniels was shocked at this information and said the reporter had never met with him or anyone in his group before writing any of the defamatory articles.

With this information, Patton knew Vince Longto had been behind the defamation of Daniels. He was the only man so inclined and clever enough to pull off such subtle, yet destructive distortions of the truth. Patton figured that Vince and Butzsaw had also biased Smyth, the hostile PSC Commissioner, possibly doing it in a similar way by threatening, telling lies, being vicious, and then being nice.

"Why don't you sue for defamation?" Patton had said to Daniels, "When the owner of the paper sees what his paper did, he'll surely settle by publishing a full retraction."

Daniels agreed that it might work. A retraction was the only thing that might allow Daniels to stay on in Rawhide. But what neither Daniels, nor Patton had considered was Vince's local Wyoming attorney, Jim Wayne, and the other members of his law firm. It represented both the newspaper, *and* Vince Longto.

Patton was well acquainted with Wayne and the other members of his law firm. Patton had used them many times in relation to his oil and gas activities in Wyoming. A couple weeks after the suit was filed, Wayne told Patton that Daniels was unethical--that he'd screwed up the PSC hearing and then he'd filed a phony defamation lawsuit just to get money. Wayne went on to say that Daniels had helped an oil company cheat the federal government out of more than $400,000 in royalties.

"Which oil company?" Patton demanded, figuring Wayne was telling the same thing to every person he saw.

"Muddy Gap, or something like that," Wayne said, obviously being evasive.

Some time later, Patton realized that Wayne was talking about Monlay-Finn Exploration. The company had been having difficulties, and finally went bankrupt when it lost a lawsuit concerning royalty valuation. The government quickly estimated what Monlay owed in back royalties and filed a claim for $400,000. The amount was later adjusted to $150,000, which Monlay paid down by half, then made further provision to pay in full in its Chapter 11 Bankruptcy plan. It showed Patton that Wayne was unethical, not Daniels.

Not more than a week later, another attorney in Wayne's law firm told Patton that Daniels' old roommate from his single days, a man named Dude Oman had been homosexual.

Patton was incredulous. Dude Oman had been a prizefighter. He regularly hit on every legal secretary in town, and ended up marrying one. The next time Patton saw this attorney, he told Patton in a low, distant, and serious voice that Daniels' ethics were suspect. Patton knew it was bullshit, and instantly realized that the Dude Oman comment was a fabrication, meant to give the impression that Daniels was gay.

"So what do you think about Daniels' lawsuit?" Patton asked, wondering if there was a party line at Rawhide's most prestigious law firm, that the attorneys had all gotten together on the way to handle Daniels.

"The man can't admit he screwed up," the attorney said, his face contorted in the pain of it all. "He has an authority-figure problem is all I can say." Patton thought about how top corporate lawyers were whores, that the more successful the lawyer, the more plastic they were and willing to adopt whatever rationale was needed to ensure success for their big clients.

"Dad," Billy said, and asked Patton another question about suing Vince Longto. Patton needed more time, said something to put Billy off, then continued thinking about Daniels.

When the newspaper wouldn't settle, Daniels tried to find a lawyer to represent him, but had no luck. Patton knew how lawyers worked in Wyoming. As soon as Daniels contacted them, they'd call a local lawyer to find out what was really going on. The law firm they contacted would have been Jim Wayne's since it was the only "A" rated firm in the area, and therefore the one with a broad, statewide practice.

It looked to Patton like every attorney in Wayne's firm knew the "party line" on Daniels, and could repeat it flawlessly.

Daniels couldn't find an attorney to represent him and had to continue as his own attorney, a move that placed him at a considerable disadvantage.

The local judge referred the case to Judge Terrell O'Toole, described by many to be the state's most conservative judge. Patton went to the hearing where the newspaper's motion to dismiss was considered. Although O'Toole appeared to be fair, it was obvious to Patton which side he was on. Every time Daniels talked about the key points of his case that clearly showed the newspaper in the wrong, O'Toole cut him off, and asked him irrelevant questions about the quality of his original case against Vince Longto. Within seconds after arguments, O'Toole ruled for the paper, then lectured Daniels on a problem he sensed Daniels had with authority, and said some other things, whose substance Patton had forgotten, but which were clearly delivered with the same cadence and intonation that Wayne and his fellow attorneys had used.

Patton suggested to Daniels that O'Toole had allowed himself to be unethically swayed by listening to someone in Wayne's firm. Daniels agreed and told Patton about a conversation he'd had with O'Toole. Judge O'Toole said he'd talked to Wayne, Vince's lawyer, at a recent lawyer's convention. Daniels said O'Toole suddenly stiffened, then looked momentarily at Daniels with a guilty look. Patton was sure it meant that Wayne had used the opportunity to deliver the party line, and O'Toole had swallowed it and allowed it to bias his thinking.

Patton could see Wayne's plan succeed perfectly. His law firm and probably even the local judge, who was more of a sheep than any of the other lawyers, had created a sea of bias which made it impossible for Daniels to get a lawyer and difficult for a contemporary judge to rule in his favor.

Patton wondered if Vince Longto had engineered the law firm's defamation of Daniels. Patton imagined a scene at Vince's mansion where Wayne was falling all over himself to kiss Vince's ass.

Daniels had to leave the state that had been his only real home since birth. Patton heard that his wife of ten years had left him shortly thereafter.

"Dad!" Billy's voice was intense. Patton startled and looked around. They were close to Cheyenne. "What about a class-action suit?" Billy said.

"Looks like you better start down." Patton paused. He'd spoken the last words like the Grim Reaper. He didn't like admitting to himself that he couldn't take on Vince Longto, and he certainly wasn't going to say as much to his boy. "Have the airport information?" he said, this time too animated.

"Aircraft are landing to the West," Billy said turning to look closely at his dad. "So, you think this trial will really last three days?" he said looking back to the direction of their travel.

"Maybe less. The judge said he might make us work evenings."

"What are your chances of getting this guy off?"

"He'll make a good witness. A lot depends on whether you can find the girl."

"You really think the Mother's hiding the Daughter to cover her lies?"

"Sure do."

"I have some good leads."

"We should break for the day at four o'clock. That's when I'll give you a ride to Laramie in the rental car. I can't believe you're already starting college." Patton gave his boy a paternal look. "You're all set up over there?"

"Sharon's driving my car down."

"Sharon, your girlfriend?" It was old ground. Billy had said they were just friends, although Patton had seen them being friendlier than that.

"I have my apartment and I'm all moved in," Billy said. "So, you think you'll tie the knot with that judge lady?"

Patton laughed. Billy was paying him back for teasing him about Sharon. Patton had been dating a thirty year-old county court judge. He liked her, but he couldn't see a long-term thing. Besides, Patton was dreaming of another girl. Sue Hansen was coming back from Russia, he'd heard, and this time, he'd vowed not to screw it up. Patton closed his eyes and recalled Sue's pretty smile and sexy eyes. When the image of her face in ecstasy appeared, he let it linger, this time without pain.

Billy parked *Sally*, then took care of most of the details of getting a rental car, enduring once again the agent's admonishment that Billy not be allowed to drive.

"So, what about a class action?" Billy said, as he drove them into town.

This time Billy's words hit Patton hard. If Patton ended up like Daniels, Sue Hansen, or any other decent woman for that matter, wouldn't give him a second look.

"You know, courts in Wyoming have changed since Sullivan got in as governor. He was a member of the most prestigious law firm in Wyoming. It represented big money and government, and he packed the courts with judges who shared his views."

"But a jury will decide it, and this is the nickel gas thing. That's in Colorado. And if nothing else, it will expose Longto for the crook he is."

"But Longto has a great public image in Colorado, too."

"So?"

"So, you'd start with a biased jury, and worse, a biased judge. Ever hear of the Missouri plan?" Patton shook his head as he remembered that Vince had been a big backer of the plan in Wyoming.

"For selecting judges? The lawyers recommend them, the governor appoints them, and every election the people decide if they should stay in office. Great idea."

"Great idea for those who are in control of public opinion--big money and government. It means that judges are responsive to the public's *perception* of things--and that's especially true since Justice Urbigkit was recalled." Walter Urbigkit had been the last liberal judge on the Wyoming Supreme Court. He dissented constantly from the majority. "Remember," Patton said, "a woman's movement got him recalled. Something to do with the constitutional rights of an accused rapist."

"Rapists don't have rights," Billy said with a gleam in his eye.

Patton sighed deeply as they parked. He gave Billy a final set of instructions, then disappeared into the courthouse.

☙ ☙ ☙

Billy completed his assignment before noon. With nothing to do, he drove around the capitol building in gradually bigger circles. Billy smiled when he thought about his unusual childhood. He wouldn't have had it any other way, he thought. He had friends his age from athletics and a lot of older friends from academics. He was mature, and he knew where he was going in life. He liked his dad's idea that he settle down and have a family, but he wondered how long it would take him to find the right person.

When Billy drove into a dead-end in an industrial area, he stopped and began to back up. Across the street was a small, disheveled-looking office building. It looked strange down near the railroad, nestled between big industrial yards. He couldn't see the sign through bushes.

As he left, he glanced back. The sign said, "Wyoming Public Services Commission." He was almost out of the cul-de-sac when it hit him. Maybe he could verify Mary White's story with records from the Colorado Public Utilities Commission? He looked at his watch, and could see that if he hurried, he could drive to Denver and be back in time to meet his dad that evening.

Before two hours were up, Billy was looking at the old drilling contract for Green Dome and a dozen more contracts concerning sales of its gas to the utility.

"Could I make copies of these?" he said to the clerk, referring to the documents he'd been looking at in the Colorado PUC office.

"Sure," she said, "twenty-five cents a copy."

Billy's eyebrows shot up.

"That's what I have to charge. Sorry."

"Could I check them out?" Billy knew where he could make copies for a nickel.

The clerk looked at Billy. He was wearing a T-shirt and old jeans, clothes he'd selected to investigate for his dad.

"It's okay," he said, showing her his card. "I work for Tom Patton, the lawyer. I'm an investigator. I'm incognito, you might say, doing investigations."

"I can check them out to your boss, the lawyer," the clerk said.

"Okay," Billy said, giving her a big smile.

His dad had accurate information. The gas *had been* locked in at a nickel. It was increased to almost four dollars apparently when a lawsuit was settled. Billy even found the contract suspension letter dated a month before the Natural Gas Policy Act went into place, just like Mary White had said.

Mary White had told Patton that she'd testify that it was phony in which case the increase was void from the beginning. But it was her word against Vince's.

Billy remembered his dad saying there was also a fraudulent lawsuit. He called the clerk of court in Rawhide and asked that a copy of the suit be made. Then he called his dad's office, and had a secretary fax it to him at the Colorado PUC.

When he got back from making copies, the fax had arrived. Again, Billy couldn't believe his eyes. It was exactly as his dad had said. Vince had sued the utility for millions in damages for theft of condensate. But there was no theft because after Vince owned the utility he filed a report saying no condensate had been stolen.

Billy did some quick figuring. The numbers were staggering. Given a successful class-action suit, Vince would have to reimburse as much as fifty million dollars to the people of Rawhide and surrounding towns.

Billy made the copies, returned the files, then got back onto I-25. He caught his dad at a short recess.

"Can't talk now," his dad said. "The judge wants to run to nine o'clock. Why don't you take the rental car to Laramie and turn it in?"

"Got hot news." Billy was anxious to tell his dad that he'd discovered that Vince was a total slime.

"It'll have to wait 'til I'm back from Salt Lake. I'll come to Laramie to see how you're doing. We'll share a six-pack and you can tell me all about it."

"Okay," Billy said. He knew a trial put a lot of demands on his dad. Patton gave Billy a little wave and headed back to the courtroom.

"Wait," Billy said. Patton turned.

"Give me a quick hug just in case I don't see you again."

Patton had said the same thing to Billy. Patton had said it as a friendly gesture. Billy said it like he meant it. Billy felt motivated by a strangely real feeling of urgency.

"Go on," Patton said, with a big smile, apparently thinking Billy was joking. With that, he was gone.

22 – Jean Butzsaw

Jean Butzsaw studied the reporter's face as he made his way to the rear cabin of Vince's jet aircraft.

"Where's Longto?" Rich Anderson said to Butzsaw. There were four seats, two facing forwards and two facing to the rear.

Butzsaw gave the reporter an icy glare. Butzsaw had obtained a psychology profile of the man from one of his former employees. It'd be difficult, she thought, but he'd break. "Mr. Longto is flying," Butzsaw said sharply. "He'll be back after he gets the plane at altitude and on course where the copilot can take over. Until then, we have some things to talk about."

Butzsaw knew Vince wasn't needed to fly, he just wanted it in the paper that he flew a jet. He only had a private pilot's license, and he had difficulty getting that. He actually only operated the controls in good weather. When they were in bad weather he talked on the radio and performed other mundane cockpit chores. Butzsaw also knew Vince's real reason for the pretense: Vince hated it that oilmen everywhere talked about how good a pilot Tom Patton was. She was aware of Vince's need to be better than Patton in every way possible.

Jean had had a long visit with Bob McCartney, a major owner of the *Herald*, and Jim Peoples, its publisher. Before talking to them, she carefully went over the law of defamation with Wartsall. It was Wartsall's specialty--not because he did a lot of work in that area, but because it intrigued him. He used it as a weapon, and commonly threatened defamation suits on his client's behalf.

"Mr. Longto cannot qualify as a public figure," Butzsaw had explained to Peoples and McCartney in their meeting. "That means if you don't print the truth, he'll have grounds to sue. There are a lot of wild stories going around about Mr. Longto. I dismiss them as nothing but jealousy spawned by Mr. Longto's incredible success."

"Miss Butzsaw," Peoples had interjected. "Rich is one of our best reporters. The last thing he has on his mind is muckraking. This is simply a personal interest story. Relax."

"I've checked on Anderson," Butzsaw had said sternly, "and I think he's intent on muckraking. I want you all to know Mr. Longto only uses the best lawyers money can buy, and if there's even a hint of falsity in this story, you'll have hell to pay."

The speech had been in accordance with a well-established Longto routine. Intimidate first, then embarrass, harass, and if necessary defame. Each lie must resemble the truth--the more truth, the easier to defend the statement.

By the time Butzsaw had departed, she had personal guarantees of accuracy from both men.

Butzsaw now sat with her legs crossed and sneered at the reporter. The jet engines were winding up for takeoff. "I've spoken with McCartney and Peoples," Butzsaw said, continuing her lecture to the reporter.

"Surely you jest," Rich said with a sarcastic smile. "Those guys don't grant interviews with just anyone."

"Mr. Anderson," Butzsaw said with an icy glare, "Vince Longto is not just anyone. He's one of the richest men in America. That spells power. If you can't understand this simple concept, maybe we should terminate this idea about an interview. His operations are international. You think the CEO of General Motors would grant you an interview, Mr. Anderson?"

Butzsaw knew he couldn't terminate the interview. How could he explain that he'd spent a day in Vince Longto's plane and didn't get an interview? Besides, if he did take her bait and cancel, she had hours to turn him back around.

"Listen, Jean--"

"Miss Butzsaw."

Rich closed his eyes and took a slow breath, "Miss Butzsaw, this is just a simple interview." Rich started to say more, but didn't.

Butzsaw could see she was beginning to gain control. "I suggest you keep that in mind," she said as if accepting a concession. "I'll tell Mr. Longto we're ready." Butzsaw went to the cockpit, closing the door on the way. Vince was waiting patiently for her report. Trooper was flying from the right seat.

"He's a slow learner," Butzsaw said. "It may take more than one try."

"We can keep him for three days if we need to," Vince said.

"Vince, Honey," Butzsaw said with a concerned look on her face, "you should wear your seat belt."

"The air's smooth as silk, and I'm always moving back and forth. It's okay."

23 – Chinese, Russian, and Spanish

"Ah, Mr. Anderson," Vince said as he took his seat. "I'm pleased to make your acquaintance."

Vince thought the reporter's cockiness had come down a notch since he came aboard. Butzsaw could do that to any man. "We have a two-day trip planned," Vince said, "maybe even three, so I'm sure there'll be plenty of time to get in all the interviewing we need."

"I understand you're a linguist," the reporter began, "that you speak several languages, and even an Asian language."

"Four Asian languages. Mandarin, Cantonese, and Russian, and I read and write Chinese, which is a language in its own right. I speak two European languages, Spanish and, of course, English."

"Isn't Russia in Europe?"

"A small portion of Russia is in Europe. The next time you consult a globe, please note that the vast majority of Russia is in Asia."

"How well do you speak Chinese?"

"I speak both Mandarin and Cantonese perfectly. You are aware, Mr. Anderson, that the two languages are as different as say, Russian and English." Vince glanced momentarily at the reporter until he acknowledged the statement. "In addition," Vince repeated, "I read and write Chinese perfectly."

"You mean you read, write, or speak perfectly?"

"All of them," Vince said, sighing his disgust.

"And your accent?"

"Also perfect."

"When did you learn?"

"When I was twenty. Mr. and Mrs. Chien, the owners of the Chinese restaurant in Grand Junction, Colorado taught me. Took them about six months. Mrs. Chien is still alive, although you would need an interpreter to talk to her."

"I studied French at the Aliance Francaise for a summer. Some people learned French without an accent, but that didn't include anyone from America. It took a year of total immersion for the brightest students to learn French fluently. Would you mind saying something for me in Chinese?" The reporter held up his tape recorder.

Butzsaw flashed him a look. Vince gestured to Butzsaw that it was okay, and grabbed the recorder. He quoted a long Cantonese poem. Yaping had used it often to sing him to sleep. Recently, Vince had obtained a book containing it. Then, in Mandarin, he quoted a few lines from a famous speech made by Mao Tse Tung.

"Who really taught you Chinese, Mr. Longto?" Rich said insistently.

Vince glowered at the reporter, and gestured to Butzsaw, who picked up the intercom, said a few words, and hung it up.

"That's it, Anderson," Butzsaw said. "This interview will continue when you learn how to behave. Stand up, please."

Rich hesitated. Trooper tapped him on his shoulder.

"Who's flying?" Rich said.

"Silence, you," Trooper said. "Stand up, and turn around."

When Rich stood, Trooper put his index finger on Rich's chest, and started instructing.

"Mr. Anderson," Trooper said, "you can sit with me in the cockpit for now."

As Trooper talked, he pushed hard enough to make Rich step back but he couldn't, because something blocked his feet. When he began to fall, he reached out to grab the door jam but, in a slick move, Trooper pushed in on his elbows, keeping him from grabbing it. As the fall continued he turned and fell onto Vince. Butzsaw had been ready with her camera and thought she'd gotten a couple good photos.

As Rich rose, Trooper struck him so hard it knocked his wind out. As he struggled to breathe, Trooper bent his arm behind him and carted him off.

"You son of a bitch," Trooper screamed, putting him in the seat Vicki had just vacated. "You attacked Mr. Longto."

"I didn't attack anyone," Rich said.

Trooper's palm crashed into his face.

"Shut up. You talk again and you're a dead man." Trooper stayed clear of the blood. "As soon as we get to Denver, you're going to jail."

Trooper handcuffed both his hands to the seat. Rich started to talk again but thought better of it.

"Sue, you aren't safe here," Trooper said. "Go on into the cabin with Jean and Vicki."

Sue took one look at the handcuffed, bleeding man and jumped up. Trooper went back to his pilot's seat.

"What happened?" Sue said as she walked into the cabin.

"That idiot attacked Vince," Jean said.

"Was he provoked?"

"Of course not," Butzsaw said, giving Sue an icy glare.

"We don't have a clue why he did it," Vince said. "But we'd like to know. Why don't you talk to him and see if you can figure it out. Take this recorder. Keep it hidden. If he says anything incriminating, we'll have it on tape."

They were just touching down in Denver when Sue returned with her report. "He says it's all a mistake, that he just fell," Sue said.

"He attacked him. I saw it," Butzsaw said. "Look at this." Butzsaw showed Sue the Polaroid she'd taken of Anderson as he came into contact with Vince. Vince wore a typical victim's look of horror, but oddly, the reporter also wore a look of horror.

"Give us the tape," Vince said. "We'll study it and see what he said."

It had already been decided that the reporter would either be allowed to cool off in jail for a night, or, if they had "evidence" of malicious intent on the tape, jail wouldn't be necessary, they'd just blackmail him. Wartsall had helped them with the plan by telling them the elements of the crime of assault.

Vince's chief of international affairs met them at the airport. It was Centennial Airport, used only by general aviation. Karam was the fellow's name, a Russian Jew. He was the only division chief Vince halfway liked. As a Jew, the KGB had bashed Karam around in Russia. He didn't let Vince's ranting and raving get to him as much as the others did.

"Hi, Karam," Vince said. "There's a fellow in the plane. He should be coming in soon. He's a reporter. Take him to your office and let him know about our foreign operations. Don't tell him about the nuclear fuels; the papers don't need to know about that; it might cause trouble."

Jean had spent a good hour on the phone with Karam the day before, so Vince was just stressing the main points.

Vince then joined Butzsaw in a nearby conference room.

"What do you have?" Vince said.

"This tape will do," Butzsaw said. "Listen to this." Butzsaw pushed the play button: "Well, yeah, I did lunge into him, but Longto had his feet against my heels so I couldn't step--." Butzsaw clicked the stop button and said with a sneer to the recorder: "We don't need your explanations, asshole." She looked at Vince. "I have it set up to get this tape edited in Salt Lake. It'll be a professional job."

Vince smiled and nodded his approval.

Butzsaw fast forwarded, and said, "And listen to this." She punched the play button: "Longto's a sorry piece of shit. Look at what he's doing."

"See, Butzsaw," Vince said with a big smile. "I told you he was planning some muckraking. We'll stop him in his tracks. Have Sue get him cleaned up, and tell him we don't think we're going to press charges. Sue bending over him and nursing his wounds should bring him back to his senses. Have Sue talk to him about being more careful."

When Rich came in with Trooper, Vince came on to him like he was the best friend he had in the whole world.

"Here's the reporter I've been telling you about," Vince said with a big smile. "Rich Anderson, meet our foreign division chief, Karam Galdfurb. Karam will be taking you on a tour of our Denver office. I have some other business. I'll meet you back here in two hours."

Vince walked over to Danny Trooper, then the two of them walked out together and jumped into a car sitting at the airport.

Vince kept cars at every city and town he flew into, each owned by a different utility. It didn't save Vince a lot of money, but it made him feel good, because every time he used one of the cars for non-utility business he was cheating every customer of the utility. He liked that.

They were going for marijuana and cocaine. It'd been years since Vince had used drugs, but lately his need had been intense.

24 – Cocaine, Airplanes, and Mary Jane

Vince and Trooper drove to Stapleton International Airport, about a half-hour drive. On the way, they stopped at a filling station. Both changed clothes in the bathroom. They emerged looking like construction workers.

"Now we need to find a *callejero,*" Vince said, upon arriving at Stapleton. "Drive over to that construction area. There should be one or more hanging around.

"*Oye tu,*" Vince yelled out to a Hispanic-looking fellow. "He's an illegal if I ever saw one," Vince said to Trooper.

When the man came over, Vince looked at him seriously.

"*Escucha lo que te voy a decir,*" Vince said, in a commanding way. The man stiffened and listened.

Vince told the man he had a job for him. The man was eager. Vince gave him a key, told him to go into the terminal, get a bag from a locker, then take it to a particular spot and leave it. The man's pleasant smile disappeared and he said he needed a hundred bucks for *this* job.

Vince gave him fifty and told him if he didn't do it just right, Trooper would find him and kill him. The man's eyes were big. He assured them he'd do it just right.

Trooper and Vince positioned themselves in different places where they could watch the man come out with the bag. They wanted to make sure he wasn't followed. The man dropped the bag, and, as per their instructions, caught a taxi and left the terminal area. Trooper got the car while Vince continued to watch. When Trooper pulled up next to the bag, Vince nodded that it was okay. Trooper threw the bag in the trunk, then drove away. Vince walked up to the passenger drop area, where Trooper picked him up.

Any one of ten different people used this car in Vince's operations. If the bag were found, they could plead lack of knowledge, a defense to a possession charge. With all the money in the world for lawyers, they'd prevail.

On the way back, they stopped and changed clothes discarding the old ones they had worn. They looked like different people again. Trooper drove right up to their aircraft and put the bag into the plane. Now it would take a search warrant to find it.

Vince jumped in and checked the contents--two kilos of high-grade grass. "God, I love this stuff," Vince said, rolling a joint.

He checked the bottom of the bag to see if everything was there. Hidden in a pocket in the bottom of the bag was a packet of cocaine. He might need it tonight, if his plans with Sue panned out. Vince placed the bag in a compartment on the plane, and locked it, then returned to the terminal just as Karam arrived with the reporter.

"Bright kid, isn't he?" Vince asked Karam, right in front of Rich.

"He sure is," Karam said, in a strong Russian accent, a big smile on his face.

"Let's get out of here," Vince said as he placed his hand on Rich's back, wondering if he was acting stoned. The marijuana was stronger than the kind he used to smoke. "You remind me of my favorite nephew," Vince said, smiling down at Rich, giving him a fatherly pat on his shoulder. "As soon as I get this baby in the air and on course with the cruise control set, I'll come back and we'll get some more good conversation in. I'm sure there's a lot more you'd like to know."

Vince looked over at Trooper with a frown. Trooper had stiffened as Vince said, "cruise-control."

"Sit in the left seat, Trooper. You can handle landing in Salt Lake, can't you?" Trooper's smile wasn't quite right. Vince thought about the two tokes Trooper had taken but figured he'd still have no problem flying. "Good. I'll get us in the air here in Denver," Vince gave Trooper a quick wink that the reporter couldn't see because Vince had no intention of flying. "It's pretty congested here. When we're on course, you can take over, and I'll go back to talk to Mr. Anderson."

Vince looked down patronizingly and made sure Rich had picked up on all that. Rich watched, but said nothing. He was learning.

"Well, young man," Vince began when he returned to the rear cabin, "What would you like to talk about?"

"Your operations in Russia are enormous, Mr. Longto. Karam says you have reserves of more than one billion barrels of oil--"

"Karam is a Russian engineer and an American accountant. I think he gets his conservatism from the accounting side. Actually, I have more than *four* billion barrels of reserves in Russia."

Vince's manner made a lie seem out of consideration.

Butzsaw rolled her eyes and squirmed in her chair.

"Isn't that right?" Vince said, looking at Butzsaw pointedly.

"No question about it." She cleared her throat, then continued a half-octave lower, "The American engineers uniformly place the Russian reserves that high or even higher."

"One hundred thousand barrels of production a day seems like a really low number compared to the size of the reserves," Rich said.

"You catch on quick. It would take more than a hundred years to get it out at that rate. Our problem has been a lack of pipeline capacity," Vince continued. "It has taken Mother Russia a while to implement the laws necessary to allow us to build a pipeline, and then for us to obtain permits. But that has finally been accomplished. In fact, we just finished a new pipeline and have been using it for a week already. Our production now exceeds two hundred thousand barrels a day. What's more, we're working to obtain new concessions."

"What will your income be on that?" Rich said.

"It's costing us five dollars a barrel to get the oil onto the freighter. Then our royalties are running twenty percent. On fifteen-dollar oil, we make about seven dollars. Our profits depend a lot on the price." Vince paused for a minute and studied the young reporter as he added the numbers up in his head. Vince could tell he didn't believe his own computations.

"So, how did you put all that together?" Rich stumbled for his words. "I mean, how did you end up with billions of barrels of reserves and hundreds of thousands of barrels of production a day?"

"I needed to understand the Russians better than the competition, that's all."

"Oh," Rich said, his jaw hanging.

When they were on the ground in Utah, Vince signaled to the reporter. "Come on," Vince said, "we'll use that helicopter over there to tour my Utah facilities. We'll look at gas wells, a drilling rig, and a gas plant. I sell the gas to utilities that I own around the country."

They quickly jumped into the waiting helicopter. Vince sat in the copilot's seat. He handed the pilot the itinerary that Trooper had made up. First, they flew low over his gas wells. He pointed one out to the reporter. Rich said he couldn't see a thing. Vince was pointing to an object smaller than a big sagebrush.

Finally, Rich said he saw. Vince didn't believe it so he ordered the helicopter to land. Vince wanted to make sure the reporter clearly saw that a gas well was nothing more than a pipe sticking out of the ground surrounded by wildflowers.

They flew toward the gas plant and arrived in less than fifteen minutes.

"There won't be time to interview any of these people," Vince said. "I'll explain it all to you when we get back into the air. This gas plant does two things. It removes H_2S from the gas and compresses the gas into the pipeline."

"H_2S is hydrogen sulfide. Isn't it poisonous?" Rich said.

"One whiff and you're dead."

"God, that stinks," Rich said as they landed. "Is that H_2S? Are we in danger?"

Vince laughed at the reporter. "You can only smell a non-lethal dose. A lethal dose instantly destroys the nerves in your nose."

"So, if I can't smell it, then I should worry?" Rich said suspiciously, but Vince was preoccupied.

The plant manager was waiting to greet them.

"Hi, Bud," Vince said. "How're you doing on your projects? You've been installing a new compressor and a new refrigeration unit."

Bud answered as they walked. The plant was large, covering forty acres. Several amine towers rose high. They removed the H_2S. A deep rumble came from the distance. It was the compressors, all housed in an enormous steel building. Pipes seemed to run in every direction, all painted different colors.

"How's that new fellow doing?" Vince said as they walked.

"Fine," Bud said.

"How's your wife and your new baby boy?"

Bud beamed. "Really well," he said.

Vince sensed a story coming and cut him off with another question. "How about that boy who got the DWI? What's his name, Garland?"

"I think he's doing all right."

They looked at the compressor installation and the refrigeration unit. It was coming along fine.

"Okay," Vince said, "let's talk to the men."

They reached the locker rooms right at shift change, just as Vince had planned. There were nine men present.

"Hi, men," Vince said. "Everything looks great. You boys keep up the good work. Anyone have any complaints? I see you don't have lockers yet. Does that bother you?"

"Sure does," one man said. "The other day I lost a watch."

"We'll get that fixed," Vince said. "Anyone else?"

"My personal H_2S sniffer's broken," another man said. "I feel pretty nervous around here without one."

"We'll get that fixed, too," Vince said. "Let's see, I need to talk to Garland."

Vince directed Garland into the office where he asked him about his drinking and explained to him that he was giving him one more chance, but that he could never tolerate a man who drank. Garland understood and assured him that he was going to his drinking classes. Vince wished him well.

Bud walked them back to the helipad. On the way, Vince made a detour and stopped at the shed where the H_2S re-injection pump was located. Once the H_2S gas was removed, it was pumped back into the formation that it came from.

"Let's take a look in here," Vince said.

Bud opened the door and showed him around.

"I need to pick up a sample of H$_2$S while I'm here."

"The chemical man came out and checked it just last week," Bud said.

Vince glowered at him.

"What could we put it in?" Bud said nervously.

"How about one of those stainless steel sample bottles that you use to sample the production gas?"

"I'd be worried pure H$_2$S would eat right through it."

Vince glowered at him again. Vince knew the H$_2$S wouldn't attack the type of stainless steel used.

Bud had reason to hesitate. Filling a bottle with pure H$_2$S was dangerous. A small amount released in an enclosure could kill every man inside. When Bud donned a mask, Vince stepped outside.

"Here she is," Bud said, bringing the bottle out. "I put quarter-inch caps on either end. The sniffer said it isn't leaking."

"Thanks Bud," Vince said, smiling. The bottle felt good in his hands.

They walked to the helipad and were in the air again in a puff of dust.

They stopped at a drilling rig where Vince studied the drilling log, then looked after the men's welfare. They were back in Salt Lake City by six o'clock.

As they landed at the Salt Lake Airport at six o'clock, Vince wondered if Trooper had gotten the reporter's phone tap installed.

25 – Ersatz Mothers

"You better take a nap." Butzsaw said when they were in their suite. "We're going out later tonight."

"Good idea," Vince replied.

He was just falling asleep when he heard the knuckles of his right hand rap the bedpost hard. Then he felt the pain.

He looked at his hand. It was against the bedpost, held tight by a rope. Bewildered, Vince looked at Butzsaw who was moving to the bottom of the bed. On the way, she grabbed a piece of rope. Suddenly Vince realized she was tying him up.

"You bitch, goddamn it!" Vince screamed.

He knew he had to be quick. Butzsaw was an expert with a rope. She could hog-tie a calf in seconds. He tried jumping out of bed, but he didn't make it. There was a noose around his right leg. Every time he moved, she pulled in a little more slack.

He reached into his pocket and pulled out a switchblade. Butzsaw didn't look concerned. She picked up a rope and formed a lasso.

Vince glanced at Butzsaw with a devilish smile. That rope in her hand wouldn't do her any good, he thought. With a flick of her wrist, she lassoed his arm to the shoulder. *No problem*, he thought. *When she pulls out slack, I'll be able to slip my hand out.* But when she pulled, the rope went toward the headboard. A second later, his left hand was tight against the corner post.

He tried to cut the rope, but couldn't reach it. He could see she'd planned it out. When Vince realized he was no longer in control, he got livid.

"You fucking cunt. You're fired."

"Fired?" Butzsaw said calmly, picking up a leather belt. "Looks like I'm the boss now." She struck Vince's face with the belt.

"Drop the knife," she said coldly.

When Vince hesitated, she struck his arm hard with the belt. A welt formed similar to the one across his face. When she raised the strap to strike again, he dropped the knife. He knew she'd beat him until he did.

She picked it up with half a smile, grabbed his shirt and began to cut.

"No, goddamn it," Vince screamed, kicking at her with his free foot. Butzsaw stuck the knife in the corner bedpost. The next time he kicked, she neatly lassoed his leg, then tied it off and pulled the slack out with his final kick. She walked around and pulled the knife out of the pole, a look of simple gratification on her face.

"What're you going to do?" Vince said, a worried look on his face.

"This isn't about what I'm going to do," Butzsaw said, calmly. "This is about what you're not going to do." Butzsaw cut his T-shirt away, then his pants and underwear. She moved close. The knife was sharp.

"Oh, Jesus, no," Vince said.

"You think I'm going to castrate you, Longto? Maybe I should. But that's not what I'm planning. You thought you were going to come here and not fuck me, didn't you? Well, it ain't never going to happen. You were going to save yourself for that little angel, huh Vince? What makes you think you can get into her pants? You're pushing what, forty? Lately you've only been good for once a night. This is gonna be your once."

"You going rape me? Where do you get these crazy ideas? You been hanging around Tom Patton? Has Vicki been talking to you? She's finished. You're all--" He froze as Butzsaw grabbed his testicles.

"God, you're stupid, Longto. Open your mouth again, and we'll be eating oysters tonight, and I don't mean the kind from the sea." Butzsaw threw the knife. It whizzed over his head and stuck in the headboard. She reached into her robe pocket and pulled out a tube of lubricating jelly, then squeezed half of it onto Vince's belly. He started to talk, then thought better of it.

She slid her robe off, scooped up a handful of the slick stuff, and started massaging his penis.

Vince felt like his body was being violated. He hated it. He wasn't going to let it happen. When he closed his eyes, he was on the lip of a volcano's crater, staring at the fiery lava as it boiled and exploded. His mission was to retrieve a sample of molten lava, and to do so he had to descend the cliff of the crater. It was working. He wasn't becoming erect. When Butzsaw quit, his eyes opened, and he looked with a smug smile. Butzsaw's strap filled his field of view the instant before it hit his face.

"Think you're being smart?" Butzsaw said, striking again, this time across his chest.

Vince looked at her face. As she wound up to strike again, he saw the determination that said she wouldn't stop beating him until she got her way. "Stop," Vince yelled.

"Well then, let's have another try." Butzsaw dropped the belt, scooped up another handful of the slick stuff and began massaging.

When he was partially erect, she stopped and offered him a snort of cocaine. He took it. She took a snort herself and went back to the job at hand. When he was fully erect, she mounted him and gave it to him just the way he liked.

"You know I love you, Vince," Butzsaw said when he was finished. "You're my favorite in the whole world," she was whispering in his ear. "No other man comes close." She kissed him softly.

These were the words Vince yearned to hear. She'd beat him for being bad, and that was fair. Her punishment had cleansed him and made him worthy of her love.

"Jean," he said, "when I'm out of town with you, you'll be the only one, I promise."

"I believe you, Honeybun," Butzsaw said, hugging him. She reached up, pulled the knife from the headboard, and with two quick swipes cut his hands free. "We have to get going now," she said, dropping the knife on his chest. Vince used the knife to finish cutting himself free.

"Jean," Vince said, through the bathroom door as he shaved. His voice carried a business tone. "Fire Bud, the gas plant manager. I told him to install lockers the last time I was here and it hasn't been done. And he doesn't have good control over his men. Two of them complained when they had the chance. They don't respect him, that's all I got to say. When men get too brave, they can cause all kinds of trouble--like forming unions. Who knows what else?"

Butzsaw smiled a happy demonic smile as she climbed into the shower. She delighted in firing men, especially managers. It gave her a feeling of control. She'd rub his nose in it first. He'd leave with his tail between his legs. She was still reveling in the idea when she stepped from the shower.

"You mind if I hang up the phone?" Vince said. When Butzsaw nodded, he tossed the receiver onto its cradle. Seconds later, it was ringing, and Vince had a quick conversation in Chinese then hung up. "It was Max, uh, I mean Trooper," Vince said. "The reporter went to a Chinese restaurant. Didn't stay long enough to eat. Then he went back to his room and called his boss, Peoples, and reported that the Chinese people at the restaurant had told him my Chinese was perfect, both Cantonese and Mandarin. The reporter and his boss couldn't believe it, and figured that I'd paid the Chinese off. Can you believe it? Why don't you check again on that big block of stock in the *Herald*? I'd like to fire those assholes."

Vince thought for a minute, then continued. "Peoples really gave reporter Rich a going-over for not asking about dead people in Russia, and how Rawhide used to have the lowest gas rates in the nation, and now the highest in the state."

"Those guys are assholes," Butzsaw said.

"The reporter promised to get to those subjects. Trooper's on his way over now to see him with the evidence of assault we have on tape and in photos. You better get on the phone and call Peoples. Do it now, so he has a chance to call the reporter before Trooper takes him to dinner. I'll shower."

Butzsaw called Wartsall first. "We have to talk to Peoples," she told the lawyer. "He's got ideas of muckraking. You want to dial him up. I'll tell you when to talk," she said.

Wartsall had conference calling ability. He did exactly as he was told.

"Hello, Mr. Peoples," Butzsaw said. "We have some serious problems here. When Mr. Longto didn't answer questions exactly as your reporter liked, he assaulted him. Vince said not to press charges, but now your reporter is making noises about bringing up some lies about nickel gas and dead people in Russia."

"Now, listen, Jean--" Peoples said in a stern voice.

"That's Miss Butzsaw, you asshole," she screamed. "We'll have your job and Anderson in jail if you print any lies."

"Miss Butzsaw, please--"

"Tell him, Wartsall," Butzsaw said.

"She's right," Poly Wartsall said, in his most sympathetic voice. "This is Jim Wartsall. We've met before." Wartsall had once successfully sued Peoples for libel. "I've looked into it," Wartsall said, "and it'd be defamation to print any of that nickel gas stuff. I've also looked into this problem with your reporter. Frankly, Jim, I think they're showing a lot of restraint in not bringing charges. As we talk, I'm faxing you a detailed report on both the assault and the defamation."

"Uh, yes, that just hit my desk," Peoples said.

"Fine, now, Mr. Peoples," Butzsaw continued. "We'll be picking up Mr. Anderson for dinner in thirty minutes. That gives you some time to go over that report from Mr. Wartsall. If your reporter brings up any old lies at dinner, it's off to jail with him."

"What she means," Wartsall said, "is that we're considering the assault charge. There's no connection between his going to jail and his bringing up trashy lies. Isn't that right, Jean? Remember, we talked about that?" Earlier, Wartsall had warned Butzsaw not to threaten blackmail. But she thought Wartsall was being overly cautious. She hated that in a lawyer. She had read the statute--it wasn't blackmail if the threat was to a third person.

"Thanks for the call," Peoples said, then cleared his throat. "We'll take a close look. Thank you."

"I think he'll come around," Wartsall said when Peoples was off the line.

"Goodbye Poly," Butzsaw said curtly as she dropped the receiver. As far as she was concerned he was a worthless piece of shit.

"So, have we got the reporter in line?" Vince said, stepping from his shower.

"Only time will tell," Butzsaw said, smiling.

"Oh, Jean, listen, I'll be back a little late tonight. You don't mind, do you?"

Butzsaw looked at Vince with the first mellow face she'd worn all day. "I've been awful selfish," she said, giving him a little hug. "You deserve to have a little fun, as hard as you've been working. Go ahead."

Butzsaw knew she didn't have to worry. This young girl couldn't give Vince what he really needed.

26 – Samurai and Flowers in Bloom

"Where we eating tonight, Honeybun?" Butzsaw said in the elevator, holding Vince's arm and cuddling up close.

"Forty-seven Samurai. It's a great Japanese restaurant. They cook the food in front of you. The cook puts on a show. They spin big salt, spice and pepper shakers like batons as they spice the food."

"Your ten-year-old is showing," Butzsaw said, sarcastically. "I don't have to eat with chopsticks, do I?"

"If you want to ruin a good Oriental meal by sticking metal into your mouth, go ahead," Vince said.

Sue and Vicki were already seated when Vince and Jean arrived. The table formed a horseshoe around the grill.

"It's difficult to imagine two prettier sights," Vince said, smiling at the girls.

Vicki was usually all business and dressed that way. Her husband was the jealous type, but he was a long way away, and tonight Vicki was in full bloom.

Vince seated Butzsaw, looked at Vicki, and excused himself. A moment later, Vicki met him in the lobby.

"It's all set up with Miss Sue Hansen, Sugar Plum," Vicki cooed.

"All set up?" Vince said.

"Well," Vicki's smile went flat and her head tilted, "you have to do something."

"What'd she say?"

"She doesn't like marijuana, but she doesn't mind if you smoke it. She's done coke, and she likes it. But she doesn't want to do any more."

"That sweet little thing? Done coke?"

"Little? She's strong as an ox. I saw her doing pull-ups in the gym, one after another. Boom boom boom. So you'd better be careful. And I hear she has some kind of a belt in karate--yellow or orange, or something."

Vince gave Vicki a disbelieving look.

"No, she doesn't look like she's full of muscle, but girls never do. She's the same size as Butzsaw, right?"

"Well, yeah, pretty much."

"Wrong. She outweighs Jean by twenty pounds."

"But she looks so good."

"Muscle's heavy. Don't forget, Vince, she was offered a tuition and books scholarship to that college in South Dakota. She could have been a swimmer or a volleyball player. It was her choice. Instead, you talked her into taking your full scholarship to the school of her choice. At Harvard she walked onto the volleyball team and ended up being their star player.

"And have you looked at her? Well, I guess you have. So, you can imagine that you're not the only swinger who's put the moves on."

"What about Tom Patton?"

"He doesn't do cocaine, Vince, Honey. Besides, he's too old for Sue." Vicki was patting Vince's bottom, pressing close. Everyone close to Vince knew Patton and he were the same age. "That's not to say there's anything wrong with Tommy Patton," Vicki said with a salacious smile.

Vince looked at her sharply. "So, what about tonight?" he said.

"I told her you might put the moves on and she better be careful."

"And?"

"She seemed to like the idea. I think she likes you. But it's all off if you don't play your cards just right."

Vince gave Vicki a disgusted look. She had just given herself an excuse in case Sue didn't cooperate. But Vince figured he had an advantage. Vince knew what Sue's life had been like in Russia. She had no close friends. The restaurants had bad food and worse service. The grocery stores were dismal affairs with nothing on the shelves. Just getting a chicken required standing in line for hours.

When Sue had gotten back just two days before, she was given an office in the Rawhide Gas building although she did no work for the utility. Her new office was full of welcome roses, all from Vince.

"What'd you tell her about Emily?" Vince said.

"Party line, baby. Told her it's in name only--that you two haven't slept together in years. Just live out your separate lives in that big old lonely mansion. Vince wants to keep it together for the benefit of the kids. He needs someone. Why shouldn't it be you?"

"You're my sweetheart." Vince hugged her in a genuine display of affection.

"Vince," Vicki said in a tone that signaled a new subject. "Would it be all right if Trooper joined us for dinner?"

Vince shot her a hateful glance. "For pollination? Absolutely not."

"Vince, Honey, don't be jealous," Vicki said. "You're my man, but a girl gets lonely sometimes and you have plans with Sue tonight. Trooper and I are just friends. Nothing will happen, I promise. I'm a married woman, remember? Besides, there should be another man at the table to balance it all out, you know--three women and three men. It'll all look *normal* that way."

Vince often had difficulty knowing what "normal" was.

"Okay. But he doesn't come to the hot tub party."

"Of course not. I thought he was going to stand guard?"

"That's right. And when you leave, it's straight to bed. Alone."

"No hanky panky, I promise." Vicki pressed against him sensuously. She was wearing his favorite perfume. She slid her body against his, hugged him then kissed him gently on his ear and whispered, "I love you. How could I help it? You're the best."

Vicki did it so well, Vince wondered if Butzsaw had helped her out.

When Vince returned to the table, Trooper was walking in with the reporter. Trooper winked at Vince. It could only mean the reporter had decided to back off. The resignation on Anderson's face confirmed it. Vicki grabbed Trooper's arm and showed him to a seat next to her. Trooper looked surprised.

Everyone drank wine but Vicki and Sue who had orders from Vince to wait. There would be champagne at the party later. The reporter started to ask questions of Vince, but Vince stopped him with a gesture.

"Mr. Anderson," Vince said, "we'll be flying to Little Rock in the morning. There'll be plenty of time to talk business."

Vince was lying. In the morning, Butzsaw would explain to the reporter that Vince had to rush off on an emergency, that it was very confidential. She'd been kind enough to make reservations for Anderson's flight back to Rawhide. She would give him all the materials he needed for his story.

When dinner was over, Vince rose and addressed the reporter. "You've been most pleasant company," Vince said, then he quickly departed with the two beautiful women. He ignored Anderson's subtle objections. Vince chuckled to himself. He knew what was going through the reporter's sick little mind. Anderson's expression said it all. He'd give anything to be able to print the "real" story of Vince and his dalliance with the two pretty women.

27 – Saunas and Dominance

Champagne was chilling in the limo. Vince poured. They toasted Sue and her return from Russia. Sue was happy from the effects of two glasses of champagne when they reached the Hilton.

"I have to get my swimming suit," Sue said as they walked toward the pool area.

Vince shot Vicki a look and she followed Sue.

"We look so nice," Vicki said to Sue. "There's *hors de oeuvres* to eat and champagne to drink. Let's stay dressed for a little while."

"You sure this isn't a set-up so Mr. Big can get into my pants?" Sue said.

"I'll be here the whole night. And I'll make excuses for you if you don't want to go into the sauna."

Sue hesitated. That word, sauna, jogged a distant memory. In Russia, Sue had a female friend from Finland. Sue went home with this friend once, and no trip to Finland was complete without a trip to the sauna.

Sue was tired when the ferry from Leningrad had reached Helsinki. She had a couple glasses of wine with her friend, then they headed for the sauna. Sue thought they'd walked in the wrong door at first. She grabbed her friend and dragged her back out.

"What's wrong?" her friend said in Russian. Her friend could speak English, but they were used to Russian.

"We went into the men's sauna," Sue said, her eyes big.

Her friend gave Sue a confused look, then said, "Yes, we have men in Finland."

"Read my lips," Sue said, pointing. "There are naked men in there."

"It is custom to be naked in the sauna."

Sue was beside herself.

At last her friend seemed to understand. "In Finland," she said, "men and women use the same sauna. You can leave your towel on if you prefer."

If Sue Hansen had just arrived from America, she would have turned around and left, but she had been meeting with entirely strange and unexpected circumstances in Russia on a daily basis, and adjusting constantly. This would just be one more adjustment. She broke out laughing. "Americans," Sue said, "we have such funny ideas."

Sue didn't bother with the towel. She didn't notice anyone giving her a second look. A good-looking Swedish man talked to her, but nothing in his look suggested that he found her more interesting because of her lack of clothes. He said in English, "You two Russian?"

"I'm American, and Anya Liisa," Sue gestured to her friend, "is Finnish."

"I never would have guessed you for an American," the Swede said, probably intending flattery.

What a way to meet men, Sue had thought. The "big" questions were answered even before the first date.

Now Sue looked at Vicki who was smiling warmly, shrugged and headed for the pool. Vince popped another bottle of champagne when they arrived. The air was warm. The conversation was good. Soon Sue was relaxed and happy.

When Vicki stood and took off her clothes, Sue watched impassively.

"I'm going for a swim," Vicki said. She looked like the blue-eyed girl from a Renoir painting. She walked to the water's edge and dove in. "Come on, Vince," Vicki yelled.

"In a minute," Vince shouted back. "Come take a toke first." Vince held up the marijuana cigarette he'd just rolled.

Vicki climbed out, grabbed a towel and walked over. Sue took it all in stride.

"Wow. This grass is dyne-O-mite," Vicki said, exhaling her third toke. She turned around, dropped the towel, and then walked slowly on her toes to the pool. Her arms waved in the air as if she were doing a ballet. She dived in and swam under the water to the other side.

"Come on you chicken," Vicki said from the far side of the pool.

"I don't have my swimming suit," Vince protested.

"I won't look," Sue said.

Vince didn't have masculine lines to complement the feminine grace of his companions. The only thing he had going for him was his air of confidence. He was soon undressed and in the pool.

"Okay, Sue, it's your turn," Vicki said.

"I won't look," Vince said.

Vince didn't watch when Sue got in but he figured Danny Trooper had. He knew about Trooper's KGB past when he was known as Maxime Efremov. Vince had seen Trooper's impressive photo collection.

Vince found himself hoping Trooper was taking pictures, and cussed himself for not thinking about it earlier. Vince wasn't concerned about his own pictures. Trooper would be the big loser if he tried using pictures against him. Trooper would lose his job, maybe even his life. Besides, who would pay good money for pictures that had no more value than the ability to embarrass?

On the other hand, Vince would pay to see Tom Patton embarrassed. Vince could have his brother, Mike, show the pictures to oil people at the Pump. Patton didn't go there much anymore, but the word would get back. Maybe Vince could even break the news in private. It would be so much fun to see the pain on Patton's face as he discovered his dream girl was nothing more than a high class call girl.

Tom, Vince could say, *we go back a long way. I knew you'd like to know about this.* Then he'd slip the best picture in front of Patton, and watch him squirm. He'd have to get tips from Trooper on the best way to do it, Vince thought. Then he could tell Patton about the pictures that had already made the rounds. *I'm really sorry*, Vince would say in his best kiss-ass voice.

As Vince reveled in these thoughts, he became even more determined to have sex with Sue. That way, he could also confess that to Patton. *She wasn't a good girl, Tom. You're better off without her. Hell, I bagged her in the sauna. Never saw a looser piece.*

Vince didn't care that Sue's reputation would also be damaged. As far as he was concerned, she was nothing but an extension of Patton. Shouldn't she be punished for preferring Patton to him?

Vince had confided to Trooper his desire to see Tom Patton dead, and Trooper had readily adopted Vince's obsession. Vince was amazed at Trooper's creativity. There were so many ways to kill a man and not get caught.

Vince knew Sue would go for Patton again when she got back from Russia. Patton was a viable male again. Vince was surprised that Patton had risen so quickly after going broke in the oil business. Vince cursed Butzsaw for not keeping him better informed. He could easily have stopped Patton's rise, even from Russia. A lawyer's reputation is such a fragile thing.

Sue dived in and swam the length of the pool underwater. Vicki and Vince watched her shadow under the water as it returned to her starting point, then back to where Vince and Vicki were standing, where she gracefully made her appearance. She looked as good soaking wet as she did all made up. She smiled as she approached her two companion nudists.

"Where'd you learn to swim like that?" Vince said, admiringly.

"My dad taught me to swim in his hot tub when I was a baby. I can't remember not being able to swim."

"Sue's a diver, too," Vicki offered. "She was state champ in high school."

"Did you dive in college?" Vince said.

"There wasn't time."

"Dive for us?" Vince said, thinking it would give Trooper great photo opportunities, hoping again he had his camera, and wondering if he could get a message to him.

"Okay," Sue said.

After a couple of beautiful dives, Sue joined up with them again.

"Are you cold, Vince?" Vicki said. "You got goose bumps all over. Come on Sue, let's warm him up, poor baby."

Vicki walked over to Vince and pressed against his side, then stretched her hands beyond him in a gesture to Sue.

Sue hesitated, then came over. "He is cold," Sue said, pressing against him.

"Come on," Vicki said, tugging on the group of huddled bodies, "let's move him to the sauna." Vicki gave Vince a look that could only mean: *I'm due for a raise, Honeybun.* Vince gave her a reassuring nod.

As soon as they were in the sauna, Sue poured water on the rocks.

"Not too much," Vince said. "That steam will burn you."

"Not if you don't move," Sue said sitting motionlessly.

When the steam subsided, Vicki began giving Vince a back rub.

"It's too hot in here for me," Vicki said. "I'll be back in a minute."

"You just want a cigarette," Vince said. "When are you going to quit that filthy habit?"

"We're from Rawhide," Vicki said. "It's the one last place in the United States where smoking's still cool."

Vince and Sue looked at each other as if to say, *That's news to us.*

"You have to finish rubbing my back," Vince said. "It feels good."

"Sue, rub his back," Vicki pleaded. "I'll be right back."

"Okay," Sue said, taking up Vicki's post.

"Hey," Vince said, "not so rough. So, I hear you used to date Tom Patton." Vince said it casually. "It ended when he went broke."

Sue smiled, "We didn't really break up. We were always just friends."

"I heard the county attorney--Porkchop, or whatever her name was--wanted to press charges but she couldn't talk your mom into signing the complaint."

In fact, it was Vince who had talked to the county attorney. Since when's being friends a crime?" Sue said pointedly.

"When it involves carnal knowledge," Vince said. "You aren't the only one, you know. He molested young girls in Denver, too."

Sue was getting irritated, and wondering what was going on.

"Do you know why Tom Patton went out of business?" Vince said.

"Why *did* he go out of business?" Sue said, getting her composure back. She was really interested in what Vince had to say.

"Mismanagement. I own all his old oil fields now, and every one is making a handsome profit."

"That's incredible," Sue said, enthusiastically, "especially when you consider the oil price is lower now than it has ever been."

"That's right," Vince said, smugly.

"Jean was telling me the oil comes out of the ground at eleven gravity or so, and when you sell it, it's thirty gravity, which sells for almost five dollars a barrel more. How do you do that?"

Vince described the device he used, in general at first. Sue engaged him in a charming way and drew a more detailed response by pretending to be interested in the science.

Tom Patton had told her all about POCUS and his perplexity at how it hadn't worked. He told her how he had hoped it would protect him from a big drop in oil prices. He told her about Vince Longto being in charge of its development. From the moment Patton had said that, Sue suspected Vince had sabotaged his plan. She had known Vince Longto. He'd frequented the Pump back in the boom days. She'd watched him, and talked to her grandpa, Tony, about him.

She wished again she hadn't taken Vince's scholarship. She thought about how she'd done it to hurt Tom Patton, who not only had broken the biggest date of her life, he'd also broken off their relationship because of something that had happened in his *business*. Surely he understood she loved *him*, not his stupid business. Thinking back now, she realized that it was probably her age that was Patton's biggest problem.

Sue looked down and recoiled at the sight of Vince's naked body. She'd heard enough, but she knew better than to let

Vince know what she thought. "What do you suppose happened to Vicki?" Sue said, feeling uneasy.

"It's been so long since she had a cigarette," Vince said, "she probably decided to have two, or maybe she's talking to Trooper. I saw them looking at each other. You want me to give you a back rub now?" Vince said.

"Okay," Sue said, thinking it would relieve her from having to look at Vince.

"Did you like the roses in your room?" Vince said as he began rubbing her back.

Sue heard something in Vince's voice and in that instant realized she'd been set up, that Vicki wasn't coming back.

"Someone as pretty as you needs nice things," Vince said. "You sure have a nice back and nice legs, too," he said as he began massaging her thighs.

Sue was becoming aroused. She liked it, and she didn't like it. She liked sex. On the other hand, she didn't like getting set up, and now she was positive she didn't like this man.

"I'm sure you won't have a problem satisfying the remainder of your contract," Vince said. When Sue had accepted the Rawhide Gas scholarship, she'd agreed to work for three years for Rawhide Gas, and if she didn't, or if she was terminated for cause, she had to repay the cost of the scholarship.

Sue understood the threat. Vince was saying if she didn't have sex with him, he'd fire her, which always included a smear campaign, and she'd owe him a hundred thousand dollars. Sue thought for a minute about Vicki, and realized that if Vicki would stoop to set her up like this, she'd also lie for Vince.

Sue thought when she signed the contract that the "terminated only for cause" provision would protect her, but she'd since learned that Vince Longto could find "cause" to discharge the Virgin Mary. He stopped at nothing to get his way. He had incredible temper tantrums just to accomplish that goal. Sue had heard about an incident a year earlier where he'd called a secretary a "stupid cunt" in front of everyone. At the sexual harassment trial, all of Vince's employees lied for him.

Now, if Sue said no, she'd be in for a fight. What the hell, she thought, wasn't he a billionaire? She stiffened at the thought. She had to get out of there. In a clear, matter of fact voice she said, "You have to use a condom. Who knows where that thing of yours has been? I could get pregnant."

She saw Vince glance around for an instant with a confused look. Sue figured it was her best chance and grabbed a towel.

"You're trying to seduce me, aren't you?" Vince said.

"It doesn't look like you're in the mood," Sue said, glancing at his partially flaccid penis, amazed at how little it was. She slipped quickly out the door.

Moments later, Vince burst from the sauna. "You're nothing but a whore. Trying to seduce me. Well then, get your ass back in here and I'll do it."

Sue could still hear him screaming as she climbed onto the elevator.

28 – Still Friends?

"Where's Vince going this morning?" Patton asked Claude, the Rawhide airport base operator. Patton had just pulled up in his airplane to a place where Claude was pumping jet fuel into Longto's sleek jet plane. It was morning and the air was still cool.

"A suit," Claude said, giving Patton a wide-eyed look. Patton usually flew in blue jeans and a leather jacket.

"I got court in Utah," Patton said, apologetically.

Patton had spoken to Vince earlier that morning at The Pump, and told Vince he was on his way to Salt Lake. Vince had said his plane was going to Seattle. Patton was curious to see if Vince had told Claude the same thing. He'd long ago learned not to believe a word Vince Longto said. Patton looked at Claude who still hadn't answered his question.

"Vince isn't going," Claude said after giving Patton a sly glance. "They're going to Seattle. Were going to stop in Idaho for fuel. Now they're stopping in Salt Lake. A girl's going."

"A girl?"

"Just back from Russia," Claude said, turning his head in a way that kept Tom Patton from seeing his expression.

"Sue Hansen?"

"I guess that's her name," Claude said, covering his face with his hand.

"How long has she been back from Russia?" Patton said, excitedly.

"Saw her a week ago--she made a trip with Vince and Butzsaw."

"How'd she look?" Patton said this with a worried look.

"You mean, is she fat?" Claude said, laughing, then pausing to study Patton's worried face. "She looked fine, just like before."

Suddenly Patton became alert and looked toward the terminal building.

"Haven't seen her this morning," Claude said.

"God, Claude, she looked so good the first time I saw her--" Patton's voice trailed off.

"That's the sort of thing that will get a fella in trouble. How can you look at a fifteen-year-old anyway?"

"She was seventeen. And it's easy. You bug out your eyes, drop your jaw, and gawk."

"Better stop drooling? You're gonna ruin your nice new suit." Claude loved teasing Patton.

"And who says anything was going on?"

Claude gave Patton a funny look. "If anyone knew, it was me. I saw you two run off in your pretty little Balanca airplane a dozen times. And since you were always sneaking around, there were probably a hundred other times I didn't see."

Claude knew Patton as well as anyone. Patton had rented Claude's back shop for a year. Claude had watched every day as Patton and his boy worked on their new plane.

"Where's the boy?" Claude said.

"Off to college," Patton said proudly.

"Already? At Wyoming like the rest of you Pattons?"

"Laramie, Wyoming. That's three generations now."

"I saw Billy wrestle at the state tournament a couple months ago. He's grown up, all right. Can he whip you?"

"I was state champ, too." Patton said with a big smile. "Boy," Patton said, changing the subject, "this sure is a pretty plane."

"Sure is," Claude answered giving Patton a knowing smile. Patton was state champion, but not with the same aplomb as Billy. Patton had barcly won his championship bout. On the other hand, Billy just went out and pinned the guy. Billy was undefeated on the year. No one came close.

"Does Vince still have that new pilot?" Patton said, brushing the windblown hair out of his eyes.

"You mean Trooper? Sure does."

"What an ass. I figured Vince would get rid of him right away."

"Me, too," Claude said. "One thing about Vince Longto--predictable he ain't."

"You sure they're going to Salt Lake?" Patton said, thinking that it would be a great place to meet up again with Sue.

"Heard Trooper call in his flight plan just minutes ago. They have to stop somewhere to re-fuel."

"When they leaving?"

"What do you care? Where you going Tommy Patton?" Claude said, chuckling again with sarcasm and shaking his head.

"Salt Lake."

"What a coincidence. Too bad they aren't staying there overnight." Claude's eyes were gleaming.

"So, when they leaving?"

"Half hour, I suppose."

Patton thought about the possibilities. If he met her that morning when she arrived in Rawhide, they wouldn't have much time. And then he'd been living in Denver before. In Salt Lake he might look like the big-city-man she'd known. He quickly turned and ran toward his plane.

"Don't you need fuel?" Claude said.

"She isn't seventeen anymore," Patton said as he pulled his canopy closed. A half-hour lead could give him enough time to beat Vince's jet to Salt Lake, he thought. He'd be standing outside the executive terminal as she approached. Maybe inside would be better--the little bit of gray he was sporting wasn't visible out of the sun.

Patton fired up his little plane, started taxiing and at the same time he started talking on the radio. "Salt Lake Center, Cozy-One-Four-Niner-Charlie-Zulu," he said, "ready to copy my instrument flight plan to Salt Lake City."

"Cozy-One-Four-Niner-Charlie-Zulu, you're cleared to Salt Lake City via Victor Two-six. Climb to sixteen-thousand-five-hundred. Report your departure on this frequency. Squawk one-zero-niner-three. Cleared for departure."

When Tom Patton heard the word "cleared," he checked for traffic, then quickly pulled onto the runway. He didn't need to write down his clearance because he had a little tape recorder wired into his audio panel that did that for him. He was at full power before he was out of his turn. Within seconds he was gear up and on course for his first waypoint en route to Salt Lake City.

She stared after Patton's plane as it departed. It wasn't what she'd imagined. Vince called it a little toy. She had been cautious of Vince's words, suspicious that he was trying to mislead her. Nevertheless, the words had an impact, and the mental picture she had of Patton's airplane had been that of a tiny thing like an ultralight with an open cockpit.

When Sue Hansen arrived at the terminal, and looked at the airplanes, her gaze locked onto Tom Patton. She liked what she saw. She wondered what he was getting excited about. She wanted to come out and say hello, but she was nervous, and Patton seemed so distracted. She thought there would be a better time.

She stared after Patton's plane as it departed. It wasn't what she'd imagined. Vince called it a little toy. She had been cautious of Vince's words, suspicious that he was trying to mislead her. Nevertheless, the words had an impact, and the mental picture she had of Patton's airplane had been that of a tiny thing like an ultralight with an open cockpit.

Patton didn't get into the air like the other airplanes, lumbering along, struggling for altitude. In seconds he was off the runway, and when the landing gear popped into the plane's belly, she looked even sleeker. When he turned, his wings snapped smartly into a forty-five degree bank, all the while gaining altitude at an incredible rate. In a moment he was out of sight. This was the kind of airplane Sue had hoped Tom Patton would be flying. She took a deep breath as she stared at the spot in the sky where he disappeared.

Sue thought back on a time they had flown to Salt Lake. He was flying in the same direction. Would she see him there?

She'd worried about him over the years. She heard he'd taken to drinking, that he was fat, bald and gray. Sue's eyes grew narrow as she realized that Vince Longto was the probable source of these negative reports. Rosy had said that Patton had been asking about her. Rosy said she could tell he still wanted her. Seeing him now she was thankful nothing had happened with Vince Longto because she knew Tom Patton would never forgive her.

29 – *Sally*

As soon as *Sally's* gear were up and she was on course, Tom Patton began turning a big red knob on the aircraft's dash. Each turn moved a butterfly gate valve located in the exhaust line five degrees and began diverting exhaust gas into the blades of a small, high-tech turbine that was connected by a shaft to a second turbine.

The second turbine compressed fresh air and fed it as "ram" air to her engine. Compression increased the amount of oxygen available for combustion and therefore increased horsepower. The ram air passed through two large radiators called intercoolers to dissipate the heat of compression.

The turbocharging system made *Sally's* engine think it was still at sea level, even when she was very high. That was important. The same horsepower at altitude, where there was less air and therefore less friction on the airframe, resulted in a higher speed.

Patton could overboost *Sally's* engine and develop even more power, but doing so caused rapid engine wear. Too much of an overboost would quickly destroy the engine.

Patton had salvaged *Sally's* engine from a wrecked Subaru Legacy. He'd found a mechanic who worked on racecars and got him to boost the little engine's horsepower.

Sally's "redline" speed was 252 miles per hour. Patton had personally tested her to that speed. She could easily reach that speed in level flight at sea level, which meant she couldn't be flown low at full power. But at 25,000 feet, and overboosted, she flew 350 miles per hour. That didn't violate the redline speed, because at that altitude, it put the same stress on the airframe as 220 miles per hour did at sea level. This is the same speed that appeared on the aircraft's airspeed indicator.

Patton was flying light. He carried no baggage and had just enough fuel to get to Salt Lake City. In this configuration, his little plane could climb almost twice as fast as Vince Longto's jet. In just a couple minutes he was level at 16,500 feet. To get the speed he needed to beat Vince Longto's jet to Salt Lake, he'd have to go higher. He called the controller.

"Salt Lake Center, this is Cozy-One-Four-Niner-Charlie-Zulu. I'd like it higher please--would flight level two-five be available?" Flight level twenty-five was the same as twenty-five thousand feet under normal conditions.

"I'm showing you as a single-engine plane. Can you go that high?"

"Shouldn't be a problem," Patton said, in his best pilotease-- kind of a singsong Arkansas accent, about half an octave lower than he normally talked. He smiled to himself as he thought about the show he'd soon be giving the controllers.

"Cozy-One-Four-Niner-Charlie-Zulu," the controller said, "climb and maintain Flight Level two-five, report when level."

Patton pulled back hard on *Sally's* stick. In seconds he converted half his considerable speed to two thousand feet of altitude, then he settled in at his fastest rate of climb for that altitude.

Patton had plenty of oxygen for the trip in the main bottle, but out of habit, he checked his little reserve oxygen tank. It worked fine.

"Cozy-One-Four-Niner-Charlie-Zulu is level at Flight Level two five," he reported.

"Cozy-Niner-Charlie-Zulu, what do you have in that thing, a rocket? The altitude read-out on my screen was changing so fast, it was a blur."

"Not exactly," Patton said, again in his best pilotease.

"I show you cruising at three hundred knots. What did you say you were, a Cozy?"

These were the moments in life Patton lived for, but he was careful not to let anyone in pilot radio-land know that. "It's a two point two liter Subaru Engine, bored to two point four liter, balanced for high RPM and normalized with a turbocharger." Patton sounded nonchalant. "It weighs less than the engine in a

Cessna one-seven-two, but develops as much horsepower as a Mooney. If I don't mind how much fuel I use, I can overboost it with the turbo and develop even more horsepower."

"What's a Cozy?"

"A big Long EZ. Burt Rutan's best ever design. A guy in Phoenix, Nat Puffer, modified the Long EZ by making it wide enough for two people in front, then named it a Cozy. It turned out to be very aerodynamic. It's actually faster than many long EZ's. I made a couple modifications. One big change was retractable gear. That increased my top end by twenty knots."

"You normally cruise at three hundred knots?"

Patton glanced at his airspeed indicator. Once level flight was achieved, airspeed gradually increased for several minutes. "I'm showing better than three hundred and fifty miles per hour, which is more than three hundred knots, which is where I cruise at this altitude," *when I'm in a big hurry,* Patton thought. He liked saying speed in miles per hour since it was a bigger number.

"How much fuel you burning?"

Fuel! To fly high or through clouds a pilot was required to have a one-hour reserve at destination. At 16,500 feet Patton had about a twenty-five minute reserve. At flight level twenty-five, his reserve was below that. Before answering the question, Patton checked his on-board computers. Fuel burn was thirteen gallons per hour. He could fly like that for fifty minutes. Estimated time of arrival was fifty-two minutes.

Boy, that's cutting it close, he thought, but he could still make it because the on-board computers didn't take into consideration the almost four miles of altitude that would allow him to glide without burning any fuel.

"Thirteen gallon an hour," Patton said. "That's half a gallon an hour more than I planned. At that rate, I'll be getting short on fuel. Would you mind making sure I get sequenced right in?"

"Should be no problem. You'll be arriving at a good time."

"There's a Citation behind me, same point of origin. If he starts getting close, would you mind slowing him down just a little for traffic? I'd sure like to beat him in."

"Well--I don't know."

"The owner's a rich oilman."

"You want to get us in trouble?"

"Don't do anything that will get you guys in trouble," Patton said tongue in cheek.

Patton usually flew past the almost 14,000-foot spire of King's peak at an altitude of 13,000 feet or even lower. He liked to come as close to the rock face as he dared. The view was breathtaking. Jagged granite pointed in all directions. There were glaciers in deep canyons. The feeling of speed was real.

But high up, the air was smooth–there was nothing to give a feeling of speed. The mountains and clouds were distant and moved by slowly. His real speed could only be read on the instruments.

As the engine droned there was little to do but watch the engine and navigation instruments. It gave him time to think. The first thing that popped into Patton's head was how much he disliked Vince's pilot, Danny Trooper. He was one of those macho hotshots--tall, good-looking, and arrogant. Around other pilots he acted like a TV news anchor in the presence of commoners. He was concerned, interested in others, and yet phony. He was paternalistic toward Patton, who normally kept his cool around anyone. But around this guy, his blood boiled.

Patton's gaze tended to fixate on the instrument that indicated rate of fuel burn. At 13 gallons per minute, he barely had enough fuel for the flight. Once in a while it would jump up or down one- and sometimes two-tenths, of a gallon. Every time it jumped up, an alarm sounded telling him he didn't have enough fuel for the flight.

He was worried that the controllers would re-route him or make him hold while another aircraft landed. To avoid that, Patton would have to declare a fuel emergency. The thought horrified him. Vince's Citation was right behind him. They'd hear it all.

Patton's fuel situation wasn't life threatening. He could land at a different airport short of Salt Lake City, or pull back on power to improve his mileage. As long as he was high, he could glide to any airport within forty miles. He had experience with forced landings.

When his boy flew along, they liked to simulate total power failure for the practice. They often glided right into an airport, and that was with a whole lot less altitude than he now had.

Sally had five fuel tanks in all. He rarely used the long-range tip tanks, but from time to time he ran fuel through them. At her normal high cruise speed of 320 miles per hour, she had a range of more than 2,000 miles. She cost a little more than a dime a mile to operate, including maintenance, and cost him less than $20,000 to build.

A nice twin like a Cessna Caravan II, with twinjet props had a price tag of more than a million dollars, but its top end was less than 300 miles per hour and it could only fly twelve hundred miles non-stop.

The gauge on the sump tank was dropping. It meant his main tanks were empty. He opened the valves to the tip tanks and left them open until all residual fuel had time to drain into the sump tank.

"Cozy-One-Four-Niner-Charlie-Zulu descend to seven thousand, this is Salt Lake Center." Patton was getting close.

"Down to seven thousand, Niner-CZ."

If he could dive with power, he could come in at a greater speed. But he had to be careful not to exceed the speed he'd tested his plane for. A control surface might flutter, just like a curtain fluttering in the wind. If that happened, his aircraft could shake to pieces in less than a second. It would look like an explosion. Wings would fall off. The fuselage might even come apart. Speed tended to induce flutter.

He pushed the nose over and got *Sally* going as fast as he dared. He was sixty miles out, burning 11.5 gallon per hour. At this speed, he'd arrive in sixteen minutes and burn 2.6 gallons, leaving two tenths of a gallon at landing. That was really pushing it. His gauges and instruments were as accurate as he could find, but still they had some error.

He pulled back on power and, as his speed bled off, he gradually trimmed her nose higher. He hated to do it, but the risk of running out of fuel was too great. He'd also need a little fuel to taxi, because running out of fuel on the taxiway could be as humiliating as declaring a fuel emergency.

When he passed through 20,000 feet, he was twenty-six miles out, close enough to coast in, and he still had more than a half gallon of fuel.

"Cozy-One-Four-Niner-Charlie-Zulu, Salt Lake approach, expect a left base for one-six right."

"This is Niner-Charlie-Zulu, you think I could land on one-six left?" Patton said, pointedly. He'd have to taxi a lot further if he landed on the right runway.

"We have a Citation coming in on one-six left, but ask the tower."

Damn, that's Vince's plane. Those guys must have left right after me. "Where's the Citation?" Patton said.

"Seven miles behind you."

He's bound by the same airport speed limit, Patton thought, so he can't catch up. Patton could still beat him to the terminal.

"Salt Lake approach, this is Citation-One-Six-Five-Victor-Lima on a fifteen mile left base for one-six left. Will that *little* plane be a problem?" It was Trooper calling from Vince's jet.

What a jerk, Patton thought. He'd overheard Patton talking to the controllers. Trooper was suggesting that Patton's plane was so slow the controller should make him go around to let Trooper in.

"I doubt it Citation-Victor-Lima," the controller said, "his speed is fifteen knots higher than yours, and we have him on the right, you're on the left. Cozy-One-Four-Niner-CZ, better slow it down."

"Niner-CZ," Patton said grinning.

"Cozy-Niner-CZ," the controller said, "contact tower, on one-one-eight point three, good day."

"Good day." Patton switched radios.

"Salt Lake tower," Patton said, "Cozy-One-Four-Niner-CZ, could I get in on the left?"

"Cozy One-Four-Niner-Charlie-Zulu," the tower guy said in an exaggerated way, "you're the guy we've been waiting for. The entire last shift from approach control is up here just to see you land. They want to see for themselves what kind of a plane you are."

Sabotaged. These guys just wanted to look at *Sally.* There was a diagonal runway that could be used as a taxiway that Patton could use to get quickly across the airport. To do so meant he had to set *Sally* down right at the end of runway one-six. The guys in the tower would have to look fast.

"One-Four-Niner-Charlie-Zulu, cleared to land one-six right."

"Thank you Salt Lake, cleared to land. Niner-CZ." Patton set her down hot on the very end of the runway. Then, holding her down with her flight controls, he turned her onto the diagonal runway. When she skidded in the turn, he pushed *Sally's* stick forward until he had enough traction to stop her from skidding.

He came out of the turn then taxied so fast, he could start flying again just by pulling back on the stick. He was burning three gallons an hour, a tenth every two minutes.

"One-Four-Niner-Charlie-Zulu, hold short of one-six right, traffic landing is a Citation."

"Damn," Patton said to himself. *He's two miles out. There's time to cross.* Patton jammed on his brakes, and barely came to a stop before the barrier. He stared wistfully at the Citation on short final and his rate of fuel burn. When it clicked off another tenth, Patton looked at the sump fuel gauge. It said the tank was empty. As he waited, he hit a fist into his hand. He watched as Vince's jet landed and turned off way before his position. When he finally added power to cross, the engine coughed, sputtered, and almost died. When he pumped the throttle the engine flared up, and he charged across the runway.

Only a little farther.

The engine sputtered, then died. He was coasting and it was quiet.

He didn't make it all the way off the runway. He jumped out and, as the Citation pulled up, he pushed his little plane--now really light with no fuel in her wings--to a spot off the runway. It wasn't a real parking spot, but good enough for a little while. He straightened his tie and headed for the terminal.

The line crew was rolling out the carpet for Vince's jet. As Patton approached, Sue Hansen's left leg stretched elegantly onto the red carpet.

30--Anticipation

Patton took a deep breath when he saw Sue. She was more stunning than the image he'd been carrying. She was more confident, her dress more refined. He felt his head, neck, and forearms tingle as thousands of individual hairs stood straight up.

"Well, hi," Sue said with obvious enthusiasm. "What are you doing here?"

"Business," Patton said, too nervous to say more, and feeling a little inadequate now that he was just a lawyer.

"Patton. Hey, little buddy," Trooper said in a semi-voice of authority and speaking with an accent that made the figure of speech sound strange, "What you doing parked way out there?" As Trooper approached, Sue turned away.

"When you have a plane like that," Patton said, "you have to get it far away from the people you *don't* want around."

"You must've left Rawhide before sunrise," Trooper said. "Here it is nine-thirty, and you're in Salt Lake already. Where'd you stop for fuel?"

Patton could feel his ears begin to glow.

A line boy pulled up with a car. "Hey, Sue," Trooper said. "Here's the courtesy car I requested. Jump in."

"Mind if I freshen up?" Sue said in a way that gave Trooper no options.

"What are you doing in Salt Lake?" Sue said, pleasantly, inviting Patton with her eyes to walk with her.

"Defamation case." She was so mature, Patton thought. He was very proud of her. Harvard. He knew she was smart, but....

"That sounds interesting," Sue said.

"I hear you're going to Seattle," Patton said.

"Where'd you hear that?"

"Vince mentioned it to me at the Pump this morning."

Sue looked at Patton in a way that reminded him that she knew exactly how he felt about Vince Longto.

"He makes a point to be friendly," Patton said. "He's probably setting me up."

"Stopped for fuel," Sue said. "We'll be here for a couple hours. Something about a problem with the cargo." Sue stopped, looked at Patton, and touched his sleeve. When he was looking, she said, "We'll be spending the night in Seattle. I hear there're a lot of nice places to eat there."

Patton hesitated for a minute, then said, "You know, I have some business in Seattle that I need to take care of. I should be able to get out of here in time. Seattle's such a nice town."

"That would be wonderful," Sue said enthusiastically. "What do you have to do in Seattle?"

"Well, you know," he stammered. Patton glanced at Sue and realized she was baiting him. She was still the same girl, and old feelings of affection were welling up. "I have some old friends there," Patton said grinning. "Was hoping we could get connected on a really good deal."

Sue smiled broadly. She looked like she was blushing. "We're going into the city," she said pleasantly, giving Patton a sideways glance. "Like a ride?"

"You bet."

"I'll be right back." She gave his hand a nice squeeze. As he watched her walk away, he thought for an instant about giving her a ride to Seattle, but they'd get there long before him, and she'd have things to do.

Patton walked over to Trooper's copilot, Dave Hech, a long-time friend. Hech was busy with the Seattle flight plan. Patton didn't say anything. His heart was pounding so hard he was worried his voice would quaver.

Dave Hech was an old Colorado rancher who'd lost too many cattle in a blizzard, and had to sell out. He'd become an aircraft mechanic and Vince had hired him in that capacity. Vince prompted him to become a pilot so he could fly as copilot when Vince didn't go. Dave had helped Patton with *Sally* in just about every phase of her construction, but especially with her power plant.

"Hi, Tom," Dave said, smiling broadly. "Cat got your tongue?" Dave was looking in the direction where Sue had disappeared. "Figuring on picking up where you left off?"

"What you carrying that's so heavy?" Patton said, glancing at Dave's weight and balance sheet.

Dave grabbed the papers, picked them up, and then slammed them down on their face. Patton put his hands up and shook his head as if to say he wouldn't tell.

"Gold," Dave said, glancing around, "supposedly, right out of Russia. But I don't know--there's something fishy about it. Weighs a whole ton."

A ton was a lot of weight for a Citation. Patton had a hunch and went into the flight planning room and found a book with performance figures on Vince's Citation. Seattle was only 700 miles away. Nevertheless, as hot as it was going to be at their planned departure time, and considering their weight, they wouldn't be able to take off with enough fuel to go all the way to Seattle.

Patton glanced at the map, and wondered what they were doing because Salt Lake was a poor choice to re-fuel. Somewhere in Idaho would have allowed a single stop.

Patton hung around the flight planning room for a minute pretending to work on a flight plan. Pretty soon Hech came in and called flight service to file his flight plan. Patton got close and copied it all down. They'd re-fuel in Walla Walla, Washington.

Patton became alert when he heard Sue coming. He absolutely could not believe how good she looked. He wished he wasn't so nervous.

They dropped Patton off at his hotel. He checked into his room and began making phone calls. First thing he had to do was get out of the court hearing he'd come for. He dialed the

number of Mike Quail, the Utah lawyer on the case Patton
was working on. "Hi, Mike--Tom Patton."

"What's going on?"

It was a pretrial hearing. Important issues would be
determined, including the jury instructions. If Patton wasn't
going to be there, he needed a damn good excuse.

"I'm not going to be able to make it, Mike. Trouble with
Sally."

"Who's *Sally?*" Quail said.

"My airplane. It's technical. But don't worry. A friend of
mine went to Salt Lake this morning on business. His plane
was full so I couldn't catch a ride, but I gave him all my
materials to bring over to you. He's going to leave them at
the front desk at the Hilton. They should be there now.
There are three mini-briefs in the materials covering the
major issues. For your arguments, you can read those briefs,
then give them to the judge. You won't have any trouble."

Mike Quail was an experienced attorney but he didn't
like the courtroom, and defamation was an especially
difficult area. Patton hadn't gotten stellar grades in law
school, but he had the right qualities to be a good trial
attorney.

Patton had competed in Golden Gloves boxing. He
usually won. Fighters like Gerry Spence, once a
heavyweight boxer, made good trial attorneys.

When Patton left the materials with the desk clerk there
was an urgent message for him from the airport. Patton
called them.

"Hey," the line boy at the airport said, "are you the guy
who parked your little plane near the runway?"

"Yeah, anything wrong with that?"

"Well, uh," the boy stammered, "the wind came up and
started to blow her away. We got her tied down."

"Thanks," Patton said, feeling silly.

"You need fuel?"

Patton liked to watch when they put in fuel, but he was in
a hurry.

"Okay," Patton said, then told the boy how much fuel he
needed. "Don't, that is, *do not* check the oil. I'll take care of
that."

Patton had survived four engine failures, and all were the result of ground crew error.

Once a ground crew let dirt and dust get into the fuel, which had clogged the fuel filter until fuel would not pass. He was flying into Salt Lake City in a rented Mooney, in the clouds over the Wasatch Mountains when the engine quit. The controllers helped him glide through a mountain pass. He never knew how close he was to the granite.

Few had so many close calls, but Patton tended to push the limits of himself and his aircraft. If a pilot is dodging mountains and running phantom strafing runs when the engine gulps a few drops of water, he has a much bigger problem than a pilot two miles high.

"That's okay by us," the lineman said cheerily, referring to Patton's request that he not check the oil. "We were wondering where you'd check it anyway. How about oxygen?"

These guys have been snooping, Patton thought. This time it seemed like a good thing, because it sounded like they could handle it. "Sure do," Patton said. "Could you fill the bottle on the top, inside the canopy?" Patton paused as the man agreed to his instructions.

"What's the deal with my airplane?" Patton said. "Why was it moving around?"

"A thunder banger came up. We chocked her, but she jumped the chocks and moseyed down the taxiway. The brakes were set, but the way she was rocking side to side, she just scooted along on tires that didn't turn. She sure seemed light."

"Thanks fellas," Patton said, genuinely thankful. "So it rained?"

"An inch or more, but your plane seems fine. Sure is a pretty plane."

Patton concluded the conversation and hung up the phone. On his way back to his room, he thought about the fact that Trooper needed to re-fuel, and wondered if it would allow him to beat Trooper to Seattle. When he got to his room, he did some figuring and discovered he could get there first, especially if he got insurance.

Patton called flight control. "Hi, this is Citation-One-Six-Five-Victor-Lima," Patton said to the controller. "I filed a flight plan for Seattle earlier. I don't have the copy of that in front of me, and I forgot where I'd planned to stop for fuel. Do you have that?"

"Looks like Walla Walla."

"I thought that's what I did," Patton said, chuckling. "I meant Chuckwalla. Would you mind changing that for me, please?" Walla Walla had twenty-four hour a day fuel service. Chuckwalla had service on call. If Trooper wanted to change that, he'd have to change his flight plan, often a thirty-minute process.

When Patton got back to the airport, men were at Vince's plane. They were moving solid-looking aluminum boxes that were quite different from the normal cardboard or wood containers used for transporting goods. Although the boxes were small, the workers were straining with them.

"What kind of cargo you guys loading?" Patton said, trying to act like a jet jockey with just a casual interest.

"Rearranging," one of the workers said. "Pilot said the weight wasn't in the right place. Don't know what it is."

Patton noticed Russian writing on one of the containers. They all had a brightly colored emblem that looked nuclear, although different from any Patton had ever seen.

"This is my friend's plane. I need to look at their approach plates for Seattle just to make sure mine are current." Patton climbed in past the workers, not waiting for a response.

"We're just loading her, fella. Far as we know it's okay." The worker paused and thought for a minute. "What is it you need?" the man said, again.

"Approach plates," Patton said, again in his best pilot-ease. "Here, I'll show you."

Patton pulled out the Seattle area maps showing the various approaches to Seaside Airport and began studying them. Patton pretended to be so intent on studying the plates and comparing them with his own outdated plates that he forgot about his promise to show them. The worker watched for a minute then went back to work.

Satisfying himself there were no major changes, Patton put the approach plates back into their case. He noticed two walkie-talkie type communicators.

The devices looked Russian, and they appeared to be equipped with scramblers. Vince had repeaters on the tops of several western mountains. A jet at altitude was always in range of one of them and Patton figured the communicators could access them. Without looking at the workers, Patton grabbed one of the communicators. He'd slip it back later, or he'd have Claude or Dave put it back for him. The information he picked up might be worth it. They may use them to talk about the Chuckwalla problem. That should provide a laugh.

Suddenly there was an angry voice. "What are you doing in my airplane?" It was Danny Trooper.

"You hauling plutonium for Vince?" Patton said firmly.

He saw a quick look of terror in Trooper's eyes before he composed himself.

"Where would Longto get plutonium?"

"Maybe Russia?"

Patton's ribbing was working far better than it should have. He wondered if there was something to the plutonium thing.

"He was looking at these maps," the workman said to Trooper. "He didn't touch nothing else."

Trooper's face relaxed.

"So what is this stuff you're transporting for Vince?" Patton said.

"This stuff is none of your business. Now sketattle."

"You mean skedaddle?"

Trooper glowered.

"You telling me I can't stand here and watch?" Patton said.

"That's exactly what I'm telling you."

Patton figured Trooper was close to losing control. Trooper was bigger, but Patton wasn't worried. He kept the button of Trooper's chin in his sights. Patton held an earlobe with his right hand so he didn't have to wind up in order to pop Trooper good. One solid punch on the button and he'd be out.

Trooper seemed to sense his status as prey and tried to move out of range, but Patton moved right with him.

"So what is it, Trooper?" Patton said when Trooper had gained some distance. "They look like plutonium caissons to me."

Patton snickered to himself as he watched Trooper fight for control. "It's not plutonium," Trooper said in a command voice, "now get you the shits out of here."

"Take it easy--I'm going. I was kidding. I mean, where would Vince get plutonium anyway?" Patton turned to walk away.

"Hey, Patton, I hear you're going to Seattle. Bet I beat you." Trooper had a sneer in his voice. "I'll spot you half an hour."

"I have a better proposal," Patton said. "I'll beat you, and you leave first. A hundred bucks says I'll win."

"You're stupid, Patton. My Citation versus your crazy little plastic toy airplane?" Trooper hesitated for a minute, then extended his extra large hand. "Ten thousand dollars says I beat you."

"Got the money?" Patton said.

"I got it, but I won't be paying."

Patton figured he'd beat Trooper by fifteen minutes given headwinds as forecast, and by five minutes even if the headwinds were as strong as fifty miles an hour--so long as Trooper stopped for fuel, and so long as they spent at least thirty minutes on the ground refueling.

Patton figured Dave Hech, Trooper's copilot, hadn't yet told Trooper about their need to refuel. Patton didn't want to take the chance that Trooper would renege.

"You put up the cash, and it's a deal," Patton said.

Trooper went into his plane, and to Patton's amazement returned with a stack of hundred dollar bills. "Ten thousand," Trooper said. "Sue can hold it. What about yours?"

"She'll have to hold my check," Patton said. When Trooper scowled, Patton said. "I'll call my bank and ask them to guarantee the funds. You can talk to my banker. Deal?"

"Deal," Trooper said. He shook Patton's hand, then broke into wild laughter.

So strange, Patton thought.

ᘜ ᘜ ᘜ

Later Patton sat in *Sally* and waited patiently. When Trooper got his instrument clearance, Patton called ground control and got cleared to taxi. Patton didn't let Trooper get more than fifty feet ahead of him as they taxied for fear another aircraft would get in between and cause him a several-minute wait. The Citation's jet wash buffeted *Sally*.

"Citation-One-Six-Five-Victor-Lima," the tower said, "cleared for takeoff. Cozy-One-Four-Niner-Charlie-Zulu, taxi into position and hold behind the Citation."

Patton would depart immediately after Trooper. As Trooper raced down the runway on his takeoff roll, Patton keyed his microphone and said, "I'll watch you land in Seattle, Trooper."

31 – Seattle or Bust

"Why don't they let us climb?" Trooper said to his copilot, Dave Hech. Dave couldn't help but notice that Trooper was fidgeting as they flew straight south, almost perfectly opposite the direction of their destination.

Trooper clenched his teeth and pursed his mouth when the tower cleared Patton on course. Dave leaned back in his seat, and gave Trooper a long curious look. He wondered what Patton had meant about watching them land and why Trooper's face got red when Patton had said it.

"We in a hurry?" Dave said. Trooper glanced quickly at Dave with an intensity Dave had never seen. Dave looked down at the map in his lap, then sat perfectly still as Trooper stared ahead.

Patton turned to the exact great circle heading to Seattle as soon as he was a thousand feet high. When he was established on course, he called flight control.

"Salt Lake Center, Cozy-One-Four-Niner-Charlie-Zulu, climbing through niner thousand. I'd like to pick up my instrument flight plan direct to Seattle at flight level two-five."

Twenty-five thousand feet was as high as Patton could go in his little airplane. To fly higher required sophisticated oxygen equipment. At 25,000 feet, a person could lose consciousness and if he got too high he could die.

"Cozy-One-Four-Niner-Charlie-Zulu, Salt Lake Center, cleared to climb to flight level two-five. Proceed direct to Seaside airport."

"Yes!" Patton said. This was perfect. The controllers were going to let him fly direct. With the recent introduction of the Global Positioning System, it was possible to fly anywhere in the world on the great circle arc. Just a few years before, the same capability could only be achieved by an inertial platform, a system costing millions of dollars and having a fraction of the accuracy of the two thousand-dollar Global Positioning System in *Sally*.

Patton had a homemade autopilot that got information from the Global Positioning System and kept *Sally* on the great circle course. He could fly for eight hours without concern for his heading.

He was able to get his altitude assignment quickly because he was far away from any of the flight paths, and he was cleared direct to Seattle for the same reason. This time he had a two-hour fuel reserve. Everything looked fine. Headwinds appeared to be a little stronger than forecast, but he should be okay.

Patton was at altitude and on course when he noticed a drop of cold water in his mouth. *Damn ground crews.* They must have gotten water in their oxygen hose when it rained so hard. Then it was pumped into the oxygen tank.

He checked the temperatures. It was fifteen below zero outside and forty-five degrees inside. He didn't feel cold because the sun shined directly on him through *Sally's* full canopy. *Sally* was made of fiberglass with a thick layer of foam sandwiched inside. The foam provided thermal insulation, and the fiberglass made her airtight. As long as the sun was shining, Patton was usually warm without the need to run his heater.

"Do we have enough fuel for this flight?" Trooper said, staring at the gauges.

"Not exactly," Dave Hech drawled. "As hot as it was and with all the weight we're carrying, we could only take on twenty-eight hundred pounds in Salt Lake. We'll refuel in Walla Walla. Could have made it from Boise. Why'd you say we changed the original plan?"

"What is Walla Walla?" Trooper said.

"God, I thought *I* was a hick from the sticks," Hech said. "Walla Walla is a beautiful little town in southwestern Washington. We're eighty miles from there, see," Dave said, pointing to the readout on their distance measuring equipment.

"We better start down," Trooper said.

Trooper called the controllers and asked for a lower altitude. That's when he found out they were going to Chuckwalla.

"So, what is this Chuckwalla?" Trooper said to the controller. He gave Dave an irritated look.

"It's a little town in central Washington," the controller said. "They have a nice airport there. You have to call in advance for fuel. Want me to call them for you?"

"We can call," Trooper said. "Have the number?" Trooper backhanded Dave indicating that he should write it down. They had equipment on board to make calls through Vince's repeater stations.

Trooper wasn't the only one writing down the number--Tom Patton was, too. He waited ten minutes, then changed frequencies and called a weather station. He was going to have the weather guy make the call for him, but they patched him through. "Hello, Chuckwalla fuel service?" Patton said in his best rendition of Hech's voice.

"I take orders and make arrangements," a voice said.

"Have you turned in the order yet for Citation-One-Six-Five-Victor-Lima?"

"I was just getting ready to call."

"We won't be needing that fuel after all. But thanks a lot."

"You aren't the same fella, who called, are you?"

"That was my captain who called. I'm the copilot." Patton thought Dave Hech would end up in trouble over this. Patton figured he would do something real nice for Dave Hech to make it up to him.

"Okay, thanks for the call," the voice in Chuckwalla said in a kind of a sarcastic farmer drawl.

What a stroke of luck. The head winds were running sixty miles per hour, considerably stronger than forecast. If it hadn't been for this break, he would have lost the race. Headwinds had a greater impact on *Sally* because of her slower speed than the Citation.

Patton wondered if Trooper knew yet that he was going to be beaten. Dave Hech knew how fast *Sally* could fly. Dave was probably over there now telling Trooper the story. Two months before, Patton had flown to Seattle especially to get *Sally* turbocharged. When Patton got back, he had gone into the terminal building at Rawhide.

"Hi, Dave," Patton had said, his chest all puffed out. Claude was reading a magazine, and Dolly, Claude's secretary, looked busy at her desk.

"What's with you?" Dave drawled. "You look like a rooster looking over a new flock of hens."

"I just flew back from Seattle Dave." Patton glanced at Claude, who looked like he was still deep in his magazine. "Took just a little over two hours. Fastest trip I ever made. Cruised at twenty-five thousand feet."

"You must have had a thousand mile-an-hour tailwind," Dave said, chuckling.

"The tailwind was pretty normal, maybe twenty miles an hour. No, I made the big change this time, got old *Sally* turbocharged. She's faster now than a King Air. I averaged three hundred and eighty miles an hour coming home." Claude seemed to bury his face deeper in his magazine. Patton could tell he was listening. "I'm having a hard time believing it myself. I left there at one-fifteen. Here it is three-thirty, and I've been on the ground for fifteen minutes."

When Dave Hech had given Patton his disbelieving look, Patton said: "Hey Dolly, what time did I call from Seattle?"

"I thought you called from Chicago."

Patton's mouth dropped.

"No, Dolly," Patton said with a half-smile. "Remember, I said I'd bought you guys some flounder? And I asked what time it was?"

"I don't like fish," Dolly said with an unusual smile. Claude and Dave were snickering quietly.

Patton looked around speechless, fighting for control.

"Oh, sure," Dolly said, finally brightening. "And you had someone on the ground there talk to me briefly, I assume so we'd know you weren't calling from the air. Claude said he loves flounder. So, did you bring some back?"

"Sure did," Patton said, beaming again and handing a package to Claude. "Baker Brother's Packing, Seattle, Washington." Patton pointed to the label.

"I even wrote down the time you called." Dolly showed everyone a piece of paper. "It was exactly one o'clock. And I wrote down the time you landed, too. It was three-fifteen."

Patton sighed deeply when he realized Dolly had been teasing him, and Claude and Dave had been in on it.

"How do we know you didn't call from Denver?" Dave Hech had said, frowning.

"Guess you'll just have to ask flight service. Well, I gotta go. Have an appointment in fifteen minutes."

Patton had sat in his car for a little while before leaving the airport. He watched the line boy go to flight service. He figured he was getting winds aloft. He had seen Claude and Dave walk over to *Sally* and look inside. He figured they were looking at his Global Positioning System that would show his time of departure, arrival, and course. They'd know exactly how fast *Sally* could fly when they were done.

𝕏𝕏 𝕏𝕏 𝕏𝕏

Now, as Trooper and Dave descended into Chuckwalla, Trooper put the plane on autopilot, and did a little calculating.

"Well, Hech, look at this. Even if it takes us thirty minutes to get fuel, Patton will have to average three hundred and forty-five miles per hour to beat us. That's gotta be a lot faster than his little toy plane can go."

When Dave sat quietly, Trooper said: "So, Dave, how fast is that little airplane of Patton's?"

When Dave finished telling Trooper about Patton's trip to Seattle, Trooper was suddenly stunned. "Land this airplane," Trooper said, grabbing the calculator. They were close to landing at Chuckwalla.

"Holy shits," Trooper exclaimed just as Dave touched down. "That fuel truck better be waiting. We can only be here for fifteen minutes. Nobody can leave the airplane." Dave taxied to the largest building. A tumbleweed rolled in front of them. No person or car could be seen, only a couple old aircraft and huge empty hangars probably left over from World War II.

When no fuel truck was in sight, Trooper's face got red. "Where's that number, Hech?" Trooper got through quickly. "It isn't canceled!" Trooper yelled. "How soon can you be out here with it? This is a situation emergency, national security. So, be pleased to hurry, *da?*" Trooper turned to Dave. His eyes were narrow. "He said you called and canceled, Hech."

"Why would I call and cancel? Looks to me like you and Patton got some kind of bet going. Maybe Patton called. He's a crafty lawyer, you know."

Trooper scowled, and stared at the emptiness outside their aircraft. As they waited he looked at his watch and fidgeted, then he turned on the radar. "Look at this," he said. "Looks like a line of thunderstorms all along the top of the Cascades."

"Sure does," Dave said. Then Dave leaned back and looked at Trooper. "You were just telling me last week how there's usually a line of thunderstorms over the cascades this time of day."

"He doesn't have radar, does he?"

"He has a storm scope."

"A storm scope isn't accurate enough to let him thread the needle, and that's what he'll have to do to get through these. He can't fly high enough to get over them." Trooper glanced quickly at Dave, apparently to confirm this statement.

"Then I imagine he'll fly through them."

"That little plane would be ripped to pieces."

"That little toy airplane is stressed for thirteen G when she's light," Dave said, "and I imagine right now he's pretty light."

"How could that be?" Trooper said.

"It's a long story, but it has to do with fiberglass being three times stronger than aluminum for its weight, but not as stiff. Since airplane wings have to be stiff to avoid flutter, Burt Rutan used a lot of extra fiberglass to gain stiffness. Patton will die from the G forces before his little airplane comes apart.

"He'd be crazy to do it," Trooper said.

"He's talked to me about it a dozen times. That's been his big deal for a while. He has thunderstorms on his brain. Kinda like a mountain climber dreaming about the big one, I guess."

"*Chert poberee. D'yavol,*" Trooper mumbled to himself.

32 – Thunder Bangers

Patton loved the freedom he felt flying miles above the earth where there was no sign of another living soul. It was almost like being in outer space.

Once *Sally* was at altitude, level and on course, pilot duties were minimal, mostly consisting of watching engine instruments and making sure the homebuilt autopilot kept her on course.

Patton wore headphones. He'd recently added a noise-cancellation system. A computer listened to the noise inside *Sally* and identified the sounds that constantly repeated like the drone of *Sally's* engine and the noise of the wind rushing by. The computer reproduced the exact opposite sound, or antagonistic sound, canceling the background noise completely.

Patton used the time to catch up on his thinking. He wondered if Vince was shipping plutonium, and whether Sue was involved. *Is there a plutonium thing?* Why would Vince take the risk? He wondered what was going to happen between him and Sue, and then drifted into a fantasy.

They had gone to dinner, drank some wine, then come back to his room on the shore of Puget Sound. The sea was shimmering. The moon and stars reflected off the water. They were on a wooden deck, dancing to soft, slow music that drifted to them from across the water. She felt good in his arms.

Her eyes were big, and she was whispering notions of love. Her hair drifted across his face in the light sea breeze. It was soft and silky and smelled as fresh as an English flower garden after a light rain.

A thick mist from the sea drifted in, obscuring the moon and the stars. The change felt right. The cool mist was on his skin and the heat from Sue's body was stronger.

Their clothes had vanished in the mist, fulfilling a silent wish. The curvature of her hip, soft and smooth, moved under his hand. Her nipples gently brushed his. Her body was as beautiful and perfect as he had imagined at least once each day for the last six years.

The melody that drifted to them was distant but clear.

The spell was broken as *Sally* bumped hard. Patton grabbed his seat belt and shoulder harness and tightened them with all his strength. He wished he had a helmet. He looked at his stormscope. There appeared to be a solid wall of thunderstorms from Canada to Northern California.

Trooper could go over the top of them, or find a way through with his radar. Patton couldn't go that high even if he had the right oxygen equipment. He had one choice if he was to win this race: go through them.

The most severe conditions a pilot can encounter are inside a thunderstorm. Some pilots think they harbor hidden tornadoes. Normal aircraft will be torn apart inside a thunderstorm.

Patton had a friend from New Zealand who was also a homebuilder. His name was Maxwell Ferguson, and he was a doctor of internal medicine and a psychiatrist. He was also an adventurer.

"The North Pole? How are you getting there?" Patton had said the last time Maxwell had called.

"Russian air force," Maxwell said in his Kiwi accent. "They'll drop us from a cargo plane, then land and pick us back up."

"What if the wind is blowing thirty miles an hour and they can't land to pick you up?"

"Can't Tommy."

"What do you mean, 'can't?'"

"Just like the wind can't blow in the doldrums at the equator. I'll explain it to you the next time I'm in your wonderful state."

Patton had wondered if he'd see him again. Maxwell had a Long EZ, a plane very similar to Patton's. Maxwell had experimented flying his plastic airplane into thunderstorms. He'd strap on a parachute and fly right into the worst looking thunderstorm he could find.

One time Maxwell was badly injured when his left shoulder harness slipped off. He hit the canopy so hard it was cracked. His scapula was broken. It was all he could do to get the plane back on the ground. Other than the crack in the canopy, the plane hadn't been damaged.

"What's it like in a thunderstorm?" Patton once asked Maxwell.

"Every trip is different. One time my entire cockpit was filled with Saint Elmo's fire. Little blue flames were everywhere. They looked like little bolts of lightning, and reached from the canopy to the instrument panel. Then with the loudest bang I've ever heard, and the brightest flash I've ever seen, they were gone."

"So, how'd you prepare your airplane?"

"Just made sure she was built to specifications. The parts I worry about most are the control surfaces. They'll take the most abuse. The elevator is most important. You can lose both ailerons and still bring her in using your rudders to steer. But lose your elevator and you're dead as a Moa. Tally ho, Tommy. Maxwell out." He said it as though they'd been talking on a radio.

Sally jolted hard. Patton was only five miles from the red dots on his storm scope. He eased back on the power. He didn't want to hit severe turbulence going fast.

He liked the idea of doing a triad: Do a thunderstorm, beat Vince's jet with his dip-shit pilot, and get the girl.

Patton thought about the last time Maxwell had called. He said he was on his way to Sicily where he would parachute into the mountains, then march to the sea.

"What happened at the North Pole, Maxwell?" Patton had said.

Patton slowed *Sally,* trimmed her for the lower speed, then thought about Maxwell's answer.

"The wind was blowing thirty miles an hour," Maxwell had said. "I slammed into a pressure ridge in the arctic ice and broke my hip. Spent a month in a hospital in Siberia. Very interesting. Tally ho, Tommy. Maxwell out."

"Bang." *Sally* shuddered as Patton flew into an enormous downdraft full of rain and hail. It felt like a giant fist slamming down on the top of *Sally*. Cracks and screeches came from *Sally's* bones. His shins smashed into the underside of the instrument panel. Blood trickled down his left leg and into his socks.

The next sound was like a rifle shot. It was a hailstone. Patton instinctively ducked, and thought about his speed. *Sally* was going more than 250 miles per hour. An instant later, it sounded like hundreds of hailstones struck *Sally* at the same time.

The noise was deafening; each strike was crisp, clear, and incredibly loud. Could the canopy break? Maxwell hadn't told him about hail. Could he survive if the canopy broke?

Suddenly he was subjected to several negative Gs in a downdraft. His shoulder harness squeezed down on his collarbones. They felt like they were ready to break.

Then it was calm. He inventoried *Sally's* parts--wings and control surfaces. They looked fine. He checked the security of the three metal bottles he had on board, two oxygen, and one a fire extinguisher. One of them flying around in severe turbulence could kill a person, or destroy the inside of an aircraft. He had the communicator in the right seat under the seat belt. He tightened it.

He had been in the clouds for ten minutes. It was so cold inside *Sally* he could see his breath. Just as he reached up to switch on the heat, a voice blasted his ears.

"Base one." The sound was loud and crisp--Danny Trooper. "Base one, this is sky one."

It took him a minute to figure out where the sound was coming from. It was the Russian communicator. Patton had hooked the communicator into his audio panel and directed it into his headset so he wouldn't miss anything if Trooper used it.

Patton looked at the little recorder on his instrument panel. The Record light was on, which meant the voice activation device was working and it was recording everything from all radio channels automatically. With difficulty, he turned the volume down.

It was really getting rough. He reduced power again to get below maneuver speed—140 miles per hour indicated. Below this speed a full movement of a control surface, like a rudder or aileron, would not result in structural damage. He dropped her landing gear. It would slow her down in a dive, he thought.

The next thing Patton heard was a foreign language. It sounded like Russian, but he wasn't sure. He was being bashed so badly by the turbulence he couldn't concentrate on what was said. He wedged his legs under the instrument panel so they didn't fly up. He held onto her stick with his left hand. To keep his right hand from flying around, he reached around his waist and grabbed the seat belt. He pressed his head firmly into the headrest.

Sally was holding together. He couldn't imagine worse conditions than those he'd just endured. When an enormous bolt of lightning exploded in his face, he did the strangest thing. He pointed and laughed, then giggled at the white plume of steam that was his breath. It was a symptom of anoxia.

Get control. There's alternate oxygen. Just turn the valve.

Suddenly another fist—this one in her belly. *Sally's* altimeter began spinning wildly. She was caught in the grip of an updraft moving at more than 100 miles per hour. Patton fell unconscious as *Sally* continued to tumble and pop and jolt.

Dark, almost black clouds surrounded her. Suddenly the clouds ahead became lighter and *Sally* burst out of the anvil on the top of the head of the storm cloud into air that was as smooth as feeling bodies could feel.

The sky was a beautiful blue-black. Thunderheads towered on *Sally's* left and right. They were brightly illuminated by the sun.

Now, in smooth air, *Sally* could do a better job maintaining her heading to Seattle. First her right wing popped up high for a five-degree turn to the left. It came down slowly. She hit her heading almost perfectly. She bobbed her left wing a couple times to tidy up her heading until she was within a half degree of the great circle heading to Seaside Airport on Puget Sound on the north side of Seattle.

Sally wasn't comfortable in the thin air because she'd been trimmed for a lower altitude. So she dipped her nose and began a slow descent. Her autopilot didn't hold altitude, but her mechanical trim system would keep her reasonably close to the elevation where Patton had last trimmed her. Her engine, with its turbocharging system, worked fine in the rarefied air although she was developing a fraction of her potential horsepower.

The controllers called repeatedly, but received no answer. Air Force jets were scrambled. They reported a lifeless passenger in a pretty little homebuilt aircraft descending slowly through 35,000 feet.

When *Sally* reached Seattle, two television crews were in the air in pressurized aircraft to welcome her. They found her in time for the evening news on the East Coast.

Before the day was over, more than five hundred million viewers the world over saw Tom Patton under *Sally's* full canopy, cruising in the vicinity of 25,000 feet, his tie ruffled, his gaze steady.

Sally's countenance wasn't as lifeless as Patton's. Her sleek, sweptback wings were bathed in bright sunlight. Her skin was soft, luxurious, and glossy. She looked like she was born to fly.

Sally flew ten miles past Seaside airport where, in accordance her autopilot program, she turned and flew back. She continued past the airport for another ten miles before turning back again. It was a safety feature of her autopilot designed to keep a sleeping pilot from continuing too far past his destination where he might fly into a mountain or out to sea.

Patton had her trimmed for a slow speed so her power was pulled back and she was only burning four gallons per hour. Her two-hour reserve had been computed assuming a much higher burn rate. As a consequence, her fuel would stretch for hours. Half the town of Seattle strained to get a view of her flying back and forth almost five miles above their city, but she was too high to be seen or heard.

Sally ran out of fuel at seven-fourteen, Seattle time. She didn't seem to mind. She began a slow descent and continued soaring back and forth. On her last circuit, she passed over Seaside airport, then she turned and glided back toward the thousands of spectators at the little airport who were standing on taxiways and on the tarmac. It was a general aviation airport, and there was no security. Anyone could walk to the aircraft.

A tall blond man stood at the front of the crowd. Everyone gave him plenty of room.

33 – Billy Patton

"Hey Billy, come get a load of this." It was Billy Patton's college roommate. "There's a dead guy flying back and forth over Seattle in a weird little airplane."

Billy continued working for a second, then stopped when the words registered. He came in and looked. Several male students were watching. His expression intensified and he felt his body react to adrenaline. It was *Sally*, he was sure. The aircraft had retractable gear, rare for that type aircraft. It had *Sally's* paint scheme and homebuilt aircraft were rarely painted alike. He listened to the words of the announcer.

"Authorities believe the pilot inadvertently flew into a thunderstorm, and was lifted above the biosphere where life cannot exist. Although the pilot appears to have died, by some miracle, the aircraft appears to be undamaged."

Billy watched with a burning intensity. He has to be alive, Billy thought. That altitude won't kill a person who's in good shape. Even if he had gone to forty thousand feet, he wouldn't have died if he had come right back down.

"Air Force jets could not fly slowly enough to get a good look at the pilot inside," the baritone voice continued.

Her gear's down and she's flying slow, Billy thought. It's the configuration his dad would use to fly through severe turbulence.

"It wasn't until *News Five's* own aircraft was scrambled were we able to get a good picture of the pilot. No one is certain, but the accident appears to be the result of pilot error. Even aircraft approved by the Federal Aviation Administration cannot fly into a thunderstorm."

Patton's inert face filled the screen. Billy looked, as if from a trance. The camera artfully panned back to show the beautiful little aircraft flying along in the background with the announcer in the foreground.

"Pilot error. What a dumb shit," a student said, then they all laughed.

"The aircraft has overflown Seattle, and it's now over Puget Sound. Authorities have no way to stop it. It will continue flying into the Pacific where it will crash and sink when it runs out of fuel."

As the broadcaster talked, the little airplane began turning. Soon it would be out of sight. The announcer turned to look. He stumbled for words until a commercial came on.

"Hell, maybe he ain't dead after all," one of Billy's roommates said as Billy headed for his car.

"It's just a homebuilt airplane. Maybe the dumb shit made it wrong," another one said, again followed by laughter.

"Hey Patton, where you going?"

Billy ignored the words and headed for his car. Soon he was on the road to Denver. He figured he'd be able to catch a flight to Seattle. His father had tried to prepare him for the day he died. *God, don't let it be now.*

When Billy arrived at Seaside airport, police were trying to seal off the entrances to the tarmac. It didn't take him long to find a place some distance from the terminal to get in. He got to the tarmac just in time to see *Sally* hit hard in the grass between runways. She bounced high, then slammed down again. Her gear was strong. With no fuel and only one passenger, she was light. She could handle a healthy impact. When she was firmly on the ground, she taxied rapidly toward the tarmac.

"She's going to run into us," one man shouted, and started running. The crowd panicked and ran. When she hit some tall grass, she came quickly to a stop about 200 yards from the scattering crowd. As the crowd ran in all directions, a lone man moved quickly toward *Sally*.

Billy was four hundred yards away on the tarmac, running hard. His vision was impaired by tears that streamed across his cheeks and into his hair and ears. Billy saw the big man reach *Sally* just as she stopped. He quickly opened her canopy, did something inside, looked at Billy who was getting close, and then moved back into the crowd. Billy could see he was blond, but not much more.

The mechanism that allowed the canopy to be opened was complicated. The big man must have been familiar with the way it worked because he opened it quickly. The spectators were still a couple hundred yards away. The people in the front had a stunned look on their faces. When Billy was within twenty yards he could see his father's blank gaze. Billy looked away. Suddenly his body's need for oxygen was intense. His knees were weak, arms shaky, and his stomach had butterflies.

The canopy wasn't latched. The blond fellow had dropped it and run. Billy avoided his father's blank gaze as he located a wrist to feel for a pulse. The hand and wrist were icy cold. Billy put his head down on *Sally's* fuselage and fought for control. When he noticed that the hand seemed stiff, he pulled hard. He knew the feel of rigormortis from hunting. It had an unmistakable quality.

Billy's legs gave out and he fell toward the ground, and as he fell seventeen years of his father's love flashed before him. For some reason his mind focused on the walks to see the shark that was never there. He buried his head in his hands, and as he did he heard a loud hiss. His body felt hot, then a tenth of a second later it felt cold. A bright light hit him. Was his father's soul rising in the light? If only he could rise with it. Is there a heaven? Would he ever see his father again?

When he finally opened his eyes, he saw legs all around. Billy fought for control. He had to know what happened. Maybe his father was murdered. *What was the blond doing?* Is this Vince Longto's doing? If the blond were the murderer, he would get away if Billy lost control.

Billy took a deep breath, then exhaled slowly. He jumped up, grabbed the canopy, closed it, and with his own key, locked it. In a booming voice of authority he said to the crowd, "This aircraft is personal property. Do *not* touch it."

He disappeared into the crowd. A couple reporters tried to block his exit, but his wrestling skills allowed him to push quickly past. It had looked like the blond man was looking for something. What could it have been?

When Billy failed to find the blond man, he returned to find that an FAA investigation team had *Sally* roped off. "It's my airplane," Billy said to the guards who acted like he wasn't there. "I have a key."

Finally, one of the FAA Inspectors appeared to hear the commotion and came over. "You have a key?" the FAA man said. Billy held up the key to *Sally's* canopy. "It's my airplane."

"We show it registered to Tom Patton."

"I'm Billy Patton, sole heir of Tom Patton. All his property has devolved to me."

The FAA man gave Billy a perplexed look. "Give me the key," the man said, extending a hand.

Billy figured the man would take the key, then leave him in the cold. Foul play was a definite possibility, and it needed to be explored. Billy had investigated a criminal case for his dad where law enforcement made big mistakes. His dad said that was normal. He didn't want this to be another one.

"May I come in?" Billy said, dropping the key to his side.

"Just a minute," the man said, then went over and talked to a short, round man.

Billy took the opportunity to take *Sally's* key off the ring and slip it into his shoe. The short, round man waddled up to Billy. "You say you have a key?" He had a barrel chest and a gruff voice. He had a heavy, black beard with more than a day of stubble.

"I sure do," Billy answered.

"Bob Kresh," the man said, extending his hand.

"Billy Patton."

"Why would you have a key?" Kresh said, glancing at the key in *Sally's* ignition, which was visible through her large canopy.

"Because I fly this aircraft all the time. Because that's my father in the aircraft. Because I helped build it. Because it's my aircraft, and I took possession when I locked it."

"You locked it?"

Billy nodded.

"You helped build it?"

"I want to cooperate, but I suspect foul play. There was a man who came up to the plane just before I locked the canopy. Maybe he took something. Maybe it was critical evidence. I could be a big help to your investigation. My dad is, ah--was a lawyer, and I worked for him as an investigator."

"You don't look old enough to be out of high school."

"I'm a senior in college. I only need three hours to graduate. I'm enrolled in graduate-level courses."

The man looked at Billy with a look of disbelief.

"I'm eighteen, but I took college courses in high school. Here, look." Billy held up his student ID. "Freshman" was scratched out and "Senior" was handwritten over it with someone's initials.

"I figure you at seventeen," the man said sarcastically looking at the ID.

"I'll be eighteen this month."

"Anyone could have changed this."

"I was a freshman until they gave me credit for the college-level work I did in high school. I had my advisor make that change. Bill Schulz is his name. He initialed the change." Billy could see Kresh was thinking that the initials "B. S." stood for *bullshit.*

Kresh stared at Billy for a minute, tapping the school ID on his thumb. "Okay," he said, "come in."

"Like I was saying, I suspect foul play."

"There's two detectives here from Seattle PD." Kresh gestured to a man standing next to him, who gave a subtle nod. "We'll look into that, but let's have the key."

"Have you dusted for prints?" The look on the men's faces told Billy they weren't prepared for a full criminal investigation. "I can't wait to tell the reporters you aren't going to dust for fingerprints." There was a look of determination on Billy's face.

Bob Kresh stared at Billy. Billy thought he knew what Kresh was thinking. This aircraft accident had been on national TV. The FAA wanted to look good. A criminal investigation could drag on forever, and if there were no quick resolution, they'd look bad. Kresh turned to the detective.

"I'll take care of it," the detective said.

"The key, please," Kresh said to Billy.

"The man I saw would have touched her on the outside. Those places should be dusted first." When Kresh looked like he was ready to explode, Billy turned and said to the nearest reporter, "Hi, I'm Billy Patton. That's my father in there. I have a key." Billy held his keys up.

Kresh grabbed him by the arm, and led him away. "What makes you think there might be foul play?" Kresh said. Billy's mind raced.

Just as he opened his mouth to explain, he realized that he had no evidence. And even with a lot of evidence, Vince Longto was too slick to get caught. Few knew him for the slime he was. If justice were to be done, Billy would have to do it himself and he could only take justice into his own hands if no one knew what he was thinking.

"My dad was an experienced flier; he wouldn't have made the kinds of mistakes necessary for this result," Billy finally said.

"I see," Kresh said, his face becoming relaxed.

"Maybe he was poisoned," Billy said.

"The autopsy will show it," Kresh said. He gave Billy a quick glance, then walked over to a reporter, a fellow he seemed to know. Other reporters gathered.

"I'm Bob Kresh, the FAA chief investigator on this crash. We don't want to leave one stone unturned. Someone approached the aircraft before anyone else, then left. In the very remote possibility there's foul play, we want to dust and see if he left fingerprints on the outside of the aircraft. I'll keep you posted as the investigation unfolds. Thank you."

When the detective with the fingerprinting kit arrived, Billy saw Kresh talk to the three police detectives.

When they dusted, Billy was disgusted with the detectives' technique. Billy knew about getting fingerprints. His dad had bought him all the equipment and a couple books. To do it right was time consuming. The detectives used too much powder, weren't careful when they used a pressurized bottle to blow it away, and didn't search with a magnifying lens. No prints were found, not even prints from Billy's sweaty fingers.

The FAA investigation didn't take long. They looked at the settings on *Sally's* electronics, especially on her Global Positioning System. Billy had to show them how to read it. It hadn't been approved yet for use in FAA certified aircraft.

They took the oxygen bottles. They wanted to fly *Sally* back to Salt Lake City, but there was a problem. No one was qualified in the airplane. Billy Patton was, and he was anxious to get her back to Colorado. He'd only agree to the flight if he got possession of *Sally*. Billy was surprised when Kresh agreed to it. Billy agreed to make *Sally* available again if they needed another look.

The next day, during the flight to Salt Lake, the inspector monitored the gases in the cockpit. He said he was especially interested in the carbon monoxide level.

"How did he use the other oxygen bottle?" the inspector said.

"Easy," Billy said. "He could switch between tanks with this selector valve." Billy tapped on a little knob.

"How'd the oxygen get from the auxiliary bottle to this selector valve?" the inspector said.

"There should be a small vinyl hose behind the instrument panel." The FAA man could feel no hose. When they landed, Billy stuck his head under the instrument panel. The vinyl hose was missing.

"I'm sorry," the FAA inspector said when he saw the sunken look on Billy's face.

The final FAA report was simple. Oxygen from the main bottle had become obstructed, probably by freezing water. Tom Patton switched to the reserve bottle, but couldn't get oxygen because the hose was missing. The aircraft was thrown upward in a thunderstorm almost to the stratosphere where the pilot died of from lack of oxygen. The conclusion: *pilot error.*

Billy Patton didn't believe it. His dad was in excellent physical condition and he was careful. When his dad knew he was going high he always checked to see that there was a flow of oxygen from both tanks. Besides, Billy figured he would have lived without oxygen even if he had gone as high as 40,000 feet, although he may have suffered with the bends.

Two days later, at the funeral, Billy saw a copy of the autopsy. Poison had been ruled out. Billy took the news hard. He went to the room his mother always kept ready for him, crawled under the covers, curled up, and didn't move.

34--Espionage

"Worry is a useless emotion," Patton had often said. "A person must first succeed over himself before he can succeed in life." Billy used these words to get through the immediate circumstances of his father's death.

As he lay in his room staring at the ceiling, it felt to him like a part of his body had been ripped away. The damage to his father's reputation hurt Billy. He was amazed at how easily a smart, capable person could instantly be reduced to a bumbling idiot.

He realized he was probably imagining things when he thought Vince Longto had something to do with his father's death. It was wishful thinking, he thought, so he didn't have to admit that his father's death was a result of negligence.

Billy's dreams and daydreams gradually focused more and more on his father's theme that "worry is a useless emotion." He'd watched his father endure and get through incredible hardship.

Day five found Billy still in bed. He awoke to a light tapping on his door. The morning sun streamed through cracks in the curtains. It was beautiful outside, but Billy didn't notice.

"Billy," his mother said, "there's a nice man here to see you."

Billy pulled the sheet over his head and curled up with his back toward the door.

"He says he's Vince Longto's pilot."

Billy took a deep breath, rolled over and opened the door.

"What does he want?" Billy said in a quiet voice.

"I'm sure he just wants to offer his condolences."

Billy opened the door wide, had his mother step into his bedroom, and wondered if the man's failure to clearly state his purpose meant he was being secretive.

"Would you entertain him while I take a bath and get cleaned up?"

"You'd better shave while you're at it," she said, tapping the fuzz on his chin. She seemed suddenly happy for the first time since Billy had been home.

Billy got cleaned up, and started down the stairs. Suddenly he froze when he heard the man's voice. It had a quality that made him feel tense. He moved quietly down the stairs and caught a glimpse of the man. He had a head of hair that resembled what he'd seen in Seattle. Billy returned to his room and thought again about the possibility of Vince Longto being a murderer. With poison ruled out, he knew his suspicions were crazy. He still couldn't shake them.

His mother's house in Metro Denver was in the suburb of Arvada in an old section of town. It was a big old house. At one time the upstairs had been a separate apartment. Billy's step-dad had it converted back to a whole house, but it still had a separate outside staircase that ended at Billy's bedroom.

He slipped down the back stairs and peeked into the kitchen from the outside. This time, when he got a better look, he felt a rush of adrenaline. The man definitely looked like the blond in Seattle. His mind flashed through reasons why Vince Longto's pilot would want to get into his father's plane, but he could think of nothing.

Billy's guts curled into a tight knot as he wondered what to do. Could the man be there to kill him? Unlikely. He had no reason, and he'd have to kill his mother, too.

Billy spotted a strange car about a half block away and went to it. It had a rental car sticker on it. There was a briefcase on the front seat, and a radio device like the one he'd found in *Sally*. The car was locked.

He returned to his mother's house and looked again to make sure the man was in the same spot. He was wearing a short-sleeved shirt. No room for a pistol. He returned to his bedroom, thought one more time about his need to be composed, and started down the stairs.

"I'm Billy Patton," Billy said, entering the kitchen.

Billy walked right up to Trooper and extended his hand as his mother made introductions: "This is Danny Trooper," she said.

Trooper's clothes were European, Billy thought, especially his shoes.

"Mr. Longto asked me to stop and give you his condolences," Trooper said.

Billy detected an accent. Was it Russian? Billy knew Vince Longto had business in Russia.

Trooper glanced over at Billy's mother. His eyes lingered on her legs. Billy felt a twinge of aggression, and fought to control his emotions when he noticed that his mother seemed to like the man's attention.

"Tom Patton's death was tragic," Trooper said. "He was a dear friend. Mr. Longto asked me to say that he will miss him greatly."

"Thank you, Mr. Trooper," Billy's mother said. "I'm sorry you had to wait so long; I know you're busy."

Billy managed a smile in spite of his disgust at the lies he knew Trooper was telling.

"Thank you, Ma'am," Trooper said. "I wonder if I could have a word with your son in private? Man stuff."

"Certainly," Billy's mother said, politely. He stared at Belle with a lusty smile as she rose.

Billy didn't like the idea of being alone with this man, so he positioned himself near the door where he could get out quickly if he needed to. Billy's agitation rose another notch as Trooper stared after his mother.

"I understand you are your father's sole heir."

Billy treated it as a statement and remained silent.

"Your father owed me ten thousand dollars when he died. He issued a check payable to me. I'd like to get it, please."

Billy remembered that a large check had been delivered to his dad's office. "What type of a debt was it?" Billy said.

"An honest debt," Trooper said sounding irritated.

"You'll have to file an estate claim with the clerk of court in Rawhide."

"I want you to take care of it now," Trooper said in a threatening way.

"Do you have identification," Billy said, "so I know I'm paying the right man?"

Trooper glowered, then pulled out a driver's license. "I am Russian," Trooper said, handing it to Billy. "My real name is Maxime Efremov. Longto gave me the name Danny Trooper. Said it would be easier on everyone."

After a lengthy pause, Billy said, "What was the nature of the debt?"

"A bet. Your father lost."

Billy's eyebrows jumped. He knew a court wouldn't enforce the collection of a bet. He also knew his father would want the bet paid if it was fairly won. Billy thought about the fact that the check was large enough to give an unscrupulous person a motive for murder. "What kind of a bet?" Billy said, wanting information.

"An honorable bet." Trooper stumbled over the word.

"What did you do to win?" Billy said as innocently as possible.

Trooper's face got red. "We were racing to Seattle. He lost."

"Why was he going to Seattle?"

"How should I know?"

"You spoke to him to make a bet. Surely he said something."

Trooper glowered and Billy waited.

"He went to Seattle because he had some crazy notion he could beat my jet, but he lost."

"Why did you run up to his airplane when it landed?"

Trooper quickly glanced at Billy with a look that sent adrenaline into Billy's veins and made him tense.

"I was nowhere around," he said, the guilty look gone.

"Didn't you say you raced him to Seattle?" Now it was Billy who sounded accusatory.

Trooper's face was red. "I landed at SeaTac, not some backwoods beef pasture."

"Why would you race to different airports?"

"You're like your father," Trooper said glowering, "and he's dead."

"Are you threatening me?" Billy said with outward calm.

Trooper's body relaxed. He smiled and put a big hand on Billy's shoulder. "Of course not. Listen, Mr. Longto asked me to get a picture for him of your father's airplane. He said it would be a way he could remember your father."

"I have photos in Rawhide," Billy said.

"I have a camera. Longto wants a recent photo."

Sally was a few miles away at the Boulder airport, tucked away in a building that wasn't a real hangar. The building looked too small to hold an airplane. Billy remained quiet.

Trooper became agitated again, and looked like he was on the verge of losing control. Billy figured it was an act. Vince Longto wouldn't send a man who couldn't keep his cool.

"My father's plane is in a hangar in Rawhide," Billy finally said.

"What hangar in Rawhide?"

"Is there a problem?"

"I said where's the airplane?"

The little scar on Trooper's lower lip stood out clearly. Billy thought that whatever he was looking for in Seattle must still be in *Sally*.

"Mr. Trooper," Billy said, walking from the kitchen and signaling Trooper with his eyes to follow, "Tell Vince how much we appreciate his condolences." Billy held the front door.

"Good day, Mr. Trooper," Billy's mother said, coming into the room in a friendly way. When she saw their faces she stopped. Trooper smiled awkwardly, then left.

"You said something to offend him. I hope you don't--" Belle stopped talking and looked at Billy as if to say she were sorry. Billy knew she was going to say: *end up like your father.*

"He was too easily offended," Billy said and went to the kitchen. He stuck his fingers inside the glass Trooper had been using, and carried it upside down, to his room.

The communicator he found in *Sally* had been hooked to a tape recorder. Maybe his dad had taken it from Vince Longto's plane? Who else would have communication devices from Russia? Maybe that's why Trooper wanted to know so badly where *Sally* was, so he could get it back: But why didn't he just ask for it back?

Billy thought about the possibility that there may still be incriminating evidence in *Sally*. Billy also wondered why there wasn't a tape in the tape recorder in *Sally*. His dad would have made a recording of anything unusual. Had Trooper taken it?

Maybe it had fallen out when *Sally* landed hard, or in turbulence. Billy remembered that the audio panel had been set up to direct traffic from the communicator to the tape recorder, and the tape recorder was set to record automatically. Did they think his dad was spying?

"Mom," Billy said, coming down the stairs, "you remember those ads about picking locks?"

"Picking locks?" Belle's eyebrows went high.

"It's a great part-time job. I knew a guy at college who made all kinds of money doing it. You know, by opening cars and houses when people lock themselves out."

"There was one in the *Herald* just this morning," she said happily as she located the paper.

Billy copied down the information and left for the library where he discovered that a routine autopsy only looks for the most common poisons like strychnine or carbon monoxide. Other poisons are only detected if they are looked for specifically.

He headed out to check on *Sally*. As he slowed to turn toward the Boulder airport, the guilty look he'd seen on Trooper's face flashed into his mind's eye. It made Billy think about the fact that he hadn't checked for a tail, and swerved from his turn back to the road. He realized that there might even be a locator device on his car. He drove on to Boulder, then called his dad's friend--the owner of the airport, a fellow named Rex Walker--and asked him if anyone had been asking about *Sally*.

"There was a blond kid here," Walker said, "a real serious type with a scar under his lip. I didn't tell him a thing." To Rex Walker, a *kid* was anyone under fifty. "Thought I better check with you first."

Billy exhaled. "God, thanks, Mr. Walker." Billy had told Walker on his return about his foul play theory, and asked him not to say anything.

Billy figured they'd eventually return to search more carefully since it was one of the closest airports to his home. He didn't want them finding *Sally* before he figured out what they were looking for.

Billy drove to Arapahoe County Airport and rented a small plane. He flew toward the mountains. When he was over the foothills, he turned north. It was getting dark when he landed in Boulder.

Sally didn't appear to be bothered. He looked around carefully, but found no tape. He closed *Sally's* canopy, then opened it, and reproduced as well as he could the motions of the man who had approached *Sally* in Seattle. First, the blond man had leaned in so far his entire weight was on *Sally*. Billy knew that from the way *Sally* dipped low. He could have been taking the vinyl tubing when he did that. Then he had done something else consistent with reaching to the middle of the dash where the tape recorder was.

Maybe, Billy thought, the tape fell from Trooper's hand. He traced with his eyes the path Trooper's hand would have taken. It went over the top of the console containing the controls, throttle, carburetor heat, and fuel mixture. There was a small opening and Billy looked into it. A tape! When Billy retrieved the tape, he was careful not to disturb any fingerprints.

Billy returned the rental plane and drove home. His palms wouldn't stop sweating. He got his fingerprinting kit and looked carefully. He found several partials. Maybe he could get a match with the prints on the glass Trooper had used?

Billy couldn't understand the tape. Part was in Russian, and part was in Chinese. Billy listened to the Chinese over and over. He couldn't quite get it all. If only he'd learned it better. Billy thought one voice sounded like Vince Longto.

He knew where he could get the Russian translated. It was another friend of his father: Yulich Gleichenhaus, a Russian immigrant. A marvelous musician, he was a popular concert conductor in Denver.

Yulich was delighted to see Billy, and offered him vodka. Yulich said he'd spent many delightful evenings drinking vodka with the boy's father.

"What can I do for you, Billy?" Yulich said.

"I need some Russian translated."

Yulich agreed readily. Billy played the tape he'd just gotten from *Sally*.

Tom Patton was heard describing his encounter with the material that he thought might be plutonium. There was routine air traffic talk, then a conversation ensued between two men speaking Russian.

"This man is KGB," Yulich said, in his Russian accent, "and he is talking to another KGB who sounds like the boss man."

"How can you tell they're KGB?" Billy said skeptically as he stopped the tape. To Billy one voice sounded like the voice of his recent visitor, Danny Trooper.

"I dealt with KGB all the time in Russia. It took me years to get permission from them to leave. They killed my father. They have an arrogance about them that no one else in Russia has. Can you hear it?"

"This one," Yulich said as the voice like Trooper's came on, "is the soldier."

"The boss guy, is he Russian?" Billy said.

Yulich stopped the recorder. "He speaks Russian with no accent," Yulich said, "I think he is Russian. Not only that, but he uses colloquialisms common to the Ural Mountain area. It would be very difficult for a foreigner to do that. A lot of KGB come from that area." Yulich started playing the recorder again.

"What are they saying?" Billy said, showing impatience.

"I can tell you what they're saying, but it might not help you much to know what they mean."

Billy gave him a puzzled look.

"The soldier says he's doing a job." Yulich stopped the recorder.

"What kind of job?" Billy said.

"He just says a job. Maybe mean he's killing someone." Yulich seemed to realize something. His eyes got big. "Does this have anything to do with your father?"

"Yes."

Billy explained the circumstances. Yulich sighed deeply, then continued. "The boss guy wants to know how he's doing the job, and the soldier replies, 'candy.' That might mean poison." Yulich looked at Billy as he reacted. "Do you suspect poison?" Yulich had big eyes.

Billy became tense and nodded solemnly. Yulich reflected for a moment, then played the tape again.

"Now, the boss man wants to know when the candy is to be taken, and the soldier says if it gets cloudy he should get it. The boss guy says to be careful because he's the only one in position to take out the big man."

Yulich looked at Billy, then went on playing the tape. Billy wondered what clouds had to do with anything.

"This isn't Russian. It sounds like Chinese." Yulich looked at Billy and shrugged.

"I know someone," Billy said.

"Billy," Yulich said, concern showing in the lines of his face. "These guys play for keeps."

"Thanks, Yulich," Billy said. He gave his dad's old friend a big hug, and departed.

In the car, Billy wondered what kind of poison would have anything to do with clouds?

The Chinese people he knew owned a restaurant on South Broadway in Denver. The family had taken care of Billy when he was a toddler as a kind of a day-care arrangement. Patton wanted him going there young, even before he could talk, but his wife would not allow it. The Chinese all understood a little English. Billy talked in English and they answered in Chinese. As a consequence, Billy learned to understand Chinese, but he didn't learn to speak it. On the other hand, his Spanish-speaking babysitter, Señora Menchaca, could understand no English, and Billy quickly learned to speak Spanish fluently.

Billy was a celebrity when he went into the Chinese restaurant. It was called The Little Shanghai on Broadway in South Denver. It was a lot bigger than it had been when Billy was there. Many people still knew him. Billy had grown up a few blocks away on east Maple on the corner of Lincoln.

At the restaurant, he found his childhood friend, Susan, and asked her to translate. Everyone said he'd taught Susan to speak English. She was the only one of the Chinese who spoke English with no accent.

"Listen to this one first," Billy said, playing for Susan the Chinese portion of the tape.

"This man's a foreigner. Probably Russian," Susan said immediately. "And this one, I think he's Chinese." Susan called to her mother, who came out from the kitchen. They talked in Chinese for a minute. Susan played part of the tape for her, then they talked again.

"Your mother thinks it's a person from Canton talking in Mandarin, right?" Billy said, beaming.

"Right," Susan said, enthusiastically. Then she gave the good news to her mother, who gave Billy a toothy grin. The family felt bad that Billy hadn't learned to speak Chinese after all the trouble Tom Patton had gone through.

"So, what are they saying?" Billy said. Billy thought one sounded like Longto and the other like Trooper.

"The Russian man is saying your father is flying back and forth over Seattle. The Chinese person asks why," Susan said. "The Russian says he has no idea, but it doesn't look good. "The Chinese person sounds upset. He says, 'I can't believe it, Maxime, Tom Patton might be dead?' See," Susan said, "I told you he was Russian. Isn't 'Maxime' a Russian name?"

Billy shrugged, then his eyes widened as he realized 'Maxime' was Trooper's Russian name.

"Now the Chinese person sounds mad. He says, 'I wanted to talk to him before he died.' Then he says some very bad words. That's it, they say goodbye."

Billy worked with his laptop, and got the translation down in writing.

"That's all?" Billy said, confused after reviewing the transcript. The two tapes seemed to conflict. In the Russian tape, the man he thought was Trooper seemed to be telling his KGB boss that he'd killed Patton with poison. In the other, Vince was surprised, even saddened at the news of Tom Patton's death. It seemed to mean that Longto had nothing to do with it. But Longto's words, "before he died," may mean that Longto was a player in a plan to kill Patton. Billy wondered about motive. The bet may have motivated Trooper, but not Longto. Billy wondered if Longto was doing something crazy with the plutonium his dad had discovered. To justify murder, he thought, it would have to be something extreme, like selling it to terrorists. He couldn't imagine Vince Longto doing such a thing. He thought about the nickel gas situation. It would amount to a lot of money, but it was a tiny portion of Longto's total wealth, and Vince didn't know they were looking into it anyway.

Before Billy left, the Chinese told him how sorry they were about his father. It was a nice reunion.

Billy drove home in a relatively good mood. He told his mother he was going to Rawhide the next day. He said he needed to clean up the loose ends of his father's estate. Before he left, he spent a day running around Denver buying special equipment. He bought motion sensors, both video and still cameras, and lock-picking equipment. He purchased the whole lock-picking home study course, including several videotapes. He bought a cellular phone, a laptop computer, two walkie-talkies, and night vision binoculars.

"Honey," his mother said as he went out the door, "take this graduation picture of you to your grandma Ann."

Billy figured his mother was testing him again. She wanted to make sure he really was going to Rawhide.

"Mom," Billy said, warmly, "you know I'd never miss an opportunity to stop and see my grandma Ann."

35 – The Stakeout

Billy found Claude as soon as he landed in Rawhide.

"You know anything about Vince's pilot?" Billy said.

"Only that I don't like him."

Billy told Claude about how he thought he had run up to *Sally* in Seattle, and Yulich thinking he sounded like a man in the KGB, and how he'd talked with a Russian boss about a job involving candy.

"I'd say Trooper did it then," Claude said, "at Longto's request. Vince Longto stabbed your dad in the back every chance he got. I heard him tell one of your dad's good clients from Denver that he should find a different lawyer because your dad was a crook. I think that's why your dad started doing business outside the state because Longto had raised so many doubts about him here in Colorado."

"Why would he do that?" Billy thought about the strange feeling he had always gotten when his dad and Vince met. Vince always seemed so nice on the surface, but by the way his dad reacted, Billy could tell his dad thought it was a show.

"Your dad didn't talk about it much. Something about their past, I'd guess. Your dad was depressed for a long time after Vince left him. Vince was different after that, too. Charlie Nugen told me that the next day, Vince went into the Devil's Kitchen and set off a bunch of explosives--enough to fill a deep ravine in Hell's Creek."

Billy stared ahead for a moment in amazement. "My dad thought Vince did that years later, when he drilled there. You sure it was right after Vince quit my dad?"

"Just heard it from Charlie the other day. Charlie said he'd never forget it. It's when the big change came over Vince, and he started getting rich."

"You know anyone who would tell me about Longto and his business?"

"Sue Hansen. Vince fired her a couple days ago, I heard because she wouldn't sleep with him. But who knows. One hears stories like that all the time about Vince."

"Know where she lives?"

"Flew out of here yesterday--I heard she was on her way to Florida."

"Know where?"

Claude shook his head. "And don't talk to her mother," Claude said. "She still works for Longto. Suppose she'll quit, but she still knows a lot of people who are close to Longto, so word might get back. I'll see if I can find out for you. Give me a call in a couple of days."

Billy thanked Claude and parked *Sally* in the open on the tarmac. Claude said he'd watch her until he left at six. Patton's Porsche was still sitting, unlocked, in the parking lot at the airport. There was a key in the ashtray. He went to his dad's office. There were still three lawyers there. Everyone was friendly.

Billy checked for files that had to do with Vince Longto. He found several old files, asked his dad's secretary to make a microfilm copy of them, and instructed her to put the microfilm in a safe deposit box. She didn't ask why. Billy went through his dad's personal things, including his recent mail. He came across some interesting credit card charges and made copies.

As Billy worked, he overheard the secretaries in the next room talking about Sue Hansen. He moved to the door and listened. Vince had used vile language with Sue in front of everyone. He'd vowed to destroy her. One secretary started to talk about Sue's *real* boyfriend, then shut up when she saw Billy. Billy wondered why it was a secret. Billy knew a little bit about Sue. She'd been a diver and a swimmer at Rawhide High. In fact, she still had the Rawhide school record for the fastest 100-meter swim. There was a picture of her in a swimsuit in the trophy case in the lobby at the high school. Billy remembered that picture. She was pretty standing there, smiling as she held a trophy--proud and confident, yet somehow demure. Billy had stopped almost daily to look at that picture. He'd heard about her going to an Ivy League school. Billy's counselor at the high school said he hoped Billy would follow in her footsteps. He wondered who the lucky man was, the one who was her *real* boyfriend.

Billy drove back to the airport. The old military hangar where he'd rented space for *Sally* was left open in the summer. In the back of the big hangar there was a row of rooms consisting of an old abandoned office, a shop, and storage. There was a large area between the roof of the rooms and the ceiling of the hangar. Billy closed the big doors to the hangar, then pulled a ladder around to the side of the rooms and went to work hauling up equipment. The room's ceiling joists were exposed, so he attached two four-by-eight pieces of half-inch plywood, giving him a floored area eight feet by eight feet.

He fashioned an enclosure out of three big cardboard boxes. It took him a while to make it look like something that belonged there. Then he set up a camera, and pointed it through a hole in the cardboard in the center of a big "O" that was part of the advertising on the box. He planned to use it to videotape any visits that *Sally* might get.

He drove over to see his grandma Ann. She was glad to see him, and she had a fresh batch of cookies ready. His mother must have called ahead. He went by his dad's house, dropped off the car and got his bicycle. He rode to a high point in the hills beyond the airport where he could see *Sally* through his binoculars. Claude waved in his direction and left for the day. He wondered who else had seen him, and returned his attention to *Sally*. He wanted to see if anyone approached her.

When it got dark, he fetched *Sally*, and parked her right in the middle of the big hangar. As he prepared to jump out, he dropped his flashlight. When he picked it up, it was shining forward on the passenger side in the foot well. That's when he spotted the missing vinyl hose that led from the reserve oxygen tank. It was coiled up on top of a brake cylinder on the passenger's side. That must have been what Trooper was trying to get in Seattle. He'd succeeded in pulling it loose from its connection behind the panel, but it was still connected to the tube that led to the reserve oxygen bottle. When it slipped out of his hands it could have snapped forward and out of sight just like a rubber band. Billy reached to grab it, but froze. It needed to be dusted for fingerprints, too. That's the next thing he'd do. He carefully collected the tube.

Billy placed several small helium balloons in the canopy. They were positioned where they would float out if the canopy were opened. Then he returned to his loft and looked down.

Sally looked pretty and poised. Billy installed a light, which illuminated her nicely.

Billy had water, a sleeping bag, his lock-picking course, plenty of "backpacker" food, and plenty of time.

He had a headset for listening to the information from the motion sensors and from the communicator. The raw data from the motion sensors went into the PC computer. It activated the video camera when it sensed motion.

The sound from the motion of a person walking was recognizable and distinctive from something else, like an owl or a coyote. With practice, it was even possible to identify the walking motion of a particular person.

Billy settled into his hideout. He looked again at the photos he'd made earlier of the fingerprint fragment he'd gotten off the tape from *Sally*. It seemed to match the photo of a fingerprint he'd extracted from the glass Trooper had used at his house in Denver. He had a new program for his computer, which would help him to see if there was a match.

It didn't take Billy long to get the hang of using the lock-picking devices. He had several small locks to practice on. When he got good at opening them, he slipped down and practiced on other things.

On the second evening, Billy was quietly working on the lock of a King Air. It was well past midnight.

He heard them as soon as they stepped onto the concrete. The gravel scrunched under their shoes. He had just opened the plane's hatch. He slipped inside, then pulled the door mostly closed behind him. Then he watched and listened from the small crack he left.

There were two of them and they moved along the wall in the shadows on the far side of the hangar. They were rummaging along the wall. Finally, Billy understood. It looked like they were looking for the switch to turn off the light that shined on *Sally*. None of the switches they found worked.

After a little while, they found the main circuit-breaker box, and with a little fumbling found the breaker that cut power to the spotlight. *Sally* still remained slightly illuminated by the area lights outside the hangar. The two men whispered to each other for a few minutes, then closed the giant hangar doors. In spite of the big doors' age, they rolled easily. They now shined their flashlights around the hangar walls. Apparently satisfied, they turned the circuit breakers back on. One activated the power circuit to Billy's stakeout roost. Instantly, a faint beep came from the back of the hangar, then another one. It was Billy's PC re-booting. The two men backed into the shadows and stood there.

Billy heard his breath coming in puffs. His heart banged like a drum in his ears. He was getting tired holding the aircraft door slightly ajar, but he couldn't move. He had to wait until they moved first. That was basic.

After a while, he saw two little flashlights moving up the ladder to his stakeout nest. He carefully pulled the hatch closed, rotated the closing mechanism, and then moved into the cabin and watched from behind the pilot's seat.

The little flashlights moved slowly to Billy's little shelter. One of the men climbed down, and walked out of the hangar. The man on top didn't move for a while, then the light started shining around again. One was watching while the other worked.

Soon one man came down the ladder carrying what appeared to be all of Billy's equipment in the same bag Billy had used.

They wouldn't know who had *Sally* staked out, but it wouldn't take a technically capable person very long to figure out whose equipment it was. When they discovered it was Billy's, would his life be in danger?

When the men left, Billy opened the hatch on the plane and slipped out. As he reached the bottom of the stairway, he heard something. He froze; his heart pounded again like it was going to burst. *They were coming back.*

This time he moved into the shadows behind the plane. A second after he moved, one of them noticed the open door on the plane and shined his light in that direction. Both of them walked up to it and talked.

Billy was close to a large drain that ran the length of the hangar. It was designed to take the water away when the floor or a plane was washed. It was shallow, perhaps twelve-inches deep, and about twenty-four-inches wide. It was covered by sections of steel grate, each about six feet long. He'd have to lift one. Some noise was inevitable.

When the two men entered the King Air, Billy slipped under the grate. They systematically searched the rest of the hangar, then stood near Billy and discussed the situation. One of them was Trooper.

They talked quietly in Russian, walking slowly in the dark, pausing on top of the grate. Their shoes were inches from his face. Trooper began pushing the button on the flashlight he was holding. It was pointed straight down. Billy's face was illuminated like a full moon every time the flashlight went on.

Could they hear his breath, his heart beating? Did they know he was there, and just toying with him? They talked for a minute, then Trooper put his hand up to his ear like he was protecting a speaker to hear better. He listened for a minute, then talked to his partner. They walked toward *Sally*.

Trooper worked on the canopy lock. Before he opened it, he noticed the balloons. The two secured them under the portion of the canopy that didn't come up, then exchanged words and snickered.

They worked in *Sally* for a minute, then opened the hangar doors.

When they were gone, Billy crawled from his hiding place. He was covered with mud and oil. He went quietly to his crow's nest, and checked for the vinyl hose. It was still there. He put it under his shirt and went to *Sally*.

He reached into a compartment in the back seat and pulled out a thin nylon cloth used to cover *Sally's* canopy when she was parked outside in the summer. He used it to protect the seat from his dirty clothes.

He got in, advanced the throttle to full power, and turned the starter. She fired instantly, promptly came up to full RPM, and lurched out of the hangar. He slowed down enough, without pulling off power, to make the forty-five degree turn onto the runway. He glanced back and saw two men standing in front of the hangar. Their mouths hung open. He was surprised at the clarity of the view until he realized the canopy was still up. He released it and dropped it.

In the process, *Sally* turned and began to run off the runway. At the last second, he pulled on her stick and she popped into the sky.

Billy wondered if he was like a World War I fighter pilot. If he could survive long enough to learn from his mistakes, he'd survive the war.

He flew to Grand Junction, a few minutes away, and filled his tanks, including the long-range tanks. He got cleaned up the best he could, then got back into the air. He didn't know where he was going, but with full fuel, he could go anywhere.

Billy figured it would be best if he got some sleep. He landed at the airport in Montrose, a little town near Grand Junction, taxied to a deserted spot on the field and slept. It was a fitful sleep. His brain struggled to make sense of all that happened in such a short time.

Suddenly he woke with a start. Using a little flashlight, he checked for the tape he'd planted in the console. It was still there. He'd also planted a new vinyl tube, and it was there. The communicator was still there also. Why hadn't they taken anything? Was his theory about the tape wrong? Would they be looking for him in Denver? He cursed the fact that he didn't get their activities on videotape.

He fired up *Sally* and got into the air, pointed her south and programmed Phoenix into the Global Positioning System. The horizon was getting light. The sky was beautiful and smooth.

He didn't have the right maps, but everything he needed was in his Global Positioning System. It had the critical information on every airport in the country.

In Phoenix, he got a motel room, took a long hot shower, then slept a fitful sleep. The visions in his dreams were troubling. His confidence had been shaken by the experience with his stakeout, especially his narrow escape. They didn't take the tape. *Why?*

He woke up at sunrise with thoughts rushing through his mind. Maybe they took the tape, and left a blank? He showered again, then got out the yellow pages and started planning his day. He had lost thousands of dollars worth of equipment in Rawhide. He hated losing money.

He cashed a $10,000 check on his bank in Rawhide. It wasn't easy. There were phone calls. They studied his ID. He hated waiting. He convinced his banker in Rawhide to make them cooperate.

When he finally he got the money, he took steps to break links with his credit cards. Someone with the right computer connections could trace his every move if he kept using them. Maybe it *was* murder, Billy thought, and if it was, they apparently thought he had evidence of it that could make him a target as well.

He went to the airport, turned in his rental car, jumped into *Sally*, and flew to another local airport where he rented another car from "Junks-R-Us," the only rental company that didn't require a credit card or have a minimum age. Billy mused over the fact it was easier for him to rent an airplane than a car. He got another motel room and went shopping. It took him all day to replace the surveillance equipment he'd lost.

He woke up early and got into the air before daybreak. This time he knew where he was going.

36 – Salt Lake City

Billy Patton didn't notice the pretty snow-capped Wasatch Mountains as he landed in Salt Lake City. He knew where his father had purchased the oxygen. It was on a credit card bill.

"Hey, we've seen this plane before," the line boy said when Billy threw *Sally's* canopy open. "Isn't this the plane that flew back and forth over Seattle for two days?"

"I don't think so," Billy said with an air of authority. "This baby has been in my dad's hangar all along. These planes all look alike. There's thousands of them."

"Guess you're right. We saw one like it yesterday."

"I don't need any gas," Billy said. "I'm looking for a job."

"You came at the right time," the line boy said. "But they only hire kids with experience."

"I worked for a base operator in Colorado while I went to high school." Billy had it set up with Claude that he'd worked for him for two years. "Who do I talk to?" Billy said.

"Bob, but he's not here. But I'm swamped, so why don't you help me out now? Since you're a pilot and experienced, I know Bob will hire you when he gets back. You sure this isn't the plane that flew back and forth over Seattle?"

"I helped my dad build this plane."

"Sure is pretty. Wasn't that something? That dumb shit running out of oxygen?"

"That was really something," Billy said, clenching his jaw.

"That guy was here just before he left for Seattle. He parked his plane way out there almost on the runway. It wasn't a parking spot at all."

"Did he buy gas?"

"Sure did, and oxygen, too. He had the funniest oxygen set-up. It wasn't a real oxygen bottle."

"You mean it wasn't one you usually see in an aircraft?"

"Yeah, I guess."

"Did you have trouble getting the oxygen into it?"

"Naw."

"What did the receptacle on the oxygen bottle look like?"

"There was a guy there helping us with it."

"A guy?"

"Another pilot. Said the plane belonged to a friend."

"Who was he?"

"How come all the questions?"

"The guy who flew back and forth over Seattle was from the same small town that I'm from. So's Vince Longto. Ever hear of him?"

"No."

"He's an oil man, comes to Salt Lake a lot. His pilot's a real macho-looking blond guy. Talks funny sometimes, wears a blue trench coat. Has a scar on his lower lip."

"What kind of scar?" the boy said, as if that meant something.

"Not a big one, but it gives him a mean look. It bobs up and down when he talks."

"Sounds like the guy who was helping us with the oxygen on the plane. When we were putting fuel in, he came up and sat in the plane. He said it was okay, that the owner was his friend."

"What was he doing?"

"Messing with things. I wasn't there all the time. When I came back, he seemed real interested in the water bottle the guy had. Then he asked if we were ready to put in the oxygen."

"Is this the oxygen tank system you used?" Billy said, walking over to a big red contraption with a lot of steel bottles.

"That's it."

"Water could get into this." Billy was showing the end that hooks up to the aircraft oxygen tank. "That is, if this cap wasn't kept on."

"The cap's always on, and we always hang the connector so it points down. The FAA guy asked us the same thing. But I can tell you we checked to make sure there was no water trapped in there. I remember looking myself just before I handed it to that blond fella."

"Could you see what he was doing?"

"Not really. His back was turned."

Billy stared off in thought.

"The guy had the farts," the line boy said.

Billy looked with big eyes and a crooked mouth.

"Smelly sulfur farts. I could still smell the sulfur stink in the plane after he climbed out."

A couple of days later, Billy re-fueled a helicopter. The pilot told him about a recent charter where he'd flown into the hills to a gas plant that smelled, "like a raunchy cabbage fart."

"Who chartered the flight?" Billy said.

"Some oil guy from Colorado," the pilot said.

Bells started ringing in Billy's head. He got the location of the gas plant and went out to visit. It was a several-hour drive.

The helicopter pilot's description of the smell was accurate. The sign on the front gate said, "Utah Gas Processors, Inc., Echo Plant, Bud Anderson, Manager." Billy had already done his research and discovered that Vince Longto was the sole owner of the stock of this corporation. He went into the office.

"Is Mr. Anderson here?" Billy said to the first person he saw.

"He got run off. Couldn't handle the job."

"Know where he lives?"

"Coalville, Utah. At least he did."

Coalville was a pretty little town in the mountains. A trout stream ran through it. Bud Anderson was loading a moving truck when Billy arrived.

"You work for that asshole, Longto?" Bud said, sneering at Billy as soon as Billy started asking questions.

"I'm an investigator for a law firm. Nothing to do with Longto."

"You don't look old enough to be out of school."

"Everybody says that. I'm ten years older than I look and I have a degree in forensics."

Bud scowled.

"An important lawyer died in an airplane," Billy said, "and I think hydrogen sulfide gas may have been involved." Billy held up the piece of vinyl tubing that he'd found in *Sally's* nose. "If this tube was full of H_2S, and a person inhaled it, would he die?"

"Instantly, if it had more than about five percent H_2S." Bud's eyes narrowed and he looked at Billy. "Did Vince Longto have a reason to kill this fellow?"

"I think so," Billy said.

"See this?" Bud reached into his pickup and pulled out a small stainless steel bottle. "Longto had me fill one of these with liquid H_2S about two weeks ago."

"Maybe he was getting it analyzed?"

"The lab sent a man around once a week to pick up samples. Longto had no reason to get it that I know of."

"What's in that bottle?" Billy said.

Bud turned the valve, and gas hissed into the air.

"God, that stinks." Then Billy's eyes got wide. "Is it poisonous?"

"Must not be. You're still standing."

"But it smells so strong."

"Your nose can detect just a few parts per million. It isn't instantly lethal until the concentration gets up to a thousand or so parts per million, the same as one percent. This gas has about 200 parts per million. It's strong. You couldn't breathe it for long, but one whiff won't hurt you."

"Would you sell me that bottle?"

"Take it. It's Longto's. It'll just get me in trouble."

Billy went straight back to Salt Lake. His friend who hired him was working.

"Smell this," Billy said, back at the airport, venting a little gas from the bottle.

"God, that stinks. What you doing?"

"Ever smelled it before?"

"Yea. It's the smell from when that guy helped with the oxygen in that homebuilt plane that looks like yours."

"Bob," Billy turned and walked over to his boss, "some bad news has come up. There's been a death in the family."

"A death in the family?" Bob said, suspiciously.

"It was my father," Billy said, showing genuine emotion.

"I'm sorry to hear that. Will you be back?"

"I don't think so," Billy said, fighting back tears.

The men at the airport stared after Billy with troubled faces as he jumped into *Sally*. She was full of fuel. He wasn't sure what his next move would be.

Billy knew how Trooper did it. He'd poured water into the oxygen hose. The water was forced into the main oxygen bottle when the tank was filled. Then, using a hypodermic needle, he'd injected hydrogen sulfide into the oxygen hose that ran from the back-up oxygen bottle. When the main bottle froze-up, his dad switched to the second bottle, took one whiff of pure H_2S gas and died. That's what they meant on the tape when they said if he flies into clouds he should get it. In the sun, *Sally* was always warm. In the clouds, the main oxygen tank froze up. Trooper wanted the vinyl tube out of *Sally* so it would look like an accident, and traces of H_2S couldn't be found embedded in the plastic.

Billy wondered about Vince. Trooper could have taken some H_2S without Longto knowing about it. Billy wanted more information. He didn't want to kill an innocent man.

Billy turned *Sally* to the southeast and programmed Fort Lauderdale, Florida, into his Global Positioning System. He wouldn't need to stop for fuel.

The job he was contemplating would require four days of surveillance, Billy thought, before he made contact.

37 – Right Place–Right Time

Sue Hansen had been devastated when Tom Patton broke their date to go skiing in Utah as her present for her 18th birthday. More than a year later, Rosy told her about the bankruptcy. Rosy said he'd be depressed for a while. She said when he got back on his feet and got his self-esteem back, he'd call. For years, Sue waited for that call.

Sue wrote, but he didn't write back. At first it made her mad. When Rosy said he might not have gotten her letters, she forgave him for that, too. When Sue got back from Russia, she was elated to hear about his success as a lawyer, and especially that he was still single. She began dreaming again about being Mrs. Tom Patton.

When they had landed in Seattle, she thought it was curious the way Trooper was smirking. When she had seen Dave Hech's concerned face, she approached him.

"Tom Patton got himself in trouble," Dave said. The next look Dave gave her was terrifying. She knew what was coming.

"It doesn't look like he made it, Sue. His little airplane is headed out to sea." Then he took her in his arms as she cried, and hugged her, and rubbed her back with his big, rough, rancher hands.

In her motel room, she sat and stared at the phone. It didn't ring. At midnight, she turned on the TV. When it came on to a picture of *Sally,* she switched it off and strode from the room. She caught a taxi and headed for the airport where she waited until four in the morning to catch a flight to Denver. She didn't know what to do. Maybe her mother would help. That's where she'd go.

A week after the funeral, she returned to work. The phone was ringing when she walked into her office. Vince wanted to see her.

As she walked through the secretarial pool, Vince came out of his office and began yelling at her. "You been pining after that dumb fuck Patton?" Vince said. "We don't give time off for such a thing." Vince was standing above everyone on a balcony that extended from his office one floor above the secretarial pool. "He was more of a sheep than a human. Spent his life searching for a way to die, and finally found one."

Sue felt hatred. She took a step backward.

"Don't even think about quitting, bitch." The last word echoed around the large room that contained more than a dozen secretaries. "How much you owe me?" Vince read from a piece of paper. "One hundred seventy-five thousand counting interest and penalties. Lot of good it did."

Sue turned to leave.

"You leave and you're destroyed. Last I heard, Mary White was working as a maid." None of the secretaries looked up. A couple continued typing. Sue heard him yelling until she closed the door to her office.

She needed her things before she was locked out. Her office was lined with pictures of a naked woman. She refused to look and began jamming her things into a plastic garbage bag.

"You don't recognize yourself?" Danny Trooper said, walking into her office.

Sue looked. The pictures were of her from the hot tub party. "Did you take these?" Sue said evenly, fighting for control.

"Nice, aren't they? Vince was mad when he heard. Told me to give them to you, including the negatives."

Sue held out her hand.

"But I understand you and Vince are no longer friends."

"What's one little spat between two close friends?" Sue said, leaving her hand out.

"But deep down, Vince is so insecure. And as for me, how could I forget that you refused to give me my ten thousand-dollar check. Now you have to prove yourself."

"How would I do that? She said, mostly out of morbid curiosity.

"You could spread the truth about Patton, that he molested you when you were a child."

As Trooper talked, he caressed Sue's cheek. It took all her willpower to keep from ripping his eyeballs out. She knew they would delight in an assault. There was probably a video camera recording everything.

"I need to make some phone calls," Sue said, guiding Trooper out her door.

There was no lock. She wanted to sit at her desk and cry, but thought again about the possibility of a camera. She didn't want to give Longto that satisfaction. Sue quickly grabbed the few personal items she had and started out the door. She stopped, took the photos down, put them in a big envelope, and threw them in the trash. What good would burning them do? she thought. Vince would make a billion copies if he thought it would tarnish Tom Patton's memory.

Sue went to stay with her mother. Vince sent flowers, and talked to her mother personally, and told her how unfortunate their misunderstandings were. Vince said Trooper would be punished--probably fired. Vince said the next time he visited he'd try to see Sue. The next day, Vicki came by insisting on seeing Sue so misunderstandings could be cleared up. Next came Butzsaw--then it started all over again, with flowers from Vince.

Sue's mother suggested she get away. Her brother was in England for a month and he needed a house sitter for his beach house in Florida. Sue left that afternoon.

For the first five days she was in Florida, Sue cried. Would she go to prison? Would she work as a maid like Mary White, for the rest of her life?

On the sixth day, Sue decided she had to quit moping around. She could go for a walk on the beach, maybe even take a swim in the ocean, but she never made it off the couch. When the doorbell rang, she was slow getting to the door, and when she did, she didn't bother looking through the peephole. She just threw it open.

A handsome boy with a hauntingly familiar face stood on her porch, stammering.

"I'm Billy Patton from Rawhide," the boy said. "Here on vacation. I stopped to see you."

He looked like the high school picture she'd seen of Patton-- handsome, muscular, and proud. She stepped out and hugged him. His body felt strong, and for an instant she felt secure. It reminded her of the hug she'd dreamed Tom Patton was going to give her in Seattle as he explained why he hadn't contacted her, and said he was sorry.

Billy Patton was the little boy she'd seen in pictures. She'd often wondered if she could be a good stepmother to Billy, and whether he would accept her.

"Come in," she said, taking his hand. Billy walked around the room and looked at several paintings. As he did, he glanced nervously at Sue.

"This one's a copy," Sue said.

"Has to be," Billy replied. "The original's in the Louvre."

The comment startled Sue. Then she remembered Tom Patton telling her that he'd shown his baby hundreds of famous paintings. Patton said it seemed to have made the child interested in art.

Sue took Billy's arm as they looked. The next time Billy talked, he was nervous.

When they sat, Sue noticed that Billy's crotch was swollen. Sue found it pleasing that the boy found her attractive. She wondered if Tom Patton had been as hot-blooded.

Sue decided she better not torture the boy and excused herself in order to change out of the bikini she was wearing. Sue fixed her hair and put on some make-up. The boy beamed when she walked into the room. Sue couldn't remember the last time she'd been pleased at such a response.

"I knew your dad well," Sue said, figuring the information might cool the boy down. "I was a seventeen-year-old waitress when we became friends. He came into the restaurant where I worked, sometimes twice a day. I always waited on him. He used to take me for rides in his pretty little plane."

Sue went on. It felt so good to talk--he was a good listener, and he had an intelligent grasp of every subject that came up.

When Billy suggested a walk on the beach, Sue was delighted to have an opportunity to get out of the house. They shared an interest in biology, and it was everywhere along the beach.

"Could I take you to dinner tonight?" Billy said as they returned to Sue's house.

"I'd love to," Sue said, thinking about how much fun he was to talk to. "But this isn't a date."

"Why not?" Billy said.

Sue giggled at his boldness. "Because I don't do babies," she said, smiling.

When Billy put on a hurt face, Sue made amends by putting her arm around his shoulder and kissing him on the cheek. Smiling broadly, she said, "Not even cute ones."

"How about crabs for dinner?" Billy said. "My dad and I used to catch Dungeness crabs in Puget Sound. He had a beautiful friend in Seattle. She'd be our guide. We'd park our camper trailer near the ocean somewhere, get a six-pack of beer--my dad wasn't a big drinker--make up a butter batter, eat crabs, and drink beer. Boy, those crabs were good."

"You mean his goddaughter from Europe?" Sue said, figuring Billy was trying to tell her that his father had a lot of girls, and she never had a chance. "The one you stayed with when you went to Germany?"

"Right," Billy said, looking both surprised and disappointed.

"There's a nearby restaurant that serves crab called *Cangrejos Para Dos*."

"Could we walk?"

"I'll change."

Sue came back wearing a snug pair of jeans.

"I'll buy," Billy said. Sue looked up to protest. "You just told me how much trouble you're going to have paying Vince Longto back for your college education. So, I'll buy, okay?"

"Okay," Sue said. His offer to buy made her feel secure again. She resisted the urge to touch his arm.

"Let me grab a windbreaker out of my car in case the breeze gets cool," Billy said. As warm as it was, Sue wondered why he needed it.

On the way, Sue told him about Russia, and Billy told her about his year in Ecuador with his father's friends where he learned to speak Spanish fluently, and his year in Germany where he learned German, and the trip to China that never materialized because of Tiananmen Square.

"My mom sent me a clipping saying you were Athlete of the Year at Rawhide," Sue said. "It said you were a diver and a two-time state champion wrestler. I was impressed."

"I wasn't much of a diver."

"State champ isn't much?"

"No competition. You have to have a feminine side to be a really good diver."

"Did you start thinking that way," Sue was being sarcastic, "when Greg Louganis came out of the closet?"

Billy glanced away with a confused look. "I used to look at your picture in the trophy case in Rawhide. In real life you're prettier."

Sue gave him a sweet smile, and resisted an urge to take his arm.

"Your father and I dated when I was seventeen."

"God," Billy exclaimed, "You know how old he was?"

"He looked good to me."

"I guess you're right. I mean, what difference does age make?" Billy gave Sue a meaningful look.

Sue smiled at his quick comeback. "Do you know why he flew to Seattle?" She said, thinking it might be a good idea to cool the boy down by telling him in so many words that she'd almost been his stepmother.

"I sure don't, and nobody else does, either. Mike Quail, the lawyer in Salt Lake City, said Dad called him from Colorado and said he couldn't come over to Utah, that he was having trouble with his plane or something. But Dad was really in Salt Lake when he called Quail--the phone call's on his bill from the hotel. Quail sure seemed upset when I told him that. Said he was supposed to help with a pre-trial hearing."

Sue felt guilty for having pulled Patton away from something important, but she'd wanted to know how much he cared, and besides, wasn't she due tribute? "We had a date," Sue said, then looked off momentarily in pain. The bastard, she thought, broke the two biggest dates of her life. Sue turned her head to hide tears.

"Were you going to sleep with him?" Billy said.

Tears flowed more freely as she thought about her plans, and how she'd vowed to make him beg for mercy.

"You all right?" Billy said.

"I must have gotten sand in my eyes," Sue said. She took a deep breath and struggled to regain her composure. She was fine when they reached the restaurant.

"Here it is," Sue said. When she saw that the waiters were Hispanic, she said, "You could talk Spanish to them."

"Most eighteen-year-olds are really dumb, aren't they?"

"Will you quit?" Sue said, her eyes shining. He was making the point that he was the exception to the rule. He was certainly different from his father, she thought. He was quicker, and more carefree. She liked that. Sue startled as Billy grabbed her.

Before she could pull away, he kissed her cheek and said, "You're pretty cute, for an older lady, that is."

Sue laughed. She could feel a wet spot.

When Sue went to the rest room, she saw Billy talking to the headwaiter, who had a look on his face like something serious was being discussed. When Billy ordered, Sue was impressed with his Spanish.

"Okay," Sue said, in the middle of their meal, "what's going on?"

"What do you mean?" Billy said.

"Waiters aren't hovering over that table over there."

"They don't speak Spanish, and they don't have the most beautiful woman in all of Florida at their table."

Sue looked away in thought, a smile on her face, her brow furrowed as she remembered the time the boy's father had said the same thing to her on the day they met.

It was a wonderful evening: the air was warm and the moon was bright. When the restaurant was almost empty, and it was quiet, Sue could hear music that drifted to them from across the bay. She was disappointed when it was time to leave, but glad that they had a long walk home.

"I might not be able to pass for twenty-four," Billy said, on the walk back, "but you could pass for eighteen."

Sue's eyes brightened, and she was about to knock this cocky little chip down another notch, but stopped when she saw a concerned look on his face. He put the hood up on his sweatshirt and tied the string.

Sue followed his gaze and found a menacing-looking man standing next to a tree, moving into their path. Billy was focused on him. "Don't say anything," Billy said to Sue. "Stay behind me."

Billy turned and gave the man a mean look.

"Hey big fella," the man said, flashing a gold-filled smile, "I hear you have a wad of hundreds in your pocket." With a flick of his wrist, a big blade popped up from a knife in his hand. "I'm here to lighten your load."

Billy showed little concern for the knife and continued toward the man who had a penetrating, determined look. Sue maneuvered around to the side as the two squared off. She was able to get into perfect position when the man paid her little heed. Her foot flashed out. The ball of her toe smashed into the man's elbow. There was a loud snap as his elbow bent backwards and seemed to wrap around her foot. The knife flew away. The man's face took on a look of horror.

Billy grabbed the man in a wrestling hold. Just before he picked the man up, Sue spin-kicked him in the temple. The kick tore a gash into the side of the man's head, and knocked him unconscious. With his head down Billy hadn't seen the kick, and appeared confused at the man's limp condition.

Billy grabbed the man's elbow, and put it behind his back. But when he tried to apply pressure, it flopped limply. Billy experimented with the arm, moving it around with a curious look on his face. The man came to and screamed in pain.

"We're calling the police unless you tell us who put you up to this," Billy said.

"It was a waiter at the restaurant," the man said.

Billy shook him. "Which waiter?"

"They all know about it at the restaurant," the man said. "The head waiter's in charge."

"What about the owner?" Billy demanded.

"The head waiter is his brother-in-law. The owner turns his head."

"Get out of here," Billy said. Billy looked around anxiously. When the man still didn't get up, Billy helped him. Finally, the man staggered off.

"We can't be calling the police right now," Billy said to Sue. "I'll explain later. Come on, we'll get to the root of this." Billy looked at Sue. "Where'd you learn to kick like that?"

Sue smiled. "What's this about a wad of hundreds?" She said.

"There's only one person who knew about it, and that's the head waiter."

"You have a pocket full of hundred dollar bills?"

Billy pulled out a wad of cash as big as his fist.

"I'll tell you later," Billy said. "So, you know karate?"

"You saw one kick," Sue said, figuring Billy must have showed his cash to the headwaiter, and promised a big tip which had resulted in their excellent service.

"You were supposed to stay back," Billy said.

"It was the charge of the light brigade," Sue said, imagining how terrible a big knife cut across Billy's face would have been. "Don't you know scissors cuts paper?" Sue gave Billy a look that said he was a real dummy.

"Kevlar," Billy said, indicating his windbreaker. "Did you see the gash in the side of his head that he got when I threw him down?"

Sue gave Billy a nice warm smile. His youthful exuberance was exhilarating. They returned to the restaurant.

The first waiter gave them a horrified look, and ran into the kitchen. Billy started barking commands in Spanish. Everyone was jumping.

When the owner came forward, he was pale. Billy grabbed the headwaiter by the arm and held him tight. The waiter went limp in his hand and slumped into a chair. *"Levante te,"* Billy commanded. The waiter came to attention. "We need to talk," Billy said to the owner.

"This way, please," the owner said, nervously. He seemed to know what was coming.

Billy explained the circumstances, still squeezing the headwaiter's arm. The silent communication between the waiter and the owner showed that the owner carried some blame. Billy sent the waiter away and closed the door to the office.

"We have a very large claim for damages," Billy said. "You're liable for the actions of your employees through the doctrine of *respondeat superior*--that includes acts beyond the scope of their employment where you condone those acts. The robber said you know what's going on and let it happen. That makes you liable for punitive damages."

The owner began to talk, but Billy silenced him with a gesture and a sharp look.

"If we bring suit, it will drag on for a year or two, and in the meantime, the police would become involved, and your reputation as a restaurateur would suffer. Your loss will be huge. Your headwaiter may go to jail, and if he implicates you, you may go, too. Our loss is small compared to your potential loss. We have suffered from the insult of being attacked. My friend's hand is throbbing from the pain of hitting the man who came at me with a knife."

Billy grabbed Sue's pretty hand. Sue winced, and feigned pain as he rubbed it. It made Sue feel a little nervous when Billy continued to rub her hand as he talked. His hands were big and strong, and she liked the feel too much. When she tried to pull away, Billy held on tight, looked at her, and smiled sweetly.

Sue relaxed, smiled back, and rubbed Billy's muscular shoulder with her free hand. When she let her hand slide across his back, she liked the feel. His shoulders were broad and strong. She laid her head on his shoulder. She was supposed to be his girlfriend, she thought. His smell captivated her, and made her feel good. She could feel the vibrations of his voice as he talked.

"In addition, we have provided a valuable service to you," Billy said. "You can nip this activity in the bud. Wouldn't you agree this is the best time to settle this?"

Sue smiled. Most men were in their thirties before they learned to negotiate.

"I'm so glad you brought this information directly to me," the owner said.

"I propose we settle now for one hundred thousand dollars," Billy said.

Sue sat up, careful not to look stunned, nodded her head, and looked resolutely at the man.

"*Señor*," the owner protested, "You can't possibly think I have that kind of money."

Billy didn't say a word. The owner attempted for a minute to deal with the silence, but could not.

"I give you what I have," he said.

He opened the safe, and pulled out the money tray.

"It's a thousand dollars. It's all I have."

He placed a bundle of twenties in front of the two. Billy looked at him with a penetrating look. Again there was silence. The owner stood over the money and gestured to it with his hands. Billy sat stone-faced.

"I remember now where there's more," the owner said, pulling out another drawer in the safe. He pulled out two more bundles of twenties. "Now, that's absolutely all I have."

Again there was silence. The owner sat quietly for a long time. Patton had shown Billy how to use the power of silence.

"I remember now where there's more," the owner said.

The owner stepped on a chair, reached up through the false ceiling, and pulled down a bundle of hundreds.

"This is ten thousand dollars. Together that makes thirteen thousand."

Billy sat for a minute. He looked at Sue, who nodded her approval of the deal.

"Do you have a piece of paper?" Billy said.

"Yes, of course," the owner said, handing him paper.

When Billy gave him a disgusted look, the owner found a pen and a large book for a surface to write on. Billy wrote: "$13,000 received in full settlement for all claims which William T. Patton III, and Susan Piserchio Hansen have against *Cangrejos Para Dos*, because of its complicity in an attempted mugging." He wrote the same thing again below, then signed and dated both, and handed it to Sue to sign.

"All that is required is your signature," Billy said, placing the paper in front of the owner and holding the pen out for him. The owner hesitated. Billy allowed the silence to hang.

"You have to sign," Billy said. "We don't want you getting us arrested on trumped-up charges of robbery the minute we walk out of here."

The owner hesitated and glanced at his phone. Billy tapped on the paper. The owner signed. "Would you have a bag for this?" Billy said, politely, referring to the money.

"Of course," the owner said. As he looked, Sue took the agreement from him and gave him his copy.

"It was a delight doing business with an honest man," Billy said. "I loved the dinner. I'll come back, you can be sure." Sue took Billy's arm as they exited the office.

"*Consigueme un taxi*," Billy said to the doorman, who didn't waste a second taking care of the demand.

Billy asked the taxi driver to take them to downtown Miami.

"Why do you know about law?" Sue said, when they were in the taxi.

"My dad was a lawyer."

Sue gave Billy a skeptical look.

"Dad wrote me stories about the law when I was a baby, even before I could read. There was *Billy Bozzle--Diamond Thief.* It was about larceny. I think that was the first one. Then there were stories about murder, kidnapping, and burglary. He must have written a hundred little books on law for me."

"But only near-geniuses are smart enough to learn law in law school," Sue said.

"Baby's are all geniuses, Dad said. He said the social rules every baby learns by the time he's seven are more complicated than the law lawyers learn in law school."

"I don't get it."

"Once I was in a restaurant with Dad. A baby was dropping her spoon. The Mother was beside herself. You could see she wanted to whack the kid, but she couldn't do it in the restaurant.

Dad said the baby was figuring out the rules, and discovering that *Thou shalt not drop the spoon* has a million meanings. At home, the rules are different. Mom gets mad and hits the baby the first time a dirty spoon is dropped on the carpet. If the spoon is clean, she just gets mad. The rules are also different for dirty spoons on linoleum.

"When Grandma's around, there's a whole different set of rules--Mom only gets mad and never hits and Grandma will smile and pick up the spoon forever. The baby's father won't pick it up at all and never gets mad except when Dad gets hit with a dirty spoon, and then only when he's wearing office clothes.

"It's why babies drop stuff, Dad said, to help them discover the rules of society. *Thou shalt not kill,* is complicated, but far simpler than *Thou shalt not drop the spoon.*"

"Never thought of it that way," Sue said. "You really learn to read when you were four?"

"Dad tell you that?"

"I was three when I learned," Sue said grinning. Sue squealed when Billy pinched her tummy.

"Girls' brains are different," Billy said.

"Right, they're wired in a way that lets them ask directions when they get lost." Sue was wearing a smile. "And they can understand simple things like scissors cuts paper."

Billy was looking at her, squinty-eyed. Sue took his hand, smiled and said, "Tell me more."

"So, I guess because of those books I was always interested in law. When my dad and I were together--which was a lot--I asked him questions about law. When I was twelve or so, I started reading my dad's law school books. At first I skimmed the material and picked out what I could.

"When I was in high school, he often took me along when he tried a case."

"That's the way it was with me and veterinary science. I guess that's why I want to be a doctor."

"You'd be better off being a physicist," Billy said. "It pays less, but they have freedom of thought. Doctors are automatons. They don't learn to think in med school. They learn to do what the pharmaceutical companies say. They're great at rote memorization, poor at analysis."

"Quoting your dad?" Sue said. "You forgot the part about them being prisoners of respectability and how they can be pushed around by anyone who threatens to use the word 'quack.'"

Billy gave Sue an amazed look.

"So, why we downtown?" Sue said after the driver dropped them off.

Billy hesitated. "If the muggers are following us, we can ditch them."

Sue sighed, and wondered what he was really up to. "What are you going to do with your share of the money we extorted from that restaurant guy?" Sue said, climbing into a taxi Billy had hailed.

"Feeling sorry for him?"

"My grandpa owns restaurants." Billy looked at her. "No, Sue said, "he doesn't assist muggers and thieves."

"I think we should spend it together. We could take *Sally* and run up to Orlando and spend a week at Disney World."

"*Sally?*" Sue had a quizzical look. It was a good way for her to buy time while she thought about his invitation.

"That's my dad's airplane. It wouldn't be a date."

Sue laughed. "I'd love to," she said.

"I'll pick you up in the morning," Billy said. "Stop here, driver."

They were still a quarter mile from Dr. Hansen's beach home.

"It's a shame to waste the beautiful evening air," he said to Sue, who looked at him with a question on her face. They got out of the taxi and Billy paid the driver.

"Why do you keep looking around?" Sue said as they walked.

"Never been to Florida."

Sue looked at him suspiciously and wondered again what was really going on.

"Could I come in?" Billy said when they arrived at her door. It was obvious from his expression what he had in mind.

"For milk and cookies?" Sue said.

"I was thinking more along the lines of honey and spice," he said, looking her up and down.

"You're so retarded," she said, laughing. "You don't even shave yet."

"What do you mean?" Billy protested. "I just shaved last week. And I'm almost two inches taller than my dad."

Sue's eyebrows shot up. He looked two inches shorter to her.

"Besides, what difference does age make?" Billy said.

Sue thought about the good time they'd had, and looked warmly into his eyes. When Billy stepped closer, she put her hand on his chest to stop him. It landed on his pectoral muscle. It was large and firm, and felt good.

She moved her hand in a quick, clumsy motion, and placed it on his shoulder, and again it felt good. As she wondered what to do, her gaze drifted into his eyes. They were dark, warm, and inviting.

Slowly he leaned forward to kiss her and, as he did, she felt her clitoris becoming engorged and her vagina lubricating. "I'll see you in the morning," Sue said, and jumped clumsily through the door.

38 – Love in the Morning

Sue was disgusted with herself when she couldn't sleep that night. The boy wasn't for her. He was too young, and she'd almost been his stepmother.

Sue awoke when she heard the sound of a person walking to the end of the diving board. She rolled out of bed and walked to the window. Billy was standing with his back to the water on the end of the board, contemplating a dive.

She focused on his abdominal muscles, one ripple after the other. Her gaze drifted to his bulging thigh muscles. Sue thought he had as good a body as she'd ever seen.

Billy launched himself into the air, spinning and turning, then ripped into the water with barely a splash. It was one of the best dives she'd ever seen. While she waited for him to surface, she replayed for her mind's eye the views of the male body she'd just seen.

The muscles in his arms looked good when he popped out of the water. As he walked in her direction, she looked at his bulging crotch, and when he climbed the ladder and walked to the end of the board, she studied his buttocks. She didn't fight it this time when she felt herself becoming aroused. She felt safe being out of sight.

Wait. The decision is made. It's final. If she couldn't control herself, they couldn't be friends. "The trip is off," Sue said out loud as she headed for the shower. Her expression showed determination.

But she couldn't keep one part of her mind from replaying the views of the body she'd just seen. As Sue showered, she became aware of her own body. She was glad she'd kept in shape. She closed her eyes and wondered for an instant what it would be like to have big strong hands rubbing soap everywhere.

Out of the shower, Sue took a long look in the mirror. A voice in her head said, *Doesn't one good body deserve another?*

She pursed her mouth. These thoughts that were welling up from the primitive part of her brain couldn't control her actions, she thought. She was too sophisticated for that. She felt smug in her feeling of conquest. A swim would be nice, she thought. She pulled on a comfortable suit and went to the pool.

Billy was drying off. The muscles in his arms were bulging. He dropped the towel and walked toward her. Billy looked taller than she remembered.

She heard her voice, as if she were a bystander. It was saying, "I have a bottle of champagne in the fridge." She looked into his handsome dark eyes. He was still moving closer.

"We aren't in any hurry," Sue's disembodied voice continued. "It might be fun to sit around and drink a little champagne before we go."

When she saw in his eyes that he had no intention of stopping, she felt a sudden need for oxygen. Her heart raced. She was not in control. When he was inches away, her eyes closed, her head tilted, and her lips parted. She couldn't speak, and she couldn't move. Finally, she felt his body, his cold mouth.

Billy slipped her suit off, then his. She reached down and held him with both hands. He felt wonderful. She wasted little time guiding him into her very wet vagina.

She was happy at last. Every part of him felt good. His body was against hers, their tummies were gently brushing, and his muscles were bulging under her hands.

It didn't last long. When she felt his body tense, she squeezed hard and tried to climax, but she wasn't ready. The second he stopped she looked around, and felt silly standing there in the open for anyone on the beach to see. When she tried to get down, he protested and held her in place.

"That's just the beginning," Billy said.

Still joined, he carried her inside, placed his back against the bar, and lowered her until her long legs touched.

"This one's for you," he said, brushing her hair back with his hands.

He kissed her face all over as he moved slowly, rhythmically. When she came to climax, he stopped and held her tight. Then he started again, slowly, rhythmically, until the next time.

And so it went until it was his turn for the second time. When Sue tried to get down, he protested again, saying, "Third time's the charm." Again holding her in place, he carried her into the living room where, still joined, he laid down on a llama fur. It was soft, lush, and warm.

Sue was brushing his hair back and kissing his face when she felt him climax for the third time. When she watched his face contort in ecstasy she noticed, as if for the first time, that he was very handsome.

"That should last you for a while," Sue said.

"How about fourths?" Billy said, a boyish gleam in his eye.

"You crazy?" I'd be sore for a week. Besides, I don't know what came over me. I could get pregnant."

"No you won't, on both counts. I picked up some lubricating jelly on my way over." Bill wore a smug look. Seeing the shock on Sue's face, he added, "We'll save it for this afternoon." Billy paused, then added, "And on the second count, I'm wearing a condom."

Sue looked at him with big eyes that turned sour when she looked at his extra-smug face.

"You came here wearing a condom? You premeditated sex with me? You actually thought I would?"

"I just thought you liked me, and I knew I liked you." Billy looked at her with soft eyes. Then he perked up and said, "So, you think you might be up for some more this afternoon?"

"We'll see," Sue said with a big smile, starting to think eighteen wasn't so bad.

"Come on," Bill said, "let's drink one glass of champagne. We have a lot to talk about. Then we have to get out of here."

"What do you mean, we have to get out of here?"

"I'll tell you all about it." He kissed her, smiled, and gave her a firm hug. Sue closed her eyes and hugged him back. His muscular body made her feel comfortable, warm, and secure. She started to think about how impossible a relationship with this young man would be, but pushed those thoughts away. It felt fine for now.

39 – The Recruitment

"Listen to this," Billy said, placing a small tape recorder on the coffee table.

"What is it?" Sue said.

"I found this tape in *Sally*. My dad recorded it on the way to Seattle." Bill pushed the play button, and his dad's voice came on dictating notes about the caissons that looked nuclear. Patton wondered if Vince was selling weapons-grade plutonium.

"What do you think?" Bill said.

"Vince bought a nuclear power plant in Washington. Nuclear fuel's expensive, so he made a deal to buy it in Russia for pennies on the dollar. There was a catch--it would take forever to get transportation permits.

"But Vince is a master at innovation. He cleaned out the plant's management so he didn't have to worry about anybody telling, then he smuggled in the fuel. He sends his spent fuel to Russia." Pain shot through Sue as she realized that her possession of this information would be a big incentive for Vince to mount a defamation campaign against her so no one would believe what she said.

"How does he know Trooper and his friends aren't selling part of it to terrorists?"

"Maybe they are," Sue said with slightly raised brows. "Vince wouldn't mind, because it might push the price of oil up." She shook her head. "Boy, am I glad to be out of that place."

"Listen to this part. It's in Russian." Billy said.

Billy pushed the play button. Something caught Sue's attention. She took the recorder, rewound and listened again. She was comfortable running the little device.

"What do you make of it?" Bill said.

"Where did you get this recording?"

"My dad had some kind of a Russian communicator device. I think he used it to make this recording when he was flying to Seattle."

"Like a walkie-talkie?"

"Sort of, yeah."

"Vince didn't use Russian radios. He said they were too unreliable."

"So, where do you suppose my dad got this thing?" Bill said.

Sue shrugged and listened to the tape.

"This sounds like Danny Trooper. He used to be KGB. The guy he's talking to sounds like Uri Novotny, Vince's head guy in Russia. This conversation must be important because they could both get fired for talking to each other." Sue listened again. As the tape played, her face contorted in pain. Sue cried. It definitely sounded like they had something to do with Patton dying.

She thought about Vince's words when he said he wanted to talk to Patton before he died. She closed her eyes. She was thankful Patton hadn't seen the photos.

Sue thought about how Butzsaw had been open in her derision of Patton--and said he'd died from an acute case of stupidity. Butzsaw knew what they had done. She knew everything Vince did. Sue's hatred grew.

Sue's mother had recently told her that Vince had been making the rounds of the coffee shops and bars talking about the tragedy, and making it sound like Patton's death was the result of his stupidity.

Sue punched the play button and listened. "Sounds like Uri Novotny is keeping tabs on his soldier," Sue said.

What does Novotny mean: "Take out the big guy?"

"You know what these tapes say?"

"I had a friend of my dad interpret them."

"Yulich?"

"You know him?"

"Drank vodka with him more than once," Sue said, ignoring Billy's surprised look. She picked up the recorder and pushed the play button. "It sounds like they're talking about killing someone else."

"The big guy? Maybe it's Vince?"

Sue shrugged.

"You think they knew my dad recorded their conversation?"

Sue realized something, and said: "The Russians probably used the communicators to talk to each other. They'd feel safer using their own scramblers. One of my jobs in Russia was to spy on the Russians to make sure they didn't mount some kind of *coup* against Vince. Your dad was in Vince's plane just before he left--maybe Trooper had two communicators. Russians have to be careful like that because their equipment is so unreliable. Anyway, they probably figured your dad had it as soon as it turned up missing. Trooper probably knew about the recorder in Tom's plane. That's probably why they wanted to find your plane, to get the communicator back, and a tape if there was one."

"Well, they found the plane, they took the tape, but not the communicator."

"That means they plan to feed information to you." Sue looked at Billy. "They took the tape we just listened to? You mean you planted a dummy?"

"Right--a copy."

"Smart b--" Sue stopped and smiled. "Smart man."

Sue stared off in thought, then looked at Billy. "What kind of poison could they have used?" She said. "Why didn't it show up in the autopsy? What about the fact that he went too high to breathe?"

Sue paused, then continued with more intensity. "If anyone killed him it would have been Vince Longto. He hated your dad." Sue started to tell Billy the rest of the story about Patton and Longto, but stopped. She looked at Bill and saw something in his face. "What else do you have?"

"You really think Vince could have killed him?"

"Vince Longto's scum with no moral restraint. What else do you have?"

"A lot," Bill said, animated as he put a briefcase on the coffee table and opened it. "See this tubing? It went to the second oxygen bottle in *Sally*. See this little hole? It's identical to one I made in another tube with a hypodermic needle. When *Sally* landed, the selector valve was in a position that would allow oxygen to be drawn through this tube. It ran to the auxiliary oxygen bottle. Dad had the main bottle filled in Salt Lake. There would have been plenty of oxygen in the main bottle for the trip, so he wouldn't have switched out of that bottle unless it froze up. Remember what the first Russian tape says? 'If he goes into the clouds, he should get it.' When he went into the clouds it got cold enough in *Sally* for the main oxygen bottle to freeze."

"None of which proves anything."

"Let me finish. Guess who hooked up the oxygen hose when they pumped oxygen into *Sally's* main oxygen tank?" Billy paused. "Danny Trooper. And guess what he was playing with at the time?"

Sue shrugged.

"A water bottle, and guess what peculiar smell the line boys smelled when Trooper was sitting in *Sally*?" Bill paused again. "Hydrogen sulfide gas. You know, one-whiff-and-you're-dead-gas. It kills more people in the oil patch than anything else. And finally, my dad didn't order oxygen on his own. The ground crew in Salt Lake asked him if he wanted it, and Trooper told them to ask."

"Rumor had it Trooper killed at least two people for Vince in Russia," Sue said.

"A hit man?"

Sue smiled and nodded.

"But Trooper's just a soldier," Billy said, sounding desperate. "We both *think* Vince did it, but without a motive, the evidence we have is too weak."

Sue leaned forward and said quietly, "Vince had a motive to kill your dad."

"Go ahead," Billy said sitting up straight.

"Your dad was digging into some old Rawhide Gas contracts that permanently fixed the price of natural gas at Vince's utility in Rawhide at a nickel."

"How'd you know he was doing that?" Billy said.

"Vince has people in the PUC in his pocket. A week before he died, Tom Patton was in the PUC office asking to see just the right documents concerning the original contract at Green Dome."

"But how could that be important enough for murder?"

"It was one of Vince's big deals. It was a possible source of intense humiliation for him. What's wrong?" Sue said, seeing Billy's distraught face.

"I'm the one who was checking out the documents. My dad didn't know anything about it, and by the way he talked about the subject, he would never have done it himself. They wouldn't check them out to me so I put them in his name. The next time I saw my dad, he was dead."

Sue gave Billy a nice hug. Tears were streaming down his face. He grabbed a tissue, cleared his eyes and blew his nose. She felt terrible for what she'd told him. She knew this wasn't Vince's paramount motive. She wanted to tell him what it was, but she'd promised Patton never to tell.

"But Vince was always so friendly and cordial toward Dad."

"It was a show," Sue said. "From the time he quit your dad, Vince hated him."

"He buried the fossil of a shark and a dinosaur the day after."

"Are you sure?" Sue said, sitting up. "The day after he quit your dad?" Sue immediately recognized its significance.

"Claude at the Rawhide airport told me."

Bill held up a tape. "This is what they put into *Sally* in Rawhide, and this is the tape they thought they took." Bill held up another tape. "Trooper's fingerprint was on it."

"How do you know all that?" Sue said.

"I'll give you the details later. But when I was a kid, Dad had me learn about fingerprinting for investigations."

"When you *were* a kid?" Sue said.

"You know, you better be nice to me," Bill said, pinching her trim tummy. Sue squealed and tried to pull away, but she was no match for his wrestling skills. He wrapped her up nicely, then kissed her and said, "The age of consent in Florida's eighteen, and that makes you guilty of statutory rape, and if you aren't careful, I'll get you busted big time.

It'll be Miami Vice all over again. They'll throw away the key on you, big girl."

"How old are you?"

"I'll be eighteen tomorrow."

"You don't scare me," Sue said, sure he was kidding, returning his kiss, and rubbing his back and buttocks. "You say you have some lubricating jelly?"

"Right here," Bill said, holding up a small tube. "But you have to wait."

"The hell I do," Sue said, pulling him close, kissing him, and then making love.

When Sue opened her eyes, she looked right into Bill's. He'd been watching her face in ecstasy. He gave her a long, warm kiss.

"Will that last you an hour while I finish explaining this really important stuff?"

"Maybe not a whole hour," Sue said, kissing his face.

"Look at this." Bill sat up and gestured to the laptop computer.

Sue looked at a whole fingerprint and two fragments.

"How old are you really?" Sue said.

Bill handed her his driver's license.

"I'm a felon," Sue said, a look of horror on her face.

"I won't turn you in, so long as you're nice to me." Bill looked at her concerned face, then added: "I don't really know what the age of consent is in Florida."

Sue started to say something, but he cut her off, indicating their need to get back to what they were doing. "This one," Bill said, indicating the whole fingerprint, "is the one Trooper left on a glass when he visited my home. This fragment is from the tape. Now watch." Bill worked the computer program until both pictures merged, one red, the other yellow. Where they matched they were green. They were identical. "This other fragment from the vinyl tube fits, too, which means Trooper had his hand on it."

"Trooper wouldn't do anything Longto didn't tell him," Sue said, looking at the computer screen.

"Here's the juiciest part," Bill said, and he explained about Vince getting a bottle full of hydrogen sulfide gas the day his dad died.

Sue sat upright. She just realized that Vince might have gotten her brother's house bugged.

"I found all the bugs and disarmed them," Bill said.

"When did you do that?"

"You don't want to know," he said. Then, looking at Sue's stern face, he added, "Okay, I'll tell you, but you have to promise not to tell."

"I promise." Sue shrugged.

"I've been watching this house for a while. After the fiasco at the airport in Rawhide, I promised myself to be more cautious. I needed to find out if they had your house staked out, so I built a blind on the beach and installed myself and some equipment."

"A blind on the beach?"

Bill gestured out the window. Sue couldn't believe her eyes. There was a big plywood box on stilts in the sea oats.

"You've been in there, looking in my window?"

"I tried not to look in your window."

"But you couldn't help looking from time to time?" Sue said with a disgusted look on her face.

"Why do you think I was so horny?" Bill offered with a sheepish look on his face. "But there's a bright side," he said, slapping her bottom and giving it a lascivious look.

"How'd you get in, and how'd you keep from setting off the alarm?"

"Lock-pick. And I just pushed this button here," Bill said, pointing to the disarming device. "I saw you do it. I found four bugs, two that looked like real bugs. One looked like a cockroach, the other like a ladybug. I recorded all the normal sounds in the house. I'm using the bugs now and broadcasting all those normal sounds back, so they won't think anything's amiss."

"So, where's this broadcast station?"

"In my crow's nest," Bill said, motioning to the plywood box out the window. "I've been borrowing power from you, see?" He pointed to an extension cord coming out of an outlet in the garden, which quickly disappeared into the sand.

"Isn't borrowing without permission stealing?"

Bill shrugged.

"I want to see this crow's nest," Sue said
"But not now. You can help me get my equipment out
tonight. We'll leave enough to keep broadcasting back to
them. They probably think I haven't found you since they
haven't heard me on their bugs."

"That's why you were so fidgety, having the cab stop a
long way away."

Bill nodded.

"If they knew you were here, they could frame us both,"
Sue said. "They could plant cocaine in the house, then tip
the police. Maybe the burglary was a KGB set-up. Who
knows? As soon as we're charged with felonies, we're
neutralized."

"You think Vince would feel that threatened about the
nickel gas thing?"

"That and plutonium, but especially murder, especially
with as much evidence as we have."

"So, what do we do?" Bill said again.

"Turn him in."

"We might end up dead before the trial, or more
probably, like you said, get our lives destroyed by felony
charges. And even if they did charge him with murder, he'd
probably get away with it."

"With all this evidence?" Sue said.

"You can't convict a, quote *good guy* unquote, on
circumstantial evidence. That's why O. J. didn't get
convicted for murder. The black jury saw him as a good guy.
They would have convicted Fuhrman on the same evidence.
The white jury convicted O. J. because they saw him as a
bad guy."

"The white jury would have let Fuhrman go on the same
evidence," Sue said resignedly.

"Right. It's something my dad talked about a lot.
Everyone interprets the facts in accordance with their own
bias."

"Why would that matter?"

"If a bad guy walks past the victim's house, that's
sinister. He's casing the place, checking to see when she's
home, right?"

"Yeah, probably."

"But if your first grade school teacher walks by the same house, she's out for an evening stroll. Right?"

"Right," Sue said, a look of amazement on her face, "but everybody knows Vince is a bad guy."

"Everybody that you know knows," Bill said. "What does the jury know? You know those big ads that Vince runs twice a week or so? Especially the ones where the little house is sitting in the middle of a big blizzard, and the only thing between it and freezing solid are Vince Longto's big warm hands? And Vince Longto is standing there with a phony smile on his phony face, wearing phony gray stuff in his hair that the hairdresser just smeared all over.

"Think about it. What if we went to the Sheriff in Orlando and told him we just discovered that Walt Disney murdered all the farmers who wouldn't sell out to him, and that's how he was able to put the block of land together for Disney World? He'd get the people who wear white coats to cart us off in straightjackets, that's what. And I guess the big point is this Sheriff has never even seen Walt Disney.

"And it's the same with Vince Longto. I mean, all that advertising has created this wonderful image. It's an image of the all-American success story of the really nice boy who has made it on his own as a result of clean, hard work. In the western slope of Colorado, and surrounding states, he's right up there with everyone's first grade teacher."

"And the really ironic part," Sue said, "is that his utilities are what built the image. And since they are utilities, Vince passed all the costs on to its customers. In essence, the public is paying for the privilege of getting screwed."

"Bottom line, we can forget going to the police." Bill paused for effect, looked at Sue, and added, "So what are we going to do?"

"Kill him ourselves," Sue said.

"Serious?"

"Vince Longto is sitting around planning how he's going to destroy us just like he did Mary White. Maybe we'll even spend time in jail."

"Maybe Vince didn't do it?"

"He did it." Sue said. "And besides, the son of a bitch has created misery for thousands of honest people, and he's stolen almost fifty million dollars from the good people of Rawhide. So, I'd say he deserves to die, and if you know a good way to do it, I'm in."

"Good," Bill said. "I'll tell you the plan in the plane."

"Plan?"

"A good one, too. We'll get out of here after it gets dark."

Sue looked relieved and nodded. Bill looked at her carefully. His expression softened. "That's a whole hour away," Bill said, making little circles on her tummy with his right hand, and on her back with his left, the circumference gradually growing bigger. "What do you want to do in the meantime?"

40 – A Pretty Summer Cabin

Sue watched as the bright lights of southern Florida were quickly consumed by the blackness of the Everglades. In just moments, they went from civilization to wilderness. The little plane was smooth, and Billy seemed to know what he was doing.

Billy said, "I know where to get a jet engine for *Sally*. That way she'll be able to fly as fast as Vince Longto's jet. We fly up behind him and blow him out of the sky. It's that simple."

"Don't you need heavy artillery to blow a jet out of the sky?"

"You know how fast the turbine in a jet turns?"

"Really fast," Sue said.

"And you know what happens when too many blades come off the turbine?"

"It vibrates a lot," Sue said, her brow furrowed.

"It explodes. It's called a rotor burst. They might take out the other engine, and they might bust up the airplane. Chances are everybody dies. My dad owned a high-powered rifle he got when he was a kid from his grandpa. You shoot into the jet engine. It blows up, the plane crashes, and everyone dies. On the way back, we toss the rifle into a deep lake."

"Where's this jet?"

"Boulder, Colorado. My dad was going to put it in *Sally*. We just borrow it. When we're done, we take it back."

"There you go again, saying 'borrow' when what you mean is 'steal.'"

"It's borrowing. My dad had a deal with the widow to buy it. He was waiting to get the money together."

"Why'd he want to buy a jet?"

"To go faster." Billy looked at Sue. Sue looked back with a continuing query on her face. "In addition to having a thing for underage women," Bill said, "he was a speed freak."

"There was something wrong with me when I was seventeen?"

"It isn't right for a thirty-three year-old man to date a seventeen year-old girl."

"How would I know that?"

"A girl's a kid at seventeen."

"Like you?" Sue said.

Bill's brow furrowed as he stared off in thought for a moment.

"Dad had *Sally* ready to go for the jet's installation," Bill said. "He'd redone all the control surfaces on the plane to make them strong and flutter-free. He had the engine mount all made and ready to go."

Sue gave him a disapproving look.

"We'll take it back," Bill said. "We can't buy it, I mean, that's our alibi--not having one. How could we shoot Vince out of the sky with *Sally* if she can't catch him? It's that simple."

"But what if we get caught stealing the engine?"

"We say we're picking it up in accordance with my dad's deal." Billy avoided Sue's look. "It'll be a lot easier than when I found the bugs in your house without you knowing it."

"Where will we go to put it in this plane?" She pointed to the control panel.

"You mean *Sally*?" He looked at her. "Say it, *Sally*. It won't hurt you."

"*Sally*," Sue finally said with a dumb look on her face.

Bill smiled. "My dad owned a piece of land in the mountains. It's really isolated. It wasn't used for forty years after a bridge washed out because it took several hours to drive to it. When we moved back to Rawhide, my dad and I went up and built a landing strip. We flew up there on the weekends. There's stuff up there to work on *Sally*. The runway's short, but it'll be okay."

"How do we keep from killing an innocent bystander?"

"The mountain cabin land is line-of-sight to the Rawhide airport, even though it's about sixty miles away. It's kind of like looking down on the world. I'll put a video camera with a zoom lens at a good place at the airport in Rawhide."

"You mean like in a big ugly plywood blind right in the middle of the airport?" Sue said skeptically.

They looked at each other and broke out laughing.

"I'll install a wireless joystick device on the video camera so we can move it around."

"I hope it works."

"We'll be in Denver in a little more than five hours. You may as well get some sleep."

Sue slept, soundly at first, but she woke up when she started having bad dreams. "Where are we?" she said.

"That's Topeka, Kansas, over there."

Sue admired the view. Lights shined everywhere beneath them and in every direction. There was a concentration of lights where the city was, similar to the concentration of stars at the center of a galaxy.

"The stars are brilliant," Sue said, staring into the night sky. "The big one there is blue-white Sirius. It's the nose of Orion's hunting dog."

"I like Betelgeuse," Bill said.

"Where is it?"

"The orange one," Bill said pointing. "It's Orion's right shoulder."

"Go on," Sue said, "I only know a couple of them."

"Betelgeuse is a giant red star. Betelgeuse, Sirius and another star, Procyon, form a big isosceles triangle. Procyon is almost as bright and white as Sirius. It's the nose of the little dog, *Canis minor*.

"But what's really unusual are the three planets right in the middle of it all. There's Mars, bright and red. It's as bright as I've ever seen it. There's Jupiter, brighter even than Sirius, and Saturn is over there."

"What about all the other bright stars?" Sue said.

Billy told her about Orion, and the messier object hanging from its belt, and all about the Greek myths associated with the stars in their field of view.

They both looked at the stars, lost in thought.

"Don't they call kids that were raised like you super babies?" Sue said.

Bill's face was illuminated by the soft red glow of *Sally's* instrument panel. "Super baby's the press's term," Bill said. "For some reason the press likes to present things that people don't understand, like infant stimulation, in a negative way. But just like a lot of other things, the press has it wrong."

"What's infant stimulation?"

"Humans are strange because they have very little instinct, which means they have to learn almost everything. No other animal is born knowing so little. We have to learn to crawl, walk, talk, see, hear, everything. A baby who's kept cooped up in a crib will be clumsy and dumb for the rest of its life." Bill gave Sue a careful look.

"Do you know why some foreigners can never learn to say certain sounds, like the 'TH' sound?"

Sue shrugged.

"It's because they can't hear the sound. The 'TH' sound is a good example. They have no idea that they're saying it wrong because they can't hear it. And they can't hear it because they didn't hear it before a critical age. The proper pathways in their brain don't exist. Their auditory operating system doesn't have a 'TH' driver. It's that simple. If you learn a language before the critical age--usually before nine--you won't speak with a foreign accent. After that you will.

"Vince Longto's really smart because he was stimulated as an infant which gave him better drivers for normal things like reading and computing, and drivers for lots of other things that don't even have names. It gave him options as an adult that most people can only dream about."

"What was special about Longto's infancy?"

"A Chinese woman took care of him when he was little. She taught him to speak and read Chinese when he was still a baby."

Sue stared in amazement.

"Vince said something to Dad that made him curious enough to investigate. Dad found and then talked to one of the Chinese women who raised Vince."

"Vince tells everyone he didn't start learning Chinese until he was twenty. A reporter said it was impossible. Butzsaw came uncorked when the reporter said that. Butzsaw argued that Vince was a kind of super-human."

"What do you think about children?" Bill said.

Sue started to smile, then looked at Bill suspiciously. "They're okay," she said, guardedly.

"Dad made me promise I'd get married as soon as I could, and have babies so he could have Grandchildren. He said he really wanted a little girl with an even disposition who would sit on his lap."

"I guess you're relieved of that promise."

"But I still feel duty-bound. I like to think he's out there watching." Bill looked at Sue.

Sue avoided eye contact, shifted uneasily, and wondered where their relationship was going. What would people say?

"There're the lights of Denver," Bill said. "The engine's at the Boulder Airport, which is at the far beacon over there against the mountains. It's an uncontrolled airport, and I doubt there will be any traffic this time of day. I'll land without any lights so we aren't seen."

41 – The Execution

Bill overflew the airport. He said he was looking for aircraft in the pattern and aircraft on the ground that were preparing to depart. When he saw none, he executed an approach to the runway.

"We'll land a little hard," Bill said. The runway lights were close.

"How hard?" Sue said with alarm.

"Not hard enough to hurt anything. Without landing lights, I won't be able to flare because I won't be able to see the runway."

Sue braced herself. *Sally* shuddered when they hit. "Not bad," Bill said. He took her hand in both of his.

She liked the feel of his strong hands. But she still didn't feel comfortable, and suddenly she knew why. "Don't you have to steer?" she said.

Billy put both hands in the air. "You steer an airplane with your feet," he said.

Sue could see Bill's legs working as *Sally* veered sharply back and forth across the runway. "I knew that," she said, wanting him to stop, but afraid to complain. She grabbed his right hand and pulled it down. Billy smiled and kissed her forehead. Then he put his left hand on the back of her hand and squeezed. She took a deep breath and relaxed.

When he left the runway, there were no lights to follow. Bill opened *Sally's* canopy and shined a flashlight. Sue couldn't see a thing and worried they would hit something. Finally, he cut the engine, set the brake and jumped out.

"Won't be more than five minutes," he said as he disappeared into the blackness. Sue looked around, but couldn't see a thing. She was feeling quite uncomfortable when Bill finally returned.

He strained to get the box he was carrying into place in *Sally's* back seat. Sue was surprised that there was enough room. Then he strapped it in with the seat belt. He started *Sally* and began taxiing.

"Can *Sally* carry this much weight?" Sue said.

"We were five hundred pounds heavier when we left Florida. Burned a lot of fuel since then. The engine and the box together only weigh about a hundred pounds. We'll be okay.

"What about other planes?" Sue said, as he closed the canopy, pulled onto the runway, and added power. She didn't like the idea that everything was happening so fast.

"I looked already," Bill said. He barely had these words out when *Sally* became airborne.

Bill said it was a short flight, but they still needed fuel, so they stopped at an airport in the Denver area. Bill filled one tank with jet fuel. He told the line boy he was transporting it. Soon they were airborne again. He said it was a half-hour's flight. Sue felt uneasy as they departed. Bill took her right hand and held it in both of his. It made her feel much better and she was able to fall asleep.

It was getting light when Sue awoke. She was startled to see snow-covered peaks towering above them. Bill said *Sally's* Global Positioning System had brought them right to the cabin in the mountains.

"See the cabin?" Bill said.

"No, and I don't see the landing strip-either."

"It's really short."

Sue strained to see. She was looking for something that looked like a real runway, only smaller. "You mean that set of ruts?" Sue said with incredulity.

"The runway is the grass strip next to the ruts. All the big rocks have been cleared out."

"It's on the side of a hill," Sue said.

"It's inclined," Bill said. "Let me concentrate."

Sue didn't say a word. The closer they got to the tiny airstrip, the smaller it seemed. Bill set *Sally* down within fifty feet of the beginning of the strip. *Sally* hit with a thud then shook and rattled a lot worse than she had at Boulder. In just a couple seconds they slowed down. Sue started breathing again when she noticed their beautiful surroundings.

Bill taxied up to the cabin. The view into the valley was incredible.

"Why didn't your dad replace the bridge?" Sue said. "A landing strip seems like a lot more trouble."

"Forest Service wouldn't let him. You as tired as me?"

Sue smiled, then wondered if he had sex on his mind.

Bill had some trouble getting the cabin door open. When they entered, it had a peculiar smell, like stale wood, Sue thought. They slept in their street clothes on a musty-smelling bare mattress until early afternoon, then worked on the installation of the jet engine, which was made easy by the fact that Patton had already made extensive preparation for its installation.

At about five, Bill jumped in the cabin Jeep and engaged the starter. It took a little while, but it finally started. Bill said it was a four-hour drive to Rawhide, only sixty miles away, so they better get going.

It was dark when they reached the airport in Rawhide. Bill installed the monitor in an old wooden hangar. He said an old spray-plane pilot owned it, but he hadn't flown in years.

Bill cut a slit near the roof in the hangar, then mounted the monitor on a power swivel. He mounted an antenna on top of the hangar. The whole installation was crude, but Bill thought it would work. They finished late that night, drove back to the mountain cabin, then slept fitfully. Bill rose with the sun and installed the receiver equipment. He seemed surprised when he actually got a picture.

"Hey, look at this," Bill said. "Claude just pulled Vince's jet out of the hangar."

Sue came over and looked at the monitor. Trooper was walking up to Vince's jet. He pulled out his keys, unlocked the hatch, and climbed in. They listened on *Sally's* radio for him to pick up his flight plan.

"There he is," Bill said pointing to a figure walking up to the jet aircraft.

"It's Vince, no question," Sue said. They watched Vince climb into the jet and closed the hatch. Shortly thereafter the radio crackled, and Vince picked up their clearance. They were going to Salt Lake City at flight level 35.

"Perfect," Bill said. "Sue, watch the monitor while I fire *Sally* up. Make sure Longto doesn't get out." Sue also knew she had to make sure no one else climbed into Vince's jet before it took off.

"What's going on?" Bill said, taxiing up close. The little jet was screaming.

"Watch the monitor"--she had to yell to be heard--"while I climb in."

Sue was taken back when she looked at *Sally*. The jet engine was sticking way out behind the place where the propeller had been. "Are you sure this is okay?" Sue said, her brow furrowed.

"The engine has to be way back there for weight and balance. It weighs a third as much as the old engine. I put a couple big rocks back there to help out. It'll be all right." Bill was watching the monitor as he talked. "They're sitting at the end of the runway. He's waiting to depart."

Bill pressed his earphones tight with his hands. "He's got his clearance," Bill said. "Watch for him to take off so we can be sure only Vince and Trooper are on board."

"What about *Sally*?" Sue said.

"She's fine," Bill said indignantly. "There they go on their takeoff roll, now follow it. Okay, it's off, let's go. Grab that video camera." Bill had been using it as a VCR to record everything. Sue realized the second he said it that the tape would have to be disposed of just like the rifle.

Bill's enthusiasm was contagious. Sue forgot her concerns and strapped herself into *Sally*. Bill taxied quickly to the takeoff point, and added power.

Right off he added too much power and *Sally* began to fishtail. Bill pulled the power way back, and she straightened out. The runway was downhill, so *Sally* accelerated quickly in spite of his inability to add full power.

As soon as he was in the air, Bill jammed the throttle forward, and *Sally* promptly spun around until she was almost at a right angle to their direction of flight. As soon as he pulled power off, she righted herself. But they were low and slow, and there were big rocks and trees all around. Bill added power again slowly, and they began to climb.

Sue sat stiffly--her hands were fists at her side. She was scared that if she screamed, it might cause them to crash. Bill gave her encouraging looks, which only made her worry that he was going to run into something.

As they climbed out, Bill experimented with power settings, control input, and speed until he said he had a good feel for the new engine. He assured Sue that he had everything under control.

When he was finally going fast enough to use full power, *Sally* climbed out at an incredible rate. Bill explained that all the new power and the engine being so far back caused *Sally* to want to spin around at slow speed.

"She works good," Bill exclaimed with exuberance.

They hadn't had time to work out the rendezvous technique. Bill looked at Vince's flight plan for Salt Lake City and took up the appropriate heading.

When they got to the "victor" flight path, he turned onto the same course as Vince's jet.

They were breathing oxygen. Bill had installed another oxygen bottle to satisfy their extra oxygen needs at the higher altitude.

Bill scanned the sky with binoculars. "There's King's peak," Bill said. "We better catch them before they start down. Get your rifle loaded and ready to go."

He had cut a small port in the fiberglass portion of the canopy just below the Plexiglas for the muzzle of the deer-rifle. It had a cork in it. Sue needed to pull the cork out, but she didn't want to.

"What's the deal?" Bill said through his oxygen mask. "You weren't afraid when that guy was coming at us with big knives."

She pulled out the rifle and inserted a small, five-round clip. She reached up and gingerly touched the cork. She expected a gale force wind to come through when she pulled it. Bill reached up and yanked it out. Nothing happened.

"It's in a low-pressure area, just like the top of the wing," he said. "It's sucking, not blowing."

Sue put her hand up and felt. Air was rushing out. "It's right in the path of the oncoming air."

"So's the top part of the wing. If it wasn't a low pressure area we wouldn't be flying."

"Let's go over this again," Sue said.

"Okay," Bill began, "When you fire, it'll be like an explosion. I used the biggest load I could. Your headgear should protect your ears, but you'll feel a sharp impact on your face, eyes, and body. Don't let that bother you. Hang onto the rifle. We don't need it flying around in here."

"I wish we'd had time to practice," Sue said.

"The instant you fire, I'll jam the stick hard. It'll be a negative three-G maneuver. If your shoulder harness and seat belt are tight, you won't hit the canopy. If your legs are braced carefully, they won't fly into the bottom of the instrument panel."

Sue lifted a leg and felt where it would hit. Her shin would contact a sharp bulkhead. "Brace them like this?" she said, looking up.

"That should work."

"Three negative Gs won't hurt the airframe?"

They had discussed this point. Three Gs in the little airplane, even negative Gs, were a long way from damaging its structure.

"We don't have to do this, you know," Bill said, gently, looking into her gray eyes. He patted her thigh.

"I'm braced in like this," Sue said, holding the rifle in position, sighting through its scope. "When the slug hits the blades in the turbine in Vince's jet, the whole engine will blow up throwing shrapnel everywhere."

"Right, the engine should fly off the aircraft, pulling big pieces with it. It will take a second for it to be accelerated toward us by the slipstream. Before it gets to our position, we duck out of the way. That's the negative three G maneuver."

There wasn't much chance she would miss when she fired at the other plane. She always got her deer with one shot, often at a range of more than two hundred yards. "I'm ready," Sue said. "Now all we have to do is find them." "Will they see us on radar?"

"Vince's radar can only see weather. A controller might see something but *Sally's* small and plastic, and she barely shows up. Here," Bill said, handing her the binoculars, "you want to look for a while?"

"There's something, over there," Sue said shortly and handed the binoculars to Bill.

"It's them. We'll catch them in about five minutes."

Gradually the speck in the sky grew larger until Vince Longto's jet was right in front of them. Sue slipped a round of ammunition into the chamber of the high-powered rifle, closed the bolt and released the safety.

When the jet loomed big in front, Bill pulled the power back just a little, and eased them into the right spot about fifty yards behind, and a little below the Citation.

"Now?" Sue, said sighting through the scope of the rifle, her finger firmly on the trigger, her legs braced.

"Now!" Bill commanded.

The cross hairs in the scope were on the jet engine. Her finger was on the trigger, slowly squeezing. Suddenly she stopped.

"I can't do this," Sue said, dropping the rifle. "Vince Longto's your uncle."

Bill gave Sue a stunned look.

"Look out!" Sue screamed.

They were on a collision course with the Citation. Without an instant to spare, Bill pushed hard on the stick. *Sally* responded crisply. At the speed they were going the maneuver resulted in several negative Gs. Sue hit the end of the travel on her seat belt hard and it cut into her shoulders. Her neck stretched. They barely missed the Citation and slipped underneath.

"What happened?" Sue said.

"He must have slowed down to begin his descent into Salt Lake," Bill said. He circled around with the power pulled way back.

"God, we'd be dead if we hadn't had our seat belts on tight," Sue said. She listened to the voice on the radio for an instant. The controller seemed upset. "Is that the controller calling Vince's plane? Why aren't they answering?" *Sally* was about a quarter of a mile behind the jet.

"Now look," Bill exclaimed.

The Citation was bouncing up and down so hard its wings were flexing in big arcs. Bill reached out and pulled all the power off in order to slow down, then he tightened his already tight shoulder harness.

"Tighten your seat belt," Bill yelled. "Hang on to that rifle and brace yourself. If we're lucky we'll slow down enough before we hit it."

"What's going on?" Sue said when nothing happened. Her hands were getting tired from squeezing the rifle.

"The way Vince's jet was bouncing up and down, I thought the wings might come off. He must have hit incredible turbulence but I guess we missed it. Didn't you tell me that Vince doesn't like to wear his seat belt?"

"That's right."

"If he didn't have it on when they went through that turbulence, he might be dead."

"Let's take a look," Sue said.

The Citation was almost out of sight. Bill pointed *Sally's* nose down and added power. The controllers were still calling the Citation. There was no answer.

"He's getting off course," Bill said. "If no one's at the controls, he'll crash into a mountain on Antelope Island in the Great Salt Lake."

When they caught up to the Citation, they could see someone in the front crumpled up facedown in the cockpit. They couldn't tell for sure, but they thought it was Longto. His arm was moving like he was trying to pull himself up. Bill grabbed the video camera, punched the record button, then placed it on his right shoulder and pointed it to where he was looking.

The body continued, with difficulty, to pull himself higher. His legs didn't appear to be working. His lower back was bent in a way that made Sue shudder. It had to be broken. Suddenly the head popped up. It was Longto, and he looked hideously deformed. His face was contorted in anger and pain. Slowly he turned and looked right into Sue's face. His surprised look quickly turned to rage.

"You're going to die, Longto," Sue said in a cocky way that she hoped Longto would understand to mean that she had something to do with his situation.

Suddenly Longto looked away from them and appeared to yell into the aircraft. Blood bubbles formed around his mouth.

Sue followed Vince's gaze and looked toward the rear of the aircraft.

"Look," Sue said, in amazement, "the hatch is opening." Bill held the camera between his head and shoulder to free his right hand so he could maneuver to a position immediately behind and below the hatch.

They stared bewildered as a figure emerged, then jumped. *Sally* was in the way. In mid-leap, he grabbed the side of the hatch, but his momentum carried his feet out the door, and he was hanging by his hands. He must have pulled the ripcord because his parachute started paying out. Bill nudged *Sally* out of the way. The chute filled and jerked the man violently away from the hatch. But part of the chute became tangled on the jet engine, and he quickly stopped again.

Bill eased away, and when he did, a mountain filled their view.

"Look out!" Sue screamed again.

The easiest way would have been to go over the top of the mountain, but the Citation was in the way. Bill turned hard. *Sally* responded crisply. They could both see they'd hit the mountain unless the turn was very tight.

The G forces pulled Sue deeply into her seat. Everything turned gray. Sue thought she would pass out. She hoped Bill didn't. The mountain seemed inches away. Just as Sue's consciousness began to slip away, the pressure eased. Sue's vision was impaired, but they must have missed it.

When Sue's vision returned to normal, all she could see was blue sky. *Sally's* nose was pointed high. Bill was wrestling with the controls. Sue was amazed to see that the video camera was still on his shoulder. It took him a couple seconds to get oriented and put *Sally* back into a normal configuration.

They were both looking for the Citation but couldn't see it.

"Look," Sue said. She was pointing to something falling rapidly. It looked like a parachute that hadn't opened. Bill looked just in time to see the person hit the jagged edge of a cliff, spin, hit again, and then disappear into jagged rocks. The chute drifted down. Bill turned toward the mountain again and climbed higher. There, beyond the mountain was the Citation, spinning like a boomerang, one wing in flames.

"He must have grazed the top of the mountain," Bill said. Before he got those words all the way out, the Citation burst into a ball of flames as it contacted the far shore of the Great Salt Lake. They stared; their jaws hung open. They looked at each other.

"Look at the boat," Bill said, pointing to a speedboat with its bow on the beach.

Sue swung around and looked with her binoculars. Bill dropped *Sally* down to the deck just a couple feet from the top of the water. Sue was looking straight ahead into the eyes of the man standing on the bow of the boat. "I don't believe it," she exclaimed. "It's Uri Novotny."

Bill gave *Sally's* stick a nudge, and she popped up just high enough to slip over the top of the boat. Then they were over the lake again, skimming the waves. After a little while, he eased off on power and *Sally* began a gradual climb.

"You going to hold that thing on your shoulder forever?" Sue said.

Bill stopped the camera, set it in his lap, then turned his neck as if it were stiff. There was a deep crease on his cheek.

"Novotny," Sue said, "is the man who was most in charge of Vince's Russian operations. You know, the man Trooper was talking to in the first Russian tape."

"Listen," Bill said, "it's Salt Lake approach. They're guiding a helicopter that was in the area to the crash site."

The helicopter asked how many were on board.

"According to the flight plan," came the answer from the controller, "there was only one."

Sue and Bill looked at each other with another look of bewilderment. They had both seen two people climb into the jet and the injured man they'd seen in the cockpit couldn't have been the man who jumped. They continued flying slowly over the Great Salt Lake.

"Got any ideas?" Bill said

"We better take the jet engine back first thing," Sue said.

"It works so well, I think I'll keep it."

"What about our alibi?"

"Don't need it any more. I'll send her a check as soon as we get back. I promise."

"You have that kind of money?"

"Before my dad went bankrupt, he gave me royalties in production where horizontal wells were planned. I have enough in the bank to put us both through medical school."

Sue looked at Billy and wished his father had been like him. But it wasn't fair to compare, she thought. Billy looked at her for a moment. He had dark, handsome eyes. Why couldn't he be older? she mused.

"We need to do some heavy-duty thinking," Bill said, "and I think best when I'm building something. *Sally's* looking pretty silly with that jet sticking out, so why don't we go back to the cabin and I'll build her a new cowling, and do some things to get more weight in the back."

"How long will it take?"

"My guess is two days. But when you're building, always multiply your first impression times three, so maybe a week."

"What if I help?" Sue said.

"Two weeks," Bill said, smiling, but when Sue wasn't amused, he added, "If you can build like you fight, maybe one-day."

Sue liked it when Bill smiled.

Bill punched in the coordinates for the mountain cabin and turned on course. He said it would be a short flight.

Uri Novotny watched as Efremov's body smashed into the rocks. It was good, he thought. Efremov knew too much and his irresponsible ways were a danger to the organization.

Novotny had seen Longto's plane graze the top of the mountain and knew it would crash. He'd return in the evening with a couple men to dispose of Efremov's body, he thought. He couldn't help it when a broad smile appeared on his face. He was very happy at the way everything was turning out.

Suddenly he caught a movement and turned. For an instant he was confused at what he was looking at. It was white and getting bigger. He raised his binoculars. It took him a moment to realize that he was looking at a small airplane and inside he saw a young man and, he wasn't sure--another person? He saw movement, then a person appeared, and he understood that the person had dropped a pair of binoculars. When he looked more closely, he looked into the familiar face of Sue Hansen, which let him understand who the boy was and the aircraft. It was the one he'd seen on national television flying over Seattle. Novotny shook his head in total disgust as he recalled the conversation where Efremov had bragged to him about killing the owner of this airplane simply because he didn't like him.

The tiny aircraft passed so close overhead that Novotny ducked. He looked with amazement at the jet engine. He couldn't understand how the two had made the little aircraft into a jet, but it must have been what they had been doing at their mountain hideaway. He wondered why they were so close to Longto's jet and decided they must have been trying to kill Efremov. Maybe they were trying to kill Longto, too, thinking he'd ordered the killing of the boy's father.

For an instant, he wished that he'd heeded Efremov's advice and let him kill the two in Florida. Novotny backed away from the island, turned to his destination and added power. He hated the idea that there had to be more violence and cussed Efremov's dead body for its necessity.

He picked up his communicator and began talking. He needed a couple small aircraft, a helicopter, and several soldiers. He was told the soldiers would have to come out of Chicago or New York City. The only thing standing between him and his grand plan was Sue Hansen and the Patton boy. He was worried, but not in despair. The two would return to the mountain thinking they were safe. The location was isolated. Their bodies would disappear without a trace.

"Now what's this about Vince being my uncle?" Bill said, his voice low and resigned.

"Your dad told me," Sue said. "I promised never to tell. I'll tell you only because he isn't here to do it himself. Your grandpa, Billy Patton, had to get married to your grandma Ann."

"I heard that."

"Did you know that he had two girls pregnant at the same time?"

Bill's brow furrowed, then his eyebrows jumped, "You mean, he was dating Linda Longto? He got her pregnant but he picked my grandma to marry?"

"That's about right. Your grandpa told your dad about his other brother when your dad graduated from college. It was no mistake that Vince went to work for your dad. Your dad searched for Vince and befriended him. When he found out how good Vince was at doing things, he talked him into going to work for him."

Bill listened carefully.

"Tom called Vince into his office and told him he wanted to offer him a partnership in his business. It's at that meeting that Tom told Vince that they were brothers. Since your dad didn't have a Brother, he really liked the idea, and he genuinely liked Vince. But at that meeting Vince changed. Your dad didn't know why, but I think I do," Sue said.

"Why?"

"When Vince was tiny, he hated his little brother, and he spent a lot of time devising ways to kill him. When he got older, he could see his little brother wasn't a real threat, and searched for ways to rid himself of his irrational desires. His Shrine in the desert allowed him to overcome his crazy hatred for his little brother. Your father had a commanding, charismatic presence. Your father had money and power and he was Vince's boss. Your father had a Mother and Father who loved him, and a good college education. Vince couldn't look at your father without feeling cheated. When he discovered that they were brothers, his hating ways came back strong."

"You think he buried his Shrine so nothing stood between him and his hatred?"

"He had to rise above your father, both by bringing himself up, and by bringing your father down, which meant he had to do things that his Shrine wouldn't let him do."

"Why didn't you tell me before?" Bill said.

"I kept thinking that a biological connection doesn't matter that much. But now I'm not so sure because they were a lot alike. They had a lot of the same motivational patterns. Vince was smarter, but your dad was awful smart, too, and his formal education sometimes gave him the advantage."

"And they looked alike," Bill said. Sue gave him a funny look. "It was in the eyes. I can't tell you exactly what it was, but I noticed it more than once."

"They were both big risk takers, and they both had big egos. But, the differences were enormous. Your dad was kind and nice and he cared about other people's feelings. Vince cheated, defrauded, and defamed. He didn't care how much pain he caused."

"He may never have learned that his actions caused others to feel pain," Bill said.

The two cruised quietly over jagged Utah mountains, neither noticing the magnificent view.

"Look at this." Bill pointed to the storm scope. "It looks like we'll have to wait to land at the cabin."

"What is it?"

"Huge thunderstorms. We can probably see them from here." He looked up from the instrument panel and peered ahead. "See those billowing clouds over there?" Bill pointed off in the distance to towering cumulonimbus clouds. They seemed to cover an area about ten miles wide.

Bill pulled the power way back. *Sally* slowed, and her fuel consumption dropped to below five gallons an hour.

"Man, look at the lightning," Sue said when they were up close.

"You know where this storm is?" Bill said. "Right over the top of Devil's Kitchen. The area never gets rain. At least not in my lifetime."

Bill pulled more power back and began to descend. He pointed *Sally* toward the deep canyon where Hell's Creek came out of Devil's Kitchen. "Where the rain ends," Bill said, "that's where I found the amber in my ring. It's just like my dad said: There's a raging river where before there was nothing."

The river exited the canyon, then fanned out over the valley. In the canyon it was a torrent, and it carried bushes, grasses, and trees. It looked dark brown like it was half mud and half water. Much of it was covered with white foam. The rain had by now let up, but thick dark clouds still loomed high.

"I guess I'll finally see the shark," Bill said. "Let's go in and take a look."

"Sounds good," Sue said, leaning forward to see better.

"I can see the place from here," Bill said. "It's only five miles away." Bill dropped *Sally* down a little lower and flew up Hell's Creek.

"There's the road that Vince used for access to his gas wells at his Enigma gas field. Look, the bridge is washed out. The water isn't so high now, but you can see how high it was from the way the area around the creek is disturbed. Okay, there's the ridgeline. Now, where it crosses the creek, that's where the shark is."

Bill stood *Sally* up on her wing so Sue could see. Then, "I don't see it," Bill said. "The place where the stream went through was really narrow. Now it's a big hole."

"Maybe the flood cut it out?"

"Don't say such a thing."

They flew by again and confirmed that the place where the shark had been had become a big, gaping hole.

"Can you imagine the amount of water it took to do that?"

Bill added power, and pointed *Sally* toward the cabin.

◎ ◎ ◎

In half an hour, the thunderstorms had dropped enough water in Devil's Kitchen to fill a medium-sized lake. The ground soaked up a little, but not much. With virtually no vegetation, big raindrops hammered the shaly ground, turning it to mud. Muddy water filled rivulets that cut scars everywhere they flowed. Rivulets flowed into gullies where the dark brown water, viscous with mud, swirled and foamed and suspended all the loose shale and dirt that had been waiting for years for this moment. In hundreds of locations, agitated water cut into gully walls causing large chunks of the hillside to cave in. In some cases, a cave-in would form a dam, only to be washed out moments later by a build-up of agitated, muddy water.

Little gullies dumped into larger gullies that dumped into Hell's Creek. Soon Hell's Creek was a churning, foaming torrent. It backed up against Vince's bridge, then flowed over and around. It undermined the bridge's foundation, then sent the bridge tumbling down the creek, disintegrating as it went.

Water quickly breached the dam made by the cast-shot that covered Vince's Shrine, the jaws of hell. Even after the dam was washed out, the cut was not large enough to carry the torrent. It undermined and busted out the section of the sandstone that contained the shark. Then, just like the bridge, the shark tumbled and disintegrated. Teeth and bones were scattered helter-skelter.

The shark and the dinosaur were relieved of their expression of agony.

42 – The Next Plan

When they were on the ground, Bill took a long-faced look at *Sally*. The sun was getting low. "I can't think," Bill said. "I know where there's a natural hot tub where we can relax." Sue smiled. "I wonder if there's anything to drink in the cabin?" Bill said. He went in, and after a while he came out with a bottle and a box of crackers.

"You think this stuff's okay?" Sue said, looking at the old bottle and trying to read its faded label.

"It's good. Has a peppermint flavor. Alcohol preserves it. Come on, I'm going to show you the most relaxing place on this planet. It's a hot spring."

"We'll need swim suits."

"Can't wear them in this hot spring on account of an old Indian curse." Billy wore a stern look.

"Okay, but don't get any ideas. We're out of condoms, remember?"

"Oh, no we're not. I found these in the bottom of an old dresser underneath an old four-inch-long hat pin."

Bill held up a couple small packets. Sue took one. *Guaranteed Fresh for Forty Years* was written on the packet. "Way to go," Sue said. "One for the hot spring and one for the cabin later on."

Bill took Sue's hand, and they walked into the forest.

The next morning they awoke refreshed and went to work. Bill referred to *Sally's* manual. He had to figure out how to move *Sally's* engine forward.

"The first thing we need to do is move as much equipment back into the engine compartment as we can, so we can move this new engine forward. Right now, it's at station two hundred and thirty, which means it's two hundred and thirty inches from the tip of the nose. We should move it forward to at least station one-ninety."

"What can we move?" Sue said.

"The most obvious thing's the battery. It weighs thirty-five pounds. Right now, it's at one-fifteen. If we move it back to station one-eighty, then we can move the engine up," Bill hesitated for a moment in thought, "almost ten inches. Then, we can move the oxygen tanks, the tool kit, and the emergency radio. That's about eight pounds. Not much weight, but now they're way up front, at station thirteen. Moving them will make a big difference. If we put them at station one-sixty, then we can move the engine forward another ten inches."

"How do you know all this?" Sue said, bewildered.

"How do I know all what?"

"How do you know that if you move the battery from--"

"From station one fifteen," Bill offered.

"--to another place, that you can move the engine--how much, ten inches?"

"I figured it out." Bill smiled broadly.

"In your head?"

"Actually, I used the semi-portable desk-top computer I keep in my back pocket."

Sue stared in awe. "It isn't normal. People can't do numbers in their head."

"Vince Longto could, and my great-grandpa, too. My dad said before there were calculators people had to be really good at figuring in their head, so his dad--my great-great-granddad--drilled him on it when he was a little boy. He could still do it when he was eighty. It really came in handy for him. He owned a car dealership in Ft. Collins." Bill looked at Sue. "I guess you knew that, huh?"

Sue smiled. "So, what's your excuse?" Sue's face brightened and she added, "Is this what you learned to do by seeing the dots?"

Bill shrugged. "That's what my dad said. He said the dots don't teach a person to do it *per se*. The dots stimulate the formation of a mathematics operating system, like a math co-processor that can be used later to build on. A math co-processor won't do you any good if you don't have the software to go with it. That's what dots do for you, give you a math co-processor. It doesn't do anything for you if you don't build on it. My dad said he was giving me options so I could do what I wanted.

"Anyway," Bill said, "we're still a long way off in getting *Sally* into balance. I guess we can put a baggage compartment back there big enough for a couple fold-up bicycles."

"Fold-up bicycles?" Sue said.

"Yeah, to get around when we go to a really weird place like Greenland."

"Greenland?"

"Sally can go anywhere," Bill said with equal enthusiasm. "That's another forty pounds, plus another twenty for little two-cycle motors, and we're in pretty good shape."

First, the motor mount was shortened--an easy task since Patton had designed it to be adjustable. Then the new baggage compartment was installed between the new engine and the firewall.

The entire engine area was covered with newspaper and masking tape. Bill brought out some stuff he called "pour foam." It was a liquid that foamed first and then became solid. He poured and sprayed the liquid foam until the engine area looked like a giant hornet's nest. Then he got out sanding boards and the two began shaping and sanding.

"Sometimes I wonder what made Vince the way he was," Sue said.

"I think I know," Bill said.

"Let's have it."

"You know how we were talking about how humans have to learn basic skills like walking, talking, even seeing and hearing--things other animals are born knowing? Animals are also born with social skills, and we call that instinct, too."

"Like all dogs seem to act like a dog even if they have never seen another dog?" Sue said. "What does this have to do with Vince Longto being a slime?"

"The strategies we humans learn are sometimes more compelling than animal-type instincts," Bill said. "Spiders are good food. Lots of protein, vitamins, minerals, carbohydrate, fat, the works. But you'd starve to death before you'd eat a bunch of them. I probably would, too. But if you learned to eat them when you were an infant, you'd love 'em."

"Most people eat bugs. We're kind of rare."

"And how about some of the religious stuff that people learn when they're young? I read once about a native fella in Africa who grew up thinking that a particular kind of a bird was sacred and if he ate one he'd die. A professor brought him to Europe. When he was educated, the professor invited him over for dinner."

"And fed him the sacred bird," Sue chimed in. "When the professor told the guy what he'd eaten, he died in a day. So, you're saying that Vince learned some really bad habits when he was raised? It's that simple?"

"That simple. My dad always told me that most successful people have just the right bad habits, sometimes called neuroses, things we do without thinking."

"That's why you have to be raised in a restaurant to be a really good at running one?"

"Exactly. In Vince's case, his obsession to cheat and defame made him rich. It was the way he operated. Cheat before you get cheated."

"But everyone says Vince was rich because he was so smart."

"You're as smart as Vince and you're not a billionaire. Two percent of the population qualifies in the genius category, which means there are millions of geniuses just here in the United States--only a tiny fraction of whom are billionaires."

"So, how did Vince get that way?"

"It's what he saw. He was cheated. His mother hated him, but loved his little brother. It was the ultimate fraud, a Mother who gave him life but not love. Every time he cheated someone, it was a victory over the fraud of his childhood."

"How can you be sure that's what happened?"

"I heard about Vince from my dad and now from you. I think it's the most likely explanation. I think the basic thesis is viable."

"You mean that fixed behavior--a person's personality for life--is learned in infancy? I guess you could be right. I read recently that babies can grow up to be aggressive because of what they learned in the womb."

"How would anyone know?" Bill said.

"Studies, I guess. I think it said that the Mother's stress was sensed by the fetus as aggression."

"Which caused its little brain to be hard-wired for aggression," Bill said. "Makes sense to me. Seems like an easy enough adaptation for evolution to build in. The Mother's stress would mean it's a hostile world out there-- *better prepare for it.*"

"Doesn't make sense to me. How can a fetus know or do, or learn anything?"

"As adults, they know if their mother tried to abort them."

Sue gave Bill an incredulous look.

"If an abortion is attempted," Bill said, "a later suicide will usually occur at the same time of year."

"Get serious."

"Scientific."

They were making progress. *Sally* was looking good. Her engine area had a nice-looking aerodynamic shape.

"So, what do you think?" Bill said. "Did Trooper murder Vince, or was it turbulence? And what was Novotny doing standing on a boat on the beach of Antelope island in the middle of the Great Salt Lake?"

"He must have been there to pick Trooper up, which means it was probably murder by conspiracy."

Bill grimaced. "What reason did the Russians have to kill Vince?" he said.

Sue thought until her face brightened. "Vince's deal with the Russians lasted for *his* lifetime only. His estate was still entitled to substantial ownership, but it was in the form of non-voting stock. All his voting shares reverted to Russia."

"So, what happens now that Russia's embracing capitalism?"

"Vince was working on that. He kept asking, and the Russians kept saying they'd deal with it when they got it. But Vince wasn't happy with that. It scared him that someone might profit from his death. Everyone thought he was being neurotic."

"Tell me about Vince's Russian operation."

"Vince hired KGB agents as executives. Everyone thinks they were involved in the assassination of the close relatives of several high-level bureaucrats."

"Maybe his Russian executives figured if Vince died they could buy his stock back from Russia. Do they have access to money?"

"They're selling two hundred thousand barrels of crude a day at fifteen dollars a barrel. That's ninety million dollars a month, and their expenses run about forty-five million."

"But do they have access to it?"

"Not really," Sue said. "It all goes directly to the bank in Denver."

"If they don't have access, how did this Novotny get the money to come to the States, and hire a boat, and who knows what else?"

"Good question," Sue said.

"My dad told me a lot about fraud in the oil patch. He said the people who had authority to spend money were under pressure to spend with a certain company. He said lots of times there were kickbacks. And sometimes a company man would even 'sell' the company's oil, for ten cents on the dollar to a crook, like that guy in Gillette, Wyoming, with the water trucks. Do you think they could've been doing that?"

"In Russia," Sue said, "if they weren't doing stuff like that, it wouldn't be normal."

"So maybe they could spend twenty thousand dollars a week on some secret project, and Vince's home office might not even know about it. On the other hand, that might not be enough to buy the voting stock."

"There are four directors, two Russian and two—Jean Butzsaw and Vince--Americans. Vince had the tie-breaking vote. So, with Vince dead, and until his seat is replaced, they can do what they want."

"They could direct the company to buy the voting stock from the Russian government. Then they could have the company sell some to them. They wouldn't need much to have control of the company because what they bought would be the only shares that could vote. They'd have control and that's almost as good as ownership. They could pay themselves almost any amount they wanted."

"And give themselves virtually any perk," Sue added.

They worked on in silence. Things were taking shape quickly. They finished the lay-up of the first thin layer of fiberglass. When it was cured, they would cover it with a releasing agent. Then they would lay up a double layer of fiberglass, and when it was cured, peel it off. That would become the cowling itself. Then the first layer of fiberglass and foam would be cut, hacked, and sawed off to reveal *Sally's* engine again. After fasteners were put in place and after painting, they would be done.

"So, it looks like Trooper filed a flight plan showing Vince as the pilot and only passenger," Sue said.

"Trooper could have filed the flight plan by FAX. Then Trooper let Vince activate the flight plan so no one would hear his voice. When Vince wasn't wearing his seat belt, Trooper beat him silly by bouncing the jet up and down. Trooper set the jet on a collision course with the mountain on Antelope Island in the Great Salt Lake and bailed out."

"Yeah," Sue said, "and since Novotny was there waiting, that means the whole Russian operation was in on it."

"And they have lots of funds and access to really well-trained bad guys," Bill said. His eyes got big. "Did that guy see you?" Bill said with sudden urgency, "the head Russian?"

"I think so. He picked up a pair of binoculars and looked at us just as I put mine down." Sue's eyes were big. "They can't have us telling about how they murdered Vince. That would spoil everything for them."

They both looked up, hearing a small plane. It flew over, then began to circle. Soon, another joined it.

"Come on," Bill said, as soon as they saw the first one, "we have to close the runway." They jumped in the cabin Jeep and rumbled over the rough road.

"How are we going to do that?" Sue said.

"You know the narrow place on the landing strip, rocks on one side, trees on the other? We need to drag a couple logs across there so they can't land."

They were none too soon getting a log in place. One of the planes was on final approach and had to go around to avoid hitting it as they dragged it into the right place.

"Bill Patton." It was a booming voice on a loudspeaker coming from one of the planes. "Sue Hansen. FBI. We have to talk to you. Open the runway."

Bill and Sue looked at each other, not knowing what to do.

"What do you think?" Bill said.

"The ex-KGB guys would lie about who they were as a matter of course," Sue said. "Let's go call them--the FBI, I mean."

"We can't do that. We just conspired to kill someone in an airplane that was modified for a firearm, and we've been moving across state lines. There's probably a dozen Federal felonies in all that, and if we get caught lying to them about it, that's another felony. I just stole a jet engine--at least until I get a chance to send the widow lady a check--and transported it across state lines. There's probably a couple more felonies in all that."

"All we have to do is get our story straight."

"But we're amateurs," Bill said. "We have to spend some time getting our story straight, otherwise we'll get caught and find ourselves in prison. It's getting dark so they'll have to drive up here now. That means we have several hours. *Sally* can easily be towed. We fold up her nose gear, then attach her nose to a point on the back of the Jeep. There's a long stretch of Forest Service road in a clearing about five miles away that we can use as a runway."

"Why don't we use our runway?"

"It'll be dark before *Sally's* ready. That runway's trouble enough in daytime."

"What if we meet them on the way in?" Sue said.

"There are several ways out. I know one that's not on the map. It's just a trail but it avoids forested areas so *Sally's* wings shouldn't be a problem. It won't take that long to get *Sally* ready to fly. We'll have to move the engine back to where it was because I haven't moved any weight back yet."

Sue gave him a worried look.

"It just has to be good enough to get us out of here."

"Let's do it," Sue said. They went right to work on *Sally*. It took them a half-hour to peel off all the foam, then another half-hour to move the engine back. They hooked her up to the pickup and started down the trail.

They were on the top of a high hill overlooking the cabin when they saw lights of vehicles approaching the cabin. When the vehicles switched off their lights, Bill pulled out his night vision binoculars.

Bill said: "There are two Jeeps with two men in each." He reported that the four men parked their Jeeps a couple hundred yards from the cabin. One stayed behind. "It doesn't look like they have any night vision equipment. I can't tell if they're armed; they're all wearing windbreakers. Here," Bill handed the binoculars to Sue, "see if you know any of them."

"I don't, but that doesn't mean much. There are thousands of out-of-work tough guys in Russia all willing to work for little or nothing, and all of them are expert killers."

"If we do it now we can disable their vehicles."

The vehicles were parked more than a mile from where the two stood. Bill and Sue went down a game trail toward the parked vehicles.

"There's a guy watching the Jeeps," Sue said, looking through the night binoculars.

"Let's go up and beat him senseless," Bill said. "I brought these nylon wire-ties along so we can handcuff him."

"What if he's FBI?" Sue said.

"What's one more felony?"

Sue's frown showed Bill she wasn't going for that plan.

"Do Russians like to smoke?" Bill said.

"They sure do, even educated Russians, and that's one reason to believe he's Russian. All those guys were smoking. I'd say we're pretty safe, but I'd like one more test. What could it be?

"Let's get down fairly close," Bill said. "Then you start cussing at me in Russian for coming home drunk. If he calls out in Russian, we've tagged him."

"What if he comes to investigate?"

"That's what this is for," Bill said, pulling a burlap bag out of his knapsack. "You hide in this while I disable their vehicles. He won't see you in this."

"You mean like they didn't find your blind at the Rawhide airport? Which brings up something that's been bothering me: After almost getting caught, why did you set up a blind in Florida?"

"It had three escape doors, one on the roof, one on the side, and one on the floor. The one on the roof went into a false ceiling where I could hide."

"Clever," Sue said. "Does this sack have an escape hatch?"

"If he finds you, I'll come to your rescue."

Sue didn't look reassured. "I guess it's better than nothing," she said. "Let's do it."

They moved closer, and found a spot with bushes where they could hide. Sue stepped into the sack and held it to her neck, ready to close it over her head. As Bill watched, she started yelling in Russian, *"You no good drunken slob, what do you think you're doing coming home drunk again. You smell like a vodka factory."*

Bill had difficulty not laughing out loud as he watched the man struggling with many emotions at once. Bill signaled to Sue to be quiet. The man stood as far from the Jeeps as he dared and shined his flashlight in their direction, but they were well out of flashlight range. The man didn't call out and he didn't leave the Jeeps. Bill told Sue to yell again, then hide. He'd go see what he could do.

The man was standing about twenty feet in front of the Jeeps. Bill circled around and sneaked up from behind, then he crawled under the first Jeep and, pulling out a pair of side-cutters, he clipped the fuel line. As he moved to the second Jeep, he pulled out the night scope, but the man was nowhere to be seen.

As Bill contemplated his situation, he became seized with fright. His heart raced and he couldn't control his breathing. He could hear his breath plainly, even his heart--could the man hear? Where did he go?

Then he saw one of them. The man was looking for Sue. The man stopped, his flashlight pointed down to where Sue was hiding. As he stood there, the man reached up with his left hand and placed it on his belt, then he began to talk like he was keying a microphone from his belt.

Soon the other two from the cabin joined him. One was still not accounted for. Bill's heart raced. His impulse was to run to help Sue, but there was something wrong. They weren't acting like they'd found a person.

Unsure, Bill waited. One of them bent over and picked up an empty sack. Another one inspected it, and threw it down. They were looking at the ground and shining their flashlights around in the direction Sue and Bill had come from. Two of them walked in that direction. The other one walked back toward Bill.

Bill crawled toward the back of the Jeep. On the way, he smelled gasoline fumes. The ground he was crawling on was wet with gasoline.

He didn't have much time; the others would be back any second. He had no choice. He made his move for the other Jeep. It wasn't far. Suddenly there was an explosion of light. A man with a flashlight was stepping out from behind the second Jeep, shining the light around. Bill rolled back under the first Jeep into the gasoline. The man walked by smoking a cigarette.

When the man was gone, Bill crawled to the other Jeep and cut the gas line. Then, with no time to spare, he crawled out the other side and into some juniper bushes. It was like crawling into cactus. He waited, not wanting to make any noise. He thought about how Sue would have been caught if she had stayed put. He moved up the slope, and watched.

Two of them stopped by the Jeep. One of them shined a flashlight under the Jeep and illuminated the stream of leaking gasoline. The three began looking around. It looked like they were looking for tracks. Bill didn't want to move any farther up the slope. It was steep, and little rocks and debris would roll down, maybe give him away.

He had just crossed a game trail. He didn't like going back down, but that's what he needed to do. It would be quieter, his tracks would not be so obvious, and it would be quicker going. When he reached the trail, two flashlights were at the bottom of the hill following his trail. He moved quickly. He hoped he was out of flashlight range.

Crossing the game trail got him time. It sent his pursuers farther up the side of the hill. It took them several minutes to find his trail again, and by then Bill had a pretty good lead. He found a trail which brought him off the slope, then he circled back to where Sue had been hiding, and looked through the binoculars. Her trail was visible in the grass, and so were the trails of the men following her. Bill began following the tracks at a run. Within a few paces, his foot fell into a prairie dog's hole and he tumbled head over heel. His head smashed into a small bush on the ground. The smell of sage was powerful. Dust got into his mouth and eyes. He set off again at a brisk walk.

When he came to a small ravine crossing his path with a mountain brook at its bottom, he stopped at a high point and looked for the best way to get across. Something was moving on the far bank. At first he thought it was a bear.

When he looked through his binoculars, he could see it was a man. It looked like his clothes were wet. Bill moved a little closer.

The man was trying to climb the bank, but he kept stumbling. His face and clothes were covered with something, blood maybe. Color was not visible in the night scope.

Bill wondered if he should handcuff the man, then decided against it. His arms were useless. He wondered if one Russian had beaten up on the other.

Bill picked up Sue's tracks again on the road heading to *Sally*. He stayed on the short grass on the side of the road to avoid leaving tracks in the soft dirt and dust in the ruts on the little Jeep trail.

When he got near *Sally*, he stopped to see if he could see anyone coming. Two flashlights were moving around at the cabin. Soon they would see the tracks of the Jeep and *Sally* and follow them.

He walked toward the rendezvous point with Sue, a point of rocks not far away. When he found her she was holding her hand.

"Where are the others?" Sue whispered, when he joined her.

"There are two at the cabin."

Sue sobbed quietly, as Bill held her.

DAN THOMAS

"I think I killed one."

"He's alive."

"Which one?"

There are two. Bill felt himself relax. It meant they were all accounted for.

"I should have told you, I got a Black Belt when I was fifteen. In Russia, I didn't have anything to do but practice karate. I'm a third degree Black Belt. Promise me you won't tell anyone."

Bill squeezed her tightly and kissed her forehead.

"I crushed the windpipe of the second one," Sue said. "He just walked up and grabbed me. Those guys all know how to fight, but they didn't take any precautions."

Bill shook his head. They must not have thought to take precautions from a pretty woman. He looked in his binoculars. Lying alongside *Sally* was the other one.

"I tried to save his life," Sue said in an apologetic tone. "I gave him a tracheotomy. But I had to wait until he passed out. Maybe it was too late."

"How'd you do that?"

"Pen-knife. Straw from the drinks we had. Vets do things a lot easier than regular doctors."

"We have to get out of here," Bill said. "The other two will be coming any time."

Bill went over their plan. The ex-KGB were good trackers, but they didn't have a vehicle, and they were missing two of their men. It would take them a little while to re-group. Bill figured he and Sue needed to get to the Forest Service road where their tracks couldn't be seen and get some distance between them and these bad guys. They made their way toward *Sally* and the man lying next to her.

"He's alive," Bill said, examining the man at the bottom of the hill. He had a soda straw sticking into his throat just above the top of his sternum. It was taped down with silver duct tape. Air could be heard moving through it.

"Be careful, then," Sue said excitedly, "his windpipe was his only injury."

"Take this gun and hold it on him," Bill said, grabbing the rifle out of *Sally*. "If he moves, blow him away."

"Okay," Sue said, then barked a command in Russian. The show of authority surprised Bill.

The man was twice as big as Bill.

Bill tried to move the man's hands together, but they wouldn't move. Sue shined the flashlight onto the man's face, then started barking commands again in Russian. With a thunderous boom, the rifle went off, and a bullet ricocheted off the ground inches from the man's head. Sue barked out more commands. The man sat up like he'd been conscious all along, put his feet together, and put both hands out in front of him in position to be cuffed. Bill stood there for a minute, his ears ringing, shaking with fright.

"You should tie him up now," Sue said, evenly.

Bill shook off his fright and put ties around the man's legs and hands. "Let's get out of here," he said, wishing momentarily that they had gotten rid of the damned rifle.

They jumped into the Jeep and began moving slowly again without lights. The moon was up--not a bright one, but good enough if they moved slowly. It was miles to the Forest Service road. The little road they were going down was just a couple of ruts. They stopped at the top of each rise, and Bill used the binoculars, but he couldn't see anyone.

It was after midnight when they found the stretch of straight road that could be used as a runway. Bill looked the area over with his binoculars. The road ran along the top of a grassy ridge. Below the ridge was a valley, and in its bottom was a stream full of trout. The valley sides were meadow-covered with grass and flowers. Several aspen groves were scattered throughout. The sides got steeper in either direction beyond the straight stretch of the road. These areas were heavily forested.

"Let's fly out of here, now," Sue said.

"I'd really like to wait for a little light. There're big mountains all around. I'd hate to hit one."

"But they found us. It's like they had radar."

"Radar," Bill said. "Maybe there's a locator device on *Sally*." It didn't take him long to find two of them, one under the cushion on his front seat, and the other one under the passenger's seat. He did a diligent search, and found no more.

"Come on," he said, "let's put these where we can watch what happens."

"Good idea," Sue said. "But what about *Sally?*" She was sitting in the middle of the road. They picked an aspen grove to hide her in, and then they took the locators and drove down the straight stretch of road they intended to use as a runway to the end of the big meadow. They bumped over the grassy meadow into the valley to an aspen grove near the little stream. It was about a mile from, and well below, the aspen grove where *Sally* was hidden.

"Let's leave the Jeep," Sue said, "we don't need it anymore, do we?"

"I guess not," Bill said, then added, "if they find the Jeep and not *Sally* they'll think we flew out of here."

They walked along the tracks in the grass the Jeep had left, then down the road to *Sally.* She was visible for a half mile in the moonlight. They spent some time covering her with boughs. She had lots of surface area.

When they were through, they climbed into *Sally.* They were asleep almost as soon as they sat down. *Sally's* seats were reclined and lined with thick, warm sheep's fleece.

At first light, a helicopter flew overhead, then flew back and forth over the grove of aspen where they'd left the Jeep and locator devices.

"They're here already," Bill said, waking Sue.

As they sat there wondering what to do, a Jeep with two people came roaring down the road, dust billowing behind. It proceeded toward the cabin Jeep.

"Let's see what they're doing," Sue said.

They climbed out of *Sally,* and took up a position behind an enormous limestone boulder. Juniper and gooseberry bushes grew around its base. The rock was white, but most of it was covered with orange, gray, or black lichens.

Bill peered through his binoculars. The bad guys were looking at the Jeep. One pulled out some kind of device and extended what looked like an antenna. The others looked at him as he worked with it. Pretty soon he turned, faced Bill and Sue, then signaled with his hand in their direction. Bill was shocked.

"Holy shit." Bill said, moving behind the boulder. "They know where we are again. They're coming this way."

"The communicator," Sue said. "That's why they didn't take it. It must have a homing device."

Bill realized she was right. "You stay here with the binoculars," he said. "I'll take it down this way." Bill pointed to a trail that would keep his movements hidden. He grabbed the communicator, ran about a half mile to the stream in the valley, dropped it off, and ran back.

"What are they doing?" he said trying to catch his breath on his return to Sue.

"The men below stopped and seemed confused when they looked at the homing device again. Now they're going to where you dropped it off."

"Let's get out of here," Bill said. Sue agreed.

They pulled the boughs off *Sally* and jumped in. To taxi in the tall grass, Bill had to use a lot of power, and *Sally's* engine screamed. Still they taxied slowly through the grass. As they turned onto the main road, Bill looked over his shoulder. The helicopter was already in the air and coming directly at them. Bill figured they'd have guns in the helicopter, maybe even a machine gun.

He looked down the road and added power. He was gaining speed nicely when the helicopter got close. Puffs of dust, indicating bullet strikes, were running toward them. In his excitement, Bill added too much power, and *Sally* started to spin to the left where there was a large drop-off. When he hit the right brake to straighten her out, her nose swung hard to the right, and kept going through the centerline. When *Sally* looked like she was going to career off the road, Bill hit both brakes hard. She skidded down the road on the gravel, rotating slowly. Bill watched in horror as she came to a rest facing the wrong direction.

There was a short stretch of road in front of them, too short for a successful takeoff roll. The helicopter had just passed overhead and was turning for another pass. Bill thought for a minute about climbing out of *Sally* and turning her around for another takeoff run in the same direction, but he could see the men from below running up, guns drawn. There wasn't enough time.

At the end of the short straightaway in front of them was a small but steep hill. On the other side of the little hill, the road turned sharply to the left to avoid going into a deep ravine. There wasn't enough room to take off, but if he could get enough elevation off the hill, and get over the small trees at the edge of the road, then he could pick up speed by diving into the ravine.

He had to do it. He added power for a takeoff roll. This time he was more cautious. The men from below were still out of range with their pistols. The helicopter was just finishing its turn and coming for a second pass.

The first part of *Sally's* takeoff roll was a little downhill, which helped. Sue sat there, not moving or speaking. As *Sally* gained speed, the helicopter made its second pass. Again, dust flew from bullet strikes. Again, a machine gun trail approached *Sally*. Bill concentrated on his takeoff roll. It had to be just right. He added more power, this time ready to pull it back if he added it too fast. Now the men from below were closer. Their chests were heaving in the rarefied mountain air.

As she picked up airspeed, *Sally's* flying surfaces gradually began contributing to her ability to be controlled. Bill glanced quickly at her airspeed indicator. It showed thirty-five miles per hour. At this altitude, his actual speed would be considerably higher. He added more power. He needed to indicate sixty-five miles per hour to fly. The hill was approaching fast. So was the helicopter with a machine gun. So were the men with pistols.

If *Sally* spun around again they'd die. He had to be careful. If he didn't have enough airspeed when she left the hill she'd crash. If they didn't die in the crash they would die at the hands of the men chasing them. Bill concentrated.

He was indicating fifty-five miles per hour when he hit the hill, still too slow to fly. As *Sally* sailed into the air, Bill added more power. He had to be careful. She had enough airspeed to give her wings considerable lift. The lift on her wings helped her pop into the air at the end of the rise. She rose high, higher than the trees in front of them, but she was going too slowly, and she quickly began to sink. She'd sink into the trees in her present configuration. Bill had few choices.

He pulled her nose higher. He was scared to add more power for fear she'd again spin out of control. He would trade airspeed for altitude, but with a loss of airspeed, he worried he wouldn't have enough control to get her nose back down.

Sally's nose was so high he could see nothing but blue sky. He looked to his side and he saw they were still sinking. Then he felt it, *kerwhap whap.* It was the tops of the trees striking *Sally.* The ground dropped away to his left. If she wasn't badly damaged, they should make it. He pushed the stick forward to dip her nose. She didn't respond. She was going so slowly her control surfaces had little effect.

He pulled off power when she felt like she was going to spin out of control again. With less power, her nose came over faster. Finally, he could see land in front, and he could see the trees and boulders very close on the other side of the valley. He added power. She responded nicely. He needed speed to maneuver. It was difficult adding power with the other side of the ravine getting closer fast, but he had to do it.

There wasn't much room, but he thought he could make it. He reached over and retracted the gear. *Sally* needed less drag.

Between her new engine and the dive they were in, she got airspeed quickly. He had to turn. He hoped she'd maneuver fast enough.

He slammed the stick over. Her wing started to rise. Too slow. He punched full right rudder. Her wing came up faster. She began to turn down the valley. He pulled her nose up to tighten the turn. She responded.

He saw big boulders and trees. They were so close they were just a blur of gray and green slipping under *Sally's* nose. Elation gripped him as he cleared the highest object in their path, a large spruce tree, and he could see that they had made it.

The standard "safe" procedure would have been to begin climbing right away, but Bill had to satisfy an urge to show off to their would-be killers. He dipped her nose back down and flew her close to the ground that was falling away quickly, placing him in a dive. In a matter of seconds her indicated speed passed 175 miles per hour, and Bill went to full power. She felt solid and responded crisply. Bill waited for a moment until his indicated speed passed 200 miles per hour, then he pulled back hard on her stick. He felt the force of several G's as *Sally* rose instantly like a rocket into the deep blue sky.

Bill looked over his shoulder and saw the men on the ground. It was the same picture he'd glimpsed when he escaped at Rawhide--the men's jaws were hanging open. They were apparently very unused to losing.

Bill rolled *Sally's* nose over to bring her into level flight, and as he did, they floated in zero G. Bill felt his spirits soar as well. He grinned at Sue, who grabbed him around the neck and squeezed in jubilation.

The lovers looked at each other. Bill wondered if anything else was in store for them.

"Look," Sue said, pointing to a neat bullet hole in the canopy.

Bill looked down to see where the bullet had exited, wondering for an instant if it had gone through one of their bodies first.

"Missed a fuel line by a fraction of an inch," Bill said, "Doesn't look like it hit anything important."

"How about this one?" Sue said, pointing to another hole in the fuselage, then another in her wing.

"I guess we're all right. Doesn't look like there's a hole in a fuel tank. Holes in the wing won't hurt much. It's just plastic, foam, and fiberglass."

43 – A Happy Ending

"Where we going?" Bill said, easing off on the power.

"Isn't a good pilot supposed to figure that out before he takes off?" They looked at each other and laughed.

"How about New York City?" Bill said.

"Why New York City?"

"Because it's big?" Bill shrugged.

"We need a lawyer. A tough one who won't be intimidated. He needs a lot of credibility so when he vouches for us they'll believe him. If he's good, he'll keep us from getting into trouble for the crimes we've committed."

"This attorney could talk to the FBI," Bill said. "He could set up the meeting places between us and them. Then part of our deal for testifying is that they pay his cost. That way we don't have to worry about big problems like protective custody or being held as material witnesses. You know a jury will convict the ex-KGB guys. They definitely have bad press."

"Sue's eyebrows dropped and she looked briefly away. "You know if we testify against the KGB guys Vince's kids will get his Russian money. Frankly, I'd rather see the KGB guys get it."

Bill looked at Sue and laughed. "They definitely worked harder for it."

"They did us a big favor when they killed Vince."

"And if we testify against them, we may be hunted for the rest of our lives."

"Maybe we should give Uri Novotny a call," Sue said. "We worked hard, too. Maybe we should get some of that stock?"

Bill laughed again, and shook his head. "I'd say a certain videotape is worth at least ten percent of it, wouldn't you agree?"

"Throw in an audio tape for another ten. What did Novotny say to Trooper? 'Save yourself for the hit on the big guy'?"

"Definitely words to that effect," Bill said laughing.

The sunrise was beautiful. *Sally's* new engine was quiet and smooth. Sue reached over and took Bill's hand, pulled it to her mouth, and kissed it gently. His big, strong hand felt good.

"You have the same name as your dad?"

"Same name."

I'd still be Mrs. William Thomas Patton, Sue thought.

"This ring is interesting," Sue said, "Is the stone amber?"

"Sure is."

"The little bug in there has its mouth bent all out of shape. It looks like it's in pain."

"That's what I've always thought, too. You know what?"

"What?" Sue kissed his hand, then looking at the stone again.

"That little critter is about a hundred million years old, and it's been screaming in agony the whole time. My dad thought it came from Vince's Shrine."

"When Vince saw he was going to crash, his face probably contorted in anguish just like this bug."

"That means his soul is contorted in anguish," Bill said. "People who die unexpectedly like that become ghosts for eternity, and they retain the emotion they die with."

"Just like this little bug," Sue said, *"eternal anguish.* We have to remember never to go camping on the shore of the Great Salt Lake so his ghost can't haunt us, or worse, possess one of us."

The two sat quietly for a moment, and then Sue spoke. "Are we still going to Disney World?"

"You bet we are," Bill said with conviction. "Great place to think."

"I've been there, and so have you."

Bill's face fell.

"You know what I'd really like to do?" Sue said.

"What?"

"Hire a guide and spend a week in the Everglades."

Bill stared off. Visions of white egrets and scarlet ibis danced in his brain. A cottonmouth displayed its big white mouth as a warning to stay away. An alligator crashed through the brush to protect her nest. Then images of sailing the world and exploring distant lands flashed through his mind's eye.

When he looked back, he was looking at the most beautiful sight he'd seen in his entire life. She was someone with whom he could enjoy life and its bounty. "Okay," Bill said, "but first two days at the Hilton in Miami."

Sue looked at him, smiled warmly, squeezed, and then kissed his hand. "That's okay with me."

◎ ◎ ◎

In that moment, when the two became bonded with love, an egg within Sue was fertilized by a tiny sperm cell. He was the hardiest of the lot. He'd out-swam all the rest.

The child would be named William Thomas Patton, IV. Tommie Patton would sit on her daddy's knee and on her great-grandpa Tony's knee and charm them with her bright, sparkly eyes.

Tom Patton would watch from beyond the wispy clouds that always seem so far away and be as proud as any Grandfather could be as his namesake was nurtured with love.

SUGGESTED READING

Cohen, Herb *You can Negotiate Anything*; L. Stuart; 1980

Doman, Glenn J. *How to Give Your Baby Encyclopedic Knowledge;* Doubleday; 1985

Doman, Glenn J. *How to Teach Your Baby to Read: the Gentle Revolution*; Better Baby Press; 1983

Doman, Glenn J. *How to Teach Your Baby Math*; Avery Publishing Group; 1994

Getty, J. Paul *How to be Rich;* Jove Books

McCoy, John *The Gift of Literacy;* Renaissance Child, Austin, Texas; 1986

McCoy, John *Curiosity, The Inborn Key to Your Child's Development;* Renaissance Child, Austin Texas; 1990

Pinker, Steven *How the Mind Works;* W. W. Norton & Company, New York London; 1997

Rankin, William H. Lt. Col. USMC. *The Man Who Rode the Thunder;* Prentice Hall, Inc.; 1960

Robin Karr-Morse and Meredith S. Wiley *Ghosts from the Nursery;* The Atlantic Monthly Press, New York; 1997

Wright, Robert *The Moral Animal;* Vintage Books, New York; 1994